Her

Minnesota

Man

Brenda Coulter

What a grand thing, to be loved!
What a grander thing still, to love!

VICTOR HUGO

Love never gives up, never loses faith, is always hopeful,
and endures through every circumstance.

1 CORINTHIANS 13:7
(NEW LIVING TRANSLATION)

ACKNOWLEDGMENTS

I am indebted to my beta readers, Valerie Comer, Kathy E. Eberly, Kate Hinke, Ginger Solomon, and Therese Travis, for their valuable feedback on this story.

Chapter One

JACKSON BELL SIGHED and set down the guitar he'd been picking as he stood alone in a dim corner of the concert venue's band room. Placing the instrument on its side, he nudged it against the painted cement-block wall so it wouldn't get stepped on. When he straightened and turned, his manager stood before him with a familiar green bottle and a generous glass of the single-malt Scotch he usually downed before a show.

"Let's lubricate those famous vocal cords." With a strained smile and a determined toss of her glossy auburn hair, Shari Daltry offered the glass.

Jeb—he liked the nickname, but allowed only four people to use it—declined the drink with an upraised hand and a brief shake of his head.

Shari's smile flattened. "Why not?" It wasn't a question, but a challenge.

Jeb just stared at her. Although he wasn't in the habit of explaining himself, he'd told her the other day that he was giving up alcohol because it was becoming a problem for him, and God couldn't be happy about that.

"Don't tell me you're still on that 'God' kick." Shari shook her head in disgust. "You're smarter than this, Jackson."

He said nothing.

The sole offspring of two atheists—a coldhearted father who'd drunk himself to death and an unremembered mother who had effected a much quicker end by swallowing a whole bottle of pills—the last thing Jeb had ever expected to become was a Bible-believing Christian. But he'd been one of those for five days now, and he was having all kinds of trouble figuring out what God expected of him.

He was determined to abandon his wicked lifestyle and become a better man. He just hoped he wouldn't have to give up his music along with everything else.

"Don't do this." Shari spoke from between clenched teeth, but kept her voice low enough to avoid being overheard by the other four occupants of the room. "Don't throw it all away."

She was about to lose her temper, but there was nothing new in that; Shari was notoriously volatile.

Jeb had never minded much. In fact, her intensity and her refusal to fawn over him were a welcome respite from the cloying behavior of the sycophants who kept trying to insinuate themselves into his life. But the main reason he put up with Shari's frequent rages was that she was the best band manager he had ever seen.

She wasn't long on personality, but she could ferret out opportunities and make things happen. During her tenure, the rock band Jeb had wryly named Skeptical Heart had produced three albums. The first two had been certified Gold records and the third had been certified Platinum.

"Just have a drink and relax," she urged, getting control and smiling again—this time with sardonic amusement. "You look like an animal desperate to claw his way out of a cage."

Well, yeah. Because he was dying for a cigarette.

And for a drink, of course.

And for some answers that he didn't know how to find.

Shari said something else, but Jeb had stopped listening. She was trying to engage him, but he had nothing to gain from an argument, so he just stared at her and waited for her to go away.

She should have gone twenty minutes ago. She knew his rule: Half an hour before the show, the room was to be cleared of everyone except the band so Jeb and the guys could get their heads into the music.

When she didn't move, Jeb looked pointedly at the wall clock and then folded his arms and raised an eyebrow at her.

She blinked furiously, her lips pressed so tightly together that they lost their color. And then with a screech of exasperation, she tossed the drink in Jeb's face.

Her angry impulse provoked a chorus of irreverent guffaws from Jeb's band mates, who had apparently picked up on the tension between their frontman and their manager and tuned in to enjoy the show.

Clamping his mouth shut to prevent himself from uttering words a Christian shouldn't, Jeb rubbed the stinging alcohol from his eyes. Then he focused his trademark laser stare on his assailant.

Jeb possessed a rare talent for killing looks. But recalling that Christians were supposed to turn the other cheek, he forced his scorching glare downward until it threatened only a worn oriental rug on the concrete floor.

A fine Christian he was turning out to be. He couldn't draw two consecutive breaths without sinning.

Shari slammed the whiskey bottle down on a cloth-covered buffet table and loosed a stream of invective that pounded Jeb's nerves like water from a fire hose. This was extreme behavior, even for her, and Jeb saw the guys exchange uneasy looks.

He wondered why none of them appeared to have

guessed why Shari was so determined to undermine his resolve to give up his hard-drinking ways. It seemed obvious to *him*. Afraid that his conversion would result in his leaving the band, Shari would stop at nothing to pull him back from the light.

Jeb peeled off his whiskey-soaked shirt and mopped his face with it. His annoyance was already evaporating, leaving behind a residue of regret. What would happen to Shari and the guys if he left the band? It didn't seem fair that his decision to begin a new life might adversely affect their careers.

Her face still contorted by rage, Shari propped a fisted hand on one slender hip and flung more words at him. "What's *wrong* with you? Why are you so different?"

"How many times do you need to hear it?" Jeb dropped his wet shirt onto a chair. "I'm a Christian now."

Five days ago in a fit of despair, he'd picked up a Bible in a Louisville hotel room and read The Gospel of John. He had ended up on his knees, and for the first time in his twenty-seven years, he had prayed to God.

A guy couldn't help being different after an experience like that.

"Hey, c'mon." Taylor Benson, a heavily tattooed drummer from Dallas, slid a placating arm around Shari's shoulders and pried the empty glass from her white-knuckled grip. "Y'all can talk about this after the show."

Shari jerked away from him. "I've all but sold my soul to make Skeptical Heart a top act! And just when we're finally getting there, our frontman suddenly turns religious"—she sneered the word at Jeb—"and wants to quit!"

Four heads swiveled in Jeb's direction, each face

registering stunned disbelief. No, the guys hadn't yet grasped that possible ramification of Jeb's conversion. Not until Shari had spelled it out for them.

Jeb had been planning to explain things after tonight's show. Shari was insane to introduce the subject mere minutes before the band was due onstage.

"He hasn't said anything about quitting," Taylor chided in his soft drawl. "He's just worn out. Five measly days off in six weeks of tourin' has been hard on all of us."

"He's going to quit!" Shari pointed a trembling finger at Jeb. "Just ask him!"

Taylor's gaze swung back to Jeb, his eyes widening in a mute appeal for reassurance.

Jeb had none to offer, as he suspected his affiliation with the band was about to become a casualty of his spiritual rebirth. His mind was groping for words to explain that when Taylor's betrayed look and the slack-jawed stares of the other three guys told him they'd finally figured it out.

Just as well. Although the critics called him a brilliant lyricist, Jeb had no talent for actual conversation. As one of his disgruntled schoolteachers had noted on a report card, he was "habitually uncommunicative, often responding to direct questions with nothing more than a stare." But Jeb had never known how to be any other way, except when he was with—

No. Best not to think about her tonight.

All four of the guys started talking at once; Shari had stirred things up good. Shaking his head, Jeb turned away from the confusion and gazed unseeing at a wall covered with graffiti and band bumper stickers.

Yes, he was worn out. That was part of what had made

him so ripe for conversion, especially after that awful show in Louisville, where a perfect storm of technical glitches had whipped the crowd into a frenzy of resentment. As Jeb grimaced at that memory, his gaze shifted and his attention was arrested by a drawing on the junked-up wall.

Between a band sticker and a crude limerick, someone had depicted a wooden cross on a rocky hilltop and neatly lettered two words beneath it: *Jesus saves.*

Had the musician who left that message of hope ever been this confused about what God expected of him? Jeb intended to follow the straight and narrow path—but where was it?

Certain that he had overlooked some important clue, he pushed his mind back to the events of five nights ago.

Demoralized by the belligerent Louisville crowd, Skeptical Heart had played the worst show of their career. Afterward, Jeb had been too disgusted to go out and drink himself stupid with the guys and their guests, so he'd accompanied them only as far as the venue's VIP entrance.

Pausing in the doorway, he turned up the collar of his leather jacket and tugged down the bill of his Minnesota Twins ball cap. Then as security guards held back a gaggle of squealing girls and the band's party piled into a rain-beaded stretch limo, he slipped unnoticed through the crowd and strode into the drizzly, ink-black night.

How could a man be lonely when he was surrounded by people? How could he feel dissatisfied when he was ripping through life at the speed of sound, a guitar in his hands and music in his heart? In the intermittent rain, Jeb walked for miles with those questions playing on an endless loop in his head. He was soaked and shivering like a half-drowned dog when he finally ducked into a convenience store to buy a cup of coffee and call a cab to take him to the band's hotel.

Hunting for the room service menu, he had discovered a Bible in the drawer next to his bed. On an impulse he still didn't understand, he had opened it to a random page, the first chapter of The Gospel of John.

Still staring at the carefully drawn cross on the band room's wall, he shook his head in amazement. What God wanted with a restive heart like Jackson Bell's was anyone's guess. But Jeb had read that even the worst of sinners was eligible to receive forgiveness and find peace.

He became aware that Taylor had out-shouted the others and gained the floor.

"No way," the drummer insisted. "Jackson would never quit on us."

Peace. The other night it had poured over Jeb like warm, healing water. But when he'd realized that resuming his normal habits would be like putting filthy clothes on a freshly washed body, that newfound peace had been swamped by anxiety.

He turned away from the wall to join the conversation.

"The thing is, guys, I—"

"You need a break." Taylor nodded encouragingly. "This tour's been amazing, but it's good we're goin' home tomorrow." He looked at the other three guys. "As for the God stuff, if he wants to read his Bible on the tour bus and pray before the shows, so what? After we all get back to L.A. and have a good rest—"

"Wake up, Taylor!" Veins bulged on Shari's forehead as she snarled the words. "He's not coming back with us. He told me this morning."

"He's staying here in Florida?" Taylor looked at Jeb, who was indulging a very unchristian fantasy about applying a dab of instant glue to Shari's bottom lip and pinching her mouth shut. "Why would he do that?"

"I didn't say he was staying here," Shari snapped. "He'll probably run home to that quaint little house in Nowheresville."

"You've been to his house?" Having somehow missed the derision in Shari's voice, Taylor eyed her like a kid who'd been denied a treat another kid was bragging about having enjoyed.

"I haven't been there," Shari admitted, watching Jeb through narrowed eyes. "But *he* hasn't been, either. Not in almost a year. And since he doesn't have a family, I don't know why he—"

"Fifteen months," Jeb corrected automatically. Every month he managed to stay away from Laney Ryland was such a hard-won victory, he couldn't help counting them.

Shari raised her chin to a mulish angle. "What's so great about some hick town in Michigan?"

"Minnesota." A shaft of longing stabbed Jeb's heart as he pronounced the word. Fifteen months was his new record. Last time he hadn't made it past eleven.

"Where *ever*. Why can't you just come back to L.A.?"

"Like Taylor said, I need a break."

Yesterday, he'd planned to head to a deserted beach he knew in Mexico to do some heavy thinking. But tonight his heart was tugging on its leash, straining toward home.

Maybe he should just give in. Laney had been a Christian all her life, so she ought to be able to help him figure out what God expected him to do next.

He'd hoped to find a clue in the Bible he'd swiped from that Louisville hotel room, but John—the guy who'd written that gospel—had been a little vague about how a twenty-first-century rock musician was supposed to extricate himself from a lifestyle that was pretty much all sin, all the time.

Absently rubbing his bare chest, Jeb looked past Taylor at the other three band members. Keyboardist Matt Holland was nursing a bottle of beer as he sprawled in a recliner, his relaxed posture at odds with the murderous glint in his eyes. Leaning against the wall, guitar genius Sean McPherson glared at Jeb while sucking viciously on a cigarette. And perched on the arm of a cracked leather sofa, bass guitarist Aaron Rice had curled his hands into fists and was staring with transparent longing at Jeb's unbroken nose.

Their animosity was understandable. If Jeb walked away now, Skeptical Heart was finished. Matt and Sean were excellent backup singers, but neither possessed the passion and power of a lead vocalist. And while Jeb valued his band's collaboration on the songs he'd written, the guys had never composed anything on their own.

He pushed his fingers through his damp hair and wondered why trying to do the right thing for once in his misbegotten life had to threaten the careers of these other people. What was God thinking, leaving their futures in his clumsy hands? He was nothing like wise, warmhearted Laney: *She* would have known the right course to steer through this mess.

All right, then.

"I'm going to Minnesota," Jeb announced. For two years he'd done his best to remain on the fringes of her life, but he needed her now, and Laney would never turn him away.

"Good idea." Taylor nodded briskly. "Let's all take a month off." Bending from the waist, he unzipped a duffel bag that lay on the floor. A moment's rummaging produced a black T-shirt, which he tossed to Jeb.

"No." Sean pushed away from the wall and moved to the buffet table, where he dropped his cigarette into Jeb's forgotten cup of coffee. "We'd lose our momentum."

"Exactly." Shari had reverted to her usual brisk, businesslike mien. "The label wants you back in the recording studio, and you'll need at least ten new songs for that." She looked around the room, assuring herself of an attentive audience before adding, "Last I heard, you only had three or four. So you don't have time for a vacation."

"Shari, I've got nothing left." Jeb pronounced the words with a solemn finality that spun the room into another shocked silence.

It was true. In the past few weeks he'd felt the creative impulse bleeding out of him like air from a slow-leaking tire. Whether that was due to exhaustion or whether God had simply revoked his gift, Jeb couldn't tell.

Laney would know. And if the answer was what he feared, Laney would help him accept it.

"So when will you be comin' back to L.A.?" Taylor asked.

Jeb expressed his resolution and his regret with a long, steady look. "I don't know."

Taylor shook his head. "But where does that leave the rest of us?"

"Nowhere!" Her dark eyes glittering with tears, Shari stormed out of the room, slamming the door behind her.

Matt swore and hurled his beer bottle at the wall.

Where are you, God? Jeb's heart squeezed out the silent

prayer as he watched foaming beer and wet glass splinters crawl down the concrete blocks to the floor. *I could use some direction here.*

He tugged Taylor's shirt over his head. Its smoky scent triggered an insane craving for the cigarettes he'd given up five days ago, but Jeb ruthlessly shut his mind against that. He had bigger problems tonight.

In a few minutes he would have to take the stage and perform songs he was beginning to be ashamed of having written, but he couldn't see any way out of that because he was under contract. He had already struck one song from tonight's set list and made a mental note to change the lyrics of two others when he sang them. He didn't know what else he could do.

He'd read in the Bible that when a man surrendered his heart to God, his old self died and a new person was born. But Jeb was hardly a naked, innocent baby. His wicked past might be forgiven, but he was still shackled by his old promises, still dragging the consequences of a thousand bad choices like iron chains behind him.

Two sharp raps sounded and the door to the hallway opened, admitting the muffled noise of a restless audience on the floor above. A harried-looking stage manager pointed at his watch and said it was time.

"We'll be there in a minute," Jeb said.

When the stage manager objected to the delay, Jeb drilled him with a get-lost glare. The guy shut both his mouth and the door with an alacrity that satisfied Jeb until he recalled his resolution to stop using his eyes as weapons.

"Jackson?" Taylor's voice broke the strained silence. "If you get off this merry-go-round, the ride's over for all of us.

You know that."

Staring at a sparkling island of broken glass in the beer puddle next to the wall, Jeb acknowledged that truth with a slow nod.

"So this could be our last show," Taylor persisted.

After a long hesitation, Jeb nodded again.

If only he could talk to Laney right now. If only he could hear her laugh. He'd close his eyes and concentrate on that effervescent sound until he absorbed it through his pores and felt it spread through his bloodstream, renewing his strength.

Too bad he'd accidentally left his phone on the tour bus.

No, it was better this way. If he didn't pull his band together in the next few minutes, there was no telling what might happen onstage.

"Guys," he began.

"Save it," Sean growled. "It's time to go."

Aaron sighed heavily and got to his feet. "Come on, Taylor." He hooked an arm around the dazed drummer's neck. "Let's be professional about this." He turned an expectant look on Sean, who in turn nudged Matt.

"Professional," Matt grumbled. "No problem. I'll just wait until after the show to rip out his vital organs."

They were filing out of the room when Jeb spotted a cell phone lying next to a plate of discarded shrimp tails on the coffee table.

"Guys, wait." As his heart beat a brutal tattoo against his ribs, he obeyed an irresistible impulse and picked up the phone.

"Oh, that's mine," Taylor said from the doorway. "Just drop it in my bag."

"Give me three minutes." Jeb tossed the words over his shoulder as he strode to the bathroom for some privacy.

He locked the door and sagged against a mirrored wall, his hands trembling as he stabbed the phone's tiny buttons to enter Laney's cell number. When he got her voice mail, he ended the connection and tried her home phone. As it began to ring, he turned toward the mirror and leaned his damp forehead against the cool glass.

He didn't have time to talk, he reminded himself as he counted electronic warbles. He'd just tell Laney he was coming home. Her squeal of delight would ease his heart enough to get him through this difficult evening.

The phone continued to ring.

"Please," Jeb whispered. Flattening the palm of his free hand against the mirror, he squeezed his eyes shut and prayed harder. "Please make her be home."

Chapter Two

"OH, FOR CRYING OUT LOUD, Francine! How could you do this to me?"

Laney Ryland was perfectly aware that sensible people didn't talk to their cars. But Francine, the old black Chevy Impala she'd inherited from her mother, was practically family.

"You knew I was waiting for a tire sale!" Laney's voice rose in a wail of despair as she brought the car to a bumpy stop on the side of a deserted gravel road between two endless cornfields just outside of Owatonna, Minnesota.

As rain pelted Francine, Laney sighed and switched off her engine. She wouldn't be stuck out here if she hadn't offered a ride to the pregnant wife and two-year-old daughter of one of her former boyfriends, a large-animal vet who had informed Laney three years ago that he wasn't ready to settle down.

He'd been mistaken about that, because he'd married her friend Megan just three months later.

And what was Laney's reward for driving Luke's family home after their car conked out, leaving them stranded while Luke was busy doctoring a sick cow at a dairy farm twenty miles away?

A flat tire in the rain.

Laney wasn't jealous of Megan, even though Luke had somehow neglected to break up with Laney before he'd begun seeing her friend. Laney had cried when she'd discovered that treachery, but Megan was perfect for Luke, anyone could see that. Laney was just having a tiny bit of trouble being patient and awaiting her own turn to get married and start a family.

Oh, all right. She was having all kinds of trouble being patient. But she was already twenty-five, and a woman who planned on having five or six children needed to marry young.

She sighed again and activated Francine's hazard lights. It was hardly rush hour out here in the cornfields, but if she didn't turn on the flashers, some distracted farmer would be sure to happen along and bash into Francine. That was the way Laney's week had been going.

She briefly considered calling her friend Ollie Lincoln, who ran a garage in town. But she'd been brought up by a courageous single mother who had never backed away from a challenge, and wimping out was no way to honor the memory of Hannah Ryland.

"So it's just you and me, Francine." Laney fingered the hem of her best black wool skirt. "And I am seriously overdressed."

It had been an unusually warm day for the first week of October in southern Minnesota, but it was evening now, and with the approaching rain, the temperature had dipped below sixty degrees. Eager to avoid a cold drenching, Laney determined to wait a couple of minutes to see if the storm would blow over.

She had a blind date with her friend Sarah Jane Swenson's cousin Eric in just half an hour, but she decided against calling him. As long as the rain stopped in the next few minutes and she got the tire changed without any trouble, she'd make it home before he rang her doorbell. And if he arrived before she'd had time to freshen up, she'd simply explain everything and ask him to give her a few minutes.

She turned on the radio for some soothing classical music but found her favorite station engaged in one of those chatty pledge drives. Twisting the tuning knob, she skipped past the rural stations' offerings of crop reports, perky polka music, and fishermen droning that record numbers of perch were being pulled out of nearby Tetonka Lake. She paused when she heard a rock ballad featuring a powerful baritone that sent a frisson of longing through her.

Jackson Bell was her best friend. At least that was what she told people, because she didn't know how else to describe their relationship.

He wasn't her boyfriend. She'd had several boyfriends, and she'd never experienced that giddy thrill with Jeb. Yet while there was no romantic component to her feelings for him, Jeb was as necessary to her life as food and water and air.

Just like Cathy and Heathcliff, a starry-eyed classmate of Laney's had sighed years ago, but that was true only to a point. Laney and Jeb *had* been extraordinarily close since childhood, but they weren't in love and they certainly didn't share the fictional couple's tendency toward mutual annihilation.

No, Laney mused bitterly, snapping off the radio in the middle of the song, Jeb was bent on *self*-destruction. Laney, he treated like hand-blown crystal.

"It's never going to stop, Francine." Staring glumly through the windshield, Laney accepted the inevitable and wriggled out of her wool cardigan so she'd have something warm and dry to put on after changing the tire. Then heaving a sigh that, if not for the pounding rain, might have been heard as far away as the Twin Cities, she opened her door and stepped out into the deluge.

She was rounding Francine's hood to inspect the right-front tire when the slender heel of one of her pumps sank into a patch of mud. The shoe stuck, but her foot kept going and she lost her balance.

She pitched forward and fell hard, crying out as tiny stones bit into her tender flesh and pain ripped through her left shoulder, which she had injured the previous night.

Fighting tears, she pushed up to her feet and gingerly brushed gravel from her scraped palms and her muddy, bloody knees. As frigid rain pummeled her, she recovered her shoe and limped resolutely to Francine's trunk.

In situations like this, Christians usually sought divine assistance. But Laney had been on the outs with God for a couple of months now, so she didn't feel right about asking him for anything.

"I can handle this," she breathed through clenched teeth as she opened the trunk and located the tools she needed. Hadn't Jeb always insisted that she was clever and stubborn enough to achieve anything she set her mind to?

Jeb.

He hadn't been home in more than a year, and it had been three months since his last phone call. Laney was hurt by his neglect, but she was also desperately worried.

The psychological wounds Jeb had suffered as a child had rendered him wary of making emotional connections with people. He had no family and Laney was his only real friend, so wherever he was and whatever he was doing right now, he was completely alone—and entirely at the mercy of his own savage spirit.

Squeezing her eyes shut, Laney pushed that awful thought aside. She had enough troubles without worrying herself sick over Jeb.

She positioned her flashlight on the ground, crouched beside the flat tire, and used the sharp end of her lug wrench to pry off the hubcap. Discovering that the lug nuts had been over-tightened by whichever hulking mechanic had put on Francine's last set of tires, she almost gave up. But she was already soaked to the skin, and annoyance fueled her determination to meet this challenge.

Grimly ignoring the pain in her shoulder, she used her whole body as leverage on the wrench and was finally able to loosen the nuts. She had a little trouble operating the jack and exchanging the heavy tires, but she finished the job.

A lightning bolt of pain shot through her shoulder as she heaved the flat tire over the lip of Francine's trunk.

At last she slithered back into the car. The sodden fabric of her skirt slapped and squished against the vinyl seat as she adjusted her position behind the wheel. She sighed over the ripped sleeve of her favorite silk blouse, and then she turned on the engine and the heater. The air that blasted her was not yet warm, so she shivered hard as she pushed dripping curls away from her face and put on the dry cardigan.

"Hot bath, here I come," she muttered, reaching for the gearshift.

Eric.

She squinted at her watch in the dim light and emitted a shriek of dismay. "Thanks a lot, Francine. By now he's thinking I just blew him off."

Laney felt terrible about not being home at the agreed-upon time for their date, but apart from calling the man earlier, what could she have done differently?

She'd just started getting dressed when the very pregnant Megan had appeared on her doorstep with a cranky toddler who needed to go potty. Their car had broken down nearby, and Luke couldn't get there for at least an hour. Since Laney hadn't been expecting Eric—who, according to Sarah Jane, was an amazingly handsome widowed dentist—for another forty-five minutes, she'd driven Megan and her daughter home.

She'd thought there would be plenty of time. She hadn't counted on having to change a flat tire in a thundering downpour.

She fished her phone out of the enormous, baby-soft leather bag Jeb had given her two birthdays ago and called Eric to apologize and explain. Surely any reasonable person would understand.

"I don't understand," Eric said. "Why didn't you call me sooner?"

"I meant to, Eric, but then I got so rattled that it just slipped my mind. I'm awfully sorry."

"All right." There wasn't even a hint of forgiveness in his tone. Was he this hard on his patients when they forgot to floss? "Go home and throw on some dry clothes. I'll let the restaurant know we're running late, and I'll be back at your house in thirty minutes."

Thirty minutes? It would take the better part of an hour for Laney to get home, wash and dry her hair, bandage her cuts, "throw on" another nice outfit, and apply the barest minimum of makeup. Why were men so obtuse about these things?

"I'm sorry, Eric, but I'm too frazzled now. Let's just reschedule, okay?"

Silence. Even the rain had stopped.

"Eric?"

"Sure. No problem." His clipped speech made it clear he resented being thrown over for a long hot bath and a cozy cup of jasmine tea. "I'll call you."

No, he wouldn't, but that was fine. Laney apologized again and said goodbye, then dropped the phone into her bag.

She didn't need this aggravation. As far as she was concerned, Eric the amazingly handsome widowed dentist could just pick one of Minnesota's ten thousand lakes and go jump into it.

Trembling from stress and annoyance as well as because she was half frozen, Laney put Francine in gear and headed home. Her shoulder continued to throb, a painful reminder of the stupid thing she'd done the previous night.

She'd been awakened by the unmistakable sound of shattering glass. Looking out her bedroom window, she'd spotted one dark-clad figure attempting to boost another through a window of the unoccupied house next door, which happened to belong to Jeb. Too shocked to think straight, she'd grabbed her old softball bat and run outside in her flannel nightshirt and knee socks, flailing and squawking like an outraged Canada goose defending her territory.

Not surprisingly, she had ended up hurt.

She sighed and rubbed her aching shoulder. No doubt this spate of disasters, which had begun on Monday when her bank denied her application for another small-business loan, was God's attempt to get her attention and bring her back into fellowship with him. But she wasn't ready to yield. She was too depressed. And, yes, she was a little angry.

She had no idea how she was going to make it without the loan. The tearoom she'd helped her mother start nearly five years ago had bled her savings dry, but she couldn't close it because she employed her three elderly great-aunts. Besides, apart from presenting the occasional talk on bridal etiquette or table manners, a sideline she'd fallen into after some friends had noted her extensive knowledge of those social niceties and recommended her to others, what else was she qualified to do?

Once, she had dreamed of going away to college. But now she was stuck in Owatonna, Minnesota watching life pass her by.

Not that she didn't love her hometown, which was full of history and charm and good people. And not that she minded looking out for her great-aunts, a set of 79-year-old identical triplet spinsters everyone called the Three Graces. And she certainly didn't regret skipping college to support her mother through the ups and downs of leukemia treatments and remissions. It was just that she'd never had a chance to spread her wings.

The second time Hannah Ryland's leukemia had gone into remission, her blood and marrow cells had returned to normal and she'd surprised everyone by giving up her job as a high-school music teacher and opening a tearoom. Caught up in her mother's enthusiasm, Laney had quit her own job as a wedding planner's assistant to help get the fledgling business off the ground.

Two years passed before Laney felt able to peruse course

catalogues from the University of Minnesota. But then the cancer returned and a few months later, her mother was gone.

Now Laney's college fund was gone, too. So was her mother's life insurance settlement, but at least the medical bills had been paid off. Laney was left with a heavily mortgaged house and a tearoom that was still struggling to break even.

Sometimes she fantasized about selling everything and going to college someplace sunny and far away, but of course she would never abandon her great-aunts. The Three Graces had plenty of friends, but Laney was their only relative, and family was everything.

Back in town, Laney turned onto Mulberry Street. Just short of her own driveway, she swung into Jeb's, pressing the remote-control device clipped to her sun visor to open the detached garage. She used Jeb's garage because she didn't have one and his would have stood empty, otherwise.

She was the caretaker of his house, a graceful three-story Queen Anne Victorian with a wraparound porch nobody ever sat on. She cut his grass, hired workmen when necessary, and supervised the cleaning crew that came every so often to freshen the inside of the showplace his mother had carefully restored and decorated some twenty years ago.

Having check-writing privileges on Jeb's local bank account allowed Laney to keep things in good order and to pay herself the monthly remuneration he insisted on. Jeb worried that maintaining his place was too much work for someone who had her own house and a tearoom to look after, but Laney always shrugged that off. Unless she kept the house from becoming a burden to Jeb, he might sell it, and then his infrequent trips home might cease altogether.

If they hadn't already.

Still shivering, Laney pulled into the garage. Her cell phone rang, but the display showed an unfamiliar number, so she decided whoever it was could just wait until she got warm and dry.

She stepped out of the garage and automatically made a quick visual survey of the back of Jeb's house. Nothing seemed amiss—she'd cleaned up the broken glass and had the new window installed before leaving for work that morning—so she closed the garage and hurried toward the much smaller brick house next door.

Approaching the back steps, she heard the shrill ring of her kitchen phone. Her answering machine had died months ago, so this caller, too, would just have to try again later.

Inside, she plopped her handbag on a kitchen chair and toed off her muddy shoes. The phone's strident ringing continued, ramping up Laney's annoyance as she eased out of her cardigan and draped it over a wood peg by the door.

"Okay, *okay!*" She strode to the old wall phone and snatched the receiver. The movement caused a painful twinge in her shoulder, so she greeted the caller with a decidedly grumpy hello.

Three seconds of startled silence ended in a familiar masculine chuckle. The sound flowed over Laney like soft warm water, soothing her rumpled spirit and generating a relief so intense she had to close her eyes in order to bear it.

"Your telephone demeanor could use some polishing," Jeb suggested.

"Hello, stranger." She endeavored to match his light tone. "I was afraid you'd forgotten this number." Did he realize how long it had been since he'd called home?

"Telephones work both ways," he said. "You could call *me*."

"I hate to bother you." Shivering, Laney plucked at her blouse, pulling the clammy silk away from her skin. "I know how busy you are."

"Laney." Jeb's deep, smoky voice held a note of reproach. "I'm never too busy to talk to you."

She pressed her lips together, preventing a bitter retort from slipping past them. Had he even noticed how time and physical distance were eroding the extraordinary connection they shared?

Her gaze settled on an old snapshot of him that she'd anchored to her refrigerator with a magnet.

His face wasn't especially handsome. "Arresting" was the word Laney had settled on years ago when she'd first noticed how women followed him with their eyes. Part of the fascination was undoubtedly due to his being much taller than average and as lean as a greyhound. But his eyes were his most distinctive feature. Under a pair of harsh, inward-slanting brows the same espresso brown as his lanky hair, Jeb's perpetually narrowed, light gray eyes glinted like chips of polished steel.

"So how are you doing?" Laney asked.

"Not too bad." There was an unmistakable note of tension in his voice.

Laney made a wry face at his picture. Had she actually expected to get a real answer without having to dig for it?

"You sound stressed out," she said.

"I'm fine," he said, too quickly.

Laney just shook her head. He was as tightly strung as

those guitars he loved so much, but he wasn't going to admit it.

If only he would come home. He was always reticent on the phone, but if he would just come home, she would stare into his eyes until his stubborn gaze faltered and he stopped insisting that he was "fine." He wasn't much of a talker, having learned as a child to suppress his emotions, so figuring out what was troubling him would be like working knots out of wet shoelaces. But Laney had been doing it for years.

She was still freezing, so she retrieved the damp sweater she had just hung up. As she poked her left arm into the sleeve, pain flashed through her shoulder and a small whimper escaped through her chattering teeth.

"What's wrong with *you*?" Jeb demanded.

"I'm shivering. It's cold and rainy outside, and I just walked in the door." Pushing her other arm into the sweater, Laney decided against mentioning that she was dripping wet and halfway to hypothermia.

"But you're all right." His anxious tone begged her to confirm that. "You're not sick or anything."

"I'm not sick, Jeb. Just cold. Where are you calling from?" The last time they'd spoken, he'd mentioned an upcoming concert tour.

"Florida," he said. "St. Peters— No, wait. That was last night. I guess I'm in Jacksonville."

Laney had always wanted to go to Florida. Or anywhere.

"Is it nice?" She hugged herself and tried to warm up by imagining a sun-baked beach like the ones in the travel magazines her mom used to pore over.

"Jacksonville?" Somehow, Jeb's shrug was audible. "It's

okay, I guess."

"I should know better than to ask an indifferent traveler like you," Laney said ruefully.

In addition to crisscrossing the U.S. more times than Laney could even recall, Jeb's band had toured Europe, Japan, South Africa, and Australia. But he'd never been much for sightseeing, and he hated going to sleep on a tour bus and waking up in a different town each morning. He tolerated the extensive travel only because he loved sharing his music with live audiences.

"This is the last night of the east coast tour," he said. "I'm supposed to be on stage right now, but . . ." He breathed a soft sigh into the phone. "Laney, I needed to hear your voice."

He *needed*? That was a startling confession from a man who was fanatically self-sufficient. In Jeb's mind, acknowledging any emotional need was tantamount to exposing his jugular vein to a vicious world.

His stubborn insistence that he didn't need anyone was an artifact of his troubled childhood. Jeb guarded his heart so aggressively that it was a wonder he and Laney had ever become friends.

There are monsters inside me, he had confided in an awful whisper when he was eleven years old. He'd meant to frighten Laney, but that bleak pronouncement and the anguish darkening his silvery eyes had aroused her pity, instead. She'd soon begun to understand that the monsters terrorizing Jeb were the tangled emotions that stemmed from a horrifying event he'd been unable to process and move beyond.

Was he battling those old monsters tonight?

"I'm always here," Laney reminded him.

"I know." He paused. "Would you mind getting my piano tuned?"

"Jeb! Would I *mind*?" Laney bounced on the balls of her feet, not-minding with all of her heart. "How soon will you be here?"

"I'll catch a flight tomorrow. The band's heading back to L.A., but I need to come home."

There was that word again. *Need.* Worry eclipsed Laney's delight.

"Jeb, tell me what's wrong."

"It's nothing that seeing you won't fix." He spoke lightly, to stop her worrying, but then his voice deepened to a more serious tone. "It's been a long time, hasn't it, princess?"

If she'd needed proof that something was troubling him, that wistful utterance had just provided it. But she wasn't going to drag any explanations out of him tonight, not over the phone, so she moved on.

"Call me tomorrow and let me know when to expect you," she said. Thinking aloud, she added, "In the meantime, I'd better see about stocking your refrigerator."

"You don't have to do that."

"You pay me to take care of your house," she reminded him. "Preparing it for your occupancy is just part of the job." And even if it wasn't, this was the kind of favor best friends did for each other. "So if you've gone vegetarian or something, you'd better tell me now."

She'd been hoping to provoke a laugh, but she was satisfied when the quintessential meat-and-potatoes man emitted a derisive snort.

"Get plenty of bacon," he said. "And ham and roast beef

for sandwiches."

Laney grinned. Some things never changed.

And some things did. Her smile slipped as she wondered again why Jeb had gone so long without calling to see if she was okay.

She wasn't okay. She hadn't been okay in a very long time. But whatever was wrong with Jeb and whatever had gone wrong between them, she'd find a way to fix it all when he came home. She'd breathe easier once she knew he was all right, and that would put her in a stronger position to attack her own problems.

Everything was going to be just fine.

"Hurry home," she said.

"Tomorrow," Jeb promised, and he ended the call.

Forgetting her chills and her aching shoulder, Laney bounded upstairs for some dry clothes. She'd call the piano tuner before it got any later, and then she'd hit the grocery store. After that, she'd put fresh soap and towels in Jeb's bathroom and make sure everything was perfect for his homecoming. She'd get him comfortably settled, and then she'd find out what was troubling him and help him deal with it.

If he gave her enough time. Jeb was as restless as the autumn wind, so he wouldn't stay long. He never did.

Chapter Three

JEB LOOKED THROUGH A WALL OF GLASS at the small regional jet he was about to board for the first leg of his trip home and shook his head in disgust. His extra-long legs demanded First Class seating, but last-minute travelers didn't always have choices about those things. If he wanted to get home today, he'd have to shoehorn his six-foot, five-inch frame into one of the toy aircraft's tiny seats.

He just hoped he wouldn't get stuck in some super-advanced yoga position that would necessitate his removal from the plane by half a dozen firefighters armed with the Jaws of Life.

Carefully avoiding eye contact with the gate attendant, Jeb presented his boarding pass and strolled down the jetway to his plane. As he ducked through the door opening, a female flight attendant looked at him and gasped. Brushing past her before she blurted his name, Jeb tugged down the bill of his Minnesota Twins ball cap, shielding his face from curious stares as he bumped and excused his way to Row 11.

Like most musicians, Jeb craved live audiences because he fed off the energy they beamed toward the stage. But after the shows were over, he had no use for fans. Celebrity hampered his freedom.

He rarely gave interviews, so the media had labeled him reclusive, which made him even more sought after. But Jeb wasn't bashful. He was just a guy from Minnesota. And when Minnesota men weren't talking about the weather or their cars, they just weren't all that big on conversation.

As for the songs the critics called "brutally honest" and

even "tortured," Jeb hated being asked where they came from and what they meant. Those answers dwelled in the darkest reaches of his mind, and he wasn't about to go poking around in there and risk stirring up all kinds of awful memories just to satisfy the curiosity of strangers.

He found his row and wedged his backpack into the overhead bin, then squeezed past a woman and her squirming baby to claim the window seat. After hitching up his seatbelt, he reached for his cell phone and entered the number of the Three Graces Tearoom in Owatonna.

The call was answered by one of Laney's great-aunts, who said Laney was on another line booking a bridal shower tea. Jeb had no idea which of the Graces he was speaking to, but it hardly mattered because identical triplets Caroline, Aggie, and Millie were identically exasperating.

"Just tell Laney I called from the plane," he said. "I should be home by—" He stopped when he heard the familiar scuffle indicating one of the Graces was attempting to wrest control of the phone from her sister.

"Is this Jeb?" Grace Number Two inquired.

"Yeah," Jeb said. "Hi. Please tell Laney I'll be—"

"Well, how ya doing, Jeb? Pretty good, then?"

"Not too bad," he replied, slipping effortlessly into his old speech patterns. "Fine, thanks" might be an acceptable answer anywhere else, but that wasn't how a Minnesotan responded to a how-are-you question. Not unless he wanted people to wonder at his exuberance. "Tell Laney that if my connecting flight gets away on time, I should be home by six."

"Here, give it to me," another Grace said.

Jeb adjusted his overhead air vent while he awaited the

outcome of the latest telephone tug-of-war.

"Jeb? It's Caroline. Will you be in town for a while, then?"

"I'm not sure," he said cautiously. A guy who made careless statements to the Graces was a guy who'd soon regret having opened his mouth. "Tell Laney I expect to be there by—"

"I guess you're coming home to list your house with a real estate agent, huh?"

"List my house?" As the baby next to him began to wail, Jeb frowned and wondered why Caroline's words sounded more like a suggestion than a request for information.

Were the Graces trying to get rid of him? They had always watched over Laney like dragons guarding a treasure, but they knew he'd never represented any danger to her. Certain other attractive young women would have been wiser to avoid him, because although he never meant to do it, he tended to leave a lot of damage in his wake. But Laney would always be safe with him.

"Sir?" The flight attendant pitched her voice to be heard over the baby's robust crying. "I need you to turn off your phone now."

"I have to go," Jeb told Caroline. "Just give her my message, okay?"

"Well, sure, Jeb. What's the message?"

Shaking his head, he pressed the Power button and slipped the phone into his shirt pocket.

The baby had the shrillest cry Jeb had ever heard. Its mother jiggled it and tried to reason with it, and by the time they were airborne, she had resorted to singing. Her absolute inability to carry a tune disturbed Jeb far more than the kid's caterwauling, so he reached for his iPod.

As he inserted his ear buds and selected the first movement of Tchaikovsky's "Piano Concerto No. 1," Jeb wondered if his mother had ever sung to him. He closed his eyes and concentrated, but the phone call he'd made on the day of her death was as far into the past as his mind could reach.

He'd been "Jackson" back then, although he couldn't remember what that name had sounded like on his mother's lips. He couldn't picture her face, either. But with a clarity that made him shudder, he recalled the awkward sprawl of her body on the kitchen floor and the terror that had gripped him as he'd pressed the numbers 9-1-1 on the phone and waited an eon for someone to answer.

"What's your emergency?" the lady asked. She had to repeat the question twice before eight-year-old Jackson found his voice.

"My mom won't wake up!" he blurted, and then he began to cry.

The house quickly filled up with adults speaking in hushed, shocked voices, but nobody told Jackson why his mother was dead. It wasn't until the next evening that he screwed up his courage to knock on the door of his father's study and ask.

"She killed herself," Jackson Senior said bluntly. "Does Mrs. Lee know you're out of bed?"

Trembling in the doorway in his pajamas, Jackson ignored the reference to the mean-faced housekeeper his father had hired just that afternoon and dared even further. "Is she in heaven?"

"No." Seated behind the desk, his father downed the last

of the whiskey in his glass and reached for the bottle. "Heaven isn't real. Only fools and cowards believe that garbage."

"Yes, Dad," Jackson whispered, trembling harder. When his father drank whiskey, he wasn't very nice. And his father drank whiskey every night.

"She's gone." Jackson Senior's hand shook as he poured more of the amber liquid into his glass. Some of it dribbled down the side, wetting a pile of papers on the desk, but he didn't appear to notice. He lifted the glass and unwrapped his long index finger from it to point at his son as he added, "She no longer exists."

"Y-yes, Dad."

A hand clamped down on Jackson's shoulder and he yelped like a startled puppy. Twisting free of Mrs. Lee's grasp, he ran to his room, where he cried himself to sleep.

The next morning he stood in front of his bathroom mirror for a very long time, staring into his puffy, red-rimmed eyes as he struggled to process his grief and confusion.

"Heaven isn't real," he whispered over and over, forcing himself to accept that horrible truth. "She isn't there. She isn't *anywhere*. Heaven isn't real."

Mrs. Lee kept a spotless house and had no patience with grubby little boys. She smacked Jackson's backside with a wooden spoon if he didn't comb his hair or get his fingernails clean. His father didn't like being disturbed, so Jackson didn't tell on her, not even when she began hitting him harder and more often, leaving angry purple marks on his back and his shoulders and his ribs.

He seethed in silence until just after his ninth birthday,

when Mrs. Lee reached for her spoon to punish him for leaving dirty socks on his bathroom floor.

"Don't you hit me anymore!" he screamed, turning on her like a wild thing, fists punching and feet kicking as she swatted at him with the long-handled spoon. "I'll call the police and show them my back and they'll make you go to prison!"

Mrs. Lee was stunned enough to stop, and she never touched him again. She continued to prepare his meals and launder his clothes, but she gave up trying to correct him and just treated him as his father did, barely acknowledging his presence in the house.

That was fine with Jackson. He could take care of himself. Except for basic material needs like school supplies and winter coats, he never asked anybody for anything. He became as sullen as his father, and continued in that bleak existence for two long years before Laney Ryland found him and changed his life.

Jeb's eyes snapped open as the back of the seat in front of him pushed against his knees. When a crabby-looking old lady peered between her seat and her neighbor's to see why she couldn't recline, Jeb behaved like a good Christian for once and refrained from assaulting her with a look.

The baby had stopped crying and was watching him, a calculating look in its bulgy blue eyes. Guessing its intent a split-second before it lunged and tried to grab the wire of his iPod, Jeb leaned out of its reach.

He had never touched a baby. He was fascinated by their jabbering and their knowing stares, but babies were too pure to be handled by the likes of him. He left the baby-touching to Laney, who'd been known to strike up conversations with stroller-pushing strangers just so she could bend down and coo at their infants. Jeb teased her about that, but there wasn't a sweeter sight in all the world than Laney cuddling a baby in her arms.

He got off the plane in Houston and headed for the designated smoking area, which was outside the terminal. He had already passed Security when he remembered he didn't smoke anymore, so with a sigh he turned around and got in line to take off his shoes and his belt and get frisked all over again.

After he put himself back together, he plopped onto the nearest chair and called Laney.

"*Houston?*" She chuckled. "I hate to tell you this, Jeb, but you're heading the wrong way."

"Don't look for logic in airline routes," he advised her. "That way lies madness."

"Will you still be home by six?" she asked.

"Looks like it. I just hope I can rent a vehicle with roof racks." Although the rental company had promised him a Ford Explorer, he knew better than to count on things like that. "But even if it means duct-taping my canoe to the top of a sub-compact, I'm going fishing tomorrow." There was no better place to think than in the middle of a quiet Minnesota lake.

"I can't wait to see you," Laney said warmly.

"Yeah. Me, too. But I'd better let you get back to work."

Forty minutes later, he boarded a normal-size plane and settled comfortably into a First Class window seat. He killed some flight time by reading part of a spy thriller he'd stowed in his backpack, and then he listened to music for a while. When he couldn't think of anything else to do, he closed his eyes and savored his earliest memories of Laney.

She had just moved into the house next door. Eleven-year-old Jackson knew her name because every evening at six her mom hollered for Laney to come in for supper. He knew her age because he'd counted nine pink birthday balloons tied to the lamppost in her front yard. The more he saw of her, the more he despised the pampered little girl whose mother escorted her to school every morning and then kissed her right there on the sidewalk, in front of the whole town.

One day as he walked past her house, Laney called his name. He was amazed by her nerve, but he kept walking.

"Jackson!" she called again. "Wait!" Her quick, light footsteps pattered like raindrops on the sidewalk behind him.

He whirled to face her, a rude word dying on his lips as he blinked in confusion at the silvery crown-thing with big fake jewels perched on top of her tangled blond curls.

"You dropped this." Laney extended a twiggy arm. Across her palm lay the pocketknife Jackson had filched from his father's underwear drawer.

He snatched it and shoved it back into his pocket.

"Why does it say 'Jeb' on it?" she asked. "Your name is Jackson."

"Those are my initials," he snapped, irritated by the reminder that he didn't have a name of his own, but had to use his old man's.

"J-E-B," she repeated thoughtfully. "What does the E stand for?"

"None of your business." Hating his curiosity about the sparkly crown-thing and about the saggy, ankle-length blue dress she wore, Jackson swept her head to toe with the insolent look he always counted on to make other kids and even adults back away.

Laney Ryland didn't back away.

"Do you like my dress?" she chirped with an innocent eagerness that sent a wave of unease through Jackson. He wasn't a good kid, but neither did he go around pulling the wings off butterflies. "It's for a play at school." She raised her arms and twirled, making the dress inflate bell-shaped around her. "I'm supposed to be a princess."

She seemed to vibrate with joy, an emotion wholly unfamiliar and therefore suspect to Jackson.

"You look dumb," he said.

She beamed at him, still amazingly unaware that she was being insulted. "I know it's too big," she said as she tugged at a sleeve that had slipped off one boney shoulder. "But my mom can fix it." She touched the sparkly thing on her head. "Isn't the tiara pretty, though?"

It was a bright afternoon, and the sunlight glinting off the silver metal and the faceted bits of glass dazzled Jackson's eyes, irritating him further. He glared at Laney and waited for her to scamper away.

She tilted her head to one side and stared calmly back at him, her elfin face alive with frank curiosity. "Why are you doing that with your eyes? It makes you look mean."

"I *am* mean." He took a threatening step toward her, but she still didn't move. She just gazed up at him, her round blue eyes suddenly full of something that looked alarmingly like pity.

Heat crept up Jackson's neck and flooded his cheeks. When cornered, he always protected himself by glaring at people until they backed off. He didn't know if Laney Ryland was fearless or just plain stupid, but his hardest stare had no discernible effect on her.

"Mrs. Lindstrom says you're so bad you can't stay in school," she said softly.

Jackson didn't know where the old lady across the street got her information, but it was true that he'd been suspended again for fighting. This time he'd thrown the first punch, but only because the other three boys had taunted him about his mother's suicide. The way Jackson saw it, they had all but begged him to shove their smug faces in the dirt.

Principal Peterson hadn't seen it that way. He never did.

"It's just a three-day suspension." Hating his defensive tone, Jackson aimed a vicious kick at a weed growing through a crack in the sidewalk.

"Mrs. Lindstrom says you're a modern-day Huckleberry Finn." Laney sucked her bottom lip for a moment before adding, "I don't know what that means."

Jackson did. He'd read the book last year, and had initially identified with Huck, the motherless child of a mean, drunken father. But as he got deeper into the story, he'd realized that he and Huck had little else in common. The fictional boy had friends, people who cared what happened to him. And Jackson Edward Bell, Jr. had nobody at all.

But so what? He didn't need anybody.

"I'm surprised Mrs. Lindstrom didn't warn you about talking to me," he sneered.

"Oh, she did." Laney's curls bounced as she nodded vigorously. "She says you're a very bad boy."

"Bad to the bone," Jackson confirmed with all the

bravado he could muster.

"Don't talk that way." Laney adjusted her slipping tiara. "My mom says you smoke cigarettes and do bad things because nobody loves you enough to make you stop. So we pray for you."

Jackson almost snorted at that piece of foolishness, but something in Laney's earnest gaze made him reluctant to hurt her feelings. He might be the meanest kid in town, but he knew a real princess when he saw one.

"Hey!" Laney's face lit up. "Do you want some ice cream?"

Jackson loved ice cream, but Mrs. Lee never bought any kind of treats, and of course he never asked her to. "I wouldn't mind some," he said cautiously.

Laney hiked up her long dress and led him to the back of her house and up the steps to her kitchen door, chattering all the way. He was very tall, wasn't he? And Jackson was a fancy name, wasn't it, but he'd been named for his father, hadn't he, so he couldn't go by Jack, could he, because everyone called his father that.

Jackson wasn't a talker, but he didn't object to Laney's garrulousness. He was too stunned by her easy acceptance of a boy everyone knew was no good.

"Mom!" she hollered, grabbing his arm and dragging him, dazed and unresisting, into her kitchen. "Can me and my friend Jeb have some ice cream?"

Jarred by several quick, hard thumps as the jet encountered some air turbulence, Jeb opened his eyes and shifted to a more comfortable position in his seat.

My friend Jeb.

With those three words, she had named him and

claimed him. In that life-changing moment, it had ceased to matter that she was a girl, that she was two years younger than he, and that she was adored and protected while he was a neglected kid on the fast track to juvenile delinquency. On that sunny afternoon, he'd been too paralyzed by wonder to offer any resistance as Laney Ryland blithely branded his heart.

Her mother had accepted him, too. Hannah was a high-school music teacher, so when she discovered Jeb's fascination with her piano, she'd begun giving him lessons. "Such a talent," she would say, shaking her head in apparent awe whenever he played one of his own compositions for her. "Such a remarkable talent."

Jeb leaned sideways in his seat, pressing his forehead against the window to get a better view of the Mississippi River, which reflected the late-afternoon sun like a tangle of brown satin ribbon. Studying its meandering course, he wondered what different turns his life might have taken if Laney hadn't befriended him all those years ago.

She and her mother were Christians, but they'd never preached at him. After he'd made it clear he didn't want to hear about their religion, they had just gone on quietly living out their faith right under his nose.

He'd thought that couldn't affect him, but now he realized God had used Hannah's kindness and Laney's fierce loyalty to prepare his heart for that encounter in Louisville.

He couldn't wait to tell Laney. While he'd become a Christian for his own sake, he also felt that he had finally done something worthy of her. Something that might begin to pay her back for befriending a worthless boy and sticking by him for sixteen years.

The cabin speakers crackled and the flight attendant instructed the passengers to turn off their personal electronic devices in preparation for the landing at Minneapolis-St. Paul. As Jeb returned his iPod to his pocket, he felt his heartbeat quicken in anticipation.

He was almost home.

* * *

Reservations were encouraged at the Three Graces Tearoom, but seating walk-ins until four o'clock still allowed Laney to get home by six most days. She wasn't taking any chances on Thursday, however, so she instructed Caroline—the Graces didn't like the formality of being addressed as "Aunt"—to put the Closed sign on the front door thirty minutes early.

By a quarter to six, Laney was darting anxious glances at her watch and trying not to resent the two parties of four that lingered in the dining room. Seated at her desk in a cramped corner of the kitchen, she tapped the keys of her adding machine to tally the day's receipts. When her mind wandered and she made an error, she ripped the tape out of the machine and crumpled it into a tiny ball.

"Laney, go home." At the prep counter, Millie paused in the act of spooning loose tea into a ceramic teapot and blinked through her eye-magnifying glasses like a worried owl. "You want to be there to welcome Jeb, don't you?"

Laney stared at the fist she'd clenched around the ruined tape. She'd been on edge all day, tormented by a feeling that some unwelcome change was in the air. She was eager to see Jeb, but she was worried about whatever was behind his sudden "need" to come home.

"I guess I could leave this for Caroline," she said. She

hated asking the Graces to do extra work, but today was special.

"We'll take care of everything." Millie lifted a kettle off a gas burner and poured steaming water into the teapot. "You go on. The day we can't finish loading a dishwasher and make a bank deposit will be the day we check into a nursing home."

"Yes, go on." Striding into the kitchen, Caroline made shooing motions with her hands. "You're not doing any good here, anyway. Instead of refilling the creamer for Table Three, you took them an extra sugar bowl. And that chicken salad you made for tomorrow? After you put it in the fridge, I found your diced apples and celery in a bowl on the counter."

"Oh." Laney dropped the ball of paper into the wastebasket next to her desk. "Did you—"

"Well, of course. I fixed everything."

"Thank you." Laney propped an elbow on her desk and rested her chin on her hand.

"Go home." The eldest of the triplets, Caroline had a mile-wide bossy streak, but Laney adored her. "We'll finish up here."

"We sure will," Millie said sweetly. While Caroline's love was often concealed behind a gruff façade and Aggie's was frequently camouflaged with humor, Millie was openly affectionate. "It's for times like this that the good Lord gave you aunts."

"*Great*-aunts," Caroline corrected.

"As opposed to ordinary, run-of-the-mill aunts," Aggie quipped as she entered the kitchen carrying a tray of dirty dishes. She caught Laney's eye and winked. "Or even pretty good aunts."

"You're the best aunts anybody ever had." Standing to push her arms into a sand-colored wool cardigan Millie had knitted for her, Laney added, "I don't know what I'd do without you."

That was the truth, and it was something she'd been thinking about a lot lately. The Graces were getting old, so unless Laney married, she'd soon be left with no family at all. She could hardly count her father, a man she had never laid eyes on.

"We slipped a white envelope into your bag earlier," Caroline said. "It's a welcome-home gift for Jeb."

Laney darted a questioning look at Aggie, who said, "Hockey tickets," out of the side of her mouth.

"For the Minnesota Wild?" Laney asked hopefully.

Millie beamed at her. "Is there any other team?"

"Not in Jeb's opinion. He'll be thrilled." She just hoped the game was soon, because Jeb never stayed in town much longer than a week.

"The other ticket is for you, of course," Millie said. "And you won't believe how good the seats are."

"Thank you. We haven't been to a Wild game in ages."

"You run along now," Caroline commanded. "It's almost six, and if his plane landed on time, he'll be home any minute."

Laney scooped her keys off the desk. "Okay, I'm gone." She puckered her lips and sent each of her great-aunts an air kiss before heading to the door.

She couldn't wait to see him. But as she drove home, she began to worry again. Why had he sounded so beaten down last night? He was always physically and emotionally drained after one of those demanding concert tours, but even then, he'd never sunk into depression. In fact, Jeb was the most stoical person she had ever seen. When troubles came his way, he never uttered a word of protest. He just accepted them as part of life. So why had he sounded so desperate last night?

Laney, I needed to hear your voice.

The band's heading back to L.A., but I need to come home.

Stopping for a red light, she promised herself that one way or another, she'd get to the bottom of things this very evening.

She was equally determined to discover why he'd been out of touch for so long, and why he seemed to be making so little effort to preserve the amazing friendship they had shared for sixteen years.

Chapter Four

ON BOTH SIDES OF I-35, vast oceans of pale yellow corn churned in the gusting wind as Jeb hurtled through southern Minnesota in a rented Ford Explorer. A long skein of Canada geese flew across the road, low enough that Jeb, with his window partway down, could hear them honking encouragement at one another.

Jeb was feeling encouraged, too.

Nearing his journey's end, he eased off the interstate to make a quick stop at a grocery store. As he placed his purchase on the counter and reached for the wallet in his hip pocket, habit made him scan the cartons in the cigarette display case. Fortunately, the store appeared to be out of his brand.

Back in the Explorer, he made for Cedar Avenue, which took him past the grain elevator towering beside the railroad tracks and just two blocks later, delivered him to downtown Owatonna.

Stopping for a red light, he cast an admiring glance at the magnificent stained-glass window gracing the front of the National Farmer's Bank Building. Designed over a century ago by the great architect Louis Sullivan, the world famous sandstone edifice was still widely acknowledged as the most beautiful small-town bank in America.

Turning left on Broadway, he glimpsed the band shell in pocket-size Central Park and recalled the free concerts he'd attended there with Laney during their growing-up years. How many sweet summer evenings had he lounged beside her on the springy grass next to the hundred-year-old fountain, licking ice cream cones and slapping mosquitoes off his bare arms as the stars came out one by one?

At last he reached Mulberry Street. The fourth house on the left, a picture-perfect Queen Anne painted slate blue and trimmed in white, was his, but Jeb barely gave it a glance. It was the neat brick two-story next door that absorbed his attention.

Laney was inside that house, and she was waiting for him.

Knowing her car would be in his garage and not wanting to block her access, Jeb swung into her driveway, which was separated from his by just a few feet. A couple of years ago, he'd finally convinced her not to evict poor Francine from his garage every time he brought home a rental car.

As he rolled to a stop in front of the dormant shrub roses hugging Laney's garden shed, he saw her kitchen door fly open.

And then there she was, leaping down the steps and running toward him, arms flung wide, her butter-colored curls streaming behind her like flags of welcome.

She hadn't changed out of her tearoom outfit, a below-the-knee floral print dress with a wool cardigan and the penny loafers she called sensible. Jeb had always thought the old-fashioned attire sweetly feminine and wholly appealing. But he tended to feel that way about any outfit that had Laney inside it.

He tossed his Twins cap onto the dashboard and made it only halfway out of the Explorer before Laney slammed into him.

Chuckling, he nudged her back so he could get both feet under him. Then he leaned down and wrapped his arms around her, resting his cheek on top of her head. Inhaling the flowery fragrance of her hair, he closed his eyes against the fierce relief that gripped his heart.

He allowed himself five full seconds to enjoy holding her, and then he called on the self-discipline he'd been honing for years and began the complicated process of withdrawing. He was as intent as any tightrope walker on finding his perfect balance. Too loose or too brief a hug might hurt her feelings, while holding her too tightly or for too long might reveal what he'd worked so hard to keep hidden from her.

He knew he'd gauged it just right, because she squeezed him hard, and then she let go and backed up, chattering the way she often did when she was excited. Jeb crossed his arms and leaned against the SUV, happily soaking up the sight and sound of her.

Her eyes were still as blue as the deepest autumn sky, her skin as pale and perfect as fresh cream. Her front teeth were a little crooked, but she had an enchanting smile—not that she had ever believed that. Laney actually thought of herself—looks, brain, and personality—as *ordinary*.

Still talking, she linked her arm with Jeb's and tried to haul him into her house. He resisted long enough to grab the plastic grocery bag off the passenger seat. Then he was hers, content to follow wherever she led, just as he had been since the day she'd gifted him with her friendship and a name of his very own.

She emitted a squeal of delight and snatched the bag from him. "Cherry Vanilla?"

"No, sorry. They were out."

She peered inside the bag and laughed. "I can't believe

you would lie to me about something as important as ice cream!"

Grinning, Jeb slung an arm around her shoulders. Didn't she know he'd have scoured every store in Minnesota to find her favorite flavor? As for lying to her, he never had and never would. There were any number of things he couldn't discuss with her, but he had never told her a lie.

That didn't mean he was above teasing her in order to provoke her gurgling laughter and see those blue eyes dance.

In her kitchen, Jeb shrugged out of his leather jacket and hung it beside the door, on the same wood peg he'd been tossing his jackets over since he was eleven. Laney set the ice cream on the counter, then removed her cardigan and handed it to him.

He draped it over another peg. "Are the Graces still knitting these things faster than you can wear them out?"

"Umm-hmm." She pushed up the long sleeves of her dress and rummaged through the commodious leather bag she'd parked on a chair. "And I still donate an old one to charity for every new one they— Yes, *here* it is." She pushed a mass of exuberant curls away from her face and flourished a plain white envelope. "They sent you a welcome-home gift."

"The Graces?" Jeb's mouth tilted into a wry smile as he took the envelope and eased his thumb under the flap. No doubt they'd sent him a selection of business cards from local real estate agents. The Graces were about as subtle as—

Hockey tickets?

Even more surprised when he noticed the seat assignments, Jeb whistled. "How did they get on-the-glass seats for the Minnesota Wild?"

"Some kind of trade, I imagine. You know how they

operate."

He knew. Nobody was better connected than the Graces. They had probably called in a favor from the second cousin of somebody's neighbor's dentist.

Looking more closely at the tickets, he found his pleasure swamped by a fast-rising tide of regret. Leaving aside the question of why the Graces, if they really were trying to get rid of him, would give him tickets to a game more than three weeks in the future, how could he risk staying that long in Owatonna? If Laney got too used to having him around, she'd be devastated when he left.

He ransacked his brain for words that would let her down gently. "Laney, I'm not sure I'll be—"

"I'll keep them." Plucking the tickets from his hand, she elevated her delicate, honey-colored eyebrows in that way she had of trying to disguise her disappointment. "If you're not here, I'll find somebody to go with me."

"I'm sorry," Jeb said. "I just don't know how long—"

She cut him off with a sharply raised hand. "You just got home, Jeb. Don't ruin it by talking about leaving, okay?" She turned away to replace the envelope in her bag.

Silently castigating himself for not handling that better, Jeb shoved his hands into his pockets and wandered through the kitchen's archway into the hall. From there he could see the living room, still furnished in the cozy style Hannah had called scruffy chic, which Laney claimed was French for "stuff bought at garage sales and refurbished." His gaze lingered for a moment on the upright piano tucked against the half-wall next to the staircase. Then his feet turned toward the dining room.

Stopping before the antique sideboard, one of the flea

market finds he'd helped Hannah haul home and refinish, he picked up a framed photograph of Laney and himself as teenagers. Unaware of the camera pointed in their direction, they'd been sharing a laugh as they laced their ice skates on the snowy bank of Owatonna's Straight River.

"Mom's favorite picture." Laney took it from him and gazed at it for a moment before setting it back where it belonged.

Turning away, Jeb noticed an assembled jigsaw puzzle on the far end of the oak dining table. A familiar scene of Paris at night, it was the single discordant note in a house full of precious memories.

"Why is that still here?" he asked.

In the last few years of her life, Hannah had begun buying puzzles—stress busters, she'd called them—depicting the European capitals she longed to visit. One by one, she'd framed her finished projects and hung them in the hallway, souvenirs of the trips she took only in her dreams.

With a stab of grief, Jeb recalled the day of her funeral. After the graveside prayers and the meal in the church basement, he'd brought Laney home. Worried by her thousand-mile stare, he'd made her a cup of herbal tea and coaxed her to sit down with him and work on the puzzle her mother had left unfinished. They had almost completed the task when they discovered a piece was missing.

Jeb had dropped to his hands and knees and searched every inch of the carpeted floor for that tiny black bit of nighttime sky, without success. In the end, a tearful Laney had decided to hang the puzzle without it.

"I thought you were going to improvise." Jeb turned to look at her. "I gave you a black guitar pick to glue behind—"

"I can't, Jeb." Her voice was heartbreakingly subdued, just as it had been on that awful day two years ago. "It doesn't feel right to put it on the wall, but I can't break it up and put it back in the box, either. I don't know why, but I'm just not ready. So there it sits."

He ached to draw her into his arms, but encouraging her to look to him for emotional support at this point was a bad idea. As soon as she answered his questions about God, he meant to slip back out of her life. She'd be hurt at first, but in the long run, she'd be happier without him.

When she hugged herself and inhaled deeply, getting control, he felt a rush of admiration tinged with foolish disappointment.

"When I have guests for supper, we eat in the kitchen," she said. "Or I just cook and serve everything at your house."

Laney loved his mother's gourmet kitchen and her antique china. She adored everything about Jeb's house, from its high ceilings and ornate period furnishings to the hot tub he'd installed on the screened porch after his father's death, so Jeb encouraged her to treat the house as an extension of her own. He liked to think of the old walls absorbing her laughter, diluting the bitterness they'd soaked up during the long years he'd lived there with his father and Mrs. Lee.

Laney still wondered why his mother had so pain-stakingly restored and decorated the house only to take her own life almost as soon as it was finished. Jeb could have enlightened her, but that memory exercise on the plane aside, he carefully avoided thinking about his parents.

Determined to haul Laney out of the melancholy mood she'd slipped into, Jeb grasped one of her corkscrew curls and gave it a teasing tug.

"You look good," he said.

She smiled. "And you look like Mowgli."

"Who?"

"The wild boy from *The Jungle Book*. Remember? Rudyard Kipling said Mowgli had long, straight black hair that fell like curtains around his face." She turned and went back to the kitchen.

Jeb tucked the "curtains" behind his ears and followed her. It was no good protesting that he'd been too busy for a haircut. That was part of it, yes. But Laney knew how much he hated sitting defenseless while a scissors-wielding stranger snipped and clipped and tried to engage him in conversations he didn't want to have.

She also knew she was welcome to get out her electric trimmer any time she wanted.

"We're grilling steaks," she announced as she stowed the ice cream in her freezer. "And I'm making your favorite garlic-and-cheddar mashed potatoes."

Jeb's stomach greeted that news with an enthusiastic tremor. He was more than ready to drag Laney's grill out of her garden shed and light a mound of charcoal, but he hadn't missed the longing gaze she'd bestowed on that carton of ice cream.

"Dessert first," he suggested.

She gave a little whoop of joy and retrieved the ice cream.

Now, his heart urged his brain. *Tell her now.*

He cleared his throat. "Laney, I have something to—"

She spoke at the same instant: "Jeb, I never told you about—"

They both stopped and shared a look of amusement.

"You first," Laney said. "I've been doing all the talking since you got here."

"Princess." Jeb shook his head at the ceiling. "You've been doing all the talking since the day we met."

He caught the bubbly laugh he'd been fishing for. He also received a playful swat on the arm. Grinning, he nudged her aside to open a drawer and collect two spoons.

"What were you going to tell me?" he asked.

"I got engaged last month." As casually as if she'd just made some unremarkable statement about the weather, she curled an arm around the ice cream's cylindrical container and pried the lid off.

Jeb had stopped breathing, but this was hardly unexpected news. The last time he'd been home, Tom Johansen had been making a nuisance of himself. Every time Jeb came over to borrow Laney's newspaper or raid her cookie jar, Tom had been here, occupying Jeb's favorite chair and hogging the sports section while he scarfed down the last of the seven-layer bars, the ones Laney always made without nuts because Jeb didn't like nuts.

"Engaged? That's great." He couldn't pull off looking delighted, but he managed what he believed to be a credible smile. "So when's the wedding? And why didn't you call me?"

"There isn't going to be a wedding." Laney's eyes gleamed with defiance. "We broke up the very next day."

Sick relief, Jeb's initial reaction to that news, was quickly replaced by self-reproach. She'd been desperately lonely since her mother's death, and she longed for a husband and children to love. Didn't he want her to be happy?

"That's too bad," he said carefully, hoping her eyes weren't about to fill with tears. "Tom was an okay guy."

"Nathan Anderson," she corrected as she claimed one of the spoons Jeb had forgotten he was holding. "Tom and I broke up on New Year's Day."

Ten months ago? Why was he just now hearing about this? Maybe he'd never come right out and asked how things were going with good ol' Tom, but why hadn't she said anything? And who, exactly, was this Nathan character?

Dazed, Jeb sank onto a chair. "Why?"

Laney set the tub of ice cream on the table and took the chair next to his. "Why did I break up with Tom?"

Tilting his head to one side, Jeb allowed her to see his exasperation. "Both of them."

She held up her spoon, the back of its bowl facing Jeb. He observed their childhood ritual by clicking his own spoon against it.

"Tom hinted about marriage," Laney said as she dug into the ice cream. "But we started arguing a lot."

"About what?" The words were barely out of Jeb's mouth before he wished he'd swallowed them, instead. He had a pretty good idea what Laney and Tom must have argued about.

"My business, for one thing," she said. "I wouldn't take his advice, and that made him mad." She slipped a spoonful of ice cream into her mouth. Closing her eyes, she moaned blissfully.

"So he told you how to run the tearoom," Jeb prompted as she went for another bite.

"He sure tried," she said with her mouth full. "I needed to extend my hours. I needed to advertise more. To hear him talk, I wasn't doing anything right."

Jeb snorted. If Tom had failed to value her strength and intelligence, good riddance to him.

"I told myself he was just trying to help," she continued. "But then he started harping on—" She hesitated. "Well, on other things."

Things like her being so emotionally attached to another man? Yes, Jeb had seen the resentment in Tom's eyes. But even before Tom, he'd been trying to distance himself from Laney, trying to become less important in her life so she'd be able to build a healthy relationship with whatever man she chose to marry.

It hadn't been enough, obviously. He was going to have to try harder. He rubbed the back of his neck and sighed.

"I'm sorry, princess."

"Don't be. He thought I was too involved with the Graces, too. He said—"

"That's ridiculous," Jeb interrupted. "The Graces are your family."

"Tom said I was a fool to tie myself to three old ladies who will just become burdens when their health fails." As she often did when irritated, Laney twitched her left shoulder. But then she grimaced as though the movement had caused her pain.

Jeb's gaze sharpened on her. "What's wrong?"

"Just a pulled muscle." She smiled ruefully and rubbed her shoulder. "It was feeling better until last night, when I strained it again changing a flat tire on Francine."

Disturbed by the thought of slightly built Laney struggling to lift a heavy wheel out of Francine's trunk, Jeb made a mental note to give her an auto club membership for

Christmas. How was it that he'd never thought of that before now?

"But back to Tom," she said. "I think I must have talked too much about Mom, and about how hard things were before she died."

"You never resented taking care of her," Jeb pointed out. "You couldn't possibly have given him that impression."

"Maybe he was just projecting. His own mother died of lung cancer a few years back." Laney shook her head. "Anyway, he said I didn't owe anything to the family of the man who abandoned my mom when she was pregnant with me."

Jeb gestured impatiently with his spoon. "He can't blame the Graces for that."

By all accounts, the triplets had doted on Ted Ryland, the son of their deceased brother. On learning that Hannah was expecting a baby, the Graces had offered their nephew a wad of cash to pay off his debts and feather his growing family's nest. But Ryland had taken the money and skipped town with a female coworker.

He had never returned to Owatonna, although he'd had the colossal nerve to phone the Graces two or three times in the intervening years. No doubt he'd been hoping to squeeze some more money out of them.

Ryland was aware that he had a daughter. He just didn't care.

The familiar outrage rose like bile in Jeb's throat, but then he remembered something he'd read in the Bible, something about not being so quick to cast stones at other sinners, and he was ashamed. Were his own transgressions any less egregious than Ted Ryland's?

"The Graces still feel bad about giving him that money, but they couldn't have known what was on his mind." Laney shook her head in disgust at her father's defection. "How a man could do that to any woman, let alone someone as sweet as Mom, I'll never understand."

Jeb longed to say that he didn't understand it, either. But the awful truth was that he did understand how a man could walk away from a woman he'd impregnated. If the man was selfish enough, he could do that.

And even worse.

"At least Mom had the Graces," Laney said softly. "In the beginning, they helped her financially. And of course they made sure I never missed having a father."

"I know." The Graces could be as irritating as a trio of tone-deaf Karaoke singers, but their faithful support of Laney and her mom had secured Jeb's undying gratitude.

He'd noticed right off that Tom Johansen didn't understand Laney's deep attachment to her great-aunts. He might have dropped the guy a hint, but no man who loved Laney the way she deserved would have needed any urging to accept the Graces as part of the package.

Shaking his head over Tom's colossal stupidity, Jeb excavated a plump cherry half and left it on the surface of the ice cream where Laney would find it.

"So what about the other guy?" he asked.

"Nathan?" Frowning, she scooped up the cherry. "He gave me a beautiful ring, Jeb, and everything was so romantic. But he's the new guy at his law firm, and he's working hard to impress the partners, so he wanted to wait a few years before starting a family. And he only wanted one baby, although he said we could talk about having two."

"That was generous of him," Jeb said dryly. So Nathan was an idiot, too. How had he failed to notice the way Laney's face lit up whenever she spotted a baby?

"I told him I wanted a big family." The corners of her mouth trembled as she tried to smile. "And he said some nasty things about me wanting to marry him to get children rather than because I was in love."

Jeb's body went rigid. Who did that jerk think he was, talking to Laney that way? "And you said . . . ?"

"That he was right." She hung her head. "But honestly, Jeb, I didn't realize it until that moment. And now I feel just awful about the whole thing."

Jeb released the breath he'd been holding. At least the guy hadn't broken her heart.

"Laney, he wasn't the right man for you. It's good you found that out before it was too late."

"I know." She shoveled a large bite of ice cream into her mouth.

Nobody seeing her slumped over a tub of ice cream and mining greedily for cherries would ever guess she'd completed an online etiquette course and occasionally gave talks on table manners to women's groups and school kids. But then, she never showed this side of herself to anyone but Jeb. She took for granted that he'd keep this secret just as he'd kept all of the others—and she was right, he would. But a little judicious teasing might lighten her mood.

"Should an etiquette consultant be eating ice cream straight from the carton?" he asked conversationally.

She rapped his knuckles with the back of her cold, sticky spoon. "Calling attention to the imperfect manners of one's dining companion is the height of rudeness," she said primly.

"Is it?" Rubbing his abused knuckles, Jeb feigned confusion. "Then why are you correcting me?"

She chuckled, and for an instant he thought he'd succeeded in cheering her up, but then her smile flattened again.

"I'm just no good at romance. I mean, look how I messed up with Tom and Nathan." She sighed. "And let's not forget Luke."

Oh, he hadn't forgotten the veterinarian who'd strung her along for the better part of a year, telling her he loved her but wasn't ready to think about marriage. If Jeb had been in Owatonna when Laney discovered the man she loved was seeing her close friend Megan behind her back, he'd have broken the jerk's nose.

"I feel so stupid." Laney shook her head sadly. "Why do I keep falling for men who are completely wrong for me?"

"Don't be so hard on yourself. You're lonely, that's all."

The thought of her marrying always made Jeb's stomach hurt. But she was a loving, giving, family-oriented woman and she deserved to be happy.

"It's more than simple loneliness, Jeb. I think there must be something wrong with me."

"There's nothing wrong with you." He pushed another cherry toward her. "You just haven't found the right guy yet."

"What if I never find him?"

"You're only twenty-five." Jeb infused his tone with a hint of impatience. "Give it time."

"You don't understand," she muttered.

He was trying to. So hard that he inadvertently allowed some extremely foolish words to slip out of his mouth.

"Tell you what. I'll help you find a husband."

Laney's gloomy expression morphed into one of wry amusement. "Oh, thank you. I'd dearly love to marry a tattooed, stringy-haired drummer who wears muscle shirts and drinks tequila straight from the bottle."

Jeb's lips twitched because she had just described Skeptical Heart's Taylor Benson, whom she had never met.

"I appreciate the thought," she went on, looking forlorn again. "But can you honestly see me with any of the guys you associate with?"

"Of course not," he said repressively. He hoped she would never guess just how much effort he expended to protect her innocence. He had even instructed his band's booking agents to avoid any venue within a three-hour drive of Owatonna, ensuring that she would never attend one of his shows and expect to go backstage and meet the band. Sweet Laney had no business anywhere near those rowdy, profane guys.

"I see you with a good Christian man," he said. Not a confused, just-barely-saved guy like himself, but a strong, confident man. One who was worthy of her admiration and love. "And I'm going to help you find one."

Just as soon as he figured out where to start looking.

Laney arched her tawny eyebrows. "Meet a lot of good Christian men in your line of work, do you, rock star?"

Jeb blinked at the bitter, mocking tone that was as foreign to her nature as the self-pity she'd displayed a minute ago. What was wrong with her? His instincts told him it was something far more serious than a little depression over her latest disappointment in love.

"Talk to me, Laney." He slipped a hand under her silky hair to cup the back of her neck and squeeze some encouragement into her. "What's going on with you, hmm?"

She bowed her head, hiding her eyes beneath a mass of flaxen curls. "Since Mom's been gone everything just seems so hard," she said quietly. "And lately I . . ." She shook her head and drew a shuddery breath.

Jeb moved his hand, tucking his knuckles under her chin to lift her face. Her eyelashes fluttered as she looked everywhere but at him.

"What is it, princess?" He'd fix it for her or he'd die trying.

"I'm having a crisis of faith," she blurted, looking miserable and embarrassed.

"A crisis of . . ." Jeb dropped his hand and struggled to process his shock. "What do you mean?"

With a visible effort, she composed herself. "You know I've always tried to be a good Christian. But lately I've been feeling . . . abandoned."

Abandoned? If God could stomach a reprobate like Jackson Bell, he'd sure never turn his back on anyone as good as Laney.

"I don't understand," Jeb said.

"I know." Her gaze skittered away again and she nibbled her thumbnail, an old nervous habit she'd outgrown years ago. "But I can't explain it to you, Jeb. It's something only another Christian could understand."

He opened his mouth, but then shut it again. If he told her he'd just joined God's team, she'd want to talk about that instead of whatever was wrong in her life. And something was very wrong.

"I haven't been to church in two months," she said around her thumb. "I thought about going last Sunday, but

I'm ashamed to show my face after staying away so long."

It was a good thing she wasn't looking at him, because Jeb wasn't sure his carefully arranged features were adequately concealing the dismay that had just steamrolled his spirit.

A crisis of faith. How on earth was he, a clumsy and clueless brand-new believer, going to help her through this?

He'd been looking forward to sharing his good news. He'd been counting on her to answer his questions and then hustle him off to church, where she'd get him signed up for the crash courses in Christian Living and Basic Goodness and so on.

But she was having a crisis of faith.

"I don't want to talk about this right now," she said.

That was a relief. Jeb just hoped that given time to ponder all of this, his beleaguered brain would come up with a plan.

"So how's the band?" Laney's chirpy tone was as artificial as her sudden smile, but Jeb didn't call her on it. When she was ready to talk, he'd listen. She knew that.

He was struggling to compose a truthful yet necessarily vague answer to her question when she spoke again, unwittingly letting him off the hook.

"You look worn out. What have you been up to?"

That, at least, he could explain. "We just did a six-week tour with only five days off," he said, watching as she slipped another spoonful of ice cream into her mouth. "We had sellout crowds at almost every venue."

She nodded, absorbing that without comment. She was fiercely proud of his musical ability, but profanity-laced, sexually suggestive songs made her uncomfortable, so Jeb could hardly expect her to root for his band's success.

They never discussed it, but she had to know he wrote and performed that hard-edged music to vent the nameless fury that had swirled inside him for as long as he could remember. Being with Laney soothed his savage heart, but every time he'd left the calm sphere of her influence, he had reverted to his wild ways.

He longed to tell her things would be different now, but that would have to wait.

"I came home for a rest," he said, hoping God would overlook a half-truth told in a good cause. He'd have to dig through his stolen Bible and see what he could find out about that.

"You were more than just tired last night," she said. "You were depressed." When he opened his mouth to speak, she shook her head at him. "And don't tell me I just imagined it. I *know* you, Jeb."

"All right." He had to give her something, or she'd never stop probing. "This past week has been . . . difficult."

Sympathy wrinkled her brow. "Problems on the tour?"

He confirmed that with a brief nod, because it was perfectly true, wasn't it? Shari Daltry had been pressing him to deny his new faith, and last night Matt, Sean, Aaron, and even easygoing Taylor had glared at him with homicide in their hearts.

Laney touched his arm. "Tell me," she urged in that honey-sweet voice that was always so hard to resist.

"I will," he promised. "But later, okay?"

"You have dark circles under your eyes," she complained in her gentle way. "And you're too thin." She smoothed his hair back from his forehead, just as her mother might have done.

If only Hannah were here right now. She'd grab both of them by the scruffs of their necks and haul them to church and get them straightened out. But Hannah wasn't here, so Jeb would just have to do the best he could.

Laney returned her attention to the ice cream, digging deep and muttering something about Jeb hogging the cherries.

Ignoring that unfair accusation, he tapped his spoon against his bottom lip, thinking hard. Finally, a memory stirred.

"Laney?" He struggled to conceal his excitement. "Doesn't your church have some kind of singles' group?"

She looked surprised by the question, and no wonder.

"There's a singles' Bible study on Tuesday nights," she said. "I went a few times before Mom died. Why do you ask?"

"We're hunting for a good Christian man," he reminded her. "Wouldn't that be the place to find one?"

Her expression had turned stony. "Right now I wouldn't be comfortable at any church function," she said as she scooped up some more ice cream. "I'm too depressed."

"Maybe if you went to some church functions you'd stop being depressed." Instantly regretting the way exasperation had sharpened his tone, Jeb offered her a lopsided grin. "Tell you what. I'll go with you. How's that for incentive?"

"*You?*" She fumbled her spoon. As it clattered on the table, its load of ice cream flew off and plopped onto Jeb's thigh.

"Why not?" With his finger and thumb, he picked up the frozen blob and transferred it to his mouth. "It won't kill me." With studied nonchalance, he licked his fingers and rubbed the ice cream smudge off his jeans before adding, "I'll even go to church with you on Sunday."

Careful not to smile at her soft gasp of surprise, he waited another heartbeat before lifting his gaze to her startled face. He'd hooked her; now all he had to do was reel her in.

"Are you serious?" she asked.

She had every reason to wonder. Unless Hannah's funeral service counted, Jeb had never been inside a church in his life.

"I'm serious." He was also a genius. There was no way Laney could reject this plan, but he endeavored to look resolute rather than exultant. "Church on Sunday, then. What time?"

Her lips curled into a mocking smile. "We'd have to leave here at nine. The service starts at nine-fifteen."

So early? Jeb was no good at mornings. But he was a Christian now, and he figured church attendance was part of the deal.

"Okay. I'll be here for coffee at a quarter to nine."

"Hah." Amusement danced in her eyes. "Remember college? You always ended up dropping your early classes because you could never—"

"I'll be here at a quarter to nine," Jeb repeated. "And don't worry about how you're going to break the ice. When people see me at church, they'll be too stunned to ask why you haven't been around lately."

"You don't have to do this, Jeb." She gave him a wistful smile. "But it means a lot to me that you offered."

"We're going to church and to the singles' thing," he said firmly. "First we'll get your faith back, and then we'll find you a nice Christian guy to m—" He was interrupted by the chiming of Laney's doorbell.

"I'm not expecting anyone." Her gaze shifted past him to the corner windows, and then her eyes widened in alarm.

Jeb swung around to look.

His rented Explorer was no longer the only vehicle in her driveway. Just behind it, he could see the front end of a black-and-white police cruiser.

And Laney had gone deathly pale.

Chapter Five

HAD SOMETHING HAPPENED to the Graces on their way home from the tearoom? All kinds of frightening scenarios involving crumpled cars and broken bodies flashed through Laney's mind as she raced to the front door. When she flung it open and recognized the big blond police officer smiling at her through the glass storm door, her trepidation receded. This was no emergency call.

She basked in that relief for about two seconds before it dawned on her that the cop must be following up on Tuesday night's burglary attempt. That was a problem because she hadn't yet told Jeb about it—and he was standing right behind her.

She'd planned to get a good supper in his belly before breaking the news. And she'd meant to avoid disclosing that she'd chased the housebreakers and ended up hurt. She didn't want Jeb driving himself crazy imagining how much worse it all might have been.

So this was going to be tricky. He wasn't good with strangers to begin with, and things could go downhill fast if Laney was forced to give her carefully edited account of the break-in in front of a third party who knew every detail and who might say something awkward.

"Officer Sayers." She fixed a bright smile on her face and opened the storm door. "Come in."

"Evening, Ms. Ryland." The cop stepped inside, glanced at Jeb and nodded politely, and then returned his attention to Laney. "I just stopped by to—" His head whipped back toward Jeb.

Wonderful.

"What can I do for you?" Laney asked, still smiling determinedly.

"Uh..." With an obvious effort, he dragged his gaze away from Jeb. "I was just in the neighborhood. Thought I'd make sure you haven't had any further trouble."

Laney's smile slipped, but at least she refrained from rolling her eyes. So he'd stopped by to flirt with her some more, had he?

He'd certainly turned on the charm the other night, but only after he'd learned who owned the house next door. Laney hadn't been fooled; it was hardly the first time someone had attempted to further an acquaintance with her in the hope of scoring an introduction to Jackson Bell.

Predictably, the words "further trouble" had galvanized Jeb. He'd just moved to her side like a well-trained attack dog.

Their arms were almost touching, so Laney eased back a little and extended her elbow to give his ribs a surreptitious poke. When he frowned down at her, she murmured, "I'll explain later" before turning back to beam at Officer Sayers.

"We're just fine here," she said. "But it was nice of you to stop by."

"No problem." He darted another look at Jeb but made no move to leave. "So how's that injured shoulder doing?"

"Injured?" Jeb rumbled like an awakening volcano. "I thought you just pulled a muscle."

Laney swallowed a groan of pure exasperation. "I did, Jeb. And it's no big deal." Trying for a nonchalant shrug, she ruined the effect by wincing at a stab of pain. Seeing his ferocious scowl, she hastily added, "Okay, it hurts. But it'll be better tomorrow."

"You were lucky," Officer Sayers said. "I just hope you understand that confronting those guys with a baseball bat wasn't your best move."

"What's he talking about?" This time Jeb's rumble was loud enough to reverberate in the high-ceilinged entryway.

"It was just a couple of boys," Laney said dismissively. "High school kids."

"What did they do?" Jeb demanded.

"Hardly anything. They broke into your house, but I scared them off. So they didn't—"

"You went after a bunch of burglars with a baseball bat?"

Laney's patience unraveled. "It wasn't a 'bunch of burglars', Jeb. It was two skinny teenage boys who were probably just after your guitars and some other souvenirs. They broke one of the bay windows, but I had it replaced and—"

"I don't care about the window!" he bellowed.

Officer Sayers stiffened visibly. When he opened his mouth, Laney forgot her manners and signaled with a sharply upraised hand that she didn't need protecting from Jeb.

"What did they do to you?" Jeb's voice had gone ominously quiet.

"When they were running away, one of them knocked me down," Laney said. "I fell on the bat and wrenched my shoulder."

Like a man suffering agonies, he pressed a hand over his eyes and groaned.

"I'm fine," Laney insisted.

Muscles twitched in Jeb's lean jaw as he lowered his hand and impaled her with a look. "It was a stupid thing to do. Why didn't you just call the police?"

"I think she's learned her lesson," Officer Sayers ventured.

"I have." Laney nodded emphatically. "I can't believe I did something that dumb."

Jeb just stared at her, his jaws flexing in a way that couldn't be good for his molars.

"Bob Sayers." Wading into the tense silence, the cop thrust his right hand toward Jeb. "I'm a huge fan."

"Thanks." Jeb's tone was dismissive, but instead of nodding curtly, his usual response to an introduction he hadn't sought, he shook the proffered hand.

Officer Sayers beamed like a kid at Christmas. "So, it's 'Jeb,' then?"

"No," Jeb said shortly. "It's Jackson."

He never allowed anyone but Laney and her family to use the name she'd given him. He loathed his real name because it had been his father's, yet anyone who dared to call him Jeb or even Jack received a flinty stare for that presumption. It was just one of the ways he kept the world at arm's length.

Officer Sayers didn't appear to be fazed by Jeb's chilly demeanor. "Last summer a friend and I drove to Des Moines and Chicago to catch your shows," he enthused. "When are you going to play the Twin Cities?"

No idea." Jeb folded his arms across his chest and glared down at the much shorter man. "Shouldn't you be out looking for the thugs who hurt Laney?"

"Jeb." Laney flung him a look of disgusted reproach,

then smiled an apology at Officer Sayers. "We'll let you know if we have any more trouble," she promised, moving closer to the door and hoping he could take a hint.

Under normal circumstances, nobody left her home without being offered a cup of coffee at the very least. But she could practically hear Jeb's nerves buzzing like high-tension wires, and she had to get him calmed down.

"Thanks for stopping by," she added.

"You bet." The cop's gaze swung back to Jeb. "You folks take care, now."

Laney opened the storm door. "You, too. 'Bye." She watched him descend the porch steps, and then she closed both doors and looked at Jeb, who was still frowning fiercely.

"I was going to tell you after supper," she said.

"You went after them with a baseball bat," he repeated incredulously.

"Don't make it sound so gruesome, Jeb. I just yelled and swung the bat to scare them off."

His head fell back in obvious exasperation. "Great plan," he said to the ceiling. "Because who wouldn't be terrified by a sweet little blonde with a baseball bat?"

"They *did* run away," Laney retorted.

His hard gaze snapped back to her. "What if they had attacked you, instead? What were you thinking, Laney?"

"I *wasn't* thinking, all right?" She hated the sudden shrillness of her tone, but made no attempt to moderate it. "I woke up in the middle of the night and saw them breaking into your house and it made me mad!"

Why couldn't he just accept that she'd made a dumb mistake and drop the subject? Shaking her head in disgust, she turned back toward the kitchen.

He captured her arm as she tried to walk past him. "Laney, you know I don't care about anything in that house," he rumbled. "You had no business risking your life to save a few stupid guitars."

She stared up at him in wordless frustration. How could she explain that she was fiercely protective of his house and its contents because sometimes it seemed they were all she had left of him?

She tugged her arm from his grasp and stumbled over to her favorite armchair. Sinking onto its marshmallow-soft cushion, she burst into tears.

"Ah, *don't*." Dropping to his knees beside her, Jeb curved an arm around her shoulders. "Please don't, princess. I'm sorry for yelling."

"It isn't that." Ashamed of her childish display, she wiped her eyes with her fingertips and rubbed her cheeks dry.

"I'm still sorry." Jeb's big warm hand smoothed the curls back from her forehead. Laney was tempted to close her eyes and lean into the caress, but she pushed his hand away.

"Jeb, don't sell your house," she blurted. "It's not like you need the money."

His dark eyebrows slanted even more sharply inward. "Have I said anything about selling my house?"

"The Graces think you're going to."

"The Graces." Jeb again lifted his gaze to the ceiling, this time like a man praying for patience. Which of course he wasn't, since he didn't believe in God.

"Laney, I am not selling the house."

"I know there's no reason for you to keep it." The property he'd inherited from his father had no claim on Jeb's heart. "And I know you think it's too much work for me." Her voice had begun to wobble, so she drew a steadying breath. "But if you sell it, you might never come back to Owatonna."

"Why wouldn't I ..." His words trailed off as his mystified expression gave way to surprise. "You think that house is what brought me back to Owatonna?"

"Jeb, I don't know what to think." All she knew was that spending time with her no longer seemed to be a priority in his life. "I hardly know you anymore."

"You know me," he insisted in a voice that was oceans deep.

"Not anymore." She shook her head and then couldn't seem to stop shaking it. "I don't know anything anymore."

"Come here."

He pulled her into an awkward sideways hug. The rigid arm of the otherwise fluffy chair dug into her ribs and she felt a painful twinge in her shoulder, but she was too upset to protest.

"That house isn't my home," he murmured into her hair. "*You* are."

Oh, really? She lifted her face to glare at him. He had some nerve, pretending nothing had changed when *everything* had changed.

"You haven't seen me in more than a year," she accused. "And not counting last night, when was the last time you called? Do you even remember?"

"Yes, I remember!" he snapped. Letting her go, he sat back on his heels and rubbed his forehead as though his head ached. Then he closed his eyes and repeated the words in a dejected, barely audible tone, "Believe me, I remember."

An awful suspicion settled over Laney. "You've been

staying away on purpose?"

He winced and averted his face. It was all the confirmation she needed.

She had to tilt her head to recapture his gaze. "Don't I deserve an explanation?"

He just stared back at her, pleading with his eyes for her to let it go, but she couldn't do that. If he wouldn't tell her what was wrong, how were they ever going to fix it?

"Jeb, *please.*"

Finally, he nodded. But when he again turned his face away from her, she was gripped by a foreboding that made her want to cover her ears and protect herself from hearing the explanation she'd demanded.

"You call me your best friend," he said slowly. "But that doesn't quite explain what's between us, does it? Do you really think a husband will accept that?" He rose to his feet and rubbed his forehead again. "Laney, we're not kids anymore. Our relationship has to change."

"No!" Her voice broke on the word, but somehow she got the rest out. "Besides, you just said I was your h-home."

"I shouldn't have said it. Things aren't that simple anymore." A bitter smile bent his lips. "We're all grown up, Laney. And this—" He spread his arms in a vague gesture that suggested he, too, was frustrated. "This is how life works. Kids grow up and move on."

"Well, sometimes life stinks," she muttered.

"Yeah." He walked over to the window. Bracing his hands on the sill, he slumped forward, his shoulders rounding as his chin sank toward his chest. "Sometimes it does."

Observing his defeated posture, Laney silently berated

herself. Her happiness wasn't Jeb's responsibility; he had his own dreams to follow. It wasn't right to make him feel guilty for leaving her behind.

He raised his head and fixed a hard gaze on something outside the window. "My calendar's clear for the immediate future," he said. "I'll stay for a while and do my best to help you get settled. But when I go, Laney, I won't be back for a long time, and I won't be calling you much, either." Sliding his hands from the sill, he turned to face her. "Tell me you can accept that."

Laney opened her mouth to protest, but then thought better of it. She'd save this fight for later, when she wasn't so annoyed with him and she'd worked out the best way to make him understand that if he had just *called* her once in a while, his emotions wouldn't have gotten into such a tangle that he'd concluded it would be in her best interest to end the most amazing friendship either of them would ever know.

Deep breath. Okay.

"I'm sorry about getting all emotional," she said with a nervous laugh. "I've been a little depressed lately, but it's nothing, Jeb, really. I'll be fine, I promise."

His troubled gaze searched her face. She stared back at him, her mind carefully blanked, until she sensed his tension receding. Only after the last glimmer of doubt disappeared from his eyes did she allow herself a slow, careful breath.

"Come on." She slapped her palms against the arms of her chair and pushed herself up. "Our ice cream is melting."

* * *

When her alarm clock buzzed at six-thirty the next morning, Laney extended a hand from her cozy, quilted cocoon and smacked the snooze button. She'd spent most of the night turning in her bed like a chicken in a rotisserie oven; it couldn't have been more than three hours since she'd stopped worrying about Jeb and succumbed to an exhausted, dreamless sleep.

She hit the snooze button twice more, and then had to rush through her morning routine. But at least the pain in her shoulder had begun to fade.

By the time she made it down to the kitchen, it was too late to brew a pot of coffee and savor her usual two cups while perusing the morning paper, so she microwaved a mug of instant espresso. She had just leaned against the kitchen counter to enjoy a few bracing sips when in the orange-pink light of dawn she saw Jeb slog past the windows, head down and shoulders hunched.

To say that Jeb wasn't a morning person was to understate the case to the point of hilarity. Laney couldn't imagine what he was doing awake at this hour, but the fact that he'd dragged himself over here could mean only one thing: She'd forgotten to buy coffee when she'd picked up his groceries.

She let him in and surrendered her mug of espresso. He grunted like an exhausted caveman and swallowed some of the hot beverage, and then he paused to stare at her in bleary-eyed puzzlement.

"It's instant," she said. "But it's fully caffeinated."

His eyes slid shut and he drank deeply.

"Look at you," she said. Outside, the grass was covered with frost, but Jeb was barefoot. He wore jeans and a plaid flannel shirt with only one button fastened—and that button had been matched up with the wrong hole, causing the shirt to hang crooked on his lanky frame. His too-long, almost-black hair, stringy and uncombed, completely hid his right eye.

"Honestly, Jeb, you need a keeper."

He grunted again and moved past her to slump onto a chair, adorably pathetic.

Shaking her head, Laney opened a cupboard and got out a can of ground coffee. A single cup of instant was never going to do it for Jeb, so she fitted a paper filter into the basket of her drip coffeemaker and loaded it up.

Filling the carafe with tap water, she looked at Jeb over her shoulder. "What are you doing up, anyway?"

"Some idiot journalist called from New York City." Scowling ferociously, he scratched the black stubble on his chin. "Who makes phone calls at seven-thirty in the morning?"

Laney opened her mouth to point out that it was eight-thirty in New York, but then she thought better of it. "People who don't realize musicians sleep in the daytime," she offered instead. "Why didn't you just turn off the ringer and go back to sleep?"

He tilted his head so that the tangle of hair flopped away from his right eye, affording Laney an unobstructed view of his indignant stare. "Because that would have meant—" He interrupted himself with a huge yawn. "—waking up twice. Once a day is bad enough."

Laney clucked in sympathy as she poured water into the coffeemaker's reservoir. She could hardly wait to see how he would handle leaving for church at nine o'clock on Sunday morning.

"And I can't turn off the ringer," he grumbled. "What if you needed to call me?"

Laney flicked the coffeemaker's switch and grabbed her heaviest wool cardigan off its peg by the door. "You're seriously underestimating my instinct for self-preservation," she said as she pushed her arms into the bulky sleeves. "I'd never call you before noon. Not even if my hair was on fire."

"Laney." His severe tone made her freeze in the act of buttoning the sweater.

Wishing she'd thought twice before teasing him at this early hour, she moved behind his chair and hugged his neck.

"It was just a joke, Jeb. You know I didn't mean it."

He patted her forearms, possibly to indicate his forgiveness but more likely to signal that he wanted to drink his coffee. Laney released him and straightened, but didn't move away. As her coffeemaker rumbled and hissed, wafting a delicious aroma through the kitchen, she finger-combed Jeb's hair.

He could talk all he wanted about childhood friends growing up and growing apart, but he was still her wild boy, still desperately in need of love and acceptance but terrified of admitting it. His taciturn nature and his piercing stare led people to believe he was dangerous, but Jeb was as sweetly vulnerable as a child.

"Call me when you wake up." Laney rubbed a silky lock of dark hair between her finger and thumb. "I wouldn't say no to a nice supper tonight." She paused. "Or do you California people call it dinner?"

He muttered something unintelligible and drank some more coffee.

"I haven't been to that French place in a while," Laney hinted. Her favorite restaurant was in Minneapolis, more than an hour's drive from Owatonna, but Jeb liked driving.

He grunted again, and Laney decided she'd better stop pestering him. Anyway, she had to get to the tearoom and start the day's baking.

"If my newspaper's not on the front porch, check the azalea bushes," she said. "And you'll find some apricot-oatmeal bars in the cookie jar. I don't suppose they'd make a bad breakfast." Not for Jeb, who could stand to put some meat on his bones. "Just be sure to have some orange juice, too."

As she worked one last tangle out of his hair, she realized there was something unfamiliar about his scent. Leaning forward, she sniffed to determine whether he was using a new shampoo. When that experiment yielded no conclusive result, she decided that her nose must still be accustomed to Nathan's expensive colognes.

She moved her hands to his shoulders and gave him two light, affectionate pats. "You have a good day," she said, and turned to go.

Jeb's hand snaked out and captured one of her wrists. He squeezed hard, for just a second, and then he released her without looking up.

"You're welcome," she said softly. "I don't know how I forgot to buy coffee for your house." She scooped up her bag and headed out the door, trusting him to switch off the coffeemaker and lock up when he left.

Having Jeb home always righted her world, but there was nothing for him in Owatonna. He needed to make music, and he couldn't do that here.

Approaching his garage, Laney pressed the button on her remote and waited while the door rumbled upward. Maybe all of this would be easier to accept if she'd had some inkling, back in those halcyon days when Jeb had been a fixture of her daily life, that things would eventually change. That his phone calls and his trips home would dwindle in frequency and duration and then stop entirely.

Last night he'd said this was simply the way of things. Maybe it was, but why did it have to hurt so much? And why did this revelation have to come at a time when her emotions were already stretched to the breaking point?

* * *

"I just can't deal with this," she muttered several hours later as she stood in the tearoom's kitchen stirring the thick batter that would become tomorrow's lemon-pecan tea bread. "If one more thing goes wrong this week, I'm going to scream."

"No, you're not," Caroline said bracingly. "You'll handle this little setback like the strong woman you are."

Little setback? This was an unmitigated disaster. The tearoom's furnace had stopped working, and where she was going to find the money to have it repaired, Laney didn't know.

She shoved the mixing bowl aside and pressed her fingertips against her eyelids until she saw sparks, but that did nothing to ease her tension headache. Neither did the low roar of the fan she'd placed in the doorway to blow the kitchen's heat into the dining room.

"Just tell me it's warm enough in there," she begged.

"It's not too bad," Caroline said. "The thermostat says it's 65 degrees, and I don't think it'll get any colder because it's 50 outside and the sun has just come out. A lady from Missouri complained about being cold, but everyone knows those people have thin blood. Aggie found her a sweater to wear at the table instead of her bulky coat, so she's all right now."

Laney stopped abusing her eyeballs to look hopefully at her great-aunt. "Was that the only complaint?"

Caroline dipped her head to peer at Laney over the rims of her glasses. "Do you honestly think Minnesotans are going to whine about having a few goosebumps?"

"I guess not." Most Minnesotans didn't even bother zipping their jackets before January, but they weren't whiners in any case, the majority of them being descendants of hardy Germans or Scandinavians. And they couldn't listen without embarrassment to people who complained about their troubles, either.

That made things difficult for a misfit like Laney, whose emotions required regular venting.

A wry smile tugged at her mouth. "So everyone's sitting out there with blue lips and frost on their eyebrows, drinking stone-cold tea and telling each other it could be worse?"

"Yeah, pretty much." Caroline gave her a look charged with meaning. "And there's a lot to be said for that attitude."

The phone rang. Grateful for the interruption, Laney grabbed the receiver.

"Good afternoon. Three Graces Tearoom."

"Hey," Jeb said. "How's your day going?"

She glanced at Caroline. "It could be worse," she said, although she really didn't see how. "What are you doing?"

"Fishing."

"That's good." Picturing him in his canoe on a tranquil lake, a hunched shoulder trapping his cell phone against his ear while he baited a hook, Laney exhaled some of her tension. "Catching anything?"

"A couple of walleyes, but they weren't keepers. Good thing I already made reservations for the French place." He paused. "Why do you sound so wistful?"

Caroline was walking away, but Laney took the precaution of lowering her voice. "Because I'd rather be with you on the lake than stuck here, tangled up in an endless string of emergencies." Unlike her mother, Laney didn't thrive on the unremitting pressure that was the small-business owner's lot.

"What's going on?" Jeb asked.

"The furnace died." Laney twisted several tight curlicues of the phone's cord around her index finger. "And I can't get anybody to look at it until tomorrow."

"I'll round up some space heaters and get there as soon as I can," he said.

"No, we're okay for now. I've had the ovens going all day, and I've got my big fan set just inside the kitchen door to blow warm air into the dining room. But thanks."

"You're stressed out," he said. "Let's do the French place another time and just go to Willie's tonight."

"Comfort food," Laney said on a grateful sigh. "Yes." One of Willie's juicy cheeseburgers and some melt-in-your-mouth onion rings sounded a lot better right now than rushing home to change before making that long drive to the Cities.

"Pick me up here, Jeb, okay?" Noticing that the tip of her finger had turned purple, Laney freed it from the phone cord's strangling coils. "Megan's car is in the shop and she had to take her mother to St. Cloud, so I let her borrow Francine."

"You're doing favors for the woman who stole your boyfriend?" Jeb's voice vibrated with disapproval. "Laney, you *cried* over that guy."

"Yes, I cried over Luke," she snapped. "I cried over Tom and Nathan, too. I thought I was in love with each of them, but I was really just trying it on, like I might try on a pretty pair of shoes and be tempted to buy them even though they pinched my toes. So now I'm frustrated and ashamed, and I can't trust myself to recognize a good fit even if I find one, and—" She stopped and pressed two fingers against her throbbing left temple. "I'm sorry. I shouldn't have gone off on you like that."

"You know I don't mind a little ranting." Jeb's voice had deepened and gentled; the warm sound was as soothing as the softly lapping waves of a tranquil lake. "But save it for tonight, when you don't have a tearoom to run."

She closed her eyes and nodded. "Okay. And on second thought, just wait for me at home. Mrs. Lindstrom is out of town tonight, and I promised to feed her cat. So I'll get the Graces to drop me off, and then—"

"The Graces?" he interrupted. "Have you lost your mind?"

"They're not that bad, Jeb." The Graces took turns chauffeuring each other around in the mile-long silver Buick they'd owned for as long as Laney could remember. Maybe they did drive a bit too fast, but they weren't as reckless as Jeb thought. "They've never had an accident."

"Only because everyone in town knows that Buick and stays out of its way."

"You're a fine one to talk about bad driving habits," Laney retorted. "You totaled two cars before your twenty-first birthday, and who knows what havoc you've been wreaking since you moved to California." Although to give him his due, whenever he drove Laney anywhere, he scrupulously obeyed the speed limit and every other law.

That was her mother's doing. Once Hannah had discovered Jeb's protective streak where Laney was concerned, she'd worked tirelessly to nurture it. She'd drilled into his head that Laney was never to be exposed to reckless driving, foul language, cigarettes, alcohol . . . The list went on and on, but Jeb had kept every rule.

"I'll pick you up at the tearoom," he said. "We'll swing by to feed the cat, and then we'll go to Willie's. Just call when you're ready."

"No, wait," Laney said before he could hang up. "Would you mind coming early? Say, five-fifteen?"

Several seconds elapsed before Jeb replied in a flat tone, "You want me to have tea with the Graces."

"Would you?" Over the years Jeb had suffered countless indignities at the Graces' hands, and he probably still hadn't forgiven them for an incident involving a pink rabbit costume. But in their own eccentric way, the Graces adored him. "They can't wait to see you, Jeb."

"Get their claws into me, you mean." He made an amused sound in his throat. "Hey, I could ask them to help me find you a husband."

"Don't even joke about that." The Graces were dears, but their matchmaking schemes were often embarrassingly obvious to the parties involved, and Laney didn't want them interfering in *her* love life.

"I'm surprised they're not already on the job," Jeb said.

Now that he mentioned it, Laney was surprised, too. Her great-aunts had never even attempted to fix her up with a man. Not that she'd have tolerated that, but still.

"Jeb, I'll see you later," she said absently, and hung up.

Why weren't the Graces trying to marry her off? Could they believe she wasn't ready for marriage? She thought about that as she greased the loaf pans for her lemon bread.

Maybe she *wasn't* ready. And maybe the reason she was having so much trouble finding the right man was that she hadn't yet found herself.

Chapter Six

STARING AT A PATCH OF BLUE SKY through the tearoom's parted lace curtains, Caroline Grace Ryland sipped tea from a china cup and smiled to herself. Being seventy-nine was a pretty good deal as long as you had a sharp mind, good health, and plenty of friends whose lives needed meddling in. Caroline had all of those things, as did her sisters Agatha and Millicent, so they had nothing to complain about.

The firstborn of a set of identical triplets who shared a middle name, a house, a car, and a job, it was Caroline who dreamed up most of their plans for improving people's lives, although Aggie and Millie often had good ideas, too.

Their favorite activity was matchmaking. None of them had ever married, but that hadn't dampened their enthusiasm for nudging others toward matrimony. Over the years Caroline and her sisters had successfully married off more couples than they could count on all six of their hands.

Too bad the match they most wanted to see was the one they couldn't actively promote. Laney disapproved of the Graces' methods, said they were heavy handed, and maintained that she'd rather die than be subjected to one of what she called her great-aunts' "unsubtle introductions."

That was unfortunate, because the Graces had already discovered Laney's perfect man. It was true that he had a few more things to learn about life and love before he'd be ready for marriage, but so did Laney. So for now, all the Graces could do was wait—and pray that the girl wouldn't do anything hasty and irrevocable, like marrying the wrong man.

"Adding candied ginger pieces to this shortbread was a stroke of genius," Millie said as she pushed a plate of cookies across the table to Caroline.

"We shouldn't be eating these," Aggie chided their younger sister. "We could have served them to the customers tomorrow."

"I thought we'd come in early and whip up a fresh batch," Millie said with an injured air. "You know I wouldn't make extra work for Laney."

"It's not just the work. Those ingredients cost money, and right now she's pinching every penny." Caroline sighed and then added, "What an awful time for the furnace to give out."

"That girl and her pride," Aggie grumbled. "She knows she'll get all of our money after we kick the bucket. Why won't she take some of it now?"

"Because she has her mother's determined streak," Caroline said approvingly.

"I guess we should be grateful she's nothing like her father," Aggie conceded.

They rarely spoke of their nephew, the scoundrel who'd charmed them out of six thousand dollars and then skipped town with that floozy from Mankato.

"Don't even mention him." Millie's tone was uncharacteristically harsh. "I know the Christian way is to forgive, but . . ." She shook her head in disgust.

Caroline had never quite forgiven him, either. But God had healed Hannah's broken heart and Laney had grown into a strong, fine young woman.

Caroline reached for the teapot and topped off her sisters' cups before refilling her own. The most enjoyable part of their day was when the last table in the dining room had been cleared and they sat down, pleasantly exhausted, to their own afternoon tea. Of course, today was different because Laney hadn't let them finish their work. Insisting that Millie looked tired, she had ordered the Graces to relax while she served the day's last customers, two young mothers with three adorable little girls.

"She needs babies of her own," Millie murmured as they watched Laney help the little girls remove the beribboned hats and long ropes of fake pearls they'd borrowed from the dress-up chest in the corner. "I wish we could hurry up and get her settled."

"I know," Aggie said. "Waiting for that girl to wake up and smell the coffee is—"

"Enough." Caroline put the teapot down with a thump. "We've discussed this to death." Reigning in her irritation, she added in a milder tone, "All we can do now is watch and wait."

"But we're women of action," Aggie complained.

"Not in this case. And it's time to face the possibility that things might not turn out the way we hope."

Millie's eyes widened. "Are you saying we might be wrong about this, Caro?"

"Wrong?" Aggie glared at Millie. "We're never wrong. Not when it comes to matchmaking."

"We're not wrong," Caroline said. "But Laney's in a hurry to get married, and that's dangerous."

"That's for sure," Aggie said. "We came close to losing her when Nathan put that gaudy rock on her finger."

Millie nibbled unhappily on a shortbread cookie. "There must be something we can do."

"We'll keep praying about it." Grasping a tiny pair of silver-plated tongs, Caroline selected two sugar cubes from the china bowl in front of her and dropped them into her tea. As she picked up her spoon to stir, a movement drew her attention to the front windows. The slanting rays of the late-afternoon sun struck a tall man from behind, casting his face in shadow, but that long, loose-limbed stride was unmistakable.

"Here comes Jeb," she said.

"Oh, good." Aggie's eyes twinkled with mischief.

"Let's go easy on him this time," tenderhearted Millie urged.

"That boy can take anything we dish out," Aggie said proudly.

They'd sure had fun with him over the years. When they had first met young Jackson Bell, they'd seen right off that although he was starved for love, he was fearful of accepting it. Not even Laney's mother had been allowed to hug him or speak tender words to him. So taking their cue from their adored elder brother's treatment of themselves decades earlier, the Graces had demonstrated their affection for Jeb by relentless teasing.

Caroline supposed that was a little nutty. But theirs was a complicated relationship because Jeb was a complicated boy. He wasn't a *good* boy, but underneath all that simmering anger he possessed a noble heart. His remarkable devotion to Laney was proof of that.

As for his steadfast refusal to engage with the rest of the world, that was no mystery to anyone who knew his background. Jeb was like a dog that had been kicked so many times he growled even when well-meaning people tried to approach him.

The Graces were under no illusions; it was solely for Laney's sake that Jeb had tolerated their shenanigans for all these years. But that wounded, bewildered boy was now a man, and men had their pride.

"Millie's right," Caroline said. "We'd better not push him too far. The consequences could be disastrous."

* * *

The trouble with the Three Graces, Jeb decided as he pulled open the glass front door of the tearoom named in their honor, was that they weren't malicious. If they *had* been, he'd have glared them out of his life years ago. But they were merely mischievous, and Laney adored them. So here he was, showered and shaved and carefully attired in black pants and a dark blue button-down shirt, bracing himself to have his manly pride sliced and diced like mincemeat for a Christmas pie.

He paused just inside the door and surveyed the familiar dining room. With its lace-curtained windows and its rosy pink walls adorned with English garden prints, the place was decidedly feminine. Only occasionally did men cross this threshold; the few who dared always looked distinctly uncomfortable as they perched on the lady-size bamboo chairs and pinched the handles of china teacups between their large, clumsy fingers.

It was different for Jeb. Laney had decorated this room, and Jeb couldn't be uncomfortable in any environment that had Laney's personality stamped all over it.

She was busy with some customers, but she'd noticed his arrival and aimed a distracted smile in his direction. He acknowledged her greeting with a slight lift of his chin. Then he squared his shoulders and made for the Graces' table.

They were still as plump as pumpkins, with finely spun clouds of white hair that reminded Jeb of the cotton candy he used to buy Laney when he took her to the pig races and lumberjack shows at the Steele County Fair. They still wore shapeless print dresses and wire-rimmed glasses and sly, knowing smiles.

Jeb had never been able to tell them apart except by looking straight into their eyes. Caroline's gaze was sharp and intelligent. Aggie's eyes glinted with mischief. And Millie always looked a little worried, as though she wanted to apologize for whatever torment she and her sisters were about to inflict on him.

He greeted each of them by name, took a seat at the table set with riotously mismatched floral china, and dragged a starched napkin over his lap.

"So, isn't your hair a little long, there, Jeb?" Aggie smiled with friendly disapproval.

"Laney will take care of it when she has time," he said.

Millie leaned toward him and patted his arm. "You still clean up real nice, though."

He did his best to look gratified by the compliment.

"Will you be in town long?" Aggie asked.

"Not sure." Jeb wondered again why they were so eager for him to leave. "But the hockey tickets were a nice surprise. Thank you."

Caroline placed a silver strainer over his cup to catch stray tea leaves as she poured him some fragrant, steaming Earl Grey. "It was our pleasure, Jeb."

Was it? If they wanted him out of town, why give him tickets for a game more than three weeks away? If not for those tickets, he might think they were trying to get rid of him so they could fix Laney up with some man they knew. Because certainly the Graces realized, even if Laney didn't, that most men wouldn't appreciate their love interest's having another man for a best friend.

Millie slipped a transparent slice of lemon into his cup. "You should come by the house and meet our new cat."

Jeb just looked at her. His memories of the Graces' *old* cat were still uncomfortably vivid. How many times had he climbed the oak tree in the Graces' front yard to rescue stupid Frankie, who always repaid him with a vicious scratching?

As far as Jeb had ever been able to tell, the Graces had made it their mission in life to keep him humble. They twisted him like a pretzel, but for Laney's sake he pretended to be about ninety percent less annoyed with them than he actually was at any given moment. He had even forgiven them—well, almost—for tricking him into wearing that pink rabbit suit.

"Too bad you weren't here in August," Aggie said. "We could have used you at the county fair."

The Graces were always up to their dimpled elbows in charitable fundraisers, and until he'd moved to L.A., Jeb had been their favorite sucker whenever they'd needed a booth manned. Seeing her great-aunts happy always put a warm glow in Laney's blue eyes, so Jeb had allowed the triplets to inconvenience and humiliate him on a fairly regular basis.

"What did you sell?" he asked, showing polite interest and wishing Laney could witness this proof that he wasn't entirely lacking in social skills.

"Hotdish-on-a-stick," Millie said.

Jeb was as familiar as any other Minnesotan with hotdish, which was essentially any casserole involving meat or poultry paired with noodles or potatoes in a binding sauce, typically canned cream of mushroom soup. But—

"Hotdish-on-a-stick?"

"You slide meatballs and Tater Tots onto wood skewers," Aggie explained. "Then you batter and deep-fry them and serve them with a cup of mushroom gravy for dipping."

"They look like lumpy corndogs," Millie added. "Laney says they're revolting, but they made us some good money for the church ladies' aid society."

"We'd have done even better with Jeb in the booth," Aggie opined. "Women love buying things from dark, dangerous-looking young men."

"Yeah, that's for sure." Millie nodded eagerly. "Put a gold hoop in Jeb's ear and dress him in one of those billowy white shirts and he'd make as good a pirate as Errol Flynn in *Captain Blood*." She looked at Caroline. "Remember that for next time."

There wasn't going to be a next time, Jeb promised himself as he drank some tea. Not even if Laney said pretty please and baked him an enormous batch of seven-layer bars without nuts. A man had his limits, after all. A man—

Oh, who was he kidding? He might wander off for a while, but all Laney had to do was tug on that invisible string she'd tied around his heart and he'd come spinning back to her like a human yo-yo, ready to do the Graces' bidding or anything else that would make her happy.

"Jeb?" Caroline was holding a napkin-lined basket containing several small, heart-shaped scones in front of him.

He hesitated. Laney and her mom had seen to it that he knew more than the average rock musician about the rituals of afternoon tea, so he expected a selection of diminutive sandwiches to comprise the light meal's first course. The scones were supposed to come next. And after that, the dainty sweets.

"We didn't have any leftover sandwiches today," Caroline explained. "But we didn't want any, and Laney told us not to make any for you because you're going out to supper."

Jeb accepted a scone, then took a spoonful of strawberry-rhubarb preserves from the bowl Millie offered and a dollop of thick Devonshire cream from the dish Aggie pushed toward him. He broke off a bite-size piece of the scone and used his knife to dab preserves and cream on it, all nice and correct. Then he popped the crumbly morsel into his mouth and savored the blended flavors and textures.

A few minutes later, Millie was easing a miniature lemon tart onto his plate and Caroline was pushing a selection of fancy cookies at him when he felt Laney's hand on his shoulder.

"Don't let them stuff you full of sweets and spoil your supper, Jeb."

Don't *let* them? She knew perfectly well that it was beyond a mere man's power to prevent the Graces from doing whatever they wanted. He turned in his chair and raised an eyebrow at her, but she didn't appear to notice.

"I have to return a call about an etiquette seminar at a bridal fair in the Cities," she said, "and then I need to make another call to finalize the menu for a baby shower tea." Tangling her slender fingers together, she looked as nervedup as she'd sounded on the phone earlier. "Do you mind waiting?"

"No, I'm fine here." If it would contribute to Laney's peace of mind, he'd sit here all night and let the Graces unravel him like a badly made sweater.

"We're concerned about that girl." Caroline said when Laney had gone.

She had Jeb's full attention, but instead of explaining her remark, she bit into a cookie and chewed thoughtfully. When neither of her sisters jumped in to elaborate, Jeb threw caution to the wind and asked.

"Why are you concerned about her?"

"Because she's unhappy," Caroline said.

Millie's head bobbed. "That's for sure."

Jeb stared at the pink roses on his teacup and waited.

"And you know why," Caroline said.

Yes. But did the Graces know, or were they just fishing?

"We need to get her married," Aggie said.

Her God problem was more urgent. But the Graces didn't go to the same church as Laney—something about wanting to encourage a young pastor up in Faribault who wasn't popular because he stuttered—so they might not be aware that Laney had stopped attending.

On second thought, someone in their vast network of friends was sure to have informed them.

"That bothers you, doesn't it?" Caroline eyed him speculatively. "The thought of Laney getting married."

Avoiding her penetrating gaze, Jeb fingered the handle of his teacup. "Why would it bother—"

"Jeb." Caroline's sharp tone sliced off the end of his question. "Stop pretending you're a stupid man."

Who was pretending? He *was* a stupid man. What other kind of man would sit down to afternoon tea with the Three Graces?

"Hey, how about those Twins?" he asked brightly. The Graces loved baseball, so maybe he could distract them. "Can you believe they ended the season with—"

"Jeb." Like a stern schoolteacher, Caroline peered at him over the metal rims of her glasses. "We need to talk about Laney's future. Now, we've given this a lot of thought, and—"

"*No.*" Jeb's backbone snapped to attention and hardened like steel. "I won't help you scheme against her."

"We're not scheming against her," Aggie said. "We're scheming *for* her."

Millie patted his arm. "She wants to get married, Jeb."

"But she doesn't want you interfering," he retorted. "And you know better than to talk to me behind her back."

Caroline's annoyed expression gave way to one of apparent satisfaction. "Yeah, those Twins were quite the deal this year," she said as she reached for the teapot. "Ready for a refill there, Jeb?"

He thanked her and held out his cup and saucer. As she placed the strainer over his cup and poured, her gaze flicked up for an instant and her wrinkly mouth curled into a smile that sent a shiver of apprehension up his spine.

Chapter Seven

HUNGRY FOR SOME OF WILLIE'S FAMOUS ONION RINGS, Laney was dismayed to find all ten of the diner's red vinyl booths occupied. When she looked at Jeb to see whether he wanted to wait for a table or go elsewhere, he pointed out two empty stools at the counter.

"Fine," she said. "Let's grab those."

As they moved in that direction, the buzz of conversation in the diner swelled like an ocean wave. All eyes had turned to Jeb, but other than a slight firming of his lips, he gave no sign of having noticed.

Laney was about to sit down when she felt his hand against the small of her back. Without a word, he steered her away from the stool whose cover had split down the middle, showing an inch-wide strip of foam padding. He settled on that stool as Laney took the good one beside it.

"I've never seen this place so busy." She pitched her voice to be heard over the jukebox that had just powered up to blare a high-energy rock song.

Jeb glanced at her to indicate he'd heard her but had nothing to add. Still willfully oblivious to the attention of his fellow diners, he plucked a dessert menu from its standing metal clip.

Laney didn't recognize the song that was playing, but she'd have known that raspy baritone anywhere. No doubt someone had made the selection as a tribute to Jeb, but he didn't enjoy that kind of attention. Laney shot a worried glance at him and wasn't surprised to see his eyebrows slanting more sharply together, a vertical groove deepening between them.

She caught the eye of the diner's bulky, grizzly-whiskered owner as he tended hamburgers on the grill. When she flicked a meaningful glance at Jeb and then at the jukebox, Willie acknowledged her silent request with a curt nod. He flipped four burgers and slapped cheese slices on top of each one, and then he stalked over to the jukebox.

The music stopped a moment later. That provoked a few groans and halfhearted protests, but the jukebox was free and everyone knew that while Willie could listen to country tunes all night long, he got cranky if the kids played too many rock songs.

Still ignoring the curious stares and raised camera phones, Jeb perused the laminated dessert menu and wondered aloud why Willie wasn't serving his homemade apple dumplings anymore. When two teenage girls sidled nervously toward him, pens and notebook paper in hand, Laney headed them off.

"I'm sorry," she said with a sympathetic smile, "but he doesn't give autographs."

So much for a relaxing supper with Jeb. She was about to suggest leaving when Willie reappeared and led the way to a back-corner booth he had just reclaimed.

"Don't know how you celebrities stand all this fuss," he grumbled as his broad forearm moved in quick strokes to wipe the table with a wadded cloth.

"Thanks for unplugging the jukebox," Jeb said.

"You bet. I don't like that noise, anyway. When you switch to country, let me know." Willie flung the cloth onto an empty tray carried by a passing server and pulled an order pad from the pocket of his stained apron. "What'll it be?"

"Cheeseburgers and rings," Laney said, amused as always by his brusque manner. "Why else would we come here?"

"Some people enjoy my sparkling personality," Willie returned without expression. He dipped his craggy head and wrote something on the pad, and then he pointed his stub of a pencil at Laney. "You still drinking diet pop?"

"Yes, thanks."

"And the rock star?"

"Just water," Jeb said.

Willie nodded and walked away. When he delivered their drinks a minute later, he muttered a gruff, "Good seeing you, Jackson" before returning to his grill.

Warmth curled through Laney as she watched him go. "I have always adored that man."

Jeb gave her a long, considering look. "I'll put him on our list of eligible bachelors, then."

"There's a list?" Laney was too startled by that possibility to react to Jeb's teasing about her supposed romantic interest in a man old enough to be her grandfather.

"There will be," Jeb confirmed. "We're going to be methodical about this."

Laney reached for her drink. "Don't even think about following me around with a checklist on a clipboard, Jeb. If I wanted to be humiliated, I'd just ask the Graces to find me a husband." She took a swallow from her glass and grimaced. "Yuck. Willie gave me sugary pop."

Jeb turned to signal a server.

"No, don't." After the day she'd had, Laney was overflowing with empathy for harried restaurant workers. "These poor people are swamped." Her gaze settled on

Willie, who was back to tending his grill beneath a hand-lettered sign reading, *If there's a line at the door, eat up and get out.*

"Have my water, then." Jeb swapped drinks with her and gulped some cola. "So how many guys go to the church singles thing?"

Laney thought for a moment. "Fifteen, maybe? But Jeb, I'm not sure this is such a good—"

"How many of them do you know?"

"Most of them, I guess, although I rarely see them except at church. But listen, Jeb, I don't—"

"Fifteen single churchgoing men." Drumming his fingers on the table's edge, Jeb was too absorbed by his own thoughts to notice Laney's growing unease. "There should be at least two or three good candidates in a group that size."

"Yes, but I really don't—" Laney broke off as a pretty redheaded teenager set a plate in front of Jeb.

Apparently unable to peel her adoring gaze off of him for even a second, the girl absently shoved the other plate in Laney's direction. It glided across the table like a hockey puck on ice, and only Laney's quick reflexes prevented it from ending up in her lap.

Amusement flared in Jeb's eyes. "Nice save, princess."

Laney would have smirked at him, but she got distracted by the tantalizing aroma of sweet onions and savory beef curling up from her plate.

"Oh, this is exactly what I needed tonight!"

"I know." Jeb's smile was broad enough to activate the dimple in his left cheek.

Their young server seemed to lose her breath at the sight. "Can I get you anything else?" she squeaked.

"He'll want some mustard," Laney said. "Thank you."

The girl pirouetted away and returned seconds later to plunk down a yellow squeeze-bottle in front of Jeb.

"Anything else?" she breathed, still trying to absorb him with her eyes.

"No, we're good." Stone-faced, Jeb stared at the girl until she blushed and scampered off.

As Laney munched a crisp onion ring, Jeb lifted the top bun of her burger and removed the tomato, which she never wanted. He added it to his own sandwich and applied some mustard.

"We eat like married people," Laney observed.

Startled gray eyes flicked up to meet hers, but Jeb offered no comment.

"That reminds me," Laney said. "Remember Sarah Jane Swenson from high school? She was in the class between yours and mine."

Jeb appeared to think about that as he gathered up his burger and took a bite. Holding Laney's gaze, he took his time chewing and swallowing.

"Cheerleader," he said finally. "Curvy brunette. Drove a black Mustang convertible."

"Count on a man to remember those details," Laney said dryly. "She was also the smartest kid in school."

He nodded. "Sarah Jane the Brain. What did she grow up to be, a rocket scientist?"

"No, an attorney. She married Alex Peterson—remember him from school? She divorced him about a year later, and then she married and divorced another guy. And now she's thinking about getting married for the third time."

"How can somebody that smart be that dumb?"

"She does seem to have trouble with commitment," Laney conceded. "But she knows a lot about men, while I . . ." Laney abandoned that sentence when she realized Jeb's attention had wandered.

He stared into space, frowning, his head tilted to one side as though he was concentrating on some faraway sound. Guessing that a lyric or a snatch of melody was jelling in his mind, Laney wasn't surprised when he abruptly set down his cheeseburger and yanked a paper napkin out of the holder on the table.

"Laney," he said urgently. "Pen?"

She delved into her bag and produced a ballpoint, and then she waited quietly while he scribbled on the napkin.

After a minute, he glanced up. "Why'd you mention Sarah Jane?"

"She lives in the Cities," Laney said. "But her mom's still here in Owatonna, and a couple of weeks ago they came to the tearoom. I said Sarah Jane was looking radiant, and she said it was the excitement of getting to know her new man."

Jeb nodded as he added guitar chords over the words he'd written on the napkin. When Laney fell silent, he looked up again. "And?"

She bit into an onion ring, then held it out and stared at the broken circle. "Getting to know a new man isn't thrilling for me. It's stressful. I always worry that I'll do or say something wrong."

"Laney." Jeb laid the pen on the table. "If a guy doesn't love you the way you are, it's stupid to change for him."

"Well, of course," she said, annoyed that he thought she needed to be told that. "I just try to show my best side, that's all. Do you think it's easy, competing in a world overrun with beautiful, fascinating women like Sarah Jane?"

Jeb made an impatient noise in his throat. "You're beautiful and fascinating." The gruff words were accompanied by an irritated look that said she was being ridiculous.

As a compliment, his response left a lot to be desired. But Laney's heart was warmed by the reminder of her best friend's unswerving loyalty.

"And when you find the right person," Jeb went on, folding the napkin and tucking it into his shirt pocket, "it'll be exciting getting to know him. Trust me."

"Trust *you*?" What could Jeb know about falling in love? Laney sat up straighter, disturbed in a way she didn't comprehend. "Are you telling me that you—"

"*No*," he said, looking appalled.

Laney's amusement and her relief at that swift, emphatic denial were quickly overtaken by regret. As much as she hated to think of him eating the tomato off some other woman's cheeseburger, Jeb deserved to fall in love like a normal person. But that would probably never happen.

What his parents had done to him was beyond tragic. If he had known any tenderness in his early childhood, the horror of his mother's suicide had wiped it from his memory. His drunken father and that coldhearted Mrs. Lee had done even more damage, forcing Jeb to bury his emotions so deep that even after years of patient digging, Laney had barely uncovered them. So it was highly unlikely that some nice woman was going to come along and persuade Jeb to risk loving her.

"All I'm saying," he continued, "is that it's a good thing you didn't marry one of those idiot boyfriends. If you want to be happy, Laney, hold out for a guy who can see what a treasure you are. That guy will be worth waiting for, so just try to be more patient."

He held her gaze for several seconds, as though assuring himself that his words had soaked into her brain. Then he addressed his supper with the gusto of a man who believed he'd just settled a problem with irrefutable logic.

What he failed to comprehend was that Laney's biological alarm clock was buzzing, and she couldn't keep hitting the snooze button forever. Not if she wanted to have five or six kids before she got too old to chase after that many.

Staring blankly at the mirrored wall next to their booth, she reached for another onion ring. Her questing fingers failed to find one, so she looked down—and saw Jeb sliding two of his own onion rings into the empty space on her plate.

"You're frowning," he said. "What are you worried about now?"

"Running out of time." Since she was filling up on onion rings, she divided her untouched cheeseburger with her knife and gave one of the halves to Jeb. "If I'm going to have a big family, I'll need to have my first baby before I'm thirty."

Jeb propped his elbows on the table and leaned in, squinting at the middle of her forehead.

"What are you looking at?" she asked.

"Just trying to read your sell-by date."

She rolled her eyes. "That is not remotely amusing, Jeb."

"Well, stop talking like you're a carton of yogurt about to go bad," he grumbled as he reached for the mustard.

Deciding she'd better change the subject, Laney pointed to the folded napkin peeking out from his shirt pocket. "Is the song any good?"

"Yeah," he said slowly, as if surprised by that. "Although it's totally unlike anything I've ever—" He stopped and shook his head. "Never mind. It needs to percolate." Applying mustard to the half-sandwich she'd given him, he asked, "Do you want your dill pickle?"

"Not as much as you do." Laney handed over the crisp green spear. "And now that you owe me a favor, how about taking me to Megan's after this so I can pick up Francine?"

He set the mustard bottle down hard enough to make the dishes rattle on the table. "I'll drive you," he said, scowling. "Just don't expect me to go to the door and exchange pleasantries with the veterinarian." He took a vicious bite of the pickle, and looked so disgruntled as he chewed that Laney had to fight a smile.

She didn't believe she was harboring any lingering resentment over her former boyfriend's betrayal—or Megan's, for that matter. But Jeb's continued indignation on her behalf was a soothing salve for her bruised pride.

They ate in silence for a couple of minutes, and then Jeb asked about the tearoom's furnace.

"I don't know what's wrong with it," Laney said on a long sigh. "But the thing's ancient, Jeb, and if it needs replacing . . ." She shut her eyes for a moment, gathering strength to continue. "Well, I just can't afford a new furnace, that's all. And the bank won't lend me another penny, so I might have to—"

No. She simply could not say those awful words.

"Sell the tearoom?" Jeb's voice was drowned out by a burst of raucous laughter from the kids at the next table, but Laney had no trouble reading his lips.

She gazed into his compassion-darkened eyes and nodded miserably. It would kill her to let go of her mother's dream, but she might not have a choice.

"I'll determine the dollar amount I can handle," she said dully. "If the estimate's under that, I'll have it fixed and just hope the dumb thing doesn't go out again this winter. Otherwise—" Her eyes were filling with tears, so she looked down at her plate and shook her head.

"Laney." Jeb's smoky voice had dropped to its lowest register. "I know you'd never accept an outright gift, so I'll make any kind of deal you want. A loan? A partnership?"

"Don't tempt me, Jeb." She tugged a paper napkin from the holder and blotted her tears. "I appreciate the offer, but it's crazy to throw money at a dying business."

"You know it would only be pocket change to me."

"That isn't the point." She unfolded the damp napkin and carefully tore an inch-wide strip off one long edge. "If I can't make a go of this on my own, then I've failed, and a cash infusion from you isn't going to change that fact."

"Just sleep on it," he urged. "Maybe—"

"No, Jeb. If the bank thinks I'm such a poor credit risk, I can't in good conscience take money from you." Tearing another neat strip off the napkin, she added, "I have to be practical. That's what Mom would have—" Her voice broke, so she gave up trying to squeeze words past the growing lump in her throat.

Jeb pushed his plate away and folded his arms on the table. "What can I do, then?"

Don't leave me, Laney's heart cried, but she forced a different set of words from her mouth. "There's nothing you can do, Jeb."

"What about the Graces?" he asked.

"They'll be disappointed. You know they see working at the tearoom as a social outlet more than anything else." Finding no relief in napkin shredding, Laney threw the whole mess onto the table. "Their house is paid for and they have their savings."

"They'll have more time for their charity work," Jeb pointed out.

"Yes. They'll be okay." If she kept reminding herself of that, the rest would be easier to handle.

"You'll be okay, too," Jeb said. "If you sell the building, you'll be able to pay off your debts and start college."

College. Laney had a knack for writing and had always wanted to take journalism classes. She'd love to be able to sell freelance articles. She could write about things like wedding traditions and etiquette, and maybe even do some light travel pieces about Minnesota tearooms and bed-and-breakfasts.

"No," she said on a sigh. "I can't leave here. Not now that Mom's gone." Even if she went no farther than the University of Minnesota, she'd be more than an hour away from the Graces—and at least twice that in snowy weather. What if something awful happened and she couldn't get home quickly enough?"

"Online courses," Jeb suggested. "You could—"

She stopped him with an upraised hand. "Not now, Jeb."

He smiled in tender amusement. "You always did insist on taking change in small doses."

"That's for sure. I'm a coward."

His dark eyebrows slammed together, forming a harsh vertical line between them. "You're no coward, Laney. And if your mom could see how hard you've worked, she'd be proud of you." His expression softened as he reached across the table to skim a clutch of curls away from her face. "Just like I am."

Startled by the intensity of his gaze, Laney stopped breathing. There was something different in Jeb's eyes. Something she'd never seen there before.

Something that made her heart begin to pound.

"How about dessert?" their young server cooed at Jeb. "We have four kinds of pie tonight. Apple, peach, lemon meringue, and pecan."

As Jeb ordered pie, Laney inhaled deeply and willed her galloping pulse to slow down. Jeb couldn't possibly have looked at her the way a man looked at a woman he wanted desperately to kiss. In her emotional state, she had just imagined that.

But what she had not imagined, and what troubled her for the rest of the night, was the undeniable thrill that had coursed through her when his warm fingertips, calloused from years of guitar playing, had caressed her cheek.

Why had that simple touch scrambled her wits?

Chapter Eight

ARRIVING HOME FROM THE TEAROOM at six o'clock on Saturday, Laney pulled into Jeb's driveway and spotted him in the open garage, a basketball tucked under one long arm as he bent to examine the contents of a row of shelves. She parked near the bottom of the driveway, allowing him plenty of access to the basketball hoop mounted below the apex of the garage roof.

He jogged over and opened her car door, his face drawn in an expression of concern. "How bad was the estimate?"

"It was just a burned-out thermostat," Laney said as she unbuckled her seatbelt. "I had enough in my checking account to cover it."

The vertical groove between Jeb's eyebrows deepened. "Then why don't you look happier?"

"Because the guy said he wouldn't trust my furnace to make it through another Minnesota winter."

Jeb turned the basketball between his large hands. "That's not good," he said quietly.

"No," Laney agreed.

He said nothing more; Jeb wasn't one to drop platitudes into uncomfortable silences. They both knew Laney had plenty to worry about, but her workweek was over, and she was desperate to forget her troubles for a while.

She got out of the car and shouldered her bag. "Were you looking for the air pump?"

"Yep." He bounced the ball between his feet.

"Bottom shelf of the workbench. Next to the bag of grass fertilizer."

Watching him walk away, Laney was conscious of a familiar regret that she knew the contents of his house and garage better than he did. It didn't bother Jeb one bit that his place was as full of treasures and as devoid of life as the undiscovered tomb of a forgotten pharaoh.

During his long absences, Laney sometimes treated herself to a late-night soak in his hot tub. As romantic shadows slow-danced on the candlelit ceiling of his screened porch, she imagined living in a house exactly like Jeb's with a husband and children. She liked to picture herself nudging aside a big, shaggy dog with her foot and sliding swollen loaves of yeast bread into the oven as small people at the kitchen table clutched pencils and asked questions about long division or Minnesota history.

Shaking her head to dismiss those thoughts, she followed Jeb into the garage, where he was already sticking a needle attached to a slender rubber tube into the basketball.

"The mail guy left a package for Mrs. Lindstrom on my porch by mistake," he said as he pumped the foot pedal, forcing air into the ball. "Would you . . . ?"

Of course she would. The judgmental old lady across the street would have a fit if "that wild Jackson Bell" showed up on her doorstep. Besides, Laney had yet to return the house key she'd used last night when she'd gone over there and scooped stinky gourmet cat food into Snowball's dish.

"Where's the package?" she inquired.

"Kitchen table." Jeb disconnected the pump and gave the ball a couple of experimental bounces. "Thanks."

Laney rummaged through her bag for Mrs. Lindstrom's spare key, and then she plopped the bag on the workbench. Heading toward Jeb's back door, she heard several quick hard thumps followed by a brief silence and then a whispery swoosh—and a masculine grunt of satisfaction.

She couldn't help smiling. She might have troubles by the truckload, but she'd be spending the next few hours with Jeb. And tomorrow morning, he would actually sit beside her in church.

She found the package and carried it across the street.

Sour-faced Mrs. Lindstrom thanked her for bringing it and for looking in on Snowball, the overfed white cat leaning against her spindly legs. Those preliminaries disposed of, she introduced her favorite topic of conversation.

"I see Jackson is home," she said in her high, nasal voice. "And you're spending too much time with him, just like you always did."

For the sake of neighborliness, Laney smiled patiently. "You know Jeb and I have always been close."

"What I know is that Jackson Bell has always been trouble." The skinny old woman pronounced the words with the relish of a small-town busybody, which she emphatically was. "Mark my words, if he doesn't end up a drunkard like his father, he'll be something even worse."

Laney's smile slipped, but she held on to her temper. "Jeb is *nothing* like his father."

"Laney." Mrs. Lindstrom gave her a pitying look. "That boy is a rock musician. Do you honestly think he doesn't take illicit drugs and consort with groupies?"

Laney refused to consider that question. "He's a sweet man," she insisted. Granted, Jeb had made some choices in life that she couldn't applaud. But he was honest and loyal and tenderhearted, and it made her crazy that people didn't know those things about him.

"Sweet!" Hugging the package to her chest as though to shield herself from such wild talk, Mrs. Lindstrom shook her head. "I just hope you know how bad it looks when he's at your house until all hours."

All hours? It was true that after last night's supper at Willie's and the trip to pick up Francine, Laney and Jeb had played Scrabble at her kitchen table. But he'd gone home at ten o'clock, just as he always did, because Laney needed her sleep.

Deciding not to waste her breath explaining that to the nosey neighbor who was obviously still maintaining full-time surveillance on Jeb from her kitchen window, Laney handed over the woman's spare house key.

"I almost forgot to give you this." Forcing a smile that felt as brittle as pond ice after a light freeze, she asked, "Did you enjoy your visit with your sister?"

"What was there to enjoy?" Mrs. Lindstrom demanded in a querulous tone. "Helen's not much of a housekeeper, and how she manages to make an ordinary pork chop so tough, I'll never know. And she brags on her grandchildren all day long, when those kids are the most obnoxious pack of brats you ever did see. And that husband of hers! If he isn't the laziest—"

"I'm sorry to interrupt," Laney said hastily, "but I have to get back." She needed this toxic conversation about as much as she needed a good poke in the eye. "You have a nice evening, okay?" Giving what she hoped would be taken for a jaunty wave, she turned and stomped back across the street to where Jeb stood waiting for her, the basketball cradled against his hip.

"Well?" His mouth curled in wry amusement. "Is she

still watching me instead of television?"

"*Yes*," Laney hissed.

All humor drained from his expression. "I shouldn't have made you go. Not after the week you've had."

"I'm okay." Laney sucked in a breath and released it slowly. "She was her usual crotchety self, that's all."

"And you defended me," Jeb guessed. "When are you going to stop rising to her bait?"

"I can't help it," Laney retorted. "She's so unfair. She doesn't understand the first thing about you."

"She might understand more than you think," he said quietly.

"Stop it," Laney commanded. "You're *not* . . . what she said. You *don't*—" She thought twice about finishing that sentence.

Jeb had gone very still, his wide-eyed gaze fixed on her with heartbreaking wariness. They had been here before, many times, and Laney had always backed away, afraid to ask questions that might elicit disturbing answers.

"Never mind," she said. "I'm just stressed out. I can't deal with stuff the way Mom did."

"Don't start that again. You're not your mother."

No, she wasn't. She could all but kill herself trying, and she'd still never be that full of wisdom and faith.

Jeb palmed the basketball and set it to spinning on his raised index finger. "We'll do something fun this weekend," he said as he pushed the ball into the air and caught it, still spinning, on the first finger of his other hand. "Anything you want."

"I want to go to church." She still hadn't made things up with the Lord, but after sixteen years of praying for Jeb, how could she ignore his sudden willingness to accompany her to church?

"That's already on the agenda." He tossed the ball up again, then clapped it between his hands and pivoted to face the goal.

Thinking some physical activity might improve her mood, Laney scrambled in front of him and flung out her arms to guard.

He stopped and stared down at her. "Seriously?"

All right, so he had fourteen inches on her, not to mention the moves of a Harlem Globetrotter. Laney dropped her arms.

"Don't feel bad," he said. "You can still crush me at Scrabble. Last night you almost had me in tears." He punctuated that outrageous statement by pushing the basketball into a perfect arc that carried it through the hoop without even touching the rim.

As he lunged forward to catch the ball, a playful autumn breeze lifted his hair and wafted a clean, spicy scent to Laney's nostrils. It was the same appealing fragrance she'd noticed yesterday morning, and it puzzled her because it carried no hint of the tobacco smell that always clung to—

Realization flashed through her like an electrical pulse.

"Jeb! When did you quit smoking?"

About to shoot again, he stopped and turned to face her, oddly hesitant. "Last week." His Adam's apple moved and then he added, "I quit drinking, too."

Laney had spent years worrying about his self-destructive habits. She'd tried countless times to dissuade him from those risky behaviors, but he would just look at her with tortured eyes that begged her not to pursue him into the dark world he couldn't seem to abandon, even for her.

"Jeb," she breathed, "that's wonderful!"

He smiled, but too faintly to show his dimple, and there was still something almost apologetic in his eyes.

Confusion dampened Laney's joy. Pressing a hand over her thrumming heart to settle it down, she asked, "What made you decide to quit?"

He shook his head. "Can't tell you just yet." Widening his stance, he dribbled the ball between his feet. "But don't worry. It's something good." He turned and took several running steps away from her before darting back toward the goal and executing a perfect layup shot.

Something good? Well, of course it was something good. But what was going on? If he had embarked on some trendy California-style health regimen, why keep it a secret? Was he waiting to see if he'd be able to stick with it?

That had to be it. Although why he'd worry about that, she had no idea, because when Jeb put his mind to something, he had tons of self-discipline. Still, if he needed time to work this out in his own way, she'd try to contain her curiosity.

She walked toward him. "At least let me give you a congratulatory hug."

He caught the ball and held it level with his face, elbows out, while she moved in and wrapped her arms around his lean middle. She saw him look up at the sky, emphatically patient, and then he sighed, tossed the ball onto the grass, and draped one arm around her shoulders to give her a brief squeeze.

Amused by his desperate nonchalance, Laney turned her face against the soft fabric of his sweatshirt to hide her smile.

"I just have a few things to work out," he said, "and then I'll tell you everything."

"All right." She let go of him and stepped back. "But isn't it a shame Mrs. Lindstrom doesn't have one of those directional listening devices that professional spies use? I'd dearly love for her to eavesdrop on this conversation."

Jeb gave her another strange look. Then he averted his face, hiding behind his lanky dark hair. The boyish, uncertain gesture was almost painfully endearing.

"Come on, Mowgli." Laney marched over to the workbench and retrieved her bag. "Let's do something about that mop of yours." When she walked past him, heading for her kitchen door, Jeb fell in behind her without a word.

In her kitchen, Laney collected her haircutting tools while Jeb tugged his sweatshirt over his head and dragged a chair to the middle of the floor. When he sat down, she tucked the edges of a towel under the neckband of his T-shirt. Splaying her fingers, she pushed both hands through his silky hair again and again, massaging his scalp. He closed his eyes and emitted a soft, deep rumble that sounded like a cat's purr.

She'd been cutting his hair since he was fifteen. On her first attempt she had nearly shaved him bald, but in time she'd become quite proficient at cutting a man's hair. Or Jeb's hair, anyway. None of the men she'd dated had ever trusted her skills enough to submit to even a light trim.

She pushed back a soft fall of shining espresso-brown hair and absently fingered one of Jeb's long sideburns. "Short layers all over?"

"Whatever," he said.

He didn't possess a particle of vanity about his looks.

His hair and clothes were always clean, and he shaved five or six days out of every seven, but beyond that he never gave his appearance a thought. He'd wear his shirts to ribbons if Laney didn't haul him up to Bloomington's Mall of America once a year to shop at the big-and-tall men's stores.

She made him buy conservative clothes so he'd look less menacing. It wasn't his fault that he towered over everyone, or that the silvery glint of his eyes and the harsh tilt of his dark brows intimidated people. As for his crushing stare, that was merely a defense mechanism, a trick he used when people scared him by getting too close. Jeb was no danger to anyone but himself, and it made Laney crazy that nobody else seemed to realize that.

She combed his hair down over his eyes and addressed its excess length with her scissors. His nose twitched like a rabbit's and she knew she'd tickled him, but he didn't move his head. She could peel him like a boiled egg and he would just sit there, silent and unconcerned.

"Let's go to the mall on Monday," she said. The tearoom was closed on Mondays, so that would be a good time to replenish Jeb's wardrobe.

Eyes still shut, he grunted his agreement.

Laney made a mental note to go through his closet and see if he needed any sport coats or ties. For all she knew, he'd taken all of his dressy clothes to California—and he'd need something nice to wear if they went to the French restaurant or perhaps to a classical music concert in the Cities.

Thinking of coats and ties reminded her of her ex-fiancé.

"I bought Nathan a beautiful silk tie for his birthday," she said, laying aside the scissors and switching on her electric trimmer. "But he never wore it."

"Nathan's an idiot," Jeb pronounced.

"No, he's brilliant. He was first in his class at law school." Nudging Jeb's head forward, Laney dragged the trimmer through his hair. "But what's even more impressive," she added with a grin, "is that he could beat me at Scrabble."

"He didn't care enough about your feelings to wear your tie," Jeb said doggedly. "That makes him an idiot."

"Maybe." But Laney had been an idiot, too. Without her best friend to talk things over with, it had been ridiculously easy to convince herself she was in love with Nathan.

Maybe she *had* been, a little. But Nathan wasn't Mr. Right, and if Jeb had been here, he'd have helped her see that.

For several minutes, the only sound in the kitchen was the pleasant hum of the trimmer that sent tufts of soft dark hair fluttering to the floor. When Laney was satisfied with the short, subtle waves that lay against Jeb's head, she removed the towel from his shoulders and brushed him off.

As she set her haircutting tools aside and washed her hands in the kitchen sink, Jeb got her broom and dustpan from the utility closet. Anyone else would have rushed to the bathroom mirror to check out his new look, but Jeb always said Laney was the only mirror he needed. If he didn't look okay, she'd fix him.

"Want to go out for Mexican food?" he asked as he plied the broom.

"No, I have other plans." Drying her hands on a dish towel, she nodded toward the items she'd assembled on the countertop that morning: two onions and two cans each of diced tomatoes and red kidney beans. Her deep cast-iron skillet stood ready on the stovetop. She glanced at her watch. "I'd better get started."

Maybe she shouldn't just assume Jeb would stick around for supper. But growing up, he'd parked his giant feet under her mother's table several nights a week, so it would feel strange to start issuing actual invitations now.

"I'll just clean this up and get out of your way," he said.

"You're not in my way, Jeb." He was no cook, but he was good company, and he never minded peeling potatoes or setting the table while Laney tended to the more challenging aspects of meal preparation. So where had he picked up the idea that she wanted him out of her kitchen?

He'd been acting oddly ever since he'd come home. She hoped it wouldn't be too long before he offered the explanation he'd promised her. He'd said it was something good, and she desperately needed to hear something good, particularly after the other night and that upsetting conversation they'd had.

"Ollie Lincoln hit a deer last weekend," she said as she lit the gas burner under her skillet. "It dented the grille of his new truck, but the carcass wasn't too badly damaged, so he butchered the meat." She opened the refrigerator to retrieve a white-wrapped bundle of ground venison, which she held up in triumph. "I'm making chili."

For a venison-loving man who had just been told he'd soon be sitting down to one of his favorite meals, Jeb didn't look pleased. The broom had stilled in his hands and a vertical furrow had appeared between his eyebrows. When Laney opened her mouth to ask what was wrong, he gave his head a small, quick shake.

"Ollie's a good guy," he muttered, and he started

sweeping again.

Did he think she was making supper for Ollie? She could see how he might have jumped to that conclusion, but why would it bother him to think of her spending an evening with a guy they'd both gone all the way through school with?

She dismissed the question with a mental shrug. Jeb's mind often moved in mysterious ways, and that head-shake he'd given her a moment ago meant she might as well forget trying to coax an explanation out of him.

"Yes, he's a good guy," she agreed. She waited for a couple of heartbeats and then deliberately added, "And his new wife is a sweetheart."

Jeb's head jerked up. "He got married?"

"A few months ago." Laney transferred the roll of ground meat to her skillet and mashed it flat with a wooden spoon. "The Graces matched him up with their neighbor's niece."

"Oh." Jeb rested his hands on top of the broom handle and stared out the window.

"I think I told you that Francine had a flat tire the other night," Laney said as she peeled the papery jacket off an onion. "On Thursday morning when I took it to Ollie's garage to see if it could be fixed, I mentioned that you were coming home. Ollie asked if you liked venison, and then he gave me some to cook for you."

"He's a good guy," Jeb repeated, this time without appearing to begrudge the words. The deep groove between his eyebrows vanished, and as he bent to sweep a mound of dark fuzz into the dustpan, his mouth relaxed into a faint smile.

Quartering her onions, Laney wondered how many more

of his smiles she'd get to see before he relegated their amazing friendship to history.

What was she going to do without him? And what would become of him after he gave up the only real friend he had ever allowed himself?

He tapped her hip, signaling her to step aside so he could open the cupboard and empty his dustpan in the trash receptacle under the sink. As Laney shifted, a hot tear rolled down her cheek and she forgot herself and sniffled.

"Crybaby," Jeb teased.

She produced a wet chuckle to support his assumption that the onion fumes were making her cry. When he went to put the broom away, she sniffled again and hacked frantically at the onions.

Why did everything good have to change? Why could she never hold on to anything that gave her any measure of peace and security?

Losing her mother had been a staggering blow, but Jeb had never been more than a phone call away, at least in the beginning. He'd talked her through a lot of sleepless nights, but then Tom had come into her life, and Jeb had gone to tour Europe and Australia with the band.

Was that when he'd begun drifting away from her like a helium-filled balloon on a summer breeze?

She broke up the meat browning in the skillet and added her onions.

It was simply the way of things, he had insisted the other night, and while he clearly didn't welcome the change, he was accepting it for her sake. That was the maddening thing about Jeb; he was forever denying his own wants and needs to do whatever he believed was best for *her*.

She had to make him see reason before they both ended up lost and alone.

Lost? Alone? Convicted by her conscience, she mentally backspaced and deleted those words. She hadn't been behaving like one, but she *was* a Christian. If she wanted to find peace and contentment, all she had to do was abandon her foolish rebellion and learn how to trust God the way her mother always had.

Jeb was the one who would be lost. He still didn't believe God existed, let alone that he desired a personal relationship with each of his children. So at least until Jeb accepted that reality, Laney was determined to reject his lame-brained plan to improve her life by bowing out of it.

Chapter Nine

HE WAS GOING TO HAVE TO ADJUST HIS SLEEP PATTERNS, Jeb realized on Sunday morning in the middle of a jaw-cracking yawn. From what he could tell, Christians were morning people who popped out of bed shortly after dawn on Sundays and trooped cheerfully off to church. Jeb wasn't optimistic about his ability to be cheerful at any hour before noon, but he was determined to participate in the Sunday morning trooping, even if that meant hitting the sack hours before his usual four A.M.

With his eyelids still at half-mast, he buttoned the blue-striped shirt he'd chosen last night to go with his black dress pants. Laney had told him a man could get away with wearing nice jeans at her church, but for once in his life, Jeb wasn't interested in getting away with anything. He wanted to do things right. Why else had he stayed up so late reading the Bible he'd stolen from that hotel in Louisville?

He still felt bad about taking it, even though he'd left a $500 check with the concierge, who had promised to send it to the people who put Bibles in hotel rooms. Jeb had taken that book like a starving man might snatch a loaf of bread, without any thought to the morality of the thing. But now he worried that he'd let God down, so he wasn't about to risk compounding his offense by wearing the wrong clothes to church.

He couldn't manage a tie at such an early hour, but he did have the presence of mind to pull on a sport coat instead of his scuffed leather jacket. Right on time, he headed over to Laney's house and tapped on the kitchen door, desperate for some coffee.

The little tyrant wouldn't give him any. Not until he exchanged his one brown shoe for another black one.

He trudged home and corrected his error, and then he returned to Laney's and presented himself for inspection. He passed, and she pressed a steaming mug of strong black coffee into his eager hands. He guzzled half of it leaning against her refrigerator, eyes shut, and then he groped his way to a chair.

He propped a hand under his chin and was close to dozing off when Laney, always excruciatingly cheerful in the mornings, jingled her car keys next to his ear.

"Time to go," she sang like a happy little bird.

During the drive to the church, Jeb woke up enough to worry. Why hadn't she told him what to expect?

"What will I have to do?" he asked as she steered Francine into the parking lot beside the steepled, white clapboard church.

Laney threw him a puzzled look. "What do you mean?"

Well, he didn't know. That was the problem. "I've never been to church," he reminded her.

"It'll be fine, Jeb." She reached over and gave his forearm a reassuring pat. "There will be a lot of singing and praying and Bible-reading, and before the sermon they'll collect an offering, but you won't be expected to participate in any of that. Not when you're just a casual visitor."

He intended to be much more than a casual visitor, but he couldn't tell her that. Not yet.

Was God okay with his holding back? It wasn't as though he was ashamed of being a Christian. He just wanted to help Laney.

"Hey." Her honey-colored eyebrows rose, etching faint lines in her forehead. "There's nothing to be nervous about."

There was everything to be nervous about. But he couldn't tell her that, so he just nodded and reached for his door handle.

* * *

Two hours later, Jeb's brain was reeling as he telescoped his long body into Francine's passenger seat. He'd been wholly unprepared for the explosions of joy that had rocked him throughout the worship service and even during the adult Sunday school class he and Laney had attended afterward. Not since that night in Louisville had he been gripped by this kind of excitement, this conviction that he might yet salvage something from the wreck he'd made of his life and become—well, not a *good* man; it was too late for that. But a far better man than he had been before.

As he buckled his seatbelt, he noticed Laney gnawing on her thumbnail and watching him with worried eyes. He gave her a pointed look and waited to hear what was troubling her.

"Was it okay?" She pulled her thumb away from her mouth. "I tried to keep the introductions to a minimum. "

"It was fine," he said, sliding his palms down his thighs to still the nervous jiggling of his knees.

"Honestly?" Her wide blue eyes begged him for reassurance.

"Honestly, princess. It was fine." Afraid he was on the verge of blurting that he'd treasured every moment of the experience, Jeb steered the conversation in a safer direction. "Did it feel good to be back?"

"Oh, yes." Her worried expression gave way to a radiant

smile that shot straight to Jeb's heart and made him want to beg her to forget about finding her perfect man and just take *him*, instead. Even though she could kiss him until her lips blistered and he would still be just a frog, never the prince she deserved.

Pulling in a slow, deep breath, he shoved those feelings back into the cobwebbed corner of his heart they had escaped from. He knew better than to yearn for things he could never have.

"Thank you for making me come," Laney said. "It was good of you, Jeb, especially when you have no interest in—"

"It was fine," he repeated, cutting her off before she said something about his beliefs that he'd be forced to confirm or deny.

Twisting to look over her right shoulder, Laney backed out of the parking space. "I just wish Mom could have seen this day," she said quietly.

Jeb gazed out his window at the white church steeple and the cerulean sky beyond it. Now convinced that heaven was a real place and that Hannah was there, he hoped she knew her prayers for him had finally paid off. He had abandoned his dissolute ways and was making an honest effort to become someone she might have been proud of.

It wasn't easy. Yet giving up his bad habits was proving far less difficult than coping with this avalanche of feelings he had no clue how to catalogue and process.

He was acutely aware that he wasn't normal. With the exception of anger, which he had always vented through his music and his reckless lifestyle, emotions terrified him.

Even when Hannah lay dying, he'd been unable to tell her that he loved her. Alone in the room with her, holding her emaciated hand, he had tried to give her that final gift. But the words had been too big for his throat and they'd gotten stuck there, stopping his breath and making him feel dizzy and sick.

As weak as she'd been, Hannah had seen his struggle and saved him. She'd given his hand a feeble squeeze and whispered, *I know, Jeb. I've always known.*

He had never said the words to Laney, either. But as damaged as he was, Laney had always accepted him. She'd loved him ceaselessly, unconditionally, until he'd given up fighting and dared to believe in her love, undeserved as it was.

It had happened exactly the same way with God.

Wonder and gratitude slammed through him in powerful waves, but Jeb stared fixedly out his window and struggled to suppress those emotions until he was safely alone.

It wouldn't do for Laney to see how deeply all of this had affected him. Not until the time was right to tell her everything.

* * *

Monday arrived bright blue and glorious, a perfect autumn day. Worrying about the tearoom had kept Laney tossing and turning for most of the night, but she was a morning person at heart, and the crisp breeze wafting through a partly raised kitchen window renewed her energy and her spirits.

She cleaned her house and did three loads of laundry before hustling upstairs to change into her favorite jeans and a rose-colored pullover sweater with delicate flowers embroidered around the neckline, yet another handmade gift from the Graces. She finger-fluffed her curls and applied only a touch of makeup, because for the first time in ages, her cheeks were glowing and her eyes sparkled with excitement.

She checked her watch, then she phoned Jeb.

"This had better be important," he growled.

"What a charming way to answer the phone," Laney said sweetly.

"Oh, it's you. Sorry." He yawned, a whining sort of roar reminiscent of Chewbacca in *Star Wars*. "What do you need?"

"It's eleven o'clock," Laney said. "You asked for a wake-up call, remember?"

"You don't have to indulge my every whim," he muttered.

Laney grinned. "Oh, this was entirely my pleasure. Now roll out of that bed. I want to get to the stores before all of the best clothes are taken."

"Very funny." He yawned again.

Marveling at her unusually buoyant mood, Laney tried to recall the last time she'd taken a full Monday off from the tearoom. She couldn't, and that meant it had been far too long.

"Get vertical, Jeb, and get over here. I'm making egg salad sandwiches."

"Fifteen minutes," he said, and hung up.

After starting a pot of coffee, Laney made one last circuit of her clean house to spray each room with honeysuckle-scented air freshener. When she entered the dining room, a shaft of sunlight was streaming through one window, spotlighting the unfinished jigsaw puzzle on the table.

It had been more than a year since she'd finished going through her mother's things and given the last boxes of music books and clothes to the Salvation Army. So why was she still unable to put this stupid puzzle away?

She ought to do it right now. She ought to get the box from the hall closet and break the puzzle apart and—

"Not today," she whispered, her shoulders slumping in defeat.

She returned to the kitchen and was preparing lunch when she heard Jeb's familiar rap on the glass portion of the door.

He hadn't shaved, she noticed when she let him in, but he smelled of spicy soap and cinnamon mouthwash. He was dressed in a decent pair of jeans and a plaid button-down shirt, but Laney frowned at the battered leather jacket he hung beside the door. If she had anything to say about it, he'd be getting a new one today.

"What's with the disguise?" she asked when he deposited his Twins ball cap and a pair of aviator sunglasses on the counter.

"We have a new music video out." He got a mug from the cupboard and helped himself to coffee. "Lots of unnecessary close-ups."

"What did you expect?" Laney asked as she arranged sandwiches and raw vegetables on a plate. "You're a star now." She popped a cucumber slice into her mouth and handed the filled plate to Jeb.

He took it and his coffee to the table and sat down.

"I just wish people wouldn't . . ." He sighed and pushed a hand through his damp, newly shorn hair, unconsciously enhancing its rumpled appeal. "I never wanted to be famous.

You know it was never about that."

Sensing that he was on the verge of revealing why he'd "needed" to come home, Laney sat down beside him.

"What *is* it about?" she asked gently. "What *do* you want?"

For a long moment, he stared at his coffee as though waiting for the answer to appear on the liquid's reflective surface. Then he shook his head.

"No. I'm not doing introspection at this hour."

As he gulped his coffee, Laney swallowed her disappointment and reminded herself that she had all day to coax confidences out of him.

Three cups of coffee later, Jeb was sufficiently alert to drive up I-35 to the Mall of America, where Laney dragged him into all of the usual men's stores to replenish his wardrobe.

"Aren't we done yet?" he asked as they entered the last store on Laney's mental list.

"Almost," she said. Why did men have so little stamina when it came to shopping? After a measly two hours, even patient Jeb started complaining.

"Laney." When she turned to look at him, he spread his arms to remind her that he was carrying six bulky shopping bags. "All these shoes and jeans are so heavy they're stretching my arms."

Hiding her amusement at his manly exasperation, Laney paused to finger the sleeve of a wonderfully supple black leather jacket. "Well, that's good, isn't it? You'll be able to tie your shoes without bothering to bend over."

"Heartless female." When she didn't respond, he nudged her shoulder with his elbow. "Come on. Let's go have some fun."

"I'm *having* fun." She shrugged away from his touch and checked the jacket's price tag. Jeb was disgustingly rich, but Laney's practical soul balked at needless overspending. "Oh, good. These are on sale." She flipped through the rack to see if they had his size.

"I don't need a new jacket." He leaned one shoulder against a mirrored wall and thrust out his bottom lip like a sulky six-year-old at bath time.

Laney sighed. "Jeb, your jacket looks like it's been fought over by a pack of wild dogs."

A hovering sales associate coughed into his fist. Probably to cover up a laugh, Laney decided as the slightly built, elegantly dressed older man ran a practiced eye over Jeb's lean frame. He selected a jacket and removed it from its hanger, holding it out to Jeb.

Jeb went statue-still and his eyes narrowed ominously. When Laney pinched the back of his arm to discourage him from firing up the Death Stare, he acknowledged defeat with a heavy sigh.

"Just go ring it up," he said to the salesman.

They hauled their purchases out to the parking lot and stowed them in the SUV. Then they returned to the mall, where they rode the indoor roller coaster and piloted World War II fighters in flight simulators. For supper, they gnawed on Tony Roma's famous baby back ribs. After that, they headed up to Level 4 and the theatres. Laney won their traditional coin toss—heads for a chick flick and tails for an action-adventure film—and chose a romantic comedy.

"Stop pretending you didn't like it," she said two hours later as they exited the theatre. Prodding Jeb's side with a playful finger, she added, "I heard you laughing."

When she tried to poke him again, he arched away from her, lightning-quick, and captured her misbehaving hand.

"I might have laughed once or twice," he said, tightening his grip as Laney tried to pull free. "But that actor put me off my popcorn."

Laney ceased struggling. "Why?"

"He looks like the veterinarian," Jeb said sourly.

Laney considered that. "Maybe. But Luke's cuter."

Jeb stopped walking to glare at her. "He wouldn't be so cute if I had broken his nose like I wanted to."

Hiding a smile, Laney glanced pointedly at the large hand engulfing her own. "Squeeze harder," she said. "One of my fingers isn't quite numb yet."

His gaze shifted to their joined hands and he reacted with patent surprise, instantly releasing her.

"Did I hurt you?" he demanded.

She laughed and resumed walking. "You're not capable of hurting me, Jeb."

"I hope you never find out how wrong you are."

This time it was Laney who halted. "What's that supposed to mean?"

He opened his mouth, but then seemed to change his mind about tendering an explanation.

"Forget it," he said. "You know talking about the veterinarian always makes me—" He shook his head.

"Turn into an animal?" Laney suggested sweetly.

He raised his hands like claws and bared his teeth.

Laney squealed and scrambled away from him. She leaped onto a descending escalator and grinned when she heard a low-pitched growl immediately behind and above her.

She had no idea what he'd been trying to tell her a minute ago. Just because she'd known him forever didn't mean she always understood him. But even at his most inscrutable, Jeb was still a more satisfying companion than any of the men she'd considered building a future with.

Never one to stand still on an escalator, Jeb walked down a few steps. Turning suddenly, he asked, "Are we still good for tomorrow night?"

So he hadn't forgotten that. "You're serious about going to the singles' group?" Laney asked.

He frowned. "Didn't I say I'd go?"

"Yes." And he never broke his word. "But it will include a Bible study, Jeb. Are you positive that you—"

"I'm positive. It's part of our plan, remember?"

"I suppose." She still wasn't sure how she felt about his plan.

"And lightning didn't strike me yesterday morning when I walked up the church steps," he added. "So I figure it's safe to go back."

He glanced over his shoulder. They were nearing the bottom of the escalator, so he turned away from Laney to step off.

She stared at his broad back and wondered what she was arguing about. If Jeb was willing to accompany her to church and to the singles' Bible study, then they ought to go. Yesterday's service had soothed her jangled nerves; surely at some point her rebellious heart would turn back to God.

Maybe Jeb's heart would begin to soften, too.

As he drove her home in a familiar, comfortable silence, Laney mulled over the other part of his plan. At supper, he had insisted that her search for a husband shouldn't be a stressful process. According to him, all she had to do was make friends with a few guys who shared her interests and values, and then just sit back and wait to see if one of those friendships blossomed into something more.

Sit back and wait? She didn't have time for that. Anyway, what was Jeb doing dispensing romantic advice when his guitars meant a hundred times more to him than any woman he had ever dated?

"Sit back and wait," Laney grumbled. "Hah."

Changing lanes on the freeway, Jeb spared her a glance. "Are you muttering at me?"

She turned an accusing look on him. "Sit back and *wait*, Jeb? That's your best advice?"

He frowned at the road. "What's wrong with that advice?"

Laney sighed. "Nothing at all, Jeb, if I wanted to catch a speckled trout. But I want to get married, and that means I'm going to have to *do* something."

"Like what?" he challenged.

She folded her arms and looked out her window.

"Exactly." He sounded annoyingly smug, but then his tone gentled. "Princess, don't make yourself crazy over this."

He was right; she was working herself into a frazzle. She did dumb things like that when she was tired. And she'd been tired a lot lately, thanks to the stress that was preventing her from getting any truly restorative sleep.

Jeb tuned on the radio and found her favorite station, which happened to be playing a Haydn piano sonata he'd learned in college. As his long fingers fluttered against the steering wheel in the remembered patterns, Laney shifted to a more comfortable position and closed her eyes. The next thing she knew, Jeb was tickling her ear and urging her to wake up because they were home.

She insisted on helping to carry the shopping bags into his house. She ended up at his kitchen table, alternately yawning and snipping sales tags off the new garments while he made hot cocoa.

"Where do I keep the marshmallows?" he asked as he set a fragrant mug of chocolate in front of her.

"You don't have any. But this is fine."

After taking a few cautious sips of the steaming, darkly sweet beverage, Laney reached for the scissors and another crisp new shirt to divest of tags. Jeb remained at her side, towering over her like a silent sentinel.

"Jeb, you're hovering," she said with a touch of fatigue-induced irritation.

"Just making sure you don't fall asleep and drown in your chocolate," he returned calmly. He pulled her jacket off the back of a chair and held it out for her. "Come on. I'll walk you home."

She took one last sip from the mug and got to her feet. "I think I can cross two driveways and a small patch of grass without assistance," she grumbled.

"Mm-hmm." He captured her groping right arm and guided it into a sleeve. She managed to insert her other arm, and then he settled the jacket onto her shoulders and turned her around. "I know you left your porch light on, but I still don't like you going into a dark house alone."

As he gathered her hair to lift it free from her collar, the warm brush of his fingers against her neck shot tingles of comfort through Laney. Sighing, she closed her eyes and sagged against his chest.

"Wake up, princess." Jeb's patient hands grasped her shoulders and eased her upright again.

"I'm awake." She spoke with conviction, even though her eyes were still closed. "And as for me going into that dark house alone, what do you think I do when you're not here?"

"I try very hard not to think about what you do when I'm not here."

The grim note in his low-pitched reply opened Laney's eyes and touched off the fuse of her resentment.

"If it bothers you to think of me being alone, that's just too bad," she snapped. "I don't have the energy to feel sorry for you. I'm too busy trying to come to terms with your unilateral decision to abandon everything we—"

She stopped, appalled by her harsh words and by the stark pain in Jeb's eyes.

What was she doing? She might be suffering from exhaustion brought on by weeks of worry-filled, sleepless nights, but that was no excuse for attacking Jeb.

She shook her head at him, her lips shaping a soundless and grossly insufficient *I'm sorry* as she backed away.

"Laney." His gravelly voice had dropped to its deepest register. "Princess. We talked about this."

And they were going to talk about it some more, but not tonight. While she regretted lashing out at him, at the moment she was too upset to discuss his ridiculous plan to help her "get settled" before disappearing from her life so she could "move on."

Best friends didn't move on. Best friends stuck together and talked things through and worked things out.

Except when they were bone-weary and frustrated half

out of their minds, in which case they called it a night so they could recover their good sense before resuming the struggle to work things out.

Laney grabbed her bag and fled.

"No, wait." Jeb caught the kitchen door as she tried to close it.

She kept going. He followed her onto the porch and stopped the screen door, too. He reached for her arm, but she twisted away and broke into a run.

"Laney!"

"Not now," she called over her shoulder. "Not tonight."

She thought he'd fallen back, but when she'd reached her door and was fumbling to fit her key in the lock, he grasped her arm and turned her around to face him.

"You said you understood!" he accused in thunderous tones. "You said you'd be okay. You said—"

"I said what you needed to hear!"

Jeb released her arm.

Laney winced as she imagined her shrill words echoing off every nearby house and tree.

"What I needed to hear," Jeb repeated in a hollow voice that told her she'd pricked his masculine pride.

His chest was rising and falling as rapidly as her own, even though they had run only a few yards. The frigid night air turned their harsh breaths into silvery ice crystals; in the pool of light on her porch they faced each other like two wary, winded dragons breathing smoke.

Somewhere a dog barked. Stirred by the light breeze, a few dry, fallen leaves scraped noisily against the sidewalk. When one of Laney's corkscrew curls blew across her face, Jeb raised a hand and smoothed it back.

"I never meant to hurt you, princess."

But he had. And what was worse, he was hurting himself.

Maybe she couldn't stop him from pushing the rest of the world away, but she wasn't about to let him shut *her* out of his life. He needed her, the impossible man, needed her to accept him and love him and discourage him from constantly waging war on himself. Why didn't he get that?

Blasting him with her own version of the Death Stare, Laney had the satisfaction of seeing him flinch. But then his chin jerked up and his expression hardened.

She wasn't surprised. Wrapping himself in a protective coat of anger had always been Jeb's way of dealing with emotions that bewildered him.

Frustrated beyond bearing, Laney just wanted to be alone. She reached for the doorknob, but Jeb captured her wrist in a firm grip.

"Here," he said roughly, pressing a velvet jeweler's box into her palm. He scowled down at her for a moment, and then he groaned and pulled her into his arms and hugged her hard.

"Don't go in there and cry." His unsteady breath tickled her hair. "Promise me you won't."

"I'm not going to cry." Laney made no effort to hide her bitterness. "What would be the point? Would it change anything?" She pushed herself out of his embrace and went inside, firmly closing the windowed door and turning the deadbolt.

"Laney."

She heard his muted voice through the glass, but she refused to look at him as she dropped her bag and shrugged out of her jacket.

"Laney, come on." He rapped on the glass. "I'm just trying to do the right thing!"

She switched off the porch light, leaving him alone in the darkness. Let him stand out there shivering; she was too disgusted to care.

She pounded upstairs and flung herself face-down on her bed. Then recalling the small velvet box in her clenched hand, she sighed and sat up to open it.

Nestled inside was a beautiful pair of sterling silver earrings that Jeb must have bought at the mall when she'd made a trip to the ladies' room. They were the dangly style that she liked, charming jumbles of shining hearts in various sizes. She lifted one cluster and couldn't help smiling when the precious metal jingled like a dozen tiny bells.

Her smile faded as she wondered if this was the last present she would ever receive from Jeb.

No, he'd send her a wedding gift when the time came—if it ever did. And if she had babies, he'd send something when each of them was born. But it wouldn't be the same.

She was terrified that nothing would ever be the same again.

She closed the box and set it on her nightstand, then kicked off her shoes and lay down again. Dry-eyed and miserable, she pulled the quilt around herself.

Laney, I needed to hear your voice.

What had upset him so much that he'd made that almost frantic phone call and then jumped on the first plane headed to Minnesota? And what good had it done him to rush home like that when he wasn't even going to tell her what was wrong?

Like a snowball rolling downhill, Laney's confusion just kept growing.

Why was he so insistent that she let go of their special friendship and "move on" with her life? She would never marry any man who couldn't accept that Jeb was like family to her. How could he imagine otherwise?

And on the subject of marriage, she never discussed spiritual matters with him, so she was fairly certain she'd never explained why she could marry only another believer. Yet he was suddenly fixated on fixing her up with a good Christian man. Wasn't that a strange goal for an atheist?

With a groan of frustration, Laney sat up to pound her feather pillow into a better shape for cradling her weary head.

Everything just felt so wrong.

In the old days, she had run to Jeb whenever she'd needed help righting her world. But what was she going to do now that Jeb had become one of her biggest problems?

Chapter Ten

TUESDAY WAS AN UNUSUALLY BUSY DAY at the tearoom, so Laney had no time to feel sorry for herself. Jeb called twice, but both times the Graces told him she was unable to come to the phone—and she honestly was. It was almost six o'clock before she returned his call.

"Laney." He exhaled her name in obvious relief. "About last night, princess, I—"

"Jeb, I'll be late getting home." She felt mean for interrupting him, but she just couldn't summon the emotional energy to pick up where they'd left off arguing last night. "If you still want to go to the Bible study, be ready at a quarter to seven."

"I'll be ready." He paused. "Laney, I—"

"Thank you for the earrings," she said quickly. He was attempting to apologize, but she couldn't bear that, not when he deserved such a huge apology from her.

"You like them?" His smoky voice betrayed a hint of anxiety that made her feel even worse.

"They're beautiful, Jeb." She fingered the cluster of silver hearts dangling from her right earlobe; they rang like precious coins. "You know I love anything heart-shaped."

His chuckle sounded forced. "Because you're an incurable romantic."

"Actually, I'm beginning to think I might be curable." She'd lain awake most of last night wondering why she was so eager to get married when she couldn't imagine ever feeling as comfortable with a husband as she did with Jeb. "But never mind that. Just be ready when I get home, okay?"

She pulled into his driveway at ten minutes to seven and found him waiting in front of the garage. She'd told him his usual T-shirt and jeans would be fine, so when he opened Francine's passenger door and ducked inside, jamming his long legs under the dash, she was surprised to note that he'd taken some trouble with his appearance. He'd shaved, and he was wearing one of his new shirts with a neatly pressed pair of khakis and his new leather jacket. He looked like a fresh-scrubbed kid on the first day of school.

"I could have met you at the church," he said.

"You wouldn't have wanted to go in alone, Jeb. You're not exactly the mixing and mingling type."

"I can adapt," he said loftily. "I realize it will take some mixing and mingling to find you a good Christian man."

She'd wait until tomorrow to break the news that she was no longer husband hunting, Laney decided as she backed out of the driveway. Just now there was too great a risk that any serious conversation with Jeb would segue into another painful exchange like last night's.

As she drove, she explained that her church's weekly singles' night began with a short Bible study and was followed by refreshments and various group activities for the college-to-age-thirty set.

"We won't stay if you're uncomfortable," she added as she claimed a space in the church parking lot.

"We're staying," Jeb said. "Where else are we going to find so many single Christian men in one place?" He opened his door and would have climbed out, but Laney touched his arm.

"This is a Bible study and fellowship group, Jeb, not a dating service."

"I get that," he said with a hint of impatience. "Now come on. We're late."

They hustled into the church and down the stairs to the basement fellowship hall, where assistant pastor Ted Vance was attempting to herd about thirty young men and women to the rows of chairs at one end of the long room.

Surprise lit Pastor Ted's round face when he saw Laney, but he smiled warmly. He waited for everyone to settle, and after welcoming Jeb and two other first-timers, he offered a brief prayer. Then he said he'd be giving a short lesson from the tenth chapter of First Corinthians.

Laney located the page and held her Bible so that Jeb could read along if he got curious enough.

"Hey, I know this!" he said in an excited whisper. "Corinthians!"

Laney's head whipped toward him. "*What* did you say?"

He cleared his throat, and then he bent to murmur in her ear. "I notice, uh, more women than men." He glanced meaningfully around the room.

"Oh. I thought . . ." Laney shook her head. "Never mind." As she returned her attention to Pastor Ted, her peripheral vision caught Jeb lifting his eyes to the ceiling like a man praying for assistance. She shook her head again and reined in her galloping imagination.

Feeling eyes on her, she looked across the aisle formed by the two blocks of chairs. Rae Cornell was staring not at her, but at Jeb, a half-smile curving her mouth as she toyed with a lock of hair that was about fifteen different shades of blond. Rae was flirting, that's what she was doing, and Laney was utterly disgusted.

Fixing her gaze on Pastor Ted, she slid her arm behind

Jeb and rested it on the back of his chair. He frowned down at her, a question in his eyes.

"Just stretching," she murmured.

"You'll make us look like a couple," he whispered back.

"Shh." Laney pointedly returned her gaze to Pastor Ted.

As the lesson continued, she sneaked a glance across the aisle to ascertain whether Rae had taken her hint and turned her attention elsewhere. It seemed that she had. But trouble arose on another front when the Bible study ended and everyone adjourned for refreshments before moving on to that evening's special event, a volleyball game in the gym of the school across the street.

Laney was saying hello to Derek Lynd, a college freshman she used to babysit, when Jeb was accosted by dark-haired beauty Amber Havlicek, who wore a clingy turquoise shirt.

"Hi, Jackson." Secure in her gorgeousness, Amber smiled and hooked a lock of gleaming chestnut hair behind one ear. "Try one of these." She moved unnecessarily close to hand him an oversize chocolate-chip cookie on a pink paper napkin. "It's my own recipe, with pecans."

Oh, for crying out loud. *This* woman was flirting, too. Something inside Laney snapped, and she went a little crazy.

"Ooh, pecans! He doesn't eat nuts, Amber, but I do." She reached for the cookie. "Thanks."

Jeb surrendered the cookie without comment, and Laney felt a stirring of remorse. She'd heard his stomach growl during the Bible study; he might be hungry enough to eat even a pecan-studded cookie. But he wouldn't do it now because he never contradicted her in public.

Salve for her guilty conscience was unwittingly provided

by Derek, who brought her a cup of fruit punch. She thanked him and took a sip for the sake of politeness, then passed the cup to Jeb. Maybe the sugary drink would stave off his hunger.

As Jeb drank, Amber's gaze fluttered uncertainly between him and Laney. Satisfied when the other woman faded back into the crowd, Laney brightened her smile for Derek and asked how his parents were doing.

"Still driving me crazy." Derek's impish grin was as adorable now as it had been when he was a freckle-faced eight-year-old. "Mom keeps reminding me to be on the lookout for a girl as perfect as Mrs. Ryland's daughter."

Laney chuckled. "How did I ever manage to fool her into thinking I was perfect?"

"That's what I'm wondering," Derek teased. "All I know is that if I'd been born seven years sooner, she'd have us married by now."

Laughing again, Laney turned to share her amusement with Jeb, but found only empty space where he'd been standing.

Afraid that he'd fall into the clutches of Amber or Rae, she anxiously scanned the room. She relaxed when she spotted him talking to two men by the door.

When he returned to her side a few minutes later, she looped an arm through his so he wouldn't wander off again.

He subtly pulled away. "What's wrong with you tonight?"

"Nothing." Hearing his stomach growl again, she said, "Here, eat this," and gave him Amber's cookie.

As he took a huge bite and chased it with the rest of the fruit drink, Laney wondered what reason she could possibly have to be jealous. When had she ever been in Jeb's company and not enjoyed his undivided attention?

Amber and Rae were hardly the first females to bat their eyelashes at Jeb right under Laney's nose. She was certain that he *noticed* women, but he never responded to their overtures when he was with her.

So what *was* wrong with her tonight?

"Don't put your arm around me anymore," he said. "One of the guys I just met, Steve somebody, asked if we were dating."

Laney rolled her eyes and wondered what kind of brain glitch had caused her to agree to let Jeb help her find a husband.

Oh, wait. She hadn't actually agreed, had she? But Jeb hadn't let that pesky detail stop him from charging ahead with a plan she hadn't liked to begin with and that she liked even less as the evening wore on.

"I think Steve's shy with women," her personal matchmaker continued. "But he introduced me to his cousin, and . . ." Jeb glanced around the room and then gestured with his empty cup. "Over there. The chirpy blonde in the tight jeans."

Laney didn't need to look. He was describing Rae. And the woman's jeans weren't merely tight—they looked like they'd been airbrushed onto her curvy body.

"The four of us should go out," Jeb said.

"The four of us?" Laney echoed faintly. Was he seriously suggesting a double date?

"Yeah." He stuffed the last of the cookie into his mouth and talked around it. "Is Saturday night good for you?"

Absolutely not. "I don't think I could stomach watching

chirpy Rae flirt with you over a meal, Jeb."

"I know we've never done anything like this, princess, but if I don't set something up, Steve might not find the courage to ask you. And even if he does, you'll still need me to help the conversation along."

"Need *you*?" Laney snorted. "Jeb, the Death Stare is hardly conducive to good conversation."

"I can be sociable if I have to. And Steve owns a hardware store and three horses. How perfect is that?"

"I give up." Noticing that Rae's head had just turned in their direction and that she was again playing with her super-highlighted hair, Laney laid a hand on Jeb's arm. "How perfect *is* it?"

He looked pointedly at her hand, and then lifted it by the wrist and pressed his empty cup into her palm.

"A hardware guy would be handy around the house," he said patiently. "And when you were going with the veterinarian, didn't you love riding his horses?" He balled up his napkin and dropped it in the cup. Then he slid his hands into his pockets, probably to prevent Laney from claiming one. "You and Steve also have that whole business-owner thing in common."

Not for long, Laney reflected morosely. The tearoom's days were numbered.

"Jeb, this doesn't feel right."

"Okay, forget Steve for the moment. See the guy he's talking to? That's Eric Swenson. Somebody said he's a dentist."

"An amazingly handsome widowed dentist," Laney said with a touch of amusement. "Yes, I know." She eyed the tall, well-dressed blond who obviously spent as much time lifting

Brenda Coulter

weights as he did drilling teeth. Sarah Jane hadn't exaggerated one bit about that chiseled jaw and those bluer-than-blue eyes.

"You know him?" Jeb sounded oddly deflated.

"Not exactly. He's Sarah Jane's cousin. We were supposed to go on a blind date, but I had to cancel at the last minute. He wasn't very understanding about it."

Jeb's head swung back in Eric's direction.

"Don't bother glaring at him," Laney said. "It was nothing. But listen, Jeb, I've changed my mind about getting married."

"What?" His gaze flew back to her and he shook his head. "No, you haven't."

"Yes, I have." Looking again at the beauteous Rae, Laney fought a surge of despair. Didn't she have enough troubles without the unreasonable jealousy she was feeling tonight? Where had this awful emotion come from?

"Could we just go home?" she asked, trying not to sound as dejected as she suddenly felt. "I can't play volleyball in a dress, and you're hungry. We could heat up that venison chili and then go for a walk or something."

His eyes searched her face. "And talk about last night."

"What's to talk about?" Laney's gaze faltered. "You know I'm sorry. I haven't been sleeping well, that's all. You know how cranky I get when I'm overtired." It wasn't much of an apology, but if she tried to give him any more right now, she'd end up in tears.

He studied her for another moment, and then he nodded. "All right. I was hoping to accomplish more tonight, but we did okay. I'm optimistic about next week."

"That makes one of us," Laney said under her breath as

she preceded him out the door.

* * *

"It's been twelve days, Jackson."

"Yes, Shari." Holding the phone against his ear with a hunched shoulder, Jeb sniffed the inside of his Thermos bottle and decided it wasn't too funky to fill with the fresh hot coffee he'd just made. "We do have calendars here in Minnesota." He moved to the sink and ran some warm tap water into the bottle.

Shari didn't immediately respond. Jeb died a little when he realized she was probably sucking on a cigarette.

He'd gone more than two weeks without one.

"You can't just leave us hanging," Shari said finally.

Jeb's temper flared. "I told you I needed to get away from the band and think. Twelve days is not an unreasonable amount of time for that." He swished the water around in his Thermos and then dumped it into the sink.

Shari started to say something else, but Jeb heard his Call Waiting signal and pulled the phone away from his ear to check the display. It was Taylor.

"Shari, I have to go. I'll be in touch." He switched to the other call. "What's up, Taylor?"

"Just called to say hey, man."

"All right, you said it." Jeb grabbed the carafe from his coffeemaker's warming plate and poured a steady stream of extra-strong coffee into the Thermos. "Just like Aaron said it yesterday and just like Shari was saying it when I hung up on her to take your call."

"Sorry, man. We're concerned, you know?"

Jeb sighed. "I know. But I can't get any thinking done with you guys hounding me like this."

"Okay, just forget I called." Taylor ended the connection.

"I'll do my best," Jeb muttered as he capped the Thermos. He dropped the phone into his pocket and rolled his shoulders to ease the tension there.

Twelve days, and he wasn't any closer to the answers he'd come home to find. He couldn't stay in Owatonna much longer because of Laney, but another week ought to be okay. After that, maybe he'd head to that deserted beach in Mexico, just like he'd planned to do before he'd decided to come home.

On second thought, there was an awful lot of tequila down there. He'd better avoid Mexican beaches until he dried out a little more.

He was reading his Bible every day. That was alternately comforting and terrifying, just like his daily forays into the mysteries of prayer. It was an awesome thing, asking Almighty God to help him, especially when he was never entirely sure what to ask for or how to format his prayers.

He couldn't wait to spill his secret and ask Laney to instruct him.

Laney. She'd spent sixteen years praying for him before it had paid off, but he'd finally seen the light and renounced his sinful ways.

Rubbing the back of his neck, Jeb wondered whether Shari and the guys had anyone praying for them.

What if they didn't?

He tucked the Thermos under his arm, grabbed a shabby old coat with a pair of canvas gloves jammed into the pockets, and hit the button by his back door to open the garage. He had some thinking to do, and thinking was always a lot easier when he held a fishing rod.

He meant to pray some, too. And not just for himself this time.

He tossed his canoe on top of the Explorer and headed over to Lincoln's GGMM—"Gas, Garage & Mini Mart"—where he stuck a gas nozzle in the SUV's tank.

The world needed more places like Lincoln's, he reflected as he stared up at the clear blue sky. Places where a guy could refuel his truck and then maybe get a quick oil change while he ducked into the Mini Mart to grab a free cup of coffee and buy some fresh hot doughnuts and a box of nightcrawlers. Places where the cashier could always tell a guy what fish were biting at the nearby lakes.

"Bell! I thought that was you!" Ollie Lincoln strode toward him from the garage, a welcoming smile on his grease-smudged face.

"It's been a long time," Ollie said as he wiped his hands on a faded red rag. Apparently unsatisfied that his right hand was clean enough for a handshake, he simply nodded at Jeb and stuffed the rag into a pocket of his coveralls.

Jeb returned the nod. "Thanks for the venison. Too bad about your truck."

"Not my favorite way to bag a deer," Ollie said ruefully. He ran a hand through his spiky red hair. "You doing okay, then?"

"Can't complain." This had already gone further than Jeb normally allowed any non-essential conversation to progress, but he was a changed man now, so he exerted himself, just as he'd done last Tuesday night and then again yesterday morning at church. "I hear you got married."

"I sure did." Ollie's ruddy complexion brightened further as he grinned. "You should give it a try."

"Marriage?" Jeb snorted. "I don't think so."

"What about Laney?"

"It's not like that with us," Jeb said.

As Ollie's eyes narrowed in what looked like amused speculation, Jeb struggled to steer the conversation past that dangerous curve. What did normal guys talk about?

Sports. He recalled Laney mentioning that Ollie was as talented with a curling stone as Jeb was with a basketball.

"You still curling?" he asked.

"You bet. Ever done any, yourself?"

"No." The gas nozzle clicked off and Jeb removed it from the tank. He'd never been especially interested in what looked to him like shuffleboard on ice, but he was determined to become a better conversationalist, so he padded his terse reply with more words. "Never thought about it."

That was all the encouragement Ollie seemed to require. He spent the next couple of minutes rhapsodizing about the sport and about his member-owned club.

"Come by any Thursday night," he said. "That's when my team practices. You could try throwing a few stones."

"I might do that," Jeb murmured, surprised to find himself actually considering it. What was happening to the guy who'd quit the high school basketball team because he'd been so uncomfortable with all that high-fiving and camaraderie?

"Great," Ollie said. "Hey, I hear you're going to church now."

Jeb hesitated. How could he respond without provoking questions he couldn't yet answer because of Laney?

In his old life, he'd simply ignored questions he didn't

like. But he was a different man now, so he should have been prepared for this. He should have realized the local grapevine would be buzzing with the news that Jackson Bell had been spotted in a house of worship, of all places. He should have known somebody would eventually corner him.

He stalled for time by removing his sunglasses and rubbing an imaginary smudge off one lens with his thumb, but God didn't take that opportunity to insert any useful thoughts into his mind. He slid the glasses back on and was opening his mouth with no earthly idea what was about to come out of it when he was saved by a guy bellowing from the garage that Ollie's wife was on the phone.

Ollie grinned. "Gotta go. Don't forget, we curl on Thursdays at eight." He turned and jogged back to the garage.

Jeb paid for his gas and bought a bag of minnows. Climbing back into the Explorer, he wondered how much longer he could avoid telling Laney he'd given his heart to God. He'd been praying about it, but he wasn't sure he was praying correctly. Neither was he certain he'd recognize an answer from God if he received one.

At least he'd gotten her back to church. If he hadn't made any other progress, there was still that. Yesterday he had accompanied her to the worship service and Sunday school class for the second week in a row. And tomorrow they'd go to the singles' thing again.

Maybe he could talk her into giving Steve What's-his-name a chance. Maybe if he prayed hard enough, she'd fall in love with Steve or with some other deserving guy. And then when she was finally headed down the road to happily-ever-after, maybe Jeb's foolish heart would stop yearning for things it could never have.

Yeah. Maybe.

He was driving past the tearoom when he noticed something was happening there, even though it was Monday and the place was closed. Laney usually did her bookkeeping and cleaning on Mondays, so it was no surprise to see Francine in the parking lot. But the Graces' Buick was there, too, and another car.

Was everything all right? Jeb turned the Explorer around and went to find out.

He parked in front of the building and was making for the kitchen entrance just around the corner when the dining room door swung open and Aggie beckoned urgently. He pivoted on the ball of one foot and walked toward her.

"You can't go in the kitchen." Behind her glasses, Aggie's blue eyes twinkled as she backed up to allow him to cross the threshold. "Laney's got a man in there."

A man? Jeb stared at the closed kitchen door and wondered why he'd been left out of the matchmaking loop.

"A real estate agent," Millie clarified, taking Jeb's arm and steering him to the Graces' favorite table, where Caroline sat. "She showed this guy around one morning last week before we got here. She didn't even tell us until hours later."

And she hadn't told Jeb at all. Poor princess. She was probably afraid he'd offer her money again.

Nodding to Caroline, he held Millie's chair while she sat down.

"First thing this morning," Caroline said, "she decided to invite him back. And this time she told us, so we came right over to give her some moral support."

"Also because we're nosey," Aggie admitted as she

settled onto her chair like a fluffy old hen.

Jeb chewed his bottom lip.

"She won't take our money," Caroline said quietly.

"Or mine." Jeb blew out a frustrated breath and carefully lowered himself onto a little bamboo chair.

Caroline gestured to the two teapots on the table, both of which were wrapped in the quilted fabric jackets Laney called tea cozies. "It's still nice and hot, but we can't go in the kitchen, so you'll have to use Laney's cup."

Jeb shook his head. "I don't want anything."

He'd never told a bigger lie in his life. He wanted *everything.* As he absently rubbed a smear of pink lipstick from the rim of the almost-empty teacup in front of him, Ollie's question rolled through his mind.

What about Laney?

It would certainly solve her money problems, and Jeb would be more than happy to give her all the babies she wanted. But she didn't love him in that way, and that was for the best. He wasn't good enough for her, and he'd promised to help her find a man who was.

Restless, he shifted on his chair. As he extended one leg beneath the table, he kicked something that sounded and felt like a cardboard box. Hearing an affronted *meow*, he jerked his foot back.

He frowned at Millie. She was clearly the perpetrator of this infraction because she was the one giving him a pleading look while the other two stared fixedly at the ceiling.

"You know Laney can't allow pets in here," he said.

"A cat in a box isn't going to hurt anything," Aggie insisted. "Besides, Frankie Five isn't used to being home alone on Mondays."

Frankie Five. It figured. Decades ago, the Graces had hit on what they believed was the perfect cat name, and they'd had nothing but Frankies ever since. Jeb just hoped this new Frankie wasn't as bad-tempered as the last one.

"Did you cut air holes in the box?" he asked.

"Well of course." Aggie harrumphed. "We're not animal abusers, Jeb."

No, they weren't. To his knowledge, the only living thing the Graces had ever abused was himself. They sure hadn't worried about him being able to breathe inside that hot, scratchy rabbit suit, had they?

"Frankie loves to crawl into a nice cozy box and take a nap," Millie explained. "So we—"

"Looks like the meeting's over," Caroline interrupted.

They all turned and watched Laney escort a portly, excessively cheerful man to the front door. The guy wore a "just trust me" suit and carried an "I'm serious" attaché case and was talking nonstop. Laney smiled and nodded, but Jeb sensed an awful tension in her.

Mr. Real Estate was plucking on her very last nerve, and that nerve was perilously close to snapping like a worn-out guitar string.

She shook the guy's hand and let him out. She locked the door behind him, and then squared her shoulders before turning and marching over to the Graces' table.

Jeb stood, offering his chair. She gave him a wan smile and sank onto it. He snagged a chair from another table and seated himself between her and Aggie.

"Thank you," Laney murmured as Millie refilled her teacup. She lifted the cup between trembling hands and sipped.

Millie drew an audible breath and started to speak, but Jeb caught her eye and shook his head urgently. She closed her mouth and slumped back in her chair.

Laney slowly returned her cup to its saucer, her eyes downcast. Tears sparkled on her lower lashes.

"I listed the building," she said in a defeated little voice that knotted Jeb's insides. "I'll tell you about it later. Right now, I just . . ." She shook her head.

The Graces responded to her announcement with a wholly uncharacteristic silence.

Laney turned her head toward Jeb but didn't raise her eyes to his. "I'll go get you a cup."

"No, I don't want any—" He aborted his protest as she sprang out of her chair and bounded away like a startled deer.

Jeb shot out of his own chair and caught up with her just inside the kitchen, where she spun around and raised her hands, palms-out, warning him to stay back.

Tears welled in her beautiful blue eyes.

Jeb was debating whether to disregard her silent order and pull her into his arms for the hug she so obviously needed when his cell phone rang.

Laney flinched at the sound. But then she pulled herself together, straightening her slim shoulders and jerking her chin up like she'd done beside the front door just a minute ago.

"I'm fine," she insisted, turning away from him to collect a cup and saucer, a napkin, and a spoon.

Jeb's phone continued to ring, but his attention remained locked on Laney.

"Maybe you should answer that," she said as she walked

past him carrying the place setting he didn't need.

As his eyes and his heart followed her retreating form, Jeb thumbed a button and raised the phone to his ear.

Chapter Eleven

"SHE'LL TAME HIM," Caroline was saying as Laney returned to the dining room. "And she'll do it without breaking his spirit."

Obviously, the Graces were matchmaking again. Laney forgot her own troubles long enough to pity the man who was being discussed as though he were a circus lion.

"And now that he's going to church," Aggie said, "there's every reason to hope the faith issue will be resolved soon."

"We'd better pray that he doesn't leave town for a while," Millie said. "He'll just get all confused again."

Oh, no. They *wouldn't.* Laney stopped walking so suddenly that the teacup she carried fell sideways on its saucer. The high-pitched clatter caused three identical heads to swivel in her direction.

"Are you talking about Jeb?" she demanded.

"We didn't know you were there," Millie said weakly.

Laney stared hard at Caroline. "You are *not* going to marry Jeb."

"Oh, he's too young for Caroline," the irrepressible Aggie quipped.

Laney shot her a quelling look.

"We won't hurt him," Millie said sweetly. "We have a plan."

No. The Graces didn't realize how vulnerable Jeb was. How easily his tender heart could be bruised by a woman who didn't understand him.

"Forget the plan." Laney had never been more annoyed with her beloved great-aunts. "Leave Jeb alone, do you hear me?"

She immediately regretted her sharp, disrespectful tone, but before she could form an apology, Caroline spoke.

"You could use some quiet right now." There was no censure in Caroline's penetrating gaze, only understanding and sympathy. "We three have to get to a church committee meeting, anyway." She smiled reassuringly. "Have some more tea. It's still fairly hot."

The Graces rose, collected their dishes, and bustled to the kitchen.

"I guess it wasn't enough being sorry for myself," Laney muttered at the fabric-covered teapot. "Now I'm ashamed of myself, too."

She refilled her cup and was raising it to her lips when Jeb reentered the dining room.

He said nothing as he resumed his seat beside her. Folding his arms, he stared out the window and sighed.

"Troubling phone call?" Laney ventured.

"Skeptical Heart's manager," he grunted. "Pressing me for a decision I'm not ready to make."

"Want to talk about it?"

"No." He turned his head to look at her. "Want to talk about the contract you just signed?"

"No."

For several minutes they sat without speaking. Laney finished her tea, and then she sighed and nudged his arm.

"We should probably stop sulking now."

He turned to her with raised eyebrows, his expression one of exaggerated innocence. "I'm not sulking. I'm just keeping you company while *you* sulk."

The wretch. He was trying to make her smile. Laney

snatched up her napkin and threw it at his face.

He ducked it and swung up to his feet, laughing. Then he grabbed her hand and yanked her up, too.

She threw a playful punch at his flat stomach and he laughed again, the white flash of his teeth an attractive contrast to the dark whiskers shadowing his jaw.

And just that quickly, Laney's black mood vanished.

"Help me clean up," she said.

While Jeb carried the last tray of dishes to the kitchen, Laney gathered the soiled tablecloth and napkins into a neat bundle. She was taking a fresh cloth from the old oak chest of drawers used for linen storage when the Graces clattered back into the dining room, coats on and purses in hand.

"Millie," Jeb said as he came in behind them, "don't forget your box."

"What box?" Laney asked.

Aggie and Millie exchanged furtive glances. Then Aggie's arm shot out and she pointed to a far corner of the ceiling.

"Goodness gracious!" she cried like a stage actress projecting to the back row. "Look at that enormous spider!"

"Where?" Laney wasn't repulsed by spiders, but she didn't want them dropping into her customers' teacups, so she looked anxiously in the direction Aggie indicated. "I don't see—"

"No, wait. It's something in my eye. Yes, that's it." Aggie thrust her small round body in front of Laney. "You'd better look." She pulled her glasses down to the tip of her nose and blinked rapidly.

Realizing that she was being conned, Laney barely glanced at Aggie's left eye. "Nope. No spiders in there."

"Check the other eye," Aggie suggested, leaning closer.

Jeb started to laugh and covered it up with a cough. As Laney turned a reproachful look on him, she saw Millie shove a cardboard box at Caroline, who hustled outside with it.

"Shotgun!" Millie yelled in another ludicrously transparent attempt to divert Laney's attention.

Aggie gave her younger sister a withering look. "You can't call shotgun when we're still indoors."

Millie flashed an unrepentant grin and hurried outside. Aggie took off after her.

Seventy-nine years old, and the Graces were still squabbling over whose turn it was to ride in the Buick's front passenger seat. Shaking her head over their silliness, Laney lifted her hand in an unnoticed farewell.

Jeb closed the door.

Having a pretty good idea what the triplets were hiding, Laney murmured, "I just hope they thought to poke air holes in that box."

"They did," Jeb said.

Through the window, Laney saw Caroline stow the box in the Buick's back seat and then slide serenely behind the steering wheel. Aggie and Millie, still playfully bickering over whose turn it was to ride shotgun, tussled next to the front passenger door.

"Somebody's going to fall and break a hip," Jeb predicted as Aggie batted Millie one last time with her handbag and then got in the back seat.

Returning to her cleanup tasks, Laney shook out the crisp white cloth and watched it flutter over the Graces' table like a collapsing parachute.

She was upset about signing that contract, but where

was the sense in risking foreclosure? Even with its pre-historic heater, this building was worth a nice chunk of change, and selling it should net her enough to get completely out of debt.

"They're up to something." Jeb turned away from the window and walked toward her.

"Besides concealing cats in my dining room?" Laney set a glass vase holding a pink carnation and some ivy in the center of the table and smoothed a wrinkle from the cloth. "Yes, Jeb, they're up to something. They're matchmaking."

"Ah." He hesitated, then cringed a little and said, "But, princess, you *do* want to get married."

Holding his gaze, Laney folded her arms. "The question is, Jeb, do *you* want to get married?"

"What kind of question is that?"

She merely raised her eyebrows and waited for him to catch on. It took a couple of seconds, but then his eyes widened and he clutched at his heart and pressed his lips together as though to form that horrible word, *married.*

"Exactly." Laney's reply was punctuated by a rubbery squeal as the Buick peeled out of the parking lot.

Jeb's mouth worked, but shock appeared to have paralyzed his vocal cords.

"Don't worry." Laney picked up the soiled tablecloth and walked past him. "I told them to back off."

"*Laney.*" He caught her arm like a shipwreck victim grabbing for something to keep himself afloat. "You're talking about the women who turned me into a pink rabbit!"

She pressed her lips together a second too late; the guffaw that slipped past them earned her an indignant look from Jeb. But how could she help laughing when she recalled how the Graces had stuffed seventeen-year-old Jeb with his favorite strawberry-rhubarb pie before requesting a "small favor"? Only after securing his promise had they revealed that they needed a tall person to wear the fuzzy pink rabbit costume they'd rented for an Easter party at a local nursing home.

The worst of it was that a full-page photograph of Jackson Bell, Easter Bunny—with a smiling elderly woman hanging on each of his long, pink arms—had somehow found its way into the high-school yearbook.

"I'm sorry," Laney managed through quivering lips.

"Yes, I can see that," he said dryly. "Now stop laughing and promise you'll save me from the Graces."

"Like I said, I already took care of it." Which was why she felt free to laugh at him now. He was just so cute: six feet and five inches of terrified male trembling at the prospect of three little old ladies foisting a fiancée on him.

"Although I can't help wondering who they had in mind," she added.

Jeb shuddered like someone who'd just had a snowball pushed under his collar. "Forget it."

Laney gave him a break and changed the subject. "Are you going fishing today?"

"Yeah. If you're okay here, I'll go toss another bag of minnows into Clear Lake."

"Try attaching them to hooks and lines before you toss them," Laney said archly. "I'd love some walleye fillets for supper."

He smiled. "I think I can promise you some, as long as you're not picky about whether I get them directly from the lake or buy them at a store." His smile faded as he caught one of her curls and twined it around his finger. "Come with me," he urged in his deepest, smokiest voice.

Gazing up at him, Laney tried to swallow and found her mouth had gone dry. When had Jeb's lean face, always dearly familiar, become so attractive? And why was that raspy voice of his suddenly so beguiling? It made her feel odd and shivery, and she had a wild desire to lay her palm against his unshaven jaw and—

"I can't," she said, averting her face to hide her sudden confusion. "I'm expecting Sarah Jane Swenson any minute, and I have a dozen other things to do here today."

He gave her curl a light tug and let it go. "See you later, then."

Just a few minutes after he left, Sarah Jane arrived to pick up the four dozen lemon tartlets and an equal number of chocolate-dipped gingersnap cookies Laney had made for a fundraising dinner Sarah Jane's mother was giving.

"I owe you one." Immaculately attired in black dress pants and a burgundy silk jacket and dripping with gold jewelry, Sarah Jane watched Laney slide the single-serving tarts into sturdy white bakery boxes. "You really should let me pay you, though." Pushing back her lush fall of chestnut hair, she smiled her cheerleader smile.

"No, I'm happy to do this," Laney said. "Children's charities have always been dear to my heart."

That was certainly true, but it wasn't the only reason she'd volunteered to provide desserts for this dinner. She'd hoped that the people who sampled her baked goods would like them enough to visit the Three Graces Tearoom for more.

Only there was no longer any point in drumming up new

business for the tearoom, was there?

"Are you okay?" Sarah Jane asked. "You look like you're about to cry."

Laney started to protest that she was perfectly fine, but Sarah Jane's coffee-brown eyes were glowing with friendly concern, and Laney had never been much of an actress, anyway.

"I'm a mess," she admitted on a sigh.

"If you need a listening ear, I could spare half an hour," Sarah Jane said.

Laney hesitated. It was a kind offer, but her current troubles weren't ones she could discuss with Sarah Jane. Still, half an hour of pleasant conversation with another woman might do wonders for her mood.

"I could do with some girl talk," she admitted.

"Good." Sarah Jane gracefully shrugged out of her silk jacket. "Why don't you make us a pot of tea?"

Laney had already consumed enough tea to float Jeb's canoe, but she put a kettle on to boil.

A short while later, sitting across a table from Sarah Jane and sipping tea for politeness' sake, she took a third piece of buttery shortbread so Sarah Jane wouldn't feel like a pig for having eaten two. She was well aware that she carried a few extra pounds on her hips; she attributed every one of them to her "Minnesota Nice" upbringing.

"I hear Jackson's in town," Sarah Jane said as she stirred milk into her second cup of tea.

"Yes. He just finished a concert tour, and he wanted some peace and quiet."

The band's heading back to L.A., but I need to come home.

When was he planning to tell her what was going on? Something was happening with the band; that much was obvious from his reaction to the phone call from his manager. But she had a feeling there was more.

"He'll find plenty of peace and quiet in pokey old Owatonna," Sarah Jane said with rueful humor.

Laney nudged the cookie plate toward her. "Try the gingersnaps," she said absently.

"We've never really talked much, have we, Laney? I wonder why." Selecting a cookie, Sarah Jane grinned suddenly. "You wouldn't believe how I envied you back in high school."

Laney had just raised her teacup to her lips; she set it down so abruptly it was a wonder her saucer didn't crack.

"You envied *me*?" she squeaked. "Sarah Jane, you were the most beautiful and popular girl in school. You were even a model student. I wanted to hate you, but you just kept on being nice to me. Do you have any idea how annoying that was?"

Sarah Jane dismissed the question with a tinkly laugh and a wave of one beautifully manicured hand. "Aren't teenagers awful?"

"*I* was," Laney said. "But you were disgustingly perfect."

"I had my faults, Laney, believe me. And I did envy you."

"Why?"

"Because I had a huge crush on Jackson."

Laney still didn't understand. "I was never his girlfriend, Sarah Jane."

"Maybe not, but he treated you like a princess. He even called you that, didn't he?"

"Still does." Laney shrugged. "It's because the first time

we met, I was wearing a princess costume, complete with a sparkly tiara." She smiled, savoring the memory. "He was eleven. He said I looked dumb."

"Well, *eleven*. At that age, they're still putting frogs down your back to show how much they like you. But Jackson was plenty attractive in high school. That high-voltage stare and that thrilling voice." Sarah Jane shuddered delicately. "Oh, I envied you, all right. Because 'just friends' or not, that intriguing bad boy would have done anything in the world for you."

Yes, he would have. That was his maddening gratitude. Believing himself to be unworthy of her friendship, Jeb had never stopped trying to compensate her for it. Sometimes he'd seemed almost desperate to make her happy, as if he feared she might abandon him like his mother had.

Things sure had changed since those days, she reflected bitterly. Now Jeb *wanted* her to abandon him. But he knew she wouldn't do that, so he meant to find a nice man to distract her while he quietly slipped out of her life.

Oh, she could just strangle him!

"I know he went out with other girls," Sarah Jane went on. "He even asked *me* out once. I said no because I knew he wanted only one thing from those other girls, and after he got it he always ran straight back to your side."

Profoundly embarrassed, Laney shifted on her chair and cleared her throat meaningfully.

"Sorry." Sarah Jane waved that elegant hand again. "Too much information, right? But why was he was so relaxed with you and so edgy with everyone else? I swear, every time I saw you sitting with him at lunch I thought of that fable about the child who pulled the thorn out of the lion's paw."

But Laney had never succeeded in pulling the thorn from Jeb's paw. She'd been trying for years to ease his suffering, to convince him that his parents had rejected him because of deficiencies in themselves, not in him. But he persisted in believing he was unworthy of anyone's love or respect.

The blockhead. If only she could hug him hard enough to squeeze all of that stupidity out of him.

"Laney?"

Her gaze, which had drifted to the windows, jerked guiltily back to Sarah Jane. "Hmm?"

"Tell the truth." Speculation gleamed in Sarah Jane's brown eyes as she leaned forward, inviting a confidence. "Haven't you ever wondered if there could be something more exciting than friendship between the two of you?"

Laney felt a hot flush spread across her cheeks. "I've wondered about it," she confessed. "Just lately."

For an instant she panicked and wished she could unsay the words and even *unthink* them. When had she turned into one of those women who sighed over Jeb's masculine appeal?

That night at Willie's, he'd looked at her in a way that had made her heart beat faster. And just now when he'd left her to go fishing, she'd felt the same breathless wonder.

What was happening here?

"My, my. Look at her eyes go all dreamy." Sarah Jane's tone was softly mocking, but there was no meanness in it. "So you've gone and fallen in love with him."

"No," Laney protested, but then honesty compelled her to amend that answer. "I mean, I've loved him since I was nine years old." She struggled to shape her thoughts into words. "But lately something has felt different. Sometimes when I look at him . . ." She faltered. How could she express her feelings when she wasn't even sure what they were?

Sarah Jane dabbed gracefully at her mouth with her napkin. "You're having romantic thoughts about him."

Laney nodded slowly.

"And you're wondering if it's the same for him."

Recalling the way Jeb had looked at her that evening at Willie's, Laney nodded harder.

"But you don't know how to find out."

"Exactly." Relief shuddered through Laney. If Sarah Jane understood all of that, surely she'd have some good advice to impart. "So what should I do?"

"It's very simple," Sarah Jane said. "Just kiss him."

"Kiss *Jeb*?" She couldn't possibly kiss Jeb. Not on the mouth. Not the way she had kissed the three men she'd talked herself into falling in love with.

Sarah Jane loosed another peal of her bubbly laughter. "If the thought of kissing him repulses you, Laney, why are we having this conversation?"

"It doesn't repulse me. It just worries me. What if he doesn't like it?"

"He's a man," Sarah Jane said dryly. "He'll like it."

"All right." Laney nodded again. She'd do it. If Jeb didn't like it, she'd find some way to laugh it off.

"Well, then." Sarah Jane lifted her teacup and swung it toward Laney in a toast. "Good luck!"

"Wait!" Laney said, panicking. "I don't know how to do it!"

Sarah Jane's perfect eyebrows rose halfway to her hairline. "You've never kissed a man?"

"Of course I have. But Jeb's a foot taller than me. What am I supposed to do, order him to stand still while I drag a stepladder in front of him?"

"You're right," Sarah Jane said decisively. "You need a plan."

A plan. Yes. She definitely needed one of those.

"Make sure he's sitting down," Sarah Jane said. "And then when the moment's right, just walk over to him and swoop in for your kiss."

Laney stared into her teacup and tried to picture herself doing that.

"Now let's think of a romantic set-up." Sarah Jane tapped her bottom lip with a slim finger. "Maybe a candlelight dinner."

No. Jeb never balked at taking Laney to elegant restaurants, but he'd didn't love the soft music and candlelight the way she did. She tried to think of something he would enjoy.

She could ask him to take her fishing, she supposed, but he'd be at one end of the canoe and she'd be at the other, and flinging herself at him in hopes of achieving lip-lock could tumble them both into a freezing lake.

"I'll give it some thought," she said.

"All right, but be bold," Sarah Jane advised. "Subtlety is wasted on men."

Bold. Okay. Somehow she'd grab Jeb and kiss him until he stopped being shocked and started wondering why they'd never thought of kissing before. And then together they might discover that what they'd felt for each other all these years had evolved into—

No.

Laney's conscience pulled her up short. What was she doing, seeking relationship advice from a woman whose manicures lasted longer than her marriages? More importantly, what was she doing ignoring the fact that Jeb didn't believe in God? She might have temporarily strayed from the path of righteousness, but she would never consider marrying a man who wasn't a Christian.

And if marriage to Jeb wasn't a possibility, then she had no business kissing him. Love wasn't a game.

She aimed a vague smile at Sarah Jane. "Listen, I don't think I'm ready for this, after all."

Sarah raised her eyebrows but said nothing. Sensing her friend's benign amusement, Laney self-consciously poured herself a cup of tea she didn't want any more than she'd wanted the first one.

"It's just that these feelings are so new," she said lamely. "I could even be mistaken about them."

"It's just a kiss, Laney. You don't have to marry the man."

"I'm not a casual kisser, Sarah Jane."

"Well, that's the difference between you and me," Sarah Jane said lightly. "So I guess that's that."

Yes, that was that. Laney sighed and drank her tea.

Chapter Twelve

AT TWO O'CLOCK ON TUESDAY AFTERNOON, Jeb stood at one of his tall kitchen windows in jeans and bare feet, his unbuttoned plaid shirt hanging loosely from his shoulders. Halfway through his third mug of wake-up coffee, he was staring at the brown blanket of fallen leaves covering his back yard and wondering what Laney usually did about it.

Hired someone, probably. She enjoyed yard work, but she didn't have much time for it these days.

Jeb yawned and scratched his bare chest. *He* had time, and some physical activity might calm his restless spirit.

He slugged down the rest of his coffee, then finished dressing and headed outside.

He found an electric leaf-blower in his garage, but it seemed wrong to use something so noisy on such a crisp, beautiful afternoon. He chose an old yard rake and set to work, humming made-up melodies as he dragged the crackling leaves into neat piles. It took him a couple of hours to finish his own yard, and then he started on Laney's.

He was working next to her front sidewalk, stuffing the last man-made mountain of leaves into the biodegradable paper bags he'd found in his garage, when a red Corvette roared past him and slid into Laney's driveway. It jerked to a stop mere inches from the Explorer's back bumper.

Jeb recognized the flashy car and its driver, a muscular blond man who emerged from the vehicle wearing a gray suit and carrying an armful of cellophane-wrapped flowers.

Muttering a word he knew he'd have to apologize to God for later, Jeb dropped his rake and stalked over to inform

Laney's ex-boyfriend that she wasn't home.

"Hello, Bell." Tom Johansen's face stretched into a patently counterfeit smile. "It's been a long time."

Not nearly long enough. And had the guy taken a bath in cologne, or what? Quashing his impulse to fan the sissy stench away with his hand, Jeb switched to breathing through his mouth. That was as much consideration as he was willing to give a guy who had failed to treat Laney like the princess she was.

"She's not home yet," he said. "And she's no longer interested, anyway." So Tommy boy could just climb right back into his little red rocket and blast off.

Tom's faux-friendly expression morphed into a sneer. "You don't own her, Bell."

"I am aware of that." Jeb felt a muscle begin to tic in his jaw. "But I won't stand by and let you hurt her again."

"I didn't hurt her," Tom shot back. "We just disagreed about a few things, and then that other guy happened along before I could work things out with her. But I hear he's out of the picture now, and there hasn't been anyone else for me, so . . ."

So he thought he would just slide right back into her life? Jeb folded his arms to stop himself from going for the presumptuous jerk's throat. "You had your chance and you blew it," he bit out. "She deserves better than you."

Tom scraped him with an appraising look. "I suppose you think you're better," he challenged.

"You suppose wrong," Jeb said through clenched teeth. He didn't need reminding that he'd never be good enough for Laney. "But you're still leaving."

"She's expecting me." Tom smiled again, this time in

smug triumph. "She said she'd be here by six."

Reflexively, Jeb glanced at his watch. It was ten minutes to six.

His heart dropped into his belly. If she had agreed to go out with Tom, the guy must still mean something to her. Why had she pretended otherwise?

And had she forgotten this was Tuesday? The singles' thing would be starting just over an hour from now.

She'd forgotten. There was no other explanation for this. And Jeb had no desire to stick around and wave goodbye as she drove off into the sunset with her boomerang boyfriend, so he turned abruptly and headed for his garage.

No, walking away wasn't the polite, Christian thing to do. But neither was slamming a fist into Tom Johansen's supercilious face, and at the moment it was all Jeb could do to resist that temptation.

He hauled his canoe out of the garage and shoved it up onto the Explorer's roof racks. He secured it with some rope and then hurled himself into the driver's seat.

With the Corvette hugging his back bumper, Jeb was compelled to make a U-turn and plow through a dormant flowerbed in order to reach his own empty driveway. If Laney's beloved pink and purple tulips failed to come up in the spring, he'd make it up to her somehow.

Carefully avoiding eye contact with Tom, he ripped past the 'Vette and out onto quiet Mulberry Street.

If Tom was what she wanted, he'd find a way to accept that. But why hadn't she told him she was giving the guy another chance? How was he supposed to help her find a husband if she wasn't going to tell him stuff like this?

It was close to sunset when he arrived at Clear Lake, so

he left his canoe on top of the Explorer and trudged down to the water's edge. Sitting cross-legged on the scrubby grass, elbows on his knees, he held his head between his hands and fought the bitterness spreading through his spirit.

Why did it have to be Tom?

Sighing, he dropped his hands, tipped his head back, and stared hopelessly at the bare, wind-whipped tree branches above him.

"Why can't it be me?"

The plaintive question startled him because he had always understood and accepted that Laney deserved to marry a truly good man—and he would never be one of those.

Sure, God had forgiven him for his wicked past. But the fact that he was now headed to heaven didn't change where he'd been before. And Laney deserved better than a guy who'd left nothing but destruction in his wake.

Tom Johansen wasn't perfect, but at least he didn't have a past that shocked and disgusted decent people. So if Laney wanted him . . .

A cold wind ruffled Jeb's shirt and found its way under his collar, stroking his back like icy fingers. Clenching his teeth, he shivered with perverse satisfaction.

He could stand this. If there was one thing besides music he was good at, it was enduring situations he didn't like but couldn't change.

Learning that lesson at a very young age had preserved his sanity. When he'd realized that crying into his pillow at night wouldn't get him a dad who took him fishing or a housekeeper who hugged him and made cupcakes for his birthday, he'd dried his tears and toughened up. Life simply was what it was; there was no point in whining about it.

He shivered again, and his hand went to his shirt pocket before he remembered that he didn't smoke anymore.

He was staring moodily at a flock of mallard ducks paddling some ten yards from the water's edge when his phone rang. He was in no frame of mind to talk to Shari again, or to any of the band guys, but habit made him check the display to see if Laney was trying to reach him.

She was, so he answered.

"Jeb, where are you?"

"Clear Lake," he said. "Where are *you*?" And what had happened to her date? If that jerk had abandoned her somewhere—

"Where do you think I am?" Her tone carried a hint of impatience. "I'm at home."

At home? Was she cooking supper for Tom, then?

She sighed. "Jeb, you said you wanted to go to the singles' meeting."

"True." He spotted a fist-size rock next to his right knee and closed his hand around it. "But I'm not the one who accepted a date with good ol' Tom." Rearing back, he pitched the rock as hard as he could.

It sailed far over the mallards' heads before dropping into the water with a resounding plunk, but it ticked them off. With fluttering wings and outraged nasally quacks, they moved their party farther down the shoreline.

"A date with Tom?" Laney sounded almost as annoyed as the ducks. "Where did you get a crazy idea like that?"

"Well, let's see." Scowling at the red sun caught in the treetops on the other side of the lake, Jeb groped the ground beside him until he found another rock. "Maybe I got that idea when I saw him wearing a suit and holding a bunch of red roses and heading for your front door. Or maybe I got it when he said you were expecting him at six o'clock. Or maybe—"

"I was expecting him, Jeb, but not for a date. What are you so irritated about?"

"We've been over this, Laney." He threw his rock so hard and with such sloppy form that he nearly dislocated his shoulder. "Tom's not the right guy for you."

"So you took off because you thought I intended to go out with Tom."

She hadn't asked a question, so Jeb didn't reply. Besides, he'd just spotted a half-buried rock that looked like it might be even bigger than the first one after he worked it out of the packed dirt.

"That's insulting, Jeb. I can't believe you thought I was ditching you to go on a date."

He gave up trying to dig out the rock and closed his eyes. "I didn't think you were ditching me," he admitted. "I just figured you'd forgotten what day it was."

"I didn't forget, Jeb." Her tone had softened; Laney was always quick to understand and forgive. "And Tom was just doing a favor for his sister. She's getting married, so she asked if she could borrow some of my etiquette books. She lives in St. Paul, and Tom's going to see her tomorrow night, so he stopped by to get the books. That's all it was."

"That's not all it was." Jeb wasn't going to let her kid herself on that score. "Princess, the guy was wearing a quart of cologne and he was holding a bunch of 'let's put the past behind us' roses. He intended to take you some glitzy restaurant and—"

"All right, so he asked." She sounded peeved again. "But I turned him down."

Because she didn't want him, or because she already had plans for the evening?

"Okay." Jeb figured he'd better back out of the argument before she told him she was entertaining thoughts about giving Tom another chance. If that was true, he didn't want to know it until he'd regained the self-control he'd lost when Tom had given him that smug look. "I'm sorry I misread the situation."

"And I'm sorry for being snippy," Laney said. "But I have to go now. Unless you want me to wait?"

"No, go ahead and leave." Jeb pushed up to his feet. "I'll miss part of the Bible study, but I'll get there as soon as I can."

* * *

Laney felt a light tap on her shoulder and turned to see Jeb sliding into the chair she'd saved for him.

"That was quick," she whispered. "And we started late, so you haven't missed much."

Realizing what she had just said, Laney looked away from him and bit her lip. It wasn't as though Jeb would regret missing a Bible lesson. Still, he was here. And maybe if he kept coming to these things for her sake, some of the truths he heard would begin to seep into his cautious heart.

Pastor Ted was teaching from Galatians. Laney's Bible lay open on her lap, but instead of following the lesson, she stared at a softly flickering fluorescent light on the ceiling and wondered again, even though she'd resolved to *stop* wondering, what it would be like to kiss Jeb.

She barely noticed when he leaned closer and then

closer still to read the verses Pastor Ted was pointing out. When he emitted a frustrated grunt and pulled her Bible onto his own knee, however, her gaze flew to his face.

He was so intent on his reading that he didn't even see her amazement.

Stung by guilt, she quickly looked away. While she'd been indulging in inappropriate thoughts about Jeb, he had been reading the Word of God.

She couldn't wait to find out what was going through his mind, but when the Bible study ended, they were caught up in the tide of chattering people flowing to the refreshment tables. It seemed like hours before she was able to maneuver him to a deserted corner of the room.

"You seemed interested in the Bible study," she said as casually as she could manage.

Jeb's silvery gaze, which had been trained on her while he drank coffee from a Styrofoam cup, dropped like a stone. Lowering the cup, he stared down into the liquid and said, "Uh . . . yeah. I guess."

All right. He wasn't ready to talk about it, and Laney knew better than to press him. "I'm glad we came," she said.

"Yeah." He looked up, his gaze touching her for only a second before moving past her. "There's rich pickings tonight. I counted at least six guys who look about the right age for you."

Somehow Laney refrained from rolling her eyes. She simply had to find a way to get him to give up this matchmaking scheme.

"We'd better split up," he said, and walked away with a purposeful stride.

For a couple of minutes Laney remained in the corner

alone, drinking coffee and watching him strike up a breezy conversation with two men. Then she gave her head a small, disbelieving shake and went to say hello to the pastor and a couple of her women friends.

She remained aware of Jeb's every move. He made contact with two more men and then politely rebuffed an overture from Amber.

It was hard to wrap her mind around: *Jeb*, being gregarious and polite. It was wonderful, but what had gotten into the man?

She saw him shake hands with Steve, the shy guy he'd suggested inviting on a double date, and then he made his way across the room and back to Laney's side. She must have had astonishment written all over her face, but he was too focused on his mission to notice.

"See that guy by the coffee urn?" he asked. "His wife died three years ago. He comes with four-year-old twin girls, which would give you a nice start on that big family you want."

"That's Paul Valenti," Laney said. "I've seen him with his daughters at the grocery store. Once, one of them dropped a jar of pickles and it shattered. And Jeb, he *yelled* at her. It was just an accident, but he called her stupid, and the poor little thing burst into tears."

Jeb shot a disgusted look in Paul's direction. "Forget him, then. As much as those kids need a good mother, I can't let you marry a hothead."

He glanced around the room. "Check out that guy with the big nose and round eyeglasses. He's assistant principal over at the high school, so he must like kids." Jeb paused and scratched his ear, apparently giving that some more thought.

"Although dealing with a whole school full of teenagers might make a man reluctant to have kids of his own. What do you think?"

Laney sighed. "I think I'm ready to get out of here." She needed go home and recover from her stressful day and the shock of watching Jeb behave like a Miss Congeniality hopeful at a beauty pageant.

"Yes, it's time." He looked around the room again. "You'll be safe with any of these churchy guys, so go pick one to drive you."

Confused, Laney shook her head at him. "Drive me?"

"To the bowling place," he said.

She'd been talking about going home, not to the bowling alley. And besides— "I'm driving Francine tonight, remember?"

"Leave Francine here. Get a lift with one of these guys. It's a short drive, but it might still give you enough time to see if the two of you are going to click."

"No, Jeb." Laney cupped a hand over the back of her neck and squeezed the knotted muscles there. "I'm going home."

"Hey." His face softened as he studied hers. "It's easy, princess. All you have to do is pick one of these guys and go smile at him. He'll take it from there."

Yeah, right. It would never occur to loyal Jeb that a man might simply be uninterested in her.

Just like it would never occur to him that she was no longer interested in any man but him.

It was crazy, but she just couldn't stop thinking about him in this new way.

He tilted his head to one side and looked her over. "That

blue shirt looks good on you, and it's a perfect match for your eyes. But you should put on some lipstick. And smile, okay?"

Laney sighed, instead.

He made a sympathetic noise in his throat. "Bad day at the tearoom?"

"Kind of." They hadn't been busy, but worry had eaten at her all day, particularly when she'd totaled the day's receipts and realized that for the fourth time this year, she was going to have to take money out of her personal bank account to pay the Graces.

"No, that's not it." Jeb eyed her shrewdly. "He upset you, didn't he? Tom."

"Annoyed me," she corrected. "With his refusal to believe that when I said "it's over" all those months ago, it really was over."

Was that a gleam of satisfaction in Jeb's eyes? She had always suspected he thought Tom wasn't good enough for her.

"No wonder you're so unenthusiastic about meeting guys tonight," he said.

Laney nodded, because that was part of it. She just hoped he wouldn't guess the main reason, that thoughts of him were crowding all other men out of her mind.

Still watching her, he ran his tongue over his bottom lip and appeared to be considering something.

"All right," he said decisively. "You can ride with me."

Laney hesitated. She was getting a headache, but if Jeb was willing to continue rubbing elbows with a bunch of Christians, shouldn't she encourage him?

"Come on. Let's just go have some fun." He held out his hand to her.

She stared at it, uncomprehending. What had happened to his concern that people might assume they were a couple?

"Come on," he repeated, waggling the fingers of his extended hand. "We haven't been bowling since high school."

Well, why not? She could always take something for her headache. Laney put her hand in Jeb's and they went out the door together.

*   *   *

It was after midnight before a mug of hot cocoa did its job and made Laney drowsy. In a faded flannel nightgown that had belonged to her mother, she padded back upstairs to return to the rumpled bed she'd left in frustration nearly an hour ago.

She paused before the bedroom window that overlooked Jeb's house. Between the curtains she never closed, she saw light pouring from his ground floor windows and smiled with sleepy satisfaction. He'd be up for another three or four hours, but the light filtering into Laney's bedroom wouldn't disturb her at all. That friendly illumination meant Jeb was home at last, and safe.

At least for now.

She fluffed her pillow and crawled back under her quilt.

For once, it wasn't worry about her financial situation keeping her awake. She simply couldn't stop thinking about Jeb.

She'd had a wonderful time at the bowling alley. Jeb had refrained from interviewing eligible men on her behalf, and yet he hadn't reverted to his usual reticence, but had actually seemed to enjoy himself with the other singles.

They had already parted for the night when Laney realized she'd forgotten to ask him why that Bible verse had captured his attention earlier. But there was always tomorrow.

Settling more comfortably on her pillow and pulling the quilt up to her chin, she smiled sleepily at the faint, shifting shadows on the wall beyond the foot of her bed.

Shifting shadows? Laney sat up.

There was no tree between her house and Jeb's. No branches to be stirred by the wind and interrupt the light from his windows and create dancing shadows on her wall. Puzzled, Laney got out of bed and crossed the room to her other window, the one overlooking Mulberry Street.

Peering out into what should have been tranquil darkness, she was momentarily frozen by horror.

Mrs. Lindstrom's house was on fire.

Chapter Thirteen

ON THE SOFA IN HIS MUSIC ROOM, Jeb was hunched over an acoustic guitar inventing a new finger-picking technique when his B-string snapped. He got up to hunt for a new one in the old walnut desk that even nine years after his father's passing, he hadn't quite made his own.

There were still three whiskey bottles in the bottom-right drawer, but Jeb wouldn't touch his old man's stash for anything. Not even tonight, when he had a powerful craving for something stronger than coffee.

He wouldn't sit in his father's chair, either, so he simply bent over it to open the center desk drawer and paw through the mess of string packets, coiled pickup cords, and small boxes of guitar picks.

Laney said the chair was a beautiful antique, elegantly crafted, so Jeb couldn't get rid of it. He was too ashamed to admit that the scared kid inside him was haunted by the notion that if he sat in that chair, he'd become as hard and cold as his father had been.

It was nonsense, of course. But while his brain accepted that truth, his deformed heart just couldn't seem to absorb it.

He was growing desperate to talk to some knowledge-able Christian about spiritual matters. He'd thought about sneaking off to visit one of Laney's pastors, but had discarded that idea because Laney deserved to know his news before any of her friends did.

He found what he needed and shut the desk drawer. Absently shoving the new guitar string into a back pocket of his jeans, he wandered over to the bay windows and stared up at Laney's dark bedroom window.

He hoped she was sleeping soundly. He cared more about her health and happiness than he did about drawing his next breath, and he hated the purple half-moons he'd been seeing under her pretty eyes lately.

Moved to pray for her, he leaned his forehead against the window. He was just about to close his eyes when he became aware of a faint, flickering light outside. Vaguely disturbed, he went to look out his living room windows, which faced the street.

What he saw from there shoved his heart into his throat. He tore out of the front door, racing in a blind panic toward Mrs. Lindstrom's burning house.

"*Jeb!*"

Laney's voice. Nothing else could have penetrated his shock and halted him. At the end of his driveway, he whirled around to locate her in the semidarkness and assure himself that she was all right.

"I'll get Mrs. Lindstrom out!" he yelled as he took off running again. "Call 9-1-1!"

Pounding across the quiet street, he noted that only one end of the long, ranch-style house appeared to be burning: its two-car garage. If Mrs. Lindstrom was in a bedroom at the opposite end, she might be okay.

Her front door was locked, naturally. Jeb kicked it as hard as he could, slamming his heel against a spot right next to the doorknob in hopes of breaking the lock.

It wasn't as easy as it looked in the movies. It took five or six tries before the door burst open.

Smoke poured into Jeb's face, making his eyes burn and water, but he didn't see any flames inside, so he plunged into the darkness. Over the shocking staccato blare of a smoke alarm, he shouted for Mrs. Lindstrom.

Something brushed past his legs. The old lady's cat?

He reached for his cell phone. Using its lighted display as a flashlight, he found the central hall.

Guessing that the kitchen would be to the right, next to the burning garage, Jeb turned left. Still yelling for Mrs. Lindstrom, he waved his phone in front of him, searching for bedroom doorways by its feeble light. He entered the first room on his left and wasted precious seconds discovering it was only a bathroom.

The next door was closed. He opened it and quickly discerned the small bedroom was unoccupied.

The smoke alarm ceased blaring, and suddenly Jeb could hear the ominous hissing and crackling of the spreading fire.

A door on the other side of the hall was open. Hurrying across the threshold, Jeb heard a faint cough. The weak light from his phone had become almost useless in the thickening smoke, so he dropped the makeshift flashlight back into his pocket. Waving his arms in front of him, he moved cautiously forward until his knees bumped a bed.

He heard more coughing. By sound and touch, he located Mrs. Lindstrom. Holding his breath to avoid inhaling any more of the dangerous smoke, he shoved the bedcovers aside and swung the nearly weightless woman into his arms.

He retraced his steps, bumping and feeling his way along the walls with his elbows as he carried Mrs. Lindstrom in his arms. At the far end of the hallway, a menacing orange light flickered.

A wave of scorching heat slammed into him as he

reentered the living room; the far wall had caught fire. His steps faltered, and he felt something press against his shins: the terrified cat, he realized.

He couldn't bend down and grab it, so he raised his knee and hooked his foot under its belly. Then he swung his leg, hurling the heavy animal toward the front door. He hoped it would land on its feet and find its way outside.

Starting forward again, he tripped over the edge of a rug. He lurched sideways, collided with a piece of furniture, and fell to one knee—all without letting go of Mrs. Lindstrom. But as he struggled back to his feet, he noticed she'd gone limp in his arms.

Despair poured through him. He had failed to save her.

He wasn't going to be able to save himself, either. Somehow he'd gotten turned around, and at some point he'd started breathing again. Now dizzy, disoriented, and with his smoke-stung eyes narrowed to slits, he was unable to find the front door.

Before he could even think the prayer, it was answered. From somewhere beyond the horrifying blackness, he heard Laney screaming his name.

Clutching Mrs. Lindstrom's lifeless body more tightly to his chest, he stumbled toward the sound.

Chapter Fourteen

OVERWHELMED BY RELIEF AND GRATITUDE, Laney couldn't stop trembling, even though Jeb stood right behind her, his long arms hugging her tightly against his warm chest as they stared at the surreal scene before them.

Several times as they'd watched firefighters battle the blaze, he'd begged her to go home to put on some shoes and grab a jacket. But she'd worn wool socks to bed, so she wasn't standing barefoot on the cold sidewalk. And she couldn't have left Jeb, in any case. Not after coming so close to losing him.

He coughed again, and her heart squeezed painfully. Closing her eyes, she sent another silent *Thank you* to God.

It had nearly killed her to turn back to call 9-1-1 when she'd known Jeb was about to run into a burning house, but she'd done it. She'd gone inside and grabbed her cell phone and was back out the door before her call was even answered. She'd given the necessary information while running across the street, her stomach clenching from fear.

She would never forget the horror of seeing that gaping doorway and knowing Jeb was inside the burning house. Screaming his name, she had charged after him, but just as her foot hit the top step of the porch, Mrs. Lindstrom's cat had rocketed out the door and tripped her.

Scrambling back to her feet, she'd screamed again for Jeb.

And then he had appeared in the doorway with Mrs. Lindstrom in his arms, just like a storybook hero.

He'd been distraught, thinking he had failed to save the

old lady, but Mrs. Lindstrom had opened her eyes mere moments after being exposed to the cold night air. The EMTs had arrived a couple of minutes later, and while Mrs. Lindstrom was clearly in shock, she had asked about her cat before being whisked away to the hospital.

Jeb had worn an oxygen mask for several minutes; he'd sat on the running board of a fire truck while Laney paced in front of him, worried sick. She'd been both relieved and annoyed when he'd torn off the mask and insisted he was fine, even though he was still coughing.

When the EMTs had finally given up trying to persuade him to go to the hospital, they'd told Laney to monitor him. If his cough worsened, or if he experienced shortness of breath or hoarseness, she was to get him to the emergency room.

"I think they've almost got it," he murmured above Laney's head as a powerful jet of water from a fire hose played over the last stubborn flames.

"Let's go inside, then." Laney patted one of the hard arms encircling her shoulders. "It's not good for you to be standing here in all this smoke."

"I'm fine, princess." His words sounded pinched; he was holding back a cough to keep her from worrying. "But you're cold, so let's go."

As they turned away from the fire, Laney remembered Mrs. Lindstrom's cat.

"One second, Jeb." In the dim light, her gaze swept the cluster of concerned neighbors until she located the kindly old woman who was cradling the corpulent feline in her arms.

"Mrs. Schultz?" Laney walked toward her. "I can take

Snowball."

"No, dear. Before they carted Ida away in that ambulance, I told her I'd look after him." Mrs. Schultz looked down at her charge. "I guess he knows me as well as anyone, since I live right next door. And Darla Frank has already offered a litter box and a bag of cat food."

"He only eats the stinky canned gourmet stuff," Laney warned.

Mrs. Schultz gave her an amused look. "We'll see about that."

Laney figured a brief stay in a less indulgent home might do the fat cat a lot of good. "Mrs. Lindstrom will be grateful," she said warmly.

"No, she won't," Mrs. Schultz contradicted with good humor. "Ida Lindstrom has never been grateful a day in her life. But she's a decent neighbor, for all that. Since my husband died, she's done all kinds of favors for me. Nobody understands like another widow."

"Well, if you're sure." Laney reached out to pet Snowball, but then decided against it because even at the best of times, the cat was as prickly as its owner. "Just let me know if there's anything I can do."

Behind her, Jeb coughed again.

"Why don't the two of you come to my house for a nice cup of tea?" Mrs. Schultz inquired. "I'll put some honey in it for Jackson's poor throat."

Laney's own throat suddenly swelled. When had any of these neighbors, even the friendlier ones like Mrs. Schultz, ever shown any concern for Jeb?

"Thank you," Jeb said, his voice even more gravelly than usual as he came to stand beside Laney. "But I'm going for a drive to get some fresh air." He looked down at Laney. "Want to come?"

She nodded hard and threaded her arm through his. It was the middle of the night, but there was no question of her going home to her snug little bed and leaving Jeb alone to deal with the emotional aftermath of this horror. Besides, somebody needed to monitor his cough.

They crossed the street together, and then she left him and rushed back to her still-open front door. Inside, she pushed her feet into a pair of snow boots and hastily pulled a goose down vest over her long flannel nightgown. She went out the kitchen door and hurried to the driveway, where Jeb was waiting next to the Explorer.

He chuckled when he saw her. "Princess, I may not know anything about fashion, but that ensemble is—"

"Shut up," she said brokenly, reaching for him. "J-just . . . shut . . . up!" She sobbed the last two words against his broad chest. He reeked of soot, but he was alive, and she didn't know how she was ever going to let him go.

His big hand palmed the back of her head and pressed her so tightly against his heart that even through his sweatshirt, she could hear its violent hammering.

"I couldn't see." His quiet words were barely audible over the rumbling engines of the fire trucks across the street. "It was so dark, and the smoke burned my eyes, and I got lightheaded and lost my sense of direction. But then I heard you screaming for me and I just followed your voice." He squeezed her hard and added, "Laney, you saved me."

"Don't talk about it." She wiped her wet face against his sweatshirt, ignoring the acrid stench. "I don't want to remember those awful moments when I thought you—" She stopped and swallowed hard. "Oh, Jeb, I thought—"

"You're right," he interrupted. "Let's not talk about it."

He stiffened suddenly and withdrew his arms. Laney looked up in confusion, and then she followed his gaze and saw they were being observed by three people on the sidewalk.

"Is he all right?" a woman called.

"Can't complain," Jeb responded like a good Minnesotan, but then he coughed.

"Try some honey and lemon juice to soothe that throat," the woman advised, and the small group moved on.

Once again, tears welled in Laney's eyes. Finally, people were looking at Jeb and seeing an actual person rather than a scandal to be gossiped about. And all he'd had to do, she reflected bitterly, was nearly get himself killed saving Mrs. Lindstrom.

"Come on," he said. "Let's go somewhere quieter."

Tugging one long flannel sleeve over the back of her hand, Laney used the soft fabric to dry her tears before climbing into the Explorer.

They drove in silence for several minutes, and then Jeb made a sound of disgust and lowered his window.

"I'll turn the heater full blast on your feet," he said, reaching for those controls. "I just need to blow some of this awful stink away. Sorry."

"I'm fine," Laney assured him.

He was safe. What did anything else matter?

Remembering the Graces, she patted the pockets of her puffy down vest before realizing she'd left her cell phone in the house.

"Jeb, do you have your phone? I should call the Graces."

"At this hour?" he asked, reaching into his pocket.

"They won't mind. People often call them in the middle of the night with emergency prayer requests, so I'm afraid they'll hear about the fire and try to reach me to make sure we're okay. And I forgot my phone because I had to set it down to put on these boots. Flannel nightgowns don't have pockets for cell phones, you know."

He made an amused sound that turned into a cough. "Should you be calling a man's attention to your nightgown?"

"It's only *you*, Jeb." She took his phone and entered the Graces' number. "Besides, I'm covered from neck to ankles in heavy flannel. Hardly the kind of thing to excite a man's interest."

He muttered something that sounded like, "You might be surprised," but she didn't have time to wonder about that because her call was answered on the first ring.

She briefly explained about the fire. Then she told Caroline she was going for a drive with Jeb to calm down.

"We'll pray for you both," Caroline promised. "And for Ida Lindstrom, of course. And don't you bother about getting to the tearoom first thing in the morning. We'll go in and get your baking started."

"No, Caroline. Thanks, but I'll be there. After a scare like this, I need to get right back into my routine."

Jeb shot her a sympathetic look. She gave him a weak smile and wished her aunts a good night.

Gravel crunched and popped under the Explorer's tires as Jeb pulled into a small picnic area next to Clear Lake. When he turned off the headlights and the engine, Laney opened her door and stepped out into the soft, welcoming darkness.

Jeb came around the hood to join her. They both leaned back against the passenger door, arms folded as they stared at the calm black surface of the lake. The moon had already set, and the inky sky was alive with stars.

"I've missed this," Jeb said quietly.

They both uncrossed their arms at the same instant. Their hands bumped, and somehow their fingers tangled, and then Jeb's big warm hand shifted to close firmly around Laney's.

A pulse of excitement surged through her, but she stared hard at the starlit lake, afraid to move or speak lest she somehow spoil the perfect moment.

Jeb cleared his throat. "Laney, I have something to tell you."

She was turning to look at him when her attention was diverted by a sudden lightening in the sky.

Jeb had noticed it, too. "Ah," he said with quiet satisfaction. "Look at that."

Far above them, a huge oval of ghostly light had suddenly appeared and was growing in intensity. Within seconds, it began to undulate, and fingers of palest green reached all the way down to the silhouetted trees on the far side of the lake. Alternately dimming and brightening, the Northern Lights fluttered like sheer curtains in a playful summer breeze.

Jeb appeared to have forgotten he'd wanted to tell her something, but she could remind him in a minute or two, after they had enjoyed this wonder together.

The lights brightened to a more definite green. Their dance became frenetic, as though to describe the emotions churning through Laney, and suddenly it was all too much.

She let go of Jeb's hand and turned toward him, wrapping her arms around his waist and pressing her face against his solid chest.

His arms circled her shoulders. "What's wrong?"

Her heart pounding, she lifted her head and gazed at the shadowed planes of her best friend's face. Here it was at last, the moment they'd been moving toward since the night he'd come home—and maybe even longer than that.

But Jeb looked puzzled, and since there was no stepladder handy, Laney summoned her courage, hauled in a breath, and said—

"Kiss me, Jeb."

* * *

"*What?*"

He stared at her, appalled. Had she fallen and hit her head while he was busy rescuing Mrs. Lindstrom? If she thought he was going to risk messing up their friendship just to satisfy some silly whim—

"Haven't you ever wondered what it would be like?" she whispered.

"No," he said shortly, and it wasn't even a lie. This was a place he had never allowed his mind to go, although it had sure tried often enough.

She held his gaze, challenging him, and for what seemed like an eternity, Jeb battled the temptation to give her what she thought she wanted.

In the end he told himself it might not be so bad. A single kiss might be enough to satisfy her curiosity, and they could go back to being friends, no harm done.

Yes, he was rationalizing. But he'd like to meet the man who could look into Laney Ryland's sweet eyes and tell her no and make it stick. He just couldn't believe anyone had *that* much self-discipline.

"Please, Jeb." She raised her arms; her soft hands touched the back of his neck.

And weak-willed moron that he was, Jeb bent his head.

His mouth settled against Laney's as softly as a butterfly landing on a rose blossom. He congratulated himself on keeping the kiss chaste, but his lips had no business touching hers to begin with. So after just a few seconds of mind-bending bliss, he marshaled his strength and withdrew.

"I knew it would be like that," she whispered, staring up at him with a dreamy expression that broke his heart.

He had to find her a husband, fast. Before she talked herself into some ridiculous romantic obsession with *him*.

He let her go and took a step away from her. "That was a mistake," he said firmly, pushing his fingers through his hair and wanting to yank it out to punish himself for his colossal stupidity. "So we're just going to forget it."

"Speak for yourself," she muttered.

"Come on," he pleaded. "You have to help me with this. You have no idea how much I—" He stopped, horrified at what he had almost said.

"How much you what?" She gazed at him in apparent fascination.

"Nothing. I'm just tired." And terrified. "We should get going." Before he lost what was left of his mind and kissed her again.

He nudged her away from the passenger door so he could open it, but she made no move to get in.

"It's very late," he reminded her.

"Jeb?"

"Laney, please." He tipped his head back and stared helplessly at the starry sky. "Please just get in and let me take you home."

She got in, and she didn't say a word all the way home. Jeb could feel the hurt rolling off her in waves, but coward that he was, he never once turned his head to look at her. When he finally pulled into her driveway, she uttered a choked, "I'm sorry," and tumbled out of the SUV almost before its tires had stopped rolling.

Jeb opened his mouth to call her back, then closed it when he realized there was nothing he could say to make this easier for her. *I'm not good enough for a woman like you* was the stark truth, but he wasn't stupid enough to say that. Not when Laney would just look at him the way Charlie Brown had looked at that pathetic excuse for a Christmas tree and think: *He needs me.*

Sighing, he climbed out of the Explorer and looked across the street. There was only one fire truck left in front of Mrs. Lindstrom's burned-out house, and the neighbors who'd stood gawking on the sidewalk earlier had all gone home to their beds. Standing alone in the darkness, Jeb tunneled his fingers through his hair and then grimaced at the stink that released.

He had almost died tonight. The thought of that happening and Laney not knowing he was safe with God had upset him so much that he'd taken her up to the lake to tell her everything. But then he'd lost his mind and kissed her.

What a screwup. He sighed again.

Laney's kitchen light went off, and Jeb imagined her weary tread as she climbed the stairs to her bedroom. It seemed to take forever for the upstairs lights to come on, and when they finally did, Jeb realized he'd been holding his breath.

She wouldn't sleep tonight, and that was his fault.

"I'm sorry," he whispered as self-loathing sucked at him like quicksand trying to drag him under.

Kissing her was a mistake he would never repeat, no matter how sorely he was tempted. Tomorrow he'd find a way to make this up to her, and then they'd go on just as if that kiss had never happened.

She would be okay.

And so would he, Jeb resolved as he turned toward his own house. He could stand being around Laney without kissing her.

Hadn't he been standing it for years?

* * *

Why had she pushed him? How could she have upset him that way? Freshly showered, bone-weary, but far too disgusted with herself to sleep, Laney flopped over in her bed and punched her pillow. How was she ever going to face Jeb tomorrow?

Maybe she should just get it over with now. Then at least she might be able to sleep. She reached for her lamp switch.

A moment later, she stood by her window, phone in hand, looking down into Jeb's brightly lit music room.

He was seated within the large semicircle of his bay windows, his profile in full view as he played the baby grand piano he'd bought the morning after his father's death.

The timing of that purchase had scandalized Mrs. Lindstrom and two other neighbors who had witnessed the instrument's prompt delivery. But eighteen-year-old Jeb hadn't been celebrating his father's demise and his own subsequent inheritance, as everyone had been so quick to assume. He'd just been trying to keep himself too occupied to reflect and remember and *feel.*

He had never admitted it, but Laney had looked into his haunted eyes often enough to know that until his father's death, the love-starved child inside Jeb had still hoped for some small sign of approval from the man.

He was so alone, she thought as she watched the fluid movements of his long hands over the piano keys. So very alone.

He stopped playing and gazed at the ceiling for several heartbeats. Then he reached for the pad of paper lying beside him on the bench and made a note.

He was writing a song, and ordinarily Laney wouldn't have disturbed him. But he must be feeling as awful as she was about what had happened at the lake, so she hit a preset key and raised the phone to her ear.

She saw him startle and then immediately turn to look up at her window. She couldn't quite make out his eyes, but knew they were locked on her face as his phone rang a second time and then a third. Finally, he reached into his pocket. The fourth ring was cut short as he raised the phone to his ear.

"Don't say a word." His voice was low and urgent. "It was completely my fault."

"I don't know how you figure that," Laney shot back. Why did he always jump in to take the blame for the stupid things she did? "I told you to kiss me."

"You wouldn't have said it unless you thought I wanted to." He walked over to the windows and stood before the center one. "So I apologize for whatever I did that gave you that message."

Laney sighed. "You didn't do anything, Jeb."

"Well, what put the idea into your head, then?"

She pressed the palm of her free hand against the window glass. "I almost lost you tonight," she reminded him in a small voice.

"Well, you *didn't* lose me, so stop thinking about it. You have to be up in less than four hours, so you'd better—"

"Jeb, are we okay?" she interrupted.

"Of course. Just like always. Now go to bed, princess."

"I can't sleep. My mind's too busy. The fire and— Well, everything."

"Warm milk," he suggested.

"Yuck. I'd rather have a lullaby, if you don't mind."

That provoked his deep chuckle. "We haven't done that in years."

"No," Laney agreed softly, remembering the balmy summer nights when he'd been home from college and she'd lie next to her open window and drift sweetly to sleep while he played soothing classical pieces on his piano. Remembering, also, how often she'd found that window tightly shut the next morning and known her mother had crept in during the small hours to make sure she was warm and safe.

Jeb tilted his head, holding the phone with his shoulder as he used both hands to raise his window sash. "The temperature's dropping," he warned. "Don't open your window very far."

"I have an extra quilt," Laney assured him. "Thank you and good night."

She put the phone down and raised her window just a

few inches. She grimaced at the charred smell that wafted in from across the street, but figured it wouldn't be so noticeable after a few minutes. She could hear the rumbling engine of the remaining fire truck, but as that vehicle was parked on the opposite side of her house, the sound was muffled to a soothing white noise.

As Jeb played the first sweet notes of Beethoven's "Moonlight" sonata, she retrieved an extra quilt from her cedar chest and added it to her pile of covers. Then she switched off her lamp and crawled into bed.

Lying on her back, she laced her fingers behind her head and closed her eyes, enjoying the nippy night breeze on her face as Jeb's skillful playing began to soothe her agitated spirit.

There could be no doubt about it after tonight. The stark terror Laney had felt when she'd realized Jeb was inside that burning house had stripped away all uncertainty.

She was in love with him.

She told herself it was for the best that he didn't feel the same way. They could never marry, not when he didn't share her faith.

The breeze from the open window chilled the sudden dampness on her cheeks, making her shiver.

As Jeb finished the Beethoven and began Debussy's "Clair de Lune", Laney dried her tears with the ruffled edge of her sheet. And then for the first time in months, she took her troubles to the Lord.

Chapter Fifteen

AT NOON THE NEXT DAY, Jeb sat at his kitchen table downing his second cup of morning coffee and doing his best to beat back a ferocious craving for a cigarette. He'd thought giving up alcohol would be the hardest thing, since he was the child of an alcoholic and had been drinking for years. But it was the cigarettes that tempted him most, and mornings were awful because nothing went better with a cup of coffee than a cigarette.

Sighing, he put his coffee down and reached for the telephone directory he'd slapped on the table a minute earlier. He located the number he needed and called the hospital to inquire about Mrs. Lindstrom's condition.

His call was answered by a cheerful young female who offered to put him through to Mrs. Lindstrom's room.

"*No,*" he said quickly, shuddering at the thought of causing the cranky old lady to have a stroke the day after he'd saved her life. "Just tell me how she's doing."

"I can't. Sorry. I'm only filling in for Mrs. B. while she goes to the bathroom." The girl was crunching on something and smacking her lips. Potato chips, Jeb guessed. "Her usual replacement is out sick, and Mrs. B. was desperate, so I offered to sit here for five minutes. I know how to transfer a call, and I could have done that for you 'cause I heard Mrs. B. tell somebody just a minute ago what room Mrs. Lindstrom is in. But I don't know how to access the patient information on this computer." More crunching and lip-smacking. "Mrs. B. will be back in five minutes if you want to—"

"This is Jackson Bell," Jeb said impatiently. He rarely

threw his name around, but this girl, who had clearly never attended one of Laney's etiquette talks, was getting on his nerves. "Maybe you could find somebody to—"

"Oh!" the girl squealed. "You don't mean *the* Jackson Bell?"

"I'm afraid I do." Jackson Bell, the hometown horror. Jackson Bell, the outrage of Owatonna. Jackson Bell, the monster who needs a cigarette so badly he's about to snap a leg off his kitchen table and start gnawing on it.

He shook his head at the ceiling. "Maybe you could—"

"You saved that lady's life, didn't you?" the girl demanded. "I heard it on the news. Hold on a sec, and I'll get somebody who knows how to use this computer. Don't go anywhere, okay?"

"Take your time," Jeb said dryly.

Five minutes later, he called the tearoom and told Laney that Mrs. Lindstrom was in good condition.

"I know." Laney chuckled. "I called the hospital first thing this morning and talked to her sister. It seems the nurses would like to stuff our cantankerous neighbor into a closet and lose the key." Her voice softened. "How are *you* doing?"

Jeb closed his eyes. Much better, now that her gentle voice was pouring into his ear and soothing his agitated nerves. "I'm fine," he said. "How are you?"

"I barely got three hours of sleep, so I'm insanely tired," she said. "But you're all right, and you saved Mrs. Lindstrom, and it's a beautiful day, isn't it?"

"Looks like rain to me." Jeb happened to be gazing out a window, and the sky was definitely darkening.

"You know what mean, Jeb. Life is good."

"You sound like your old cheerful self," he said with warm approval. "It must be all that time we've been spending at chur—" He was interrupted by a loud crash, the unmistakable sound of a tray of dishes hitting the floor.

"Jeb, I have to go," Laney said, and she ended the call.

Poor princess. He hoped she hadn't lost too much of her flowery china. But even if she had, he'd put a smile on her face when she got home tonight. The minute she pulled into his driveway, he was going to flag her down and tell her what he would have told her last night if he hadn't been sidetracked by that kiss.

That kiss. It had been pure and sweet and hands-down the most thrilling ten seconds of his entire life.

"Stop it," he said under his breath. He propped his elbows on the table and pressed the heels of his hands over his eyes. "Just stop thinking about it."

He poured himself another cup of coffee and went to the dining room to finish a project he'd begun yesterday: sorting his music CDs. He'd collected the discs from his bedroom and the music room, tossing them into a big cardboard box, which he had then emptied onto his dining room table.

He sat down and put the box next to his feet. Evaluating one CD at a time, he made small towers of "safe" music on the table while tossing a staggering percentage of his collection into the trash box.

Profane cover art. Lewd lyrics. Songs celebrating casual sex and illicit drug use. Jeb was seeing all of it through new eyes, and he understood why it was unacceptable to God. But what, exactly, was a Christian man supposed to listen to when his heart still beat to rock music?

He needed some air. Abandoning the mess in his dining

room, he grabbed his jacket and went out the kitchen door. He strode across the porch and gave the screen door an impatient shove; it slapped shut behind him.

In front of Laney's place, his restless steps slowed and then halted as he took a good, long look at the burned-out house across the street.

God had spared him last night, no doubt about it. But for what purpose? Who was Jackson Bell meant to become?

He resumed walking, and although he'd had no destination in mind, he wasn't surprised when he ended up downtown, staring through the front window of Clark's Music, the store he'd haunted as a teenager.

He went inside. The place hadn't changed a bit.

"Be right with you," somebody called from the direction of the cash register as Jeb honed in on the array of electric guitars mounted on the back wall.

Spotting a vintage Fender Stratocaster in candy apple red, the exact twin of his very first instrument, Jeb reached out and stroked its neck with a loving hand.

His father could easily have afforded the guitar, but Jeb had never liked asking for anything, and the old man hadn't been one to give birthday gifts. So when thirteen-year-old Jeb had fallen in love with the red Strat, he'd seriously considered stealing it.

Laney had saved him from that folly.

It had been winter, so she'd suggested that Jeb earn money by shoveling snow off the neighbors' driveways and sidewalks. Excited by that idea, he'd knocked on the doors of at least ten houses.

Nobody wanted to hire the neighborhood bad boy.

Laney had been outraged. She'd pulled on her boots and

grabbed a snow shovel and dragged Jeb after her. They hadn't rung any doorbells, but simply cleared snow off of five driveways. And after finishing at each house, they'd taped a neatly printed note to the front door.

Jeb still had one of the notes. He'd carried it in his wallet for years. Below his phone number, Laney had written:

This nice clean drive way is a free gift from Jackson Bell Jr. He needs an electric gitar. You can call him the next time it snows and he will do your drive way for money next time. Thank You.

Her plan had worked. Several neighbors had given Jeb regular snow-removal work and other odd jobs, and by the end of that winter he'd earned enough to make the red Strat his own.

He'd played that thing day and night. And when the fingertips of his fretting hand had blistered and bled, Laney had wrapped strips of moleskin around them and carefully taped it so he could keep playing.

He'd bought at least fifteen guitars since then. But the red Strat, stolen years ago in a sleazy club Skeptical Heart had played in its early days, would always hold a special place in his heart.

"Go ahead," a voice urged from behind him. "Take it down and try it."

Jeb removed his hand from the instrument and shook his head.

"We give lessons here at the store," the unseen clerk offered encouragingly. "Anyone can learn."

"That's what I've heard." Jeb turned and found himself eye-to-eye with a pimply blonde guy nearly as tall as he was, but who didn't look a day over 18. The kid wore a friendly expression and a T-shirt that said, "Jesus Rocks."

"Welcome to Clark's Music. What can I help you with?"

"I could use some guitar strings," Jeb said.

"Sure. You bet." Confusion flickered in the kid's eyes. "Have you been in here before?"

"Not lately." Deciding to practice his new conversation skills, Jeb added, "I grew up here. Used to come in this store a lot when I was a kid."

The clerk's jaw went slack and he raised an index finger as though silently requesting a moment to process a complicated thought. "You know," he said finally, "if your hair was longer, you'd look exactly like—"

"Yeah," Jeb said. "I get that a lot."

"You *are*! You're Jackson Bell!"

Jeb heard an electronic beep and glanced toward the front door. Two other guys had just come in. "I'd appreciate it if you'd keep that to yourself," he said. "I'm kind of on vacation right now."

"But you're Jackson Bell!" the kid informed him in a loud whisper. "Wow! I can't believe Jackson Bell is standing right here in our store! My dad says you bought your first guitar here, but—" He stopped and smacked the side of his head, apparently to help his brain take in this great wonder. "Oh, this is so unbelievably cool!"

"I'm just an ordinary guy," Jeb protested. He had never understood why people went into these transports of delight when they met him. "I put my guitar strings on one at a time, same as everybody else."

"I'm in a band," the kid blurted. "There are five of us, just like Skeptical Heart." He laughed nervously. "Well, not *just* like Skeptical Heart. We're nowhere near as good as you, and we play Christian rock. We've been all over Minnesota, playing at churches and Christian camps, and we even—"

"Christian rock?" Jeb interrupted. "Listen, uh . . ." His eyes briefly dropped to the kid's name badge. "Daniel. So you're a Christian, huh?"

An hour later, Jeb had a new friend and a bag full of Christian rock CDs hand-selected by Daniel, who had earnestly explained that while he loved Skeptical Heart's sound, he was so troubled by some of the songs' lyrics that he had ended up throwing away one of the two CDs he'd bought.

Walking home, Jeb reflected on the disquieting fact that people were at that very moment being corrupted by songs he'd written. He had perverted his God-given talent, and no matter how sorry he was about that now, he couldn't stop people from buying and listening to that music.

As he reached Mulberry Street and crossed to his own side, a gust of wind stirred some dried leaves in the gutter. They swirled around his feet like the fans who'd clamored to see him, touch him, hear him, when he'd never been anyone worth seeing or touching or hearing at all.

Thunder boomed directly overhead. When he looked up at the scudding gray clouds, a windblown leaf smacked his face as though in accusation.

A gentle rain began falling just as he unlocked his kitchen door, reminding him of the drizzly night he'd given his heart to God.

He understood that he was forgiven. He just wished he could somehow repair the damage he'd done.

He went to his music room and spent two hours sampling his new CDs. Most of them were good; Daniel had a decent ear. As for the songs' lyrics, they tugged at Jeb's heart and made his throat swell with gratitude to God.

Before coming home, he'd worried that he'd never write music again. But since his return, he'd written several songs about the new hope in his heart. They were good, but he wasn't planning to share them with anyone. Who'd want to hear "God" songs by the former frontman of Skeptical Heart?

Laney would, he realized. He could play them for her tonight.

His cell phone rang and he pulled it out of his pocket to check the display. Smiling, he punched the Talk button.

"Hey, princess. Sorry about your broken china."

He heard a rush of air and pictured her extending her bottom lip and blowing out a breath that ruffled the curls on her forehead.

"Aggie tripped," she said. "She wasn't hurt, but I lost a whole tea set. And Jeb, you wouldn't believe how expensive those are, even when I'm able to find them secondhand. But I guess that's not a problem anymore, is it? Not when I'm going to end up closing this place."

Jeb frowned at her bitter tone, but then he remembered how exhausted she was. "Do you want to order pizza tonight?" he asked.

"That would be good, thanks, but after work I'm planning to buy some flowers and take them to Mrs. Lindstrom. I'm calling to see if you'll come with me."

To inflict his presence on the woman who must be resenting the fact that *he* had been the one to save her life?

"I don't think so," Jeb said shortly. "But put the flowers on my credit card. Just don't tell her I had anything to do with them, or she'll toss them out the window."

"No she won't, Jeb. She can't possibly hate you now."

"She can hate me if she wants," he said easily. "But say yes to the pizza plan, because I want to talk to you about something."

"Yes to the pizza plan," Laney said obediently. "But as for the talk, Jeb, I'm afraid I'm not in the mood to discuss your matchmaking schemes tonight."

"It's not about that," he said. "It's about something good. Something you'll really—"

"Jeb, I have to go," she interrupted. "Millie's on the other phone and there seems to be some kind of problem. I'll try not to be too long at the hospital, okay?"

"Take your time," he said. "And give Mrs. Lindstrom my best wishes."

The crabby old lady was never going to change. But she mattered to God, and now she mattered to Jeb, too.

* * *

"How are you feeling?" Greeting her longtime neighbor with a determined smile, Laney set a vase containing three yellow roses with some greens and baby's breath on the table beside the hospital bed.

"I can't complain." Mrs. Lindstrom pressed a button; the bed whirred softly as it moved her to a more upright position, from where she frowned at the flowers. "Yellow. Those are almost as nice as pink ones, I guess. Thank you."

"You're welcome," Laney murmured. She'd purchased the modest arrangement with her own hard-earned cash rather than with Jeb's credit card, and now she almost wished she hadn't bothered.

Her day had begun well, but then she'd had a rotten afternoon, and now she just wanted to go home and cry her eyes out. But no, she'd had to come here and be nice to Mrs. Lindstrom.

"The lady over there." Mrs. Lindstrom gestured to the empty and neatly made-up bed next to her own. "She had a dozen pink roses, but she took them with her when she left this morning. I don't know why she didn't just leave them for the sick people to enjoy."

Laney had been acquainted with sulky Mrs. Lindstrom all her life, but she still didn't know how to respond to statements like that, so she just smiled harder and tried to hold on to her patience. Ten minutes, fifteen at the most, and she'd be out of here.

"Where's Jackson?" Mrs. Lindstrom demanded.

"He wasn't sure of his welcome," Laney said carefully. "But he sends his best wishes."

"Not sure of his welcome." Mrs. Lindstrom harrumphed. "That boy saved my life!"

Laney's heart warmed several degrees. "So you think he might be good for something, after all?"

The old woman bristled. "I hope I'm a big enough person to admit when I'm wrong. I guess he isn't like his father, and you can tell him I said so." Her gaze dropped to her fingers, which were plucking at the bedcovers. "You can also tell him Snowball and I said thank you."

As Laney's heart swelled, Mrs. Lindstrom looked up sharply and waved a cautioning finger. "But if he expects sugar syrup from me, he's going to be disappointed."

Laney's smile died. "You don't have to worry about that," she said with a touch of asperity. "In his whole life, Jeb has never expected 'sugar syrup' from anybody."

Mrs. Lindstrom eyed her shrewdly. "You love him," she

said with evident satisfaction. "I always thought you did."

"Not the way you're thinking," Laney said without experiencing even a tingle of guilt over the lie. It was true, heartbreakingly true, that what she now felt for Jeb was the kind of love she'd sifted through a long parade of nice men to find. But there was no way she was going to confess to Mrs. Lindstrom what she was trying so hard to teach her own heart to forget.

Chapter Sixteen

"JEB, I KNOW IT'S UNFAIR to dump this burden on you," Laney said as she stepped wearily inside his brightly lit screened porch. "But if you don't make me smile right this instant, I'm going to burst into tears."

Sitting cross-legged on a padded wicker chaise, an acoustic guitar resting on one long thigh, Jeb looked past her and ran the tip of his tongue over his bottom lip.

"Okay," he said finally, his gaze shifting back to her face. "Have you heard the one about the wildly talented guitar player and the depressed but beautiful and brilliant tearoom owner?"

She chuckled. "No, I haven't heard that one."

He hunched over his guitar and began picking out a complicated melody.

"I'm waiting," she reminded him. "What's the punch line?"

He looked up, all innocence. "Hmm?"

"What's the punch line?" she repeated.

He feigned surprise. "Princess," he said with exaggerated patience, "that joke was so good it didn't need a punch line. You laughed, didn't you?"

"You're deranged." Chuckling again, she set her bag on a side table and sank onto one of the massive wicker chairs, her black mood already several shades lighter.

As he watched her, Jeb's self-congratulatory smile faded. "Did Mrs. Lindstrom upset you?"

"No more than usual." Laney crossed her legs and tugged the hem of her floral "tearoom" dress down over her knees. Leaning back in the chair, she rested her elbows on its broad arms and inhaled deeply, willing herself to relax.

Catching a wisp of rising steam in her peripheral vision, she looked at the hot tub. Jeb must have been in it last night; he was always forgetting to replace its energy-conserving cover.

"Yeah," he said, following her gaze. "I'll get that in a minute. How's Mrs. Lindstrom doing?"

Recalling their neighbor's ungracious acceptance of the expensive roses and her expressed hope that Jeb wouldn't be expecting any "sugar syrup", Laney sighed and said, "Oh, she can't complain."

"Yes, she can." One side of Jeb's mouth hitched up. "And she does. Incessantly."

Laney snickered, but then carefully tamped down her amusement. She ought to be more charitable toward Mrs. Lindstrom, especially after what the poor old woman had gone through last night.

Jeb's thoughts must have been moving in the same direction, because he quickly sobered. "She's okay, then?"

"Just fine. They'll release her in the morning."

"To go where?"

"Right next door."

Jeb's eyes widened in alarm.

"Not *my* house," Laney said quickly. "The brick house next door to hers. Remember Mrs. Schultz? Her husband died about five years ago, and she hates living alone. So she's invited Mrs. Lindstrom and Snowball to move in with her."

"Was the house insured?"

"Yes. But she won't rebuild because she was already thinking about trading down to a condo. She seems to be dealing with the shock okay. As much as she likes to complain about little things, she's really a strong woman."

Jeb unfolded his legs and bent down to set his guitar on the floor. When he straightened, he studied Laney's face for a moment and then said, "So why'd you come in here threatening me with Kryptonite?"

"Kryptonite?"

"Tears," he said gruffly. "You know what it does to me when you cry."

A gust of nippy autumn air pushed through the wall of screens behind Laney, making her shiver.

"Let's go inside," Jeb said.

"Not yet. Maybe this fresh air will revive me." As she spoke, Laney grasped the edges of her cable-knit cardigan and tugged until they overlapped against her chest, making a double layer of warmth. She tucked her hands under her armpits, and then lifted her chin to accept the brisk evening breeze on her face.

Other people seemed able to function on just a few hours of sleep, but Laney didn't have that knack. She'd started the day with a cheerful outlook, but exhaustion had claimed her after just a few hours. And thanks to that disturbing phone call, she'd been extra grouchy all afternoon.

Jeb continued to watch her, waiting for an answer to his question. Staring back at him, Laney fiddled with the top button on her sweater and wondered how to broach what was always a difficult subject, even with Jeb.

"Just spill it, princess."

"All right." Like a swimmer about to plunge off the high dive, she deliberately filled her lungs. "Remember on the phone today when I said Millie was on the other line and seemed to be upset?" She waited for Jeb's cautious nod before continuing. "She was talking to my father."

Jeb huffed out a breath; his disgust was palpable. "What's it been? Ten years since his last phone call?"

"Something like that." Laney had never understood how a man she'd never met could hurt her so much. "I guess he hinted about needing money again."

"Where does he find the nerve?" Jeb muttered.

Laney shrugged. "All I can figure is that he thought the Graces might be getting too old to remember how he took their money and—"

"They haven't forgotten, Laney."

"No," she agreed. "Caroline says he's not even mentioned in their wills. I'm their sole beneficiary."

That thought warmed her, even though she'd never see any of the Graces' money. What they didn't spend on their charities, they'd surely use up in their old age, but that was fine. The gesture itself meant the world to Laney.

Jeb scooted to the end of his chaise to sit directly in front of her. Leaning forward, he rested his forearms on his knees.

"Did he ask about you?"

"Millie didn't say. But why would he, when he never has before?"

She had never seen her father, never spoken to him on the phone, never received a card or a letter from him. She was nothing to him. Nobody.

"I don't know why I let this upset me," she said bitterly. "I've done just fine without a father. I don't *want* him in my life. A man who can turn his back on a woman who's pregnant with his child is no man at all."

Jeb blanched, and she realized that talking about her father had dredged up his own unhappy memories. She leaned forward to lay a hand over one of his wrists.

"I'm sorry, Jeb. I know it was ten times worse for you."

She'd suffered by her father's complete lack of interest in her, but his cruelty wasn't personal. How could it be, when he'd never even seen her? Jeb's father, on the other hand, had rejected a son he'd seen every day. *That* was personal.

And mind-numbingly brutal.

"Let it go," Jeb said quietly.

"Not this time." She squeezed his wrist, determined to break this familiar impasse and help him begin to heal. "Jeb, I'm no expert on fathers, but I can tell you that yours wasn't normal. I'm not talking about the alcoholism, but about the way he—"

"*Don't.*" Jeb pulled away from her grasp and sat up, stiffening his back like a soldier at attention.

"He was emotionally deformed," Laney insisted. "I don't know how or why. But you have to stop thinking that you somehow deserved his animosity. A normal man doesn't treat his son the way your father treated you."

"Actually . . ." Jeb drawled the word, imbuing it with wry resentment. "He believed I was his brother's son."

"*What?*"

"He told me when I was seventeen. He was drunk, naturally. He said his brother died in a car wreck the week before my mother—" Jeb stopped abruptly, averting his gaze. Nearly two decades after the fact, he still couldn't bring himself to say the words, *my mother killed herself.*

So Laney said them for him. "You mean he actually implied that your mother killed herself because she'd had a—

an illicit relationship—with his brother, and she couldn't go on living without him?"

"There was no 'implying' about it. That's what he said."

"And you never told me," Laney breathed.

"It doesn't matter." He slid his hands behind him on the chaise and leaned back on his braced arms, assuming a relaxed posture that didn't fool Laney for a second. "I don't know if it's true or not," he added. "But I never mentioned it to you because I didn't care."

Of course he cared. He'd deny it to his last breath, but he did care.

"Your parents didn't deserve you." She meant the words to be comforting, so she flinched when they elicited a derisive snort instead.

"Oh, I'm sure I was exactly what they deserved." Jeb gave her a cynical, tight-lipped smile. "What is it Mrs. Lindstrom always says? That the apple doesn't fall far from the tree?"

"Stop it," Laney commanded. "You're a wonderful, caring person. If the world didn't see that before you ran into a burning house to save a crabby old woman who never had a kind word to say about you, they've sure figured it out now. It's all over the news that you're a hero."

"I'm no hero," he said harshly. "In fact, I'm just like your father."

"Don't be ridiculous, Jeb. You're no more like my father than you're like your own. You're kind and thoughtful and—"

"Yeah, I'm a real prince." He spat the words. "Two years ago I got a woman pregnant, and then I—"

"Jeb!" she gasped. "*You have a baby?*"

She couldn't like the way the child had come into the

world, as a consequence of casual sex rather than as a blessing to multiply the joy of a married couple, but she'd love Jeb's baby with her whole heart. He had to know that. So why had he kept this news from her?

"No," he snapped. "I don't have a baby."

"But you just said you—"

"I said I helped *make* one." He glared at her, daring her to understand.

To forgive.

She pressed a hand against her stomach, which suddenly felt full of butterflies. Had Jeb abandoned his baby? Was that what he'd meant when he'd said he was just like her father?

No, that wasn't possible. Jeb adored babies. He'd never said so, but whenever Laney held one in her arms and smiled up at him to share her delight, his face always softened in the most wonderful way.

"W-where is it?" she asked faintly. "How old is it? Is it a boy or a—"

"Don't you understand?" He flung the words at her. "It's gone!"

Gone? Laney could do no more than mouth the word.

"It wasn't my choice." Jeb heaved himself to his feet and strode angrily to the far end of the porch, where he stood with his back to her and stared out into the darkness. "But that doesn't make me any less guilty, especially since I paid for her to—" He halted and released a ragged sigh. When he turned and looked at Laney with tortured eyes, she knew with an awful certainty what he had done.

"She wasn't like you." His deep voice throbbed with an infinite, gut-wrenching sorrow. "Laney, she wasn't anything like you. She didn't want a baby. And I . . ." He lifted his eyes to the ceiling, his Adam's apple rising and falling as he struggled for control. "I was relieved. So I gave her money for the—the procedure, plus some extra so she could take a nice trip somewhere and forget." He shook his head. "But people don't forget that kind of thing, do they?"

"No," The word barely squeaked out of her throat. "I don't think they do, Jeb."

He closed his eyes and rubbed his forehead with his fingertips. "So tell me again what a good man I am." He barked out a savage laugh. "Tell me again that I'm a hero."

His self-loathing broke Laney's heart. Tears blurred her vision, but she did her best to blink them away.

She had to make him understand that he could have forgiveness for this. She hadn't forgotten her old agreement to refrain from proselytizing him, but things were different now. He'd been going to church with her, and last night at the Bible study, he had actually held the Word of God in his hands and followed along as Pastor Ted pointed out verses in Galatians.

He opened his eyes and regarded her with a sad smile. "Look at you," he said softly, wonderingly. "I've committed about the worst sin a fatherless girl like you can imagine, and you don't even hate me for it."

"I hate what you did." Laney swiped a tear from her cheek. "But I could never hate you, Jeb. And—" She hesitated for only an instant. "Sins can be forgiven, you know."

His mouth fell open and his head tilted back, as though he'd just recalled something important. When he spoke, it was with quiet conviction.

"Yes. I know."

Hope unfurled in Laney's heart. Did he mean that the way it sounded? Had the Tuesday night Bible lessons and the Sunday morning sermons begun to sink in?

He returned to the chaise but stood behind it, his hands resting on its tall back. "My father taught me there was nothing worth believing in," he said with obvious difficulty. "Not God. Not love." His hands curled around the chaise's braided wicker edging and Laney heard a faint crackling as he squeezed it. "But then you barged into my life. And there was your mother, too. And both of you . . . loved me. Even when I did stupid things."

"Real love isn't conditional, Jeb. You don't stop loving somebody when they disappoint you."

"I think you've proven that." His hands visibly relaxed on the back of the chaise. "Still, apart from the two of you, I've never believed in or trusted anybody." His gaze drifted away as he added, "Until just recently."

Trepidation folded icy arms around Laney. Was Jeb talking about a woman? After all these years, had he finally met someone special and fallen in love? And if so, why had he denied it that night at Willie's?

"Laney." He paced back to the far end of the porch. "There's something I need to tell you. The reason I came home."

No. She wanted to stop her ears, but she made herself sit still and wait.

He turned to face her. "I meant to tell you as soon as I got here. And then every day after that. But the time just never seemed—" He dropped his head and rubbed the back of his neck. Then he caught her expression and grinned. "Don't look so worried. It's something good. You're going to be happy for me."

Happy for him. Yes, she would try.

Oh Lord, she pleaded silently, desperately. *Help me to be happy for him, even if it breaks my heart.*

He walked past her again. Laney had to bite her lip to keep from snapping at him to just stand *still* for a minute and spit out whatever it was that he meant to tell her. This agony was unbearable.

He stopped in front of the hot tub and turned suddenly, decisively. "Laney, five days before I came home, I gave my heart—"

She fought the impulse to squeeze her eyes shut. She could stand this. She could stand anything if it made Jeb happy.

"—to God," he finished.

"To—" No, she couldn't have heard that correctly.

Grinning, he spread his arms like a circus performer inviting applause. "So I'm a Christian now."

"Oh," Laney said faintly. It seemed to take forever for her mind to switch gears, and then—

"*Oh!*" she squealed. "Oh, Jeb!" She rocketed out of her chair to give him a hug.

As she collided with him, he laughed and staggered back a step. Realizing that she'd knocked him against the side of the hot tub, which was no higher than his knees, she immediately let go and backed away so he could regain his balance.

He didn't. For a breathless instant his long arms windmilled frantically, and then he pitched over the edge. He hit the water with a mighty splash and went under.

As giant waves sluiced over the rim of the tub, Laney

had the presence of mind to snatch his guitar from the tile floor before the spreading puddles could reach it.

Jeb came up laughing. "I was perfectly willing to be baptized, princess, but you could have given me some warning." Tilting his head to one side, he twisted a finger in his ear to dislodge some water.

Instead of climbing out, he took a seat on the far side of the tub. Stretching his arms along its rim, he smiled serenely.

Laney's gaze clung to his for several seconds, and then with calm deliberation, she laid his guitar on the chaise. She shucked her cardigan and dropped it there, too, and then she slipped out of her loafers. As Jeb watched silently, his dark eyebrows elevated in amusement, she mounted the three steps on the outside of the tub and slowly descended into the hot water.

Unlike Jeb, who was a plunger, Laney was a toe-dipper who needed time to get used to the water's temperature. Going down another step, she sucked a sharp breath through her teeth. *Hot.*

Gritting her teeth, she adapted to the shock. Then she stepped all the way in. Carefully arranging the skirt of her dress so it wouldn't billow immodestly around her, she took a seat opposite Jeb.

"Tell me everything," she urged. "Every single thing, from the beginning."

"From the beginning," he repeated thoughtfully. With both hands, he skimmed back his dripping hair. "'In the beginning was the Word. And the Word was God, and the Word was with God. And—'"

"That's the Gospel of John!" Laney pressed her hands

over her heart, which seemed to be trying to thump its way right out of her chest.

Jeb talked nonstop for several minutes. Amazed and delighted by his news and by his unprecedented volubility, Laney could have listened for hours. But when he reached the end of his story, he got up, held out a hand to her, and said she'd better go home and change into some dry clothes.

"I have a bunch of questions for you," he added as they climbed out of the tub, water running off their clothes and splashing noisily onto the already wet floor. "But they'll keep. You couldn't have slept much last night, and you've had a rough day."

"I'm fine, Jeb." She grabbed two plush towels from the stack on a nearby shelf and pushed one at his chest.

"Princess, you're exhausted." He shook the folds out of the towel she'd given him and swung it around her shoulders like a cape. "Go and get changed while I order our pizza and clean up this mess." He began unbuttoning his sodden flannel shirt. "You should have something to eat and then make it an early night."We can talk more tomorrow."

"No, tomorrow night I'm going to the Cities with Megan. She won two tickets to the Saint Paul Chamber Orchestra, and Luke hates classical music. She's really looking forward to it, Jeb, and there's nobody else to go with her."

He peeled off his shirt and let it fall to the floor, where it landed with a heavy splat. "Friday, then."

Laney's mouth opened, but her train of thought was derailed when she noticed how his wet T-shirt clung to the fascinating contours of his chest and shoulders. She'd seen him in a swimsuit lots of times, but somehow she had never realized he was so—

She yanked her mind off that thought and carefully fixed her gaze on his face. "Sorry, but on Friday I'm having a working supper with my accountant at the tearoom."

"Saturday. The French place?" He crossed his arms over his chest. For warmth, no doubt, but Laney was grateful for the move because it helped her remember to keep her eyes above his neck.

"Saturday is my friend Diana's wedding. And even if I could talk you into going, I didn't R.S.V.P. for a guest." Laney shivered as another gust of cold air swept across the porch and went right through her wet dress.

Frowning, Jeb took the towel she'd forgotten she was holding and put that one around her, too. "But we're going to church on Sunday."

"Absolutely!" Laney grasped the edges of the towels and pulled them more tightly around her. "Maybe we could have a celebratory brunch after. But I have a baby shower at four o'clock."

"Of course you do," he said dryly.

She grinned. "I know. When did I get so popular, right? My schedule's just unusually full for the next several days. In fact, I won't even get my day off on Monday because I'm participating in a wedding planning seminar at a country club in Minneapolis." Tilting her head to one side, she gave him a hopeful look. "But I should be home by five, so we could have supper at Willie's. And I won't be so busy next week, so—" She stopped, puzzled by the wariness creeping into Jeb's silvery eyes, and then it hit her: He had already been home for two weeks, and his visits rarely lasted even that long.

She bit her lip and stared down at her hands, which were

clutching the towels around her. Her knuckles looked white.

"We'll have to play that by ear," Jeb said quietly. "I'm still trying to figure out what to do about the band. My attorney's on vacation in South America and won't be back for a few more days, so at this point I don't even know what my options are."

He put a finger under Laney's chin and lifted her face. His gaze dipped briefly to her lips, then snapped back to her eyes. Was he thinking about kissing her, or was he just remembering—and regretting—last night's kiss?

"I'll go to church with you again this Sunday," he said. "I hope to stay longer, but I can't promise anything right now."

Yes, all right. She wouldn't make herself crazy watching the calendar and wondering how much longer he'd stick around. After the good news she'd heard a little while ago, she ought to be rejoicing, instead.

He must have seen that resolution in her eyes, because he lowered his hand and smiled. "Now get out of here."

She crammed her wet feet into her loafers. Holding her towel-cape secure with one hand, she scooped up her bag and her sweater and hurried out the door Jeb held open for her.

She was freezing, so she broke into a run. And with every long, pounding stride, she gave thanks to the Lord.

Chapter Seventeen

ON SUNDAY AFTERNOON, Laney sat on the grass near the rocky shore of Lake Kohlmier, her arms wrapped around her drawn-up knees as she watched scores of ducks and geese paddle on the water's sun-burnished surface. She'd meant to take a long walk, but she'd become lost in her thoughts and had ended up here at the large pond on the southwest side of town.

Since Jeb's amazing revelation, she'd had little time to herself. He'd known she was worn to a frazzle, so after treating her and the Graces to a leisurely after-church brunch, he'd taken her home and insisted that she have a long nap or read a novel or just sit and think for a while.

She'd protested that she had barely seen him since Wednesday. He'd countered that she was running herself ragged, and that she needed some time alone to collect her thoughts.

He was right. Since his homecoming, she'd been through one emotional upheaval after another, and she was a person who needed time to adjust to any kind of change. So even the wonderful news of his salvation had to be examined from every angle before her fluttery heart would calm down.

How would his life be different now? How might their relationship change? Might he, now that he had opened his heart to God, be able to fall in love with her?

She shook her head impatiently. She hadn't known he was a Christian that night when they'd kissed, but *he* had known, and he'd still called the kiss a mistake.

Was he worried about their ability to manage a long-distance romance? Because long-distance, it would definitely be. How could it be anything else, given his career and her need to be near the Graces?

While he would almost certainly break with Skeptical Heart, Jeb couldn't live without his music. He hadn't said anything about joining a Christian band, but surely it would come to that. And there just weren't a lot of Christian bands in Owatonna, Minnesota, were there?

"I'm not going to think about that right now," Laney muttered as a quacking flotilla of ducks cruised past her, the ruffles of their wake catching and reflecting rays from the weakening sun.

The temperature was dropping. When a gust of wind tugged at Laney's hair and made her shiver, she straightened her knees, pushing her legs out in front of her, and slid her hands into the pockets of her down vest.

Somewhere nearby, a car door slammed. Laney heard the soft slap of shoes on the paved park road behind her, and then the sound changed to whispery footfalls in the dry grass. She was about to turn her head to see who was approaching when she heard the reassuring rumble of Jeb's voice.

"I wondered if this was still your favorite thinking spot." He reached over her shoulder to wave a lidded paper coffee cup under her nose.

In the steam curling up from the plastic sipping spout, Laney recognized the tantalizing aroma of a mocha cappuccino. She jerked to life, ripping eager hands out of her vest pockets to claim the treat.

"Thank you," she breathed, wrapping her hands around the warm cup.

"I saw you go out with nothing warmer than that vest on." Jeb lowered himself to the ground beside her. "And two hours later, you still weren't back, and I worried about you freezing."

He set his coffee on the grass and then leaned sideways, reaching into his jacket pocket. He produced a black knit cap, which he proceeded to fit onto Laney's head.

"Who are you?" She was amused by, but didn't resist his ministrations. "The fourth Grace, come to mother-hen me?"

"Something like that." He tucked her ears under the cap, and then he sat back and watched her take a cautious sip of coffee. "Are you okay?"

"I am now." She saluted him with her cup, conveying her gratitude for the coffee and the warm hat. "I was just about to head back to get ready for the baby shower, but now that I've got a ride, I'd love to sit here for a few more minutes."

"I'm on foot." Jeb stretched out his long legs and crossed them at the ankles. "Ollie stopped by to borrow my canoe. He'd promised to take a cappuccino home to his wife, so I rode over to Starbucks with him and then had him drop me off here."

"I'm glad you're spending time with him," Laney said. Ollie's church was a different denomination from hers, but he was a fine Christian all the same, and could offer Jeb some good fellowship.

They were silent for a few minutes, drinking their coffee, and then Jeb set his cup on the grass again. Leaning back on his hands, he gazed up at the sky.

"Who's having a baby?" he asked.

"You don't know her," Laney said. "I just met her a few months ago." Remembering how she'd found young Jenna

Harris crying her eyes out before the home pregnancy test kits at the drug store, Laney sighed. "Poor little thing."

Jeb turned his head and looked at her, amusement lifting his dark eyebrows. "Explain to me how *you* could feel sorry for a woman who's having a baby."

"She's not married, Jeb. She's a college kid, barely nineteen, and her parents are making her feel like trash. And the baby's father has agreed to share the financial burden, but he refuses to be involved in any other way. So Jenna's all alone."

Like her mother and the Graces, Laney had never been able to turn her back on anyone in need. So she'd taken Jenna to Willie's for a milkshake and had listened to the girl's sad tale. A few days later, she had invited six of her own friends to a gratis Sunday afternoon party at the tearoom in order to introduce Jenna.

Crystal Lincoln, Ollie's new wife, had been charmed by the girl and had decided on the spot to throw her a baby shower.

"I still don't understand." Staring at a black duck dabbling near the water's edge, Jeb spoke as though to himself. "How could I have spent so much time with a truly good person and never believed in God until now?"

Laney huffed impatiently. "I'm no Mary Poppins, Jeb. I'm not Practically Perfect in Every Way."

He looked at her. "Close enough."

"*No*, Jeb. I'm a sinner, just like you."

"Not like me."

Scowling, he picked up his coffee cup, swirled it as though trying to gauge how much was left, and then tossed his head back and drank deeply.

On the verge of becoming mesmerized by the movement of his throat, Laney blinked hard and switched her focus to the black duck, which was again going bottom-up in search of food.

"Princess, you are nothing like me." The heartbreaking conviction in Jeb's voice drew Laney's gaze back to his face. "Sassing your mom when you were a kid was nothing compared to—" Shaking his head, he crushed the coffee cup in his fist. "I've done some awful things, Laney. Things I'll never tell you about because you don't need those ugly images in your mind."

Do you honestly think he doesn't take illicit drugs and consort with groupies?

Mrs. Lindstrom's rude question buzzed like a troublesome insect inside Laney's head, but she mentally swatted it away.

Jeb wasn't that man anymore. He had turned his back on his old life and accepted God's forgiveness.

"You're missing the point," she said. "My disrespecting Mom was one of the sins Jesus died for. Maybe your sins have been more—" She paused to search for the word. "More blatant than mine. But are they worse than mine?" She gave her head an emphatic shake. "Sin is sin, Jeb. It's rebellion against our heavenly Father. He doesn't smile and say, 'Well, that was only a *little* sin. At least Laney Ryland isn't as bad as that awful Jackson Bell.'"

Jeb's mouth twitched, but his amusement was both faint and fleeting. "Pastor Jerry said something like that."

He'd met the head pastor of Laney's church just a few hours earlier, when Laney had introduced them after the worship service. On learning that Jeb was a new Christian with a lot of questions, Pastor Jerry DeSantis had offered to speak with him in private. Laney had quickly excused herself, and Pastor Jerry had clapped a fatherly hand on Jeb's shoulder and led him away.

Jeb hadn't even flinched at the unexpected touch. Clutching her Bible to her chest as she stood staring after them, Laney had been so overcome by wonder and gratitude that she'd ended up dashing to the ladies' room for a handful of tissues to mop up her tears.

"I didn't understand until just now," Jeb continued in a low voice. "Thank you."

Laney nodded, then drank some coffee to ease the sudden swelling in her throat.

Childish laughter rang out behind them, and Laney immediately looked over her shoulder. She heard Jeb's amused snort and ignored it. Could she help it if small children drew her attention like magnets?

On the other side of the park road, a little girl who appeared to be three or four years old was frolicking with a huge dog. While an older couple, perhaps her grandparents, sat on a bench and watched with fond smiles, the child threw a spindly leg over the dog's back, mounting it like a pony.

"Go dis way, Benny!" she urged, flattening herself against her pet's back and tugging on its left ear. "Go *dis* way!"

The dog carefully lowered himself to the ground. When the girl sat up and nudged his flanks with her tiny heels, "Benny" turned his head and regarded her with patient curiosity.

Remembering Jenna's shower, Laney checked her watch and then got to her feet. "Come on, Jeb. I need to get home."

He rose, but he couldn't seem to tear his eyes away from the little girl. Laney tapped his left elbow to get his attention.

"Oh," he said brightly, turning toward her, his eyes round with fake innocence. "Do you want me to go *dis* way?"

Laney laughed and gave him a playful shove.

They dropped their coffee cups in a trash receptacle and walked home in an easy silence, Jeb slowing his steps as usual to accommodate Laney's much shorter stride.

When they reached Mulberry Street and Mrs. Lindstrom's charred house came into view, Laney shuddered and looked up at Jeb.

He wasn't looking at the house, but straight ahead, and he was smiling broadly enough to reveal his dimple.

"Share," Laney demanded.

He chuckled. "That little girl and that poor dog. It was like watching a video of you and me."

"Oh, stop." Laney did her best to kill a grin. "You might have given me a piggyback ride once or twice, but I'm sure I never kicked you in the ribs to hurry you along."

"Maybe not," he said, amusement still lurking in his eyes. "But you know I wouldn't have objected. You were the princess and I was your devoted slave."

Stopping on the sidewalk in front of her house, at the very spot where their friendship had begun all those years ago, Laney gazed soberly up at him.

"The princess was equally devoted, Jeb. She still is."

His smile turned disturbingly wistful. "Do you still have that tiara? And the blue dress?"

Laney nodded. "Mom packed the whole costume away years ago. She said she was saving it for her granddaughters."

"I wish she could have lived to see you with children." Jeb's voice had gone husky.

"Yes." Hit hard by a wave of longing for her mother, Laney squeezed her eyes shut. She wasn't sure what happened after that, whether she'd reached blindly for Jeb or whether he'd been the one to move, but suddenly she was in his arms and it was right, so very right.

And then it was even more right, because he whispered her name and slid his warm fingers under her chin to lift her face. She opened her eyes, and they gazed at each other for a long, perfect moment. Then he lowered his head and—

Abruptly let her go and stepped back.

Laney nearly stamped her foot in frustration.

A rueful smile lifted one corner of Jeb's mouth. "I just realized we're standing directly opposite Mrs. Schultz's kitchen window. And didn't you say Mrs. Lindstrom is staying with her?"

"Oops." Laney's hand flew to her mouth and she giggled behind it. "I'll bet her nose is pressed against the glass right this min—" She broke off as a gleaming silver Cadillac glided past them and pulled into Jeb's driveway. "Who's that?" she asked.

"No idea."

The vehicle stopped. The driver's door opened. A pair of outrageously long, slim, tanned female legs slid into view.

Jeb groaned.

Laney glanced up and saw his expression darken like a sky filling with thunderclouds. "Who is it?" she asked again.

"Shari Daltry."

He sounded about as pleased as Laney felt at tax time when her accountant gave her the bad news, so she figured the woman must be from the media. Yet Jeb avoided those people, and would never have invited one to interview him in Owatonna. So why wasn't he throwing an arm around Laney's shoulders and hustling toward the privacy of his house or her own?

The woman emerged from the Cadillac and balanced gracefully on her mile-high legs, which rose from a chunky pair of shoes with the tallest heels Laney had ever seen. She wore a black leather jacket and the merest suggestion of a skirt, and when she flipped back her luscious auburn hair, Laney saw red.

The fashionable female had spotted Jeb and was staring at him in the determined way of an ex-girlfriend come to reclaim her man.

"Laney." Jeb spoke softly, but with obvious agitation. "Go inside."

"No way," she muttered. She wasn't proud of her jealousy, but he had almost kissed her a minute ago, and her emotions were still in overdrive. So she wasn't going anywhere until she found out exactly what he had to say to this woman who'd chased him all the way to Owatonna.

Fixing a bland expression on her face, Laney endeavored to keep her lips from moving as she lowered her voice and asked, "So who's Shari Sultry?"

"Shari Daltry," Jeb corrected without a hint of amusement. "My manager."

His manager. Of course. Why had she assumed Jeb would have a doughy, middle-aged, *male* manager like all the other rock stars?

The woman closed her car door and continued to stare expectantly at Jeb. He didn't budge, so she stepped onto the sidewalk and headed their way.

"Laney," Jeb said tightly. "Please go in the house."

Throwing him a mutinous look that he failed to catch because his gaze was locked on the other woman, Laney folded her arms and stayed right where she was. If he wanted to have a private conversation with the person at the end of those freakishly long legs, he was going to have to make a proper introduction and then ask Laney to excuse him.

Hey, she didn't make the rules. It was basic etiquette.

"Hello, Jackson," the woman purred as she neared them.

"Shari." His voice was hard enough to slice diamonds. "What are you doing here?"

"Sightseeing." Coming to a stop a few feet away, she swept Laney from head to toe with an insolent look. "And I can't say I'm all that impressed with Minnesota."

Mortified, Laney snatched Jeb's knit cap off her head and stuffed it into a pocket of her vest. As she hastily finger-fluffed her curls, she hoped the blush heating her cheeks would be taken for windburn.

"Why are you here?" Jeb rumbled.

"I came to see if you were writing songs or just—" Flicking another glance at Laney, her lips curled in derision. "—wasting time."

Jeb's jaw flexed, and Laney instinctively touched his arm to settle his temper. He looked down at her, his harsh features instantly softening in the way she knew so well. But then he shocked her by grasping her shoulders and hauling her against him. And right there in full view of the rude woman and Mrs. Lindstrom, whose nose was no doubt glued to Mrs. Schultz's kitchen window, he lowered his head and claimed Laney's lips in a soft, achingly sweet kiss.

It couldn't have lasted more than four seconds, but it thrilled Laney right down to her toes, which were barely touching the ground. And when Jeb set her down and steadied her on her feet before letting go, she stared dazedly into his silvery eyes and read some very exciting promises there.

"All righty, then." She hardly recognized the breathless, high-pitched voice as her own. "I'll just wait for you inside, Jeb, okay?" She aimed a dreamy smile in the general direction of his manager and completely forgot to excuse herself before turning toward the house.

Chapter Eighteen

JEB BIT BACK A GRIN as Laney walked away with the cutest little swing to her step.

Kissing her had been a crazy impulse, and he could hardly believe he'd done it in front of Shari and probably in full view of Mrs. Lindstrom. But she'd been jealous just now, and while that had caused the most primitive part of Jeb's brain to hum with masculine satisfaction, he'd moved quickly to reassure her.

She was falling in love with him, and he was beginning to think that might not be such a terrible thing. Granted, he didn't deserve her and he never would. But he loved her and he understood her, and that had to count for something.

He'd done some heavy thinking and praying since Wednesday night, when he'd told her about his conversion, and it had paid off. Just a little while ago, the jangling in his head had suddenly ceased and he had become aware of having made two very good decisions: one about the band and one about Laney.

"She's not much to look at," Shari commented.

Laney was beautiful, inside and out, but Jeb wasn't going to discuss her with Shari. He propped his fisted hands on his hips and waited for his manager to get to the point of this unwelcome intrusion.

"Are you coming back?" she asked.

Looking straight into her eyes, he slowly shook his head.

Her lips pinched together and her eyes glinted, but she said nothing.

"I was planning to call you and the guys tonight," Jeb

said. "And first thing tomorrow, I'm calling my attorney to see what my legal options and obligations are."

Shari made an impatient noise in the back of her throat. "We beat the odds, Jackson. With the third record and this last tour, Skeptical Heart has built up some serious momentum. If you quit now, there's no second chance. It will take the fans this long—" She snapped her fingers in his face. "—to forget you."

"I know. But I don't think God wants me to go back to Skeptical Heart."

Stepping closer and fingering the zippered edge of his open jacket, Shari tilted her head to one side and lowered her voice to a seductive purr. "God wants you to be successful, Jackson."

He couldn't believe she was making a move on him. But she probably didn't have any ideas left.

He calmly removed her hand from his jacket. "Maybe God's definition of success isn't what you think, Shari."

Her eyes flashed. "What am I supposed to tell the guys?"

"If they want to go on," Jeb said with quiet assurance, "they'll have to do it without me."

"Skeptical Heart can't go on without you," she grated out. "You own the trademark, remember?"

That was one of the things he meant to speak to his attorney about. Skeptical Heart was, in every sense, *his* band. He'd formed it and he'd chosen its name and he'd registered the trademark. But he wanted to be fair to Taylor, Matt, Sean, and Aaron, who had worked their tails off to make the band a success.

If he signed his rights over to the guys, they could replace him and probably retain a large portion of Skeptical

Heart's fan base. But wouldn't it be a mistake to offer that kind of assistance to a band that would continue to mock the faith Jeb had so recently embraced?

He shoved his spread fingers through his hair and sighed. "Look, Shari, I haven't got it all worked out yet. Don't tell the guys about my decision. They deserve to hear it from me, and like I said, I plan to call them tonight. As for the other stuff, I should be able to tell you something in a few days."

Her nostrils flared, but she spoke in a moderate tone. "This is not an insurmountable problem, Jackson. You handled that last show just fine, changing those lyrics that you suddenly found so offensive. Nobody objected to that. So you could write a couple of God songs, nothing too blatant, and slip them in with the rest. Other bands have done it, and if it's handled carefully, the fans will hardly notice. So—"

"*No.*" How many times did she need to be told that his new faith had radically changed his heart and mind? "I'm a different man now. I can't just pull on a 'Jesus Rocks' T-shirt and go back to—"

"Let me finish," she insisted, halting him with a raised hand. "We'll have your publicist put it out that you've had a spiritual awakening. And then—"

"I said *no.*"

"So you're going to throw it all away!" Shari flung out her arms and let them fall back to her sides, her palms noisily slapping her thighs. "Everything we've worked for. You don't want it, but you're not going to let *us* have it, either. Is that it, Jackson?"

"No, that's not it," he said wearily. "I don't want to hurt anybody. I'm just trying to do what's right."

"For *yourself*," she retorted. "Excuse me, but I thought Christians were supposed to care about other people more than themselves. But this is all about *you*, isn't it, Jackson?"

"You shouldn't have come here," he said.

She jerked a shoulder in irritation. "My brother's getting married in some tiny town on the northern border of Iowa, and it was easiest to fly into Minneapolis. And I had to drive right past Owatonna."

Compassion overtook Jeb's annoyance and he nodded. "I guess you had to give it a shot. But I've got nothing for you, Shari. I'm sorry."

She just looked at him for a moment. Then without another word, she turned on her heel and strode back to her rental car.

As Jeb watched the Cadillac back out of his driveway, Taylor's words echoed in his head: *If you get off this merry-go-round, the ride's over for all of us. You know that.*

The Caddy's tires squealed as Shari gunned it down Mulberry Street.

Jeb sighed. He'd been hoping to find a way to soften the blow of his defection from the band. But if a guy was earnestly trying to please God, and if certain other people believed that guy's devotion was wrecking their own plans, maybe those people ought to take that up with God.

So that was it. He was off the merry-go-round. Feeling pounds lighter, he jogged around to the back of Laney's house and bounded up her porch steps.

"It's open," she called when he rapped on the kitchen door.

He entered and found her seated at the table, her board-straight back facing the window from where she might have observed him and Shari, had she pressed her nose to the glass and looked toward the street. He knew she hadn't done that—his Laney was no snoop. But considering how transparently jealous she'd been out there on the sidewalk, she must have been tempted.

She was pretending to read her newspaper, and when she turned a page with exaggerated indifference, Jeb had to swallow a laugh. It was rotten of him, but he was thrilled by her prickly reaction to Shari's visit. This show of jealousy confirmed it: Laney was beginning to care about him in an exciting new way.

She'd lost her confidence out there, and Jeb hadn't thought twice before laying that reassuring kiss on her. It had seemed to do the trick, but it had apparently worn off after she'd come inside. Alone in her kitchen, determinedly avoiding that window, she must have gone right back to wondering and worrying.

Hey, no problem. If her confidence required additional bolstering, Jeb was her man. She could have as many of his kisses as she needed. Now that God accepted him, there was no reason he couldn't offer himself to Laney.

But right now she needed to talk, so he sat down beside her and waited for her to begin.

"So that's your manager." She closed the newspaper and then straightened the edges and folded it with great care. "She's beautiful."

"No, she isn't." Jeb scooted closer and laid his arm across the back of her chair, cupping her shoulder with his palm. "Not in any way that matters."

While the rigid line of her back hadn't softened at his touch, at least she didn't shrug away from him. Her gaze remained fixed on the neatly folded paper as her pretty eyebrows rose and the shoulder beneath Jeb's hand twitched, conveying an adorably desperate nonchalance. He knew what was coming, and he had to mash his lips together to hold back an exultant laugh.

"Was she your girlfriend?"

"No," he managed with a straight face.

"No?" She was nibbling that thumbnail again, and Jeb's amusement swiftly died.

"No," he repeated. "There has never been anything between Shari and me but business."

She turned her head and looked into his eyes. "Then why didn't you introduce us?"

"I didn't want you exposed to her nastiness. She's been under a lot of stress lately, and her temper gets out of hand. As a matter of fact, the last time I saw her, she threw a glass of whiskey in my face."

"So you were trying to protect me." Irritation flared in the China-blue eyes so close to his own. "I know Mom expected a lot from you, Jeb, but you can stop shielding me now. I'm not a kid anymore."

"Believe me," he drawled, "I am very aware of that."

"Are you?" she demanded. "Because that's not what it feels like to me. You're still pulling a curtain over a huge part of your life because you're terrified that the pampered princess might be tainted by—"

"*Yes.*" He stared at her, baffled by her irritation. "Yes, I've shielded you from the unsavory parts of my life. Yes, I was trying to protect you from Shari's caustic tongue out there. But come on, Laney." He tried to pull her into a hug, but she resisted. She was still looking at him, though, so he went on. "You've always been good at understanding, and I really need you to understand now. This new life isn't easy for me. I'm trying to get it right, but I'm confused about a lot of things. So if I messed up, I'm sorry."

Her stiff shoulders suddenly relaxed. "No, I'm the one who's sorry. I don't know what's gotten into me lately." Sliding down in her chair, she pillowed her head on the crook of his arm and stared at the ceiling. "You think people who have been Christians for a long time have it all figured out, don't you? You think we never do or say stupid things. But that couldn't be further from the truth, Jeb. Just look at *me*."

He was looking, and he had never loved her more.

There were so many things he longed to tell her. Questions he couldn't wait to ask. Promises he looked forward to making. But the time wasn't right for any of that, not yet, so he just said, "Don't beat yourself up, princess. I think we're supposed to forget what's behind us and just keep moving toward our goal."

She turned her beautiful blue eyes on him. "You've been reading Philippians."

"Have I?" He shook his head, confused. "I thought it was something that guy Paul wrote."

Laney smiled. "The Epistle to the Philippians is an actual letter from the apostle Paul to the church in Philippi, a city in Macedonia. You're thinking about a passage in Chapter Three."

"Ah," Jeb said, but his thoughts had already slipped off the Bible and settled on the woman whose nearness was making his heart pump faster.

He wanted to kiss her again, and he felt guilty about

that. A good Christian man would have occupied his mind with Bible verses and other serious thoughts, but Jeb's mind kept getting stuck on things like Laney's guileless blue eyes and her soft cloud of curls and her perfectly imperfect smile and her sweet, womanly curves.

Oh, yes. Those curves were a problem.

Exasperation flared and Jeb gazed helplessly at the ceiling. *Well, if you don't want me noticing things like the way she fills out a pair of jeans, why did you have to go and make her so beautiful?*

He thought for another minute and concluded that there couldn't be anything sinful about his physical desire for the woman he loved. Not as long as he stayed within the boundaries of chaste behavior—and he was determined to do that for her sake as much as his own. So even if his self-discipline proved inadequate to the task, his horror of tempting Laney to do anything that would ultimately leave her ashamed and filled with regret would keep them out of trouble.

He shifted, curling his arm more tightly around the back of her head so he could stroke her wind-tousled curls and breathe in their delicate floral fragrance.

He couldn't get enough of that smell. Every time he inhaled, he wished he could hold the breath and trap Laney's scent inside him and never let it go.

"This is so nice," she murmured, eyes still closed. "Let's just sit here forever."

"Forever?" Dangerously close to blurting things about his feelings that she wasn't ready to hear, Jeb made a desperate dive into levity. "I don't know. My arm's already half asleep, and my back's starting to cramp up from leaning at this awkward angle."

"Complain, complain," she teased in a singsong voice. "Why can't you just enjoy the moment and—"

She broke off with a screech of surprise as he swiftly and without premeditation grabbed her by the waist and hauled her onto his lap. She resisted, giggling, and asked what he thought he was doing, but when he stopped her mouth with a kiss, her response was immediate and deeply gratifying.

She settled herself more comfortably, balancing sideways on his thigh with both legs dangling between his, and kissed him as sweetly and as ardently as she'd done in all of those dreams he'd tried so hard not to have about her.

Laney.

He wanted to lash his life to hers and never look back. He wanted the two of them to belong to each other and only to each other until death they did part, amen.

But right now, he needed to end this kiss before it got out of hand.

To his mingled amusement and frustration, Laney was no help at all. When he moved his head back, she simply leaned forward, eyes still tightly shut, her dewy, softly parted lips following and attempting to recapture his retreating mouth.

Good thing he'd been honing his self-discipline for years. With a rueful grin, Jeb palmed the back of her head, raised his chin, and tucked her safely beneath it.

"Jeb?" Her voice was muffled against his jacket.

"Hmm?" He splayed his fingers and pushed them into a mass of fluffy curls until his hand was pleasantly trapped.

"What changed your mind?" She turned her head slightly, allowing her words to become more distinct. "That night at the lake, you were sorry about kissing me. You said it was never going to happen again"

There was an unmistakable remnant of hurt in her voice, but Jeb wasn't sure how much to explain at this point. He could confess that he'd been in love with her for years, but wouldn't that put undue pressure on her at a time when she was just beginning to explore her own feelings?

The last thing he wanted to do was push her into a romance. If something was going to happen between them, he wanted it to unfold naturally, like a flower opening itself to the sun. So for now . . .

"Could we just agree that I was stupid, and leave it at that?"

"Yes," she said happily, nestling closer. "You were stupid, Jeb." She sighed, and for a few profoundly beautiful moments they breathed in tandem. Then she suddenly went rigid.

"Oh!" she cried, and shoved herself out of his arms.

Worry zinged through Jeb. "What's wrong?"

"Jenna's baby shower!" Laney scrambled to her feet. "I'm late!" She tore out of the kitchen like a small tornado and thumped up the stairs.

Jeb started to leave, but then he decided to stick around for a goodbye kiss.

She returned after just a couple of minutes, her arms filled with a black blazer, a wrapped shower gift, a multicolored scarf, and a pair of high-heeled shoes, all of which she dumped on the table. She hadn't changed out of the crisp indigo jeans she'd worn to the park, but she had exchanged her flannel shirt and down vest for a wine-colored blouse that shimmered and clung sweetly to her curves.

She hopped on one foot and then the other, charmingly clumsy as she tugged off her sneakers and socks, chattering all the while about the who and where and when of the baby shower, and how late she was going to be. Jeb barely heard her; he was too busy admiring the way she pushed her slender bare feet into the feminine high-heeled shoes.

She wound the scarf around her neck twice, deftly knotted the ends, and then shimmied into the blazer. After finger-fluffing her glorious curls, she rummaged in the bag she'd left on the chair nearest the door and produced a tube of lipstick and something that jingled like a handful of tiny silver bells before she dropped it into the left pocket of her blazer.

She rolled up the lipstick and turned away from Jeb to hunch over the counter next to the refrigerator. Peering into the mirror-like side of her toaster, she applied a luscious pink tint to her amazing mouth.

Jeb had never been more fascinated in his life.

Oblivious to his admiration, Laney mashed her lips together a couple of times and then straightened and turned back toward him, her hand plunging into her pocket. There was more of the delicate jingling, and then she pushed the stem of one of the earrings Jeb had given her through the tiny hole in her left ear.

"How's that for a quick change?" she asked as she attached the second earring.

Jeb was too enchanted to breathe, let alone answer questions. Good thing she didn't seem to be awaiting a response.

"That's yesterday's paper," she said, pointing to the one she'd so carefully folded minutes earlier. If you want today's, it's in the living room." She shouldered her bag and scooped up the shower gift and hustled to the door. "Bye!"

"Wait!" Jeb yelped, coming out of his chair.

She halted, breathless and beautiful, her hand on the doorknob as she watched him approach. "What's wrong?"

He came to a stop before her. "Since you're already late, you might as well take a minute to kiss me goodbye."

She blushed and tried unsuccessfully to kill her smile. "I really don't have a minute, but I suppose I could give you ten seconds." Eyes alight with mischief, she set the gift on the counter and then reached up and grasped Jeb's ears and pulled his face down to hers. "So make it count, mister."

He wasted at least a third of his allotted time chuckling, but then he "made it count" until she giggled into his kiss and beat his chest with her fists and made him let her go.

After she left the house, Jeb helped himself to a can of pop from her refrigerator. He knocked back half its contents in a single breath, and then he stood staring out a window, his fingertips tapping the can in a rhythmic pattern as he pondered his next move.

Laney was falling in love with him. If he didn't screw this up, he just might end up married to her.

Unfortunately, he seemed to have a real flair for screwing things up. And he didn't have a single clue how to romance a woman.

He racked his brain to recall what Laney had said about being engaged. Something about Nathan giving her a beautiful ring and about it all being "so romantic." Knowing Laney, it wasn't the ring that had impressed her, but whatever Nathan had said and done when he'd presented the thing.

Jeb felt a twinge of jealousy, but quickly tamped it down. She wouldn't have been happy with Nathan—or with Tom, or even with the veterinarian—and she saw that now. But she was big on romance, and Jeb was determined to make every one of her dreams come true.

He gulped the rest of his drink and crushed the can in his fist. Where could he find out what he needed to know about romance? It didn't seem like the kind of thing a guy could Google.

He could ask Ollie Lincoln. After Ollie stopped laughing, he'd probably be willing to share some pointers. But what if the techniques that had won Ollie a wife weren't the right ones to use on Laney?

Not Ollie, then. Someone with a broader understanding of romance and a deeper knowledge of Laney, herself. Someone who—

"*No*," Jeb groaned as his thoughts coalesced on a single, ludicrously unacceptable solution. "Absolutely not." There was no way he was going to go crawling on his knees to—

He sighed and gave in. He would do anything for Laney. Anything at all.

"Even this," he muttered as he walked out her back door.

Chapter Nineteen

"JENNA WANTS ANOTHER PIECE," Laney said to Crystal Lincoln, Ollie's brown-eyed sprite of a wife, who stood at her dining room table cutting slices from a sheet cake that resembled a baby carriage. Glancing over her shoulder into the crowded living room she'd just left, Laney chuckled and added, "Now that she's had a piece for herself, she wants to eat one for the baby."

Smiling, Crystal eased a square of cake onto the plate Laney held out. "Jenna's going to be just fine now that she knows she has friends who care about her."

"I think you're right. Thanks for hosting this shower, Crystal."

"Thank *you* for giving that tea party and introducing Jenna to all of us."

"She's a sweetheart," Laney said thoughtfully. "Why she didn't already have tons of friends is a mystery to me."

"Her parents are rather controlling." Crystal's tone held a note of apology; she wasn't one to speak ill of anyone.

Peals of laughter floated in from the other room. Laney and Crystal glanced toward the doorway and then exchanged smiles.

"Everyone's having a good time," Laney said.

"I hope so." Crystal put the cake knife down and straightened a skewed stack of paper napkins. "Too bad the Graces couldn't come."

"Sunday afternoon is their quiet time," Laney explained. "They're on the go all week long, so they're very protective of their Sunday afternoons. But they adore Jenna, and I know they already gave her some nice gifts. They even got her to promise to go to church with them next Sunday."

"That's wonderful," Crystal said. "And speaking of taking people to church, what's this I hear about Jackson Bell? Is it true he's become a believer?"

"Yes." Joy shivered through Laney.

"I'm so glad. I'd like to meet him sometime. That is, if you think he wouldn't mind. Ollie says he's—" Crystal looked uncomfortable again. "Well, 'difficult to know' is what Ollie says."

"He's a very private person." It was Laney's standard response. While she wished people could understand why Jeb avoided social interaction, she would never betray his trust by divulging that he'd been neglected and abused as a child.

"But he's famous." Crystal's brow furrowed. "How can a shy person—"

"He's not shy," Laney interrupted. "Not the way you mean. He's just not much of a talker."

"Ollie likes him," Crystal said. "In fact, the night before Mrs. Lindstrom's house burned down, Ollie got mad when somebody we know said Jackson was a sociopath. Ollie said that just because a guy keeps to himself, that doesn't mean he despises people and lacks empathy."

"Jeb doesn't despise people," Laney said with feeling. "He's just never been comfortable in social situations." Although since he'd become a Christian, he'd been making an amazing effort. He was even thinking about taking Ollie up on an invitation to try some curling.

"Well, the next person who calls him that ugly name is going to get a piece of *my* mind," Crystal said staunchly.

"Sociopaths don't run into burning houses to save old ladies."

"He even saved her cat," Laney pointed out. "Jeb's a hero, just like the newspaper said."

Crystal tilted her head forward, looking at Laney from under raised eyebrows as a knowing smile curved her mouth. "Am I picking up a romantic vibe here?"

Recalling those soul-stirring kisses in her kitchen, Laney couldn't flatten her answering grin any more than she could banish the blush that suddenly warmed her cheeks. "Let's just say I'm hopeful. But this is a very recent development, Crystal, so please keep it to yourself."

That Jeb had initiated those kisses was a strong indication that he, too, was falling in love. But he still had a lot of decisions to make about his new life. So while Laney had begun to cherish a secret hope about marrying him, she was still a practical woman who understood that dreams didn't always come true.

"I won't say a word." Crystal came around the table and reached out for a hug. "And I'll be praying for you both."

Holding Jenna's cake plate safely to one side, Laney leaned toward Crystal and gave her a one-armed squeeze.

"Crystal." Sarah Jane Swenson entered the dining room, an empty glass cup in her hand, and gestured to the punch bowl at one end of the table. "Before I help myself to more of this wonderful stuff, please tell me there are no calories in it."

"There aren't." Crystal shared an amused look with Laney. "At least, not compared to the cake."

Already ladling punch into her cup, Sarah Jane loosed one of her silver-bell laughs.

"I'll go see if anyone needs more coffee," Crystal said. Reaching for the plate in Laney's hands, she added, "And I'll deliver this cake to our mom-to-be."

"Thank you," Laney said with quiet intensity and a significant look to convey her gratitude for the promised prayers.

"I was hoping for a minute alone with you," Sarah Jane said when their hostess had gone. "What are you looking so delighted about? Have you sold the tearoom already?"

Shaking her head, Laney wondered why Sarah Jane would imagine she'd be delighted about that. On second thought, now that she had accepted the inevitability of the sale, a good offer for the place probably *would* give her a thrill. After all, she'd finally be able to pay off her debts.

"No, I haven't even had an offer yet. But the agent is showing it again tomorrow, and he thinks it'll sell quickly."

"But you're positively glowing." Sarah Jane moved toward Laney and linked an arm through hers. "So I thought . . ." She shook her head, but a second later her puzzled expression morphed into a smile. "I know what it is!" she crowed, and then she lowered her voice to a confidential whisper. "You kissed Jackson, didn't you?"

Laney fought a grin.

"Good girl!" Sarah Jane squeezed her arm and then sipped some punch, her brown eyes twinkling as she watched Laney over the rim of the cup. "Tell me everything."

Laney chuckled. "In your dreams, Sarah Jane."

Her friend smiled back. "I gather he didn't hate it?"

"He didn't hate it," Laney acknowledged. "But that's all you're getting out of me."

It had been just two hours since those amazing kisses—

she was determined to forget that disastrous one at the lake—and two of Laney's friends already knew something romantic was happening between herself and Jeb. That could prove awkward if things didn't work out the way she hoped, so from this moment, her lips were zipped.

If Jeb came to love her the way she loved him, maybe they could build a life together. But if he couldn't love her that way, or if the Lord had a different plan for each of them . . .

Well, then she would just do her best to trust God and be content with the life he gave her.

That was what her mother had done. Even though her snake of a husband had ultimately divorced her, Hannah Ryland had never looked at another man. She had always maintained that as long as she kept her eyes on the Lord, she was perfectly content.

"So you're not going to spill any juicy details?" Sarah Jane pretended to pout. "In that case, we might as well get back to the party."

Laney concurred and followed her friend into the other room.

* * *

"This is insane," Jeb muttered as he stood on the Graces' front porch, his right index finger hovering nervously above the tiny round doorbell button.

He had never visited this house without Laney to watch his back. But while she was occupied at the baby shower, he meant to put one simple question to her great-aunts. Was it too much to hope that just this once, they might resist the temptation to toy with him and just give him an answer that made sense?

Suppressing a shudder of apprehension, he rang the bell.

The Graces were delighted to see him; they beckoned him inside like a trio of bored cats who'd just discovered a fat mouse bumbling into their domain. As they tugged off his leather jacket and hauled him back to their over-warm kitchen, Jeb braced himself to endure their relentless hospitality.

He didn't resist when they pushed him onto a chair at a table covered with a red-and-white-checked cloth and strewn with piles of yarn and knitting needles. Neither did he object when they set a mug of black coffee and a massive triangle of cherry pie in front of him.

No sane person ever said no to the Graces' pie, anyway, and even Laney's coffee couldn't touch the robust stuff her great-aunts brewed.

"Sorry the pie's not strawberry-rhubarb," Millie said. "We know that's your favorite."

"I like this, too," Jeb said. "Thank you."

Beaming at him, the Graces settled around the table and resumed the knitting session he had apparently interrupted. On the floor, a smoke-colored cat batted halfheartedly at a ball of yarn before yawning and slinking into a cardboard box that lay on its side next to the refrigerator.

"Frankie Five loves his boxes." Millie's knitting needles clacked rhythmically as she bestowed an indulgent smile on the cat. "Maybe he'll let you hold him later," she added, as though that would constitute a rare treat.

Jeb forked up several bites of pie before he found his nerve and announced, "I came here to ask you something."

Three sets of knitting needles stopped moving. Three

identical pairs of faded blue eyes blinked patiently behind wire-rimmed glasses. Even Frankie Five padded out of his box and meowed inquisitively. But Jeb's mind had suddenly gone blank.

Caroline's crinkly mouth curved in undisguised amusement. "Finish your pie," she said. "A man can get himself into all kinds of trouble asking questions on an empty stomach."

Jeb sighed and poked another bite of pie into his mouth. Laney's great-aunts went back to knitting noisily, the delicate clacking of their needles filling the brief, infrequent pauses in their chatter.

"There now." Millie slipped something that looked like a small round potholder off of her needles. "That's another little hat done. Now I'll make the booties to match."

"I already made two pairs out of that yellow yarn," Caroline said. "But we have two white hats and no booties to go with them, so you could make some white ones. Or start on another sweater. We only have four of those."

Apparently, the Graces' latest charitable endeavor was outfitting a brigade of babies. Replete with cherry pie and feeling unaccountably mellow, Jeb reached for his coffee mug.

"Here's a thought," Aggie offered. "Let's make matching sweaters for Laney and the baby out of that rainbow yarn."

About to take a drink, Jeb halted the coffee mug an inch from his mouth. Staring at Aggie, he waited for his brain to make sense out of her odd suggestion.

"Oh, what a cute idea!" Millie said. "But let's make two or three different sizes for the baby, so Laney can enjoy playing look-alike for more than just a month or two."

"Why would Laney play look-alike with somebody else's baby?" Jeb asked before setting the mug to his lips.

"These things we're making," Millie said with a beatific smile, "are for Laney's baby."

Jeb choked on his coffee.

As he coughed and gasped, Aggie sprang out of her chair and thumped him repeatedly between the shoulder blades.

"Laney's *what*?" he demanded as Aggie beat him like an old rug at spring cleaning time. "She's not even—" *Cough, cough.* "—married yet!"

"She will be soon," Caroline said composedly as she continued knitting. "You okay there, Jeb?"

"P-perfectly fine." He coughed again and then looked over his shoulder to raise a stern eyebrow at Aggie, who had stopped pounding his back to nudge her arms beneath his and dig her small fists into his solar plexus.

"Sit down, Aggie," Caroline said. "He doesn't need a Heimlich hug. He just swallowed his coffee wrong."

"Oh, shoot." Aggie withdrew her arms and subsided onto her chair. "I always wanted to try that."

"So what's with the baby stuff?" Jeb addressed the question to Millie because when it came to giving a straight answer, she was far more reliable than devious Caroline and mischievous Aggie.

"We're working ahead," Millie explained. "Because even if Laney were to get married in the next few months, it could still be a couple of years before she has a baby. And we're not getting any younger, you know. We might be gone to Glory by that time, or just not able to knit anymore. And we've been knitting for Laney since *she* was a baby. So do you think we'd risk failing to provide her first child with a box of cute little things made with a bit of yarn and a lot of love?"

Caroline and Aggie nodded their matter-of-fact approval to that poignant little speech.

"I guess that makes sense," Jeb said carefully.

"It's just insurance," Aggie said. "Pure and simple. But don't you breathe a word about it to our girl. When we finish this layette, we'll pack it away until it's needed."

Jeb wasn't sure what a "layette" was. But since he hoped to be the man who married Laney, it was entirely possible that the Graces were unwittingly knitting booties for a bouncing baby Bell.

He was careful to conceal his amusement. The Graces might appear harmless as they sat there crafting garments for Laney's first child, but they were like Miss Marple in triplicate. Their agile brains continually made all sorts of scary connections, and they could wreck a man's self-confidence faster than they could roll out the crust for one of their mouthwatering pies.

He folded his arms on the table and cleared his throat. "Speaking of starting families," he began with what he felt was remarkable aplomb, considering his history with these women, "I know you three are scheming to marry me off."

Once again, their knitting needles stilled.

"I'm not mad." Jeb regarded the bemused trio with a genial smile. "In fact, I agree that I'm ready for marriage."

Millie gasped. Aggie's jaw dropped. And for the very first time in Jeb's memory, Caroline Grace Ryland looked flummoxed.

"But you can just forget about whatever match you're planning for me." Jeb pulled in a deep breath, and then he laid his heart right there on the table. "Because I want

Laney."

"Laney!" the Three Graces cried in unison.

He'd known this would shock them, but after all they'd done to him over the years, the Graces had at least one good shock coming. Ever since the day they'd made him kneel on their living room rug so they could zip him into that pink rabbit suit, Jeb had been dreaming of payback.

"Yes," he said. "Laney." He narrowed his eyes to show he was no longer a man to be messed with. "Are you going to have a problem with that?" he challenged.

Millie darted a nervous glance at Aggie. Aggie started to speak, but was silenced by a tiny shake of Caroline's head.

"Not necessarily." Caroline had resumed her usual sphinx-like expression. "Go on, Jeb."

His confidence was already beginning to ebb. He pushed his fingers through his hair and tried to think, but when Caroline dropped her chin and peered at him over her glasses, he was unnerved enough to blurt, "I know I don't deserve her."

"No," Caroline agreed calmly. "You don't."

"But nobody understands her like I do," he insisted, "and no man could ever love her more. I'll treat her right, Caroline. You know I will."

Caroline's gaze dropped to the table, where she lightly scratched a fingernail against the red-checked cloth, tracing little shapes that might have been hearts.

"So your mind's made up, then?" she asked in that casual tone that could scare the socks off a man.

"You don't want anybody else?" That was Aggie.

"You're absolutely positive?" Millie.

"My mind's made up," Jeb confirmed. "I don't want

anybody else. I am absolutely positive."

A cold sweat erupted on the back of his neck as the Graces regarded him in silence, weighing his worthiness as a life mate for their girl. He pressed his lips firmly together; while their blessing would mean the world to him, he wasn't going to beg for it.

On second thought, a little begging wouldn't kill him.

"I know this isn't what you wanted for her," he said. "I know you were hoping I'd sell my house and get out of her life. But you know I'm a Christian now, and—"

"About your house." Aggie halted him by raising a stubby index finger. "We never wanted you to sell it. We just planted the idea in your head because we knew you'd hate it, and then you might stop and think about why you haven't been coming home very often."

"Stop and think?" he echoed. If they only knew how desperately he'd wanted to come home. Staying away for as long as a year at a time had strained every atom of his self-control.

"You don't belong in California," Millie said with un-characteristic firmness. "You're a Minnesota man, and it's high time you realized that."

"But I—" He broke off as something nudged his left ankle. Looking down, he met the enigmatic stare of Frankie Five. He was in no mood to discover whether this Frankie was as irascible as the previous model, so he slid his foot further under the table and refocused on the Graces.

"I stayed away for Laney's sake," he said baldly. "Because I was no good for her. But things are different now, so if she can love me the way I . . ." He wondered at the sudden warmth in his cheeks. Was he blushing?

Caroline put her knitting aside and folded her gnarled hands on the table. "When did you decide all of this?" she inquired with the equanimity of a courtroom judge.

"I've loved her forever," Jeb admitted. "But I never allowed myself to dream about marriage. Not until now."

"Well, then," Caroline said with that unnerving composure. "I gather you'd like us to talk to her."

"No!"

Caroline's lips twitched at his horrified reaction. "Then what do you—"

"I don't know anything about being romantic," he blurted. "All I know is that flowers and chocolate are involved." Feeling a tug on his shoelace, he gave his foot a gentle shake to dislodge Frankie Five. "And French restaurants, and—"

Aggie snickered.

Jeb's cheeks grew even hotter. "Laney loves French food," he said defensively.

"All right." Caroline aimed a quelling look at Aggie. "We'll advise you, Jeb."

"Thank you," he breathed. With the Graces on his side, how could he lose? He leaned back in his chair, not even minding when Frankie Five mistook the move for an invitation and hopped onto his lap. "So what should I do?" he asked as he scratched behind the cat's ears.

"Be patient," Caroline said. "She's had three romantic relationships, and she was even engaged to one of those men, if only for a day."

Jeb's hand stilled on the back of Frankie Five's neck. "She was never seriously in love with those other guys," he protested.

"We're aware of that. But she tried to be, and that's significant."

Frankie Five squirmed under Jeb's hand, demanding attention. Jeb complied, absently stroking the cat's smooth back while staring at a smudge of cherry pie filling on his plate and mentally digesting Caroline's words.

Judging by those kisses, Laney was already more than half in love with him. But he didn't want her leaping into a romance with him only to regret it later.

"I take your point," he said at last. As difficult as it had been to humble himself before the Graces, seeking their advice had been a good move. Lifting his gaze from his plate, he eyed the three wise women with deepening respect.

"So what she needs is time," Millie said gently.

"And space," Aggie put in. "You don't have to be with her every single minute."

"And forget the kissing," Caroline said.

"*What?*" Obviously, he'd been too hasty in ascribing wisdom to the Graces. "That makes no sense at all!"

"Spoken like a man," Caroline observed dryly.

"I *am* a man," Jeb shot back. "Why can't I kiss her?"

"Time and space," Caroline reminded him. "Don't rush her. Don't crowd her. That's very important, Jeb."

"All right," he said unhappily. He couldn't tell them that he had already kissed their girl pretty thoroughly, and that he had no idea how he was going to fend her off the next time she grabbed his ears and pulled his face down to hers. But he would do his best to follow their advice, especially as he still had a lot of things to work out before he could ask Laney to marry him.

"Do this right," Aggie said, "and you'll find yourself

wearing a wedding ring. Then you can kiss the daylights out of the girl whenever you feel like it."

"For the rest of your lives," Millie added dreamily, both plump hands pressed over her heart.

Figuring he'd better get out of there before they changed their minds about supporting him, Jeb carefully tipped Frankie off his lap.

"All right," he said again. He pushed back from the table, his chair's legs screeching against the oak-plank floor. "Thanks for the pie. And the talk."

The Graces stirred, but Jeb put out a hand, palm down, and signaled them to remain seated.

"I can let myself out," he assured them. "I'll think about all of this and talk to you more later."

He exited the kitchen and headed for the hall closet, where he retrieved his jacket. Sliding his arms into that garment, he marveled that his talk with the Graces had gone even better than he'd dared to hope.

He was whistling as he went out their front door.

* * *

Jeb was barely out of the kitchen before Caroline began to shake with silent laughter. If there was anything more adorable than a proud young man humbling himself for love's sake, she sure didn't know what it could be.

"How the mighty art fallen," Aggie murmured, and then she giggled behind her hand.

"Hallelujah!" Millie agreed in a noisy whisper, and then she giggled, too.

"Shh!" Caroline stabbed a finger toward the hallway, where Jeb could be heard opening the closet to get his jacket. Aggie and Millie pressed their hands over their mouths and endeavored to contain their mirth.

Caroline cocked her head, listening intently to make sure Jeb didn't hear the commotion and return to the kitchen to see if anything was wrong. She was relieved when he shut the closet door and continued down the hallway, treading on the squeaky board next to the staircase before his footsteps were abruptly silenced by the living room carpet.

He started whistling. The cheery tune wasn't one that Caroline recognized, but Jeb had been making up his own songs for years. She would have liked to hear more of this one, but the front door banged shut.

And Laney's thoroughly vetted, fully approved suitor was gone.

Aggie and Millie gave themselves over to riotous laughter that nearly toppled them from their chairs.

"D-did you see his face when Caro told him to f-forget the k-kissing?" Aggie was chuckling too hard to talk straight, let alone mimic Jeb's slack-jawed, disbelieving stare, but she did her best.

"Yes!" Millie slumped forward, elbows on the table as she held her grinning face between her palms. "That was more fun than chasing a g-greased pig on the F-fourth of July!" she stammered between fits of giggles.

"You two are acting like silly schoolgirls," Caroline admonished, even as the corners of her own mouth turned up.

Oh, well. This kind of joy was what kept them all young.

Still smiling, Caroline got up to make a fresh pot of coffee. When her sisters calmed down, they'd all join hands and express their gratitude to the Lord.

And then they'd have some more coffee and get back to their knitting.

Chapter Twenty

THE SUN WAS SHINING BRIGHTLY in a cloudless blue sky, but that wasn't what dazzled Jeb's eyes as he stood on the sidewalk in front of Willie's Diner at ten o'clock on Monday morning. No, the dazzler was Laney. Achingly beautiful in a demure black dress, her wool coat draped over one slender arm, she bent next to Francine's front door and peered into the outside mirror to apply some sweet pink lipstick.

Jeb longed to kiss that lipstick right back off, but he was resolved to keep his mouth to himself, at least for the present. As much as he hated to admit it, the Graces had been right to caution him against overwhelming Laney with passion. She needed a slow, patient wooing, and Jeb was determined to give her that.

She wasn't making it easy. Last night when she'd showed up at his place after the baby shower looking gratifyingly eager for more of his kisses, he'd had to distract her by asking some questions about the Bible. Then he'd reminded her of the late hour, and of the panel discussion on weddings she was to participate in this morning at some Minneapolis country club. Before she could argue, he'd hustled her out the door with a quick kiss on her forehead and a promise of breakfast at Willie's before she took off for her etiquette gig in the Cities.

He hadn't dared to walk her home. He'd just stood on his back steps and watched until her kitchen lights came on.

She must have wondered what was going through his mind, but she hadn't asked. That moment was surely coming, however, so Jeb's brain was scrambling to formulate a plan for handling it.

Maybe he could think up some more questions about apostles and epistles to distract her with.

She finished dragging the lipstick over her luscious mouth and met his eyes in the mirror. When she mashed her lips together, parted them, and then mashed them again, Jeb nearly lost control and reached for her. Was that alarmingly sexy lip action somehow necessary to set the color she'd just applied? Or had she noticed how his gaze was riveted to her mouth and decided to torture him?

Recapping the lipstick, she straightened and turned and smiled up at him, her blue eyes sparkling in the sunlight. When she dropped the lipstick into the bag swinging from her shoulder and edged closer, angling for a kiss, Jeb's mind went blank.

If she reached up and grabbed him by the ears, his willpower was going to sizzle and evaporate just like the drops of water Willie threw on his griddle to test its readiness for pancakes.

Her flirty, confident smile wavered. She was about to ask what was wrong, and all Jeb could do was stand there stupid, paralyzed by panic.

She opened her mouth, but then closed it and gave her head an almost imperceptible shake. Sensing her mental shrug, Jeb guessed she had concluded he was too shy to kiss her in broad daylight on the sidewalk in front of Willie's.

Too shy! He might have laughed out loud if he hadn't been so relieved. As she pulled her handbag in front of her body and rummaged for her car keys, Jeb chewed the inside of his cheek and wondered if he could avoid being alone with her for a few days. Just until he figured out how to deal with all this excruciating temptation.

Producing her keys with a jingling flourish, she looked up and smiled again. "I'm still amazed that you got up so early just to have Willie's French toast."

"I didn't." Jeb croaked the words out of a mouth gone dry from watching her put on that lipstick. "I got up early to have Willie's French toast with *you*."

"Your voice sounds funny." She gave him another of those puzzled looks. "But I guess you're not used to talking this early in the day, are you? I'm sorry for being such a chatterbox in there."

"I like hearing you chatter." He waited for her to step aside, and then he opened Francine's door.

She tossed her coat and bag onto the passenger seat and was about to slide behind the wheel when two sharp blasts from a car horn drew her attention to the street.

As she straightened and waved and called a cheery greeting to the veterinarian, who was passing in his pickup truck, Jeb felt the familiar resentment twist his gut. But when she nudged his arm, wordlessly encouraging him to lift his own hand and wave, he actually did it.

Because she was right; it was past time to let go of the old grudge. Staring at the truck's brake lights as the veterinarian—okay, *Luke*—slowed for a turn, Jeb recalled what Jerry DeSantis, the head pastor of Laney's church, had said in yesterday's sermon: *The best way to demonstrate your gratitude for God's forgiveness is to forgive others.*

"Ugh!"

Startled by the feminine exclamation of disgust, Jeb jerked his gaze back to Laney and found her scowling at her reflection in a dark-tinted window of the Explorer, which he'd parked next to Francine.

Finger-combing the sun-drenched curls surrounding her face, she muttered, "This hair is out of control."

She said that like it was a *bad* thing. If she only knew how ardently Jeb longed to push his own fingers into that delightful riot of curls.

"You look good," he said carefully. In fact, she looked *too* good. He needed her to be on her way before he forgot his noble intentions and kissed her breathless.

She expected to be home by five o'clock, and she'd asked Jeb to bring her back to Willie's for cheeseburgers tonight. That meant he had just seven hours to figure out how to make it through the entire evening without kissing her.

If only he could catch a cold. If he started coughing and sneezing all over the place, she wouldn't be so eager to swap germs with him.

She gave up trying to fix whatever she thought was wrong with her hair and turned to look at him. "Don't worry if you notice some activity at the tearoom. The real estate guy will be showing the building today." She nibbled nervously on her thumbnail.

"Are you okay with that?" Jeb asked.

She pulled her thumb away from her mouth and nodded determinedly. "It's time, Jeb. I have to let go."

He was so proud of her. He probably could have bought her tearoom with the wad of emergency cash he kept in his sock drawer in L.A., but she didn't want him bailing her out. She had courage, his Laney.

Making a loose fist, he brushed his knuckles against her velvety cheek. "You're going to be just fine, sweetheart."

Her eyes widened at the endearment. No, he'd never used it before, but after yesterday's kisses, why should it surprise her? He hadn't given her an *I love you*, not yet, and he wouldn't be in a position to offer marriage until he'd settled some questions about his career and had a better idea where he was headed in life. But hadn't she guessed how he felt about her?

"Jeb, I'm going to put the puzzle away." She spoke quickly, as though determined to get the words out before she changed her mind.

He didn't hide his surprise. "You don't want to hang it on the wall with the others?"

"No. I'm not even sure why I've kept it on the table all this time."

"You were angry," he said, understanding at last. "Mad at God for taking your mom."

It had been a long roller-coaster ride of hope and despair: Cancer and remission. More cancer. Another remission. And then Hannah had gotten sick for the third and final time.

"You're right." Distress puckered Laney's forehead and her beautiful blue eyes glistened with tears. "Leaving that puzzle on the table was a way of . . . reproaching God." Her voice dropped to a horrified whisper. "Oh, Jeb, that's so wicked! How could I have presumed—"

He stopped her words by gently pressing the pad of his thumb against her lips. "We can't do this now, princess. Save it for tonight."

She nodded, getting control. "Yes, all right."

He simply had to lean down and kiss her. But remembering just in time that her mouth was off limits, he altered course and touched his lips to her cheek, instead.

Her mood changed in an instant. "Not much of a goodbye," she pouted prettily.

"Sorry." Jeb glanced at his watch. "But I'm due at the gym."

"Pastor Jerry!" she cried. "I forgot all about your meeting, and now I've made you late."

"Not yet, you haven't." Sliding a hand under her elbow, he urged her into the car. "Drive carefully."

"I will. And you go easy on Pastor Jerry, okay? He's a lot older than you, and—"

"I won't hurt Pastor Jerry, princess. Now hit the road." He waited for her to settle into her seat, and then he shut the door.

She blew him a flirty kiss and backed out of her parking space. And then she drove away, leaving him staring after her with a sappy grin on his face and a heart overflowing with joy and wonder and gratitude.

* * *

"Are you all right?" Standing in the center of the basketball court, Jeb tucked the ball under his arm and eyed his panting, beet-faced opponent with concern.

"You bet!" Pastor Jerry DeSantis wheezed cheerfully.

The guy had some skills, but he'd have to look over his shoulder if he wanted to see forty-five again. And although years of smoking hadn't done Jeb's endurance any good, basketball was still his game.

Even so, the head pastor of Laney's church had thrown his whole heart into their play, and Jeb admired that.

After yesterday's worship service, Jeb had spent thirty minutes closeted with the affable man whose face drooped like a bulldog's. They were just beginning to discuss some heavy issues when Jeb noticed the time and remembered his and Laney's promise to meet the Graces for brunch.

"I hear you know what to do with a basketball," Pastor Jerry had said as they shook hands in parting. "Care to show me tomorrow morning? We could play some one-on-one and then talk further."

Jeb had eagerly agreed.

So they'd met, and they'd played, and just now the guy had groaned and slumped forward, hands braced on his knees as he fought to catch his breath.

Jeb eyed him uneasily. "How about a break?"

"I'm fine, the pastor gasped. "I just wish you weren't so tall. And so fast. And so disgustingly young."

Jeb couldn't hold back a grin. "Let's go sit down," he suggested. "I can't kill Laney's pastor. She'd never forgive me."

Pastor Jerry nodded toward the bench on the sidelines where they'd left their gym bags. "Go have a seat. It shouldn't take me more than ten minutes to crawl over there and join you."

Jeb laughed and took the long way, dribbling several figure eights before lighting on the bench.

"Showoff." Pastor Jerry plopped down beside him with a grunt and then tugged up the hem of his T-shirt to wipe perspiration from his forehead.

"You've got some moves," Jeb offered.

"Twenty years ago, maybe." Pastor Jerry leaned over and rummaged in his gym bag. Producing a plastic water bottle, he sat up and popped the cap. "Now that I've proved I'm just an ordinary middle-aged guy who's losing his hair and gaining a paunch, let's move on to the counseling."

"Not until you stop looking like somebody about to have a heart attack," Jeb said, only half joking. "Drink your water."

While Pastor Jerry tipped his bottle and noisily rehydrated, Jeb tapped his fingers against the basketball he held on his knees and gazed up at the gym's steel roof joists and prayed for the poor old guy's health.

"Want to talk now?" Pastor Jerry asked after a minute.

"If you don't mind," Jeb said.

Pastor Jerry nodded. "Yesterday you indicated that you're confused about a number of things. Maybe you'd like to start with whatever's weighing heaviest on your mind right now."

"My music," Jeb said without hesitation.

Except for Laney, he had never had a confidant. But even though he'd known Jerry DeSantis for a mere twenty-four hours, he felt that he could tell the guy anything. The pastor had heard some very blunt talk yesterday morning—in a church, no less—but he hadn't even flinched at references to things like illegal drug use and sex with women whose names Jeb had never bothered to ask.

"Go on," Pastor Jerry urged.

Still holding the ball, Jeb slumped forward and propped his elbows on his spread knees. "I don't know how I'm going to spend the rest of my life without music."

"I'm not following." Pastor Jerry recapped the water bottle and tossed it back into his gym bag. "Yesterday you said you intended to call it quits with your band, but I didn't get the impression that you meant to give up music entirely."

"I thought I could let go of the band but keep making

music," Jeb confessed. Staring at the basketball as he turned it around and around between his palms, he did his best to explain. "I thought, what about a different band? A band that wasn't so . . ." He twitched a shoulder, annoyed that he wasn't expressing himself better. "But last night I realized I've been thinking like an alcoholic who insists he can manage his drinking problem when everyone else knows he can't." He shook his head. "I can't manage this."

He was as close to tears as a guy like him ever got, but he made himself continue. "So I guess I'm afraid. What if I give up music and find there's nothing left of *me*?" He thrust the ball away from him, watched it bounce several times and then roll to the other side of the court.

"Why are you assuming God wants you to give up music?" Pastor Jerry asked. "What if he just wants you to make music that glorifies him?"

"Christian music?" Jeb pushed unsteady fingers through his sweat-dampened hair. "I thought about it. Briefly. But it could never work."

"Why not?"

Making no effort to conceal his irritation, Jeb turned to stare at his companion. "Come on, Jerry. You know what I am. Where I've been. A guy like me doesn't have any right to—"

"What you *are* is a Christian," Pastor Jerry said firmly. "As to where you've been— That's all forgiven now."

"I tried writing a few songs," Jeb admitted. "But it's clear I'm no preacher."

"You don't have to be. Just be honest."

Jeb sighed. "If only it could be that simple."

"It *is* that simple. Jackson, your talent is a gift from God.

Don't close your mind to the possibility that he might be calling you to use it for his own purposes."

"But I'm not worthy. I've done awful things."

"We're all of us sinners, Jackson."

"Yeah, but my case is different." Staring at the wall on the far side of the basketball court, Jeb struggled to articulate his biggest worry. "I know God has forgiven me. But I've done a lot of bad things that can never be made right, and I'm still profiting financially from that old life."

"Are you talking about royalties from your records?"

At last, the guy was catching on. "I have three albums out," Jeb said. "I'm ashamed of them now, but they're insanely popular, and I can't stop them from being sold. So I'll just keep getting richer, and that's not right."

"I see." Rubbing his jaw, Pastor Jerry appeared to give that some thought. "If it were me," he said slowly, "and if I couldn't stop those records from being sold, I might think about giving my royalties to worthy causes."

"It's dirty money," Jeb reminded him.

Pastor Jerry shrugged. "It was earned legally. And as you say, you can't turn off the spigot and stop that money from flowing into your bucket."

Could that be the answer? In the past few years, Jeb had contributed to quite a few charities—mostly ones benefitting children, because Laney was so nuts about kids. He couldn't even count the times he'd whipped out his checkbook after seeing her cry over one of those TV commercials about starving children. So why couldn't he just sign over all of his future Skeptical Heart royalties to people who would use that money to feed kids and tell them about God?

He wouldn't starve. And neither would Laney, if she

married him.

Although he'd made several million dollars from his music, he'd never been interested in accumulating things like exotic cars, glass beach houses, fine art, and designer clothes. As a matter of fact, his material needs were so few that he could give away every penny he made and go back to living on the modest inheritance he'd received from his father.

And then he could start over, this time with a Christian band.

"Yes," he breathed. Possibilities exploded like beautiful fireworks inside his head. "*Yes*."

He stood and grabbed his gym bag. "I need to get home and make some arrangements," he said distractedly. "Thanks for meeting me today." He took several long strides toward the exit and then halted.

A quick glance around him confirmed that he and the pastor were still the only people in the gym. Feeling oddly self-conscious as he walked back to the bench, he had to force himself to meet the older man's questioning gaze.

"Pastor Jerry?" He pushed the words out before he lost his nerve. "Will you pray with me?"

A wide smile transformed the man's droopy face. "I'd be honored, Jackson."

Chapter Twenty-One

IN THE MUSIC BUSINESS, everyone knew somebody who knew somebody, so Jeb had to make only three calls before one of the somebodies he knew put him in touch with the president of a major Christian record label. Jonathan Rice seemed deeply interested in Jeb's conversion experience, and by the end of a ten-minute phone call, he had invited Jeb to meet him in Nashville on Wednesday.

Since Jeb intended to fly to Nashville and back on the same day, he decided not to tell Laney about the meeting until his return, when he hoped to have some good news to report.

He worried that she would sense his elation and ask what was going on. But as it turned out, she was late getting home on Monday evening, and nearly fell asleep over her onion rings at Willie's, so they didn't talk much.

She was breathless and distracted when she called him at six-thirty on Tuesday and said a large bridal shower was still underway at the tearoom. She told him to leave for the Bible study without her, and he did, but not before saying a prayer that things would go smoothly at the tearoom, and that she'd make some good money from that large party.

Pastor Ted had finished speaking and was taking questions when she finally slid onto the empty chair next to Jeb's and flashed him a weary but triumphant smile. Sensing her eagerness to speak, he leaned toward her, offering an ear.

"We had twenty-one people for the bridal shower," she whispered as she unbuttoned her coat. "They ran the Graces and me ragged, but they spent a fortune on food, and they were all so nice about everything."

She was having trouble wriggling out of the coat, so Jeb helped get her arms unstuck and then assisted in draping the garment over the back of her chair. She was still vibrating with excitement, so he leaned down again.

And almost died from delight when her sweet, soft lips accidentally brushed his ear.

"I think they had a good time," she whispered, "and they left a fantastic tip."

Jeb turned his head to share a smile with her.

"God bless 'em, every one!" she murmured.

"Amen," Jeb mouthed. She'd be able to pay some bills this month. He sat back in his chair and gave silent thanks to God.

After the Bible lesson, they were having coffee and mingling when Jeb happened to look over the back of Laney's head and saw a blushing, stammering Steve trying to ask her out.

Steve seemed like a good guy, but he'd missed his chance; Laney Ryland was now taken. Moving to stand just behind her left shoulder, Jeb caught Steve's eye and raised his chin a notch.

Get lost.

Steve mumbled an apology and took off like a startled rabbit.

"I was handling that," Laney said over her shoulder. "You didn't have to give him the Death Stare."

"I didn't give him the Death Stare," Jeb retorted. "You don't shoot a rabbit with an elephant gun."

The instant the words left his mouth, he realized he was

behaving like a jerk. He wasn't surprised when Laney whirled to face him, eyes narrowed in indignation.

His mouth worked, but his voice had deserted him, and he didn't blame it. He'd been Laney's boyfriend for just two days, and he had already screwed up.

She folded her arms. "Did you expect your kisses to rock my world and make me never want to look at any other man?"

Jeb stopped breathing. Expect? No. He'd just hoped, that was all.

"Because they absolutely *did*," she went on, a spark of deviltry lighting her pretty blue eyes. "But still," she added more seriously. "You shouldn't have done that to Steve."

"Or to you," Jeb said, breathing again. "I'm sorry for interfering. But I've never had a girlfriend before, so I'm not totally clear on how these things are supposed to work."

"Don't worry." Wry humor edged her tone. "I'm making allowances."

"Laney, about those other guys," he blurted. "Tom and Nathan." He hated asking in a room full of people, but the information might help him avoid messing up again, so he couldn't afford to wait for a more opportune time. "Where did they go wrong? I mean, how did they lose you?"

Her face softened. Her sweet blue eyes grew even more luminous, and her strawberry-colored lips curved into a tender smile.

"Laney!" A woman on the other side of the room waved and started toward them.

Laney waved back. Then she crooked a finger at Jeb, signaling him to bend down.

"They weren't *you*, Jeb," she said in his ear. "That's all.

They lost me because they just weren't you."

As he stood there dumbfounded and so grateful he almost cried, she patted his shoulder and turned away to greet her friend.

The evening's planned social activity was a roller-skating party. Even after her exhausting day, Laney insisted on participating, so Jeb drove her to the rink. And then he publicly declared his new status as her boyfriend by holding her hand as they skated in big circles on the old wood floor.

He left her side only once, when he bribed a bored-looking DJ to dim the lights and play the Righteous Brothers' "Unchained Melody", a song more than twice Laney's age, but one she'd fallen in love with as a teenager. He scored even more points for singing it to her as they skated arm-in-arm. And when she looked up at him and smiled, he just knew that that the stars in her eyes were because of him and not mere reflections of the mirrored disco ball twirling above their heads.

"I never dreamed you could be so romantic," she said, and his heart jumped over the moon.

He had to kiss her when they parted for the night. Just a little bit.

Then he kissed her a little bit more, and he wasn't even sorry. If the Graces had seen the way she'd been looking at him all evening, they would have understood.

* * *

Awakened by his jangling alarm clock at 6:45 on Wednesday morning, Jeb flung off his covers and leaped out of bed.

He sang in the shower.

Dressed and ready to go, he poured some coffee and sat

down at his kitchen table with his Bible. When he realized he wasn't craving a cigarette, he laughed out loud.

He'd finished three mugs of coffee and two long chapters in Psalms before a faint rumbling told him Laney was opening his garage door. He waited until she'd left for the tearoom, and then he headed out his back door, guitar case in hand.

His flight to Nashville was an hour late, so he had two more cups of coffee while he waited. On the plane, he drank another cup in the packed First Class cabin, his knees jiggling nervously as he stared out his window and mentally reviewed what he planned to say to the record mogul.

He made it to downtown Nashville right on time for his appointment. He presented himself at the headquarters of Bright Hope Records and was immediately ushered into a cavernous office, the walls of which were plastered floor-to-ceiling with gold and platinum records and other awards.

Behind a massive desk, a man of enormous girth hung up a telephone and rose like a full moon, soundless and unhurried.

Becoming aware of an uncomfortable churning in his belly, Jeb wished he'd had something besides coffee for breakfast and lunch. Caffeine jitters aside, he was just plain nervous. After nearly two decades of uncompromising self-reliance, he was about to humble himself and ask a complete stranger to assist him in building a new career.

"I'm Jonathan Rice." The big man approached Jeb for the requisite handshake. "Can we get you some coffee?"

"No," Jeb said quickly. "Thank you."

Jonathan shook his head at the woman who had escorted Jeb into the office and lingered in the doorway. She withdrew, closing the door behind her.

"Have a seat, Jackson."

"Thanks. It's good of you to give me some time today." The words rolled smoothly off Jeb's tongue. After years of watching Laney be polite to people, it was no great trick to emulate her good manners. He just had to remember that people liked to be answered with words, and not stares.

He set down his guitar case and was about to lower himself onto a heavily padded leather chair when he spotted a familiar music CD lying on a corner of Jonathan Rice's immaculate desk. He froze, dread trickling through him as he stared at the mocking, accusing cover of Skeptical Heart's third album.

Jonathan followed his gaze. "Ah, yes. Your latest." He walked back to his desk and picked up the CD. "I had my assistant run out and get it this morning." Extending his broad arm, he dropped the CD into the trash container next to his desk, where it landed with an embarrassing *thunk*.

Jeb swallowed hard. Why had he allowed himself to believe that he might find acceptance as a Christian recording artist? As long as radio play and record sales were beyond his control, he could no more distance himself from his old music than he could unzip his skin and step out of it.

"I listened to four tracks." Jonathan pointed at the trash container. "And I have to tell you, Jackson, that's not an album I'd want my sixteen-year-old daughter singing along with."

Jeb's gaze faltered. "I understand," he mumbled, shame heating the back of his neck.

How was it that he had always taken such care to preserve Laney's innocence but had never spared a thought for anyone else's? How many young minds had he corrupted with his songs?

As he stared at his shoes, the churning in his stomach reached an alarming intensity. "Coming here was a mistake," he said hoarsely. "I apologize for wasting your time." He grabbed his guitar case and headed for the door, dizzy and sick and praying he could find a men's room before it was too late.

"I don't believe we're finished," the big man boomed.

Jeb halted. He was trembling and sweating, but he turned and forced himself to meet Jonathan Rice's un-yielding gaze. Raising his chin a notch, he braced for the rebuke he so richly deserved.

"You have a remarkably expressive voice," Jonathan said, "and fantastic tone. You have an ear for melody and you write a great hook. Your lyrics—" He shrugged. "Well, apart from all the anger and vulgarity, they have a literary quality that's all too rare in this business. They're imaginative and evocative, and they hint at a very appealing vulnerability. Even your guitar playing is extraordinarily good."

Compliments? Jeb shook his head. "I don't under-stand."

Jonathan folded his arms. "To put it bluntly, Jackson, you're probably the best all-around artist who ever walked into this office. Too bad you've been squandering your God-given talent."

Too overcome to speak, Jeb simply nodded his un-derstanding.

He'd been a fool to imagine he could get a do-over for the years he'd wasted going his own stubborn way. He was a high-profile recording artist who had sinned so blatantly that any attempt to cross over to the Christian market would naturally provoke questions about his sincerity.

"You must be wondering why I invited you here today," Jonathan went on, "if all I was going to do was tear you down."

No, that was no mystery. "You were aware of my band's success and wanted to meet me," Jeb said dully. "But you'd never actually heard any of the music until today, when you sampled that CD."

"True. But I would have invited you here even if I'd heard the music before."

"Why?" The word twisted itself out of Jeb's throat.

Jonathan's lips quirked. "Because I'm a businessman, Jackson. A very successful businessman."

Jeb was again crushed by disappointment. Was money everything, then? Was this man, the president of a Christian label, no different from the greedy record executives Skeptical Heart had dealt with?

"I should explain that everything you see here—" Jonathan made a sweeping gesture with one thick arm, indicating his spacious, luxuriously furnished office. "—has come to me from the hand of God. And since he can take it all away in the blink of an eye, I try to keep my success in perspective. But I hope he keeps letting me make money because the more money there is, the more Christian music we can send out into the world."

He seemed to be waiting for a response, but Jeb was too overcome by relief and admiration to speak.

Jonathan unbuttoned his suit jacket and shoved it aside so he could thrust his hands into his pants pockets. "That's where I stand, Jackson. Where do *you* stand?"

Jeb hadn't been so humbled since the night he'd given his heart to God. "In all honesty, Jonathan, I haven't got the knack of 'standing' yet. I've been trying to figure out what's right, but I'm not finding all of the answers I need. So—" Jeb had to stop and clear his emotion-clogged throat. "So mostly I just keep falling on God's grace."

For several seconds Jonathan stared at him without expression, weighing that bald response. Jeb knew he'd failed to deliver the correct answer, and he was about to leave when Jonathan's wide face broke into a smile.

"I assume you're still contracted?"

Surprise delayed Jeb's answer for several seconds. Then he nodded and named his record label.

Jonathan removed his hands from his pockets and leaned over his desk to press an intercom button. "Sarah, ask Troy Bangs to come in here. And get Jolene and Michael, too. And Char Blacklick, if she's in town." Removing his finger from the button, he spoke to Jeb again. "My people will look into it. If you can stomach losing a great deal of money, we can probably get you out of your contract."

"It was never about money," Jeb said. "All I ever wanted was to make music."

Jonathan waved a hand to indicate a large seating area near the office's corner windows. "Then suppose we make ourselves comfortable, Jackson, and have a serious talk about your future."

Chapter Twenty-Two

"WHY ME?" LANEY GROANED as she swirled a rag mop over the flooded tile floor of the customers' restroom, sopping up water.

An adorable 4-year-old had apparently tired of the pink feather boa she'd borrowed from the dress-up chest, because she'd tried to flush it down the toilet. Squealing with delight at the miniature Niagara Falls she'd created, the child had flushed again and again before her blithely inattentive mother caught her.

During the ensuing commotion, a party of obnoxious college girls from Chicago had skipped out without paying their $92 bill. All three of the Graces had been busy elsewhere when Millie had noticed the empty table and spotted the snickering miscreants hurrying out the door.

"Mercy, but those mean little girls were fast!" a visibly shaken Millie had told Laney afterward. "I couldn't even get their car's license number."

After she'd soothed Millie, Laney had been heading back to the bathroom to sop up the sixth Great Lake when her real estate agent had phoned with the disheartening news that he'd just received an insultingly low, take-it-or-leave-it offer for the building.

"Although after another day like this one," Laney grumbled as she wrung out her mop over a plastic five-gallon bucket, "I might be willing to *give* this place away."

"Laney?" Aggie poked her head in the doorway. "How are you doing?"

Laney thrust her bottom lip forward and blew out a

breath, ruffling the curls that had flopped across her brow. "I can't complain," she said wearily.

"Sure you can." Flashing a conspiratorial grin, Aggie stepped into the room and shut the door. "Just don't let Caroline hear you." She reached for the mop.

Laney tightened her grip and swung the mop to one side, out of her great-aunt's reach. "No, Aggie, I've got this. But thank you."

"Why don't you go home as soon as you finish in here?" Aggie stepped gingerly around the puddle and backed up against the sink counter, out of Laney's way. Folding her plump arms, she added, "We'll close up today. You go have an early supper and a hot bath and then tuck yourself in bed with a good book."

That sounded like heaven, but Laney gave her head a resolute shake and returned to her mopping. "Thanks, but I can hold it together for another couple of hours. Besides, we're running low on cookies, and if I don't get some made today, I'll have to come in extra early tomorrow morning."

"But you look worn out," Aggie protested.

"I am, but it's my own fault. We didn't leave the skating rink until midnight, when it closed, so I barely had five hours of sleep."

Several times, Jeb had suggested she'd been working too hard to stay out so late, but she hadn't wanted the magical evening to end. He'd looked so happy, and it had all been so romantic.

Laney's mop slowed as she remembered the tender kisses they'd shared at her kitchen door. Afterward, she'd gone upstairs and donned a long white nightgown and twirled around her bedroom just like Audrey Hepburn, hugging her pillow and singing that bit from *My Fair Lady* about how she could have danced all night.

Then morning had come, and climbing out of her cozy bed had required tremendous willpower. She'd made it to the tearoom at her usual time, but she'd been slogging through a marathon of disasters ever since.

"Aggie, why am I like this?" she asked suddenly. "Why do I get bent out of shape over things like a flooded bathroom? Mom never lost control the way I do. What was her secret?"

Tilting her head to one side, Aggie regarded her with a sober expression. "It was no secret, Laney. She told you often enough. Why don't you just slow down for a minute and think about it?" She pushed away from the counter and quietly left the room.

"I'm too tired to think about it," Laney muttered, but as she again wrung out her mop, she recalled her mother's frequent reminders about the importance of maintaining a habit of gratitude.

"That's my problem," Laney murmured as she mopped around the base of the toilet. "Lord, please help me be more aware of my blessings."

For the rest of the afternoon, she paused every few minutes to think of at least one blessing and breathe a quiet prayer of thanks. When she forgot to set her oven timer and ended up burning a batch of delicate almond cookies, she was dismayed for only a moment. Then she remembered how much fun baking with her mother had always been, and how their mistakes had always seemed so hilarious, and she felt another warm rush of gratitude.

At last she headed home. She couldn't wait to tell Jeb

about her breakthrough, but when she pulled into his driveway, the Explorer was nowhere in sight.

Her first thought was that he'd gone fishing. But as the garage door rumbled open, she saw his canoe still hanging from its hooks on the wall—and Jeb rarely went fishing without it.

Maybe he was spending some more time with Pastor Jerry or with one of the men he'd made friends with at church. He'd had a lot of "guy time" in the past few days, and the fellowship and instruction appeared to be doing him a lot of good.

Laney shrugged off her disappointment and went inside. Wherever he was, he'd be home before too much longer. If he'd made any plans for the evening, he'd have told her. Jeb was thoughtful that way.

After a quick look at her mail, she jogged upstairs and wriggled out of her vintage floral "tearoom" dress and into her favorite jeans—the ones that did absolute wonders for her too-plump backside. Grinning at her reflection in her full-length mirror, she buttoned herself into the clingy wine-colored blouse Jeb hadn't seemed able to peel his gaze away from the other night.

She pushed her fingers through her unruly curls, but as usual, it didn't help. Good thing Jeb liked her crazy hair.

She rummaged in her makeup drawer and found a pot of shimmery lip gloss, which she applied with her pinky. Jeb's gaze had been straying to her mouth a lot lately, and she couldn't resist the feminine urge to drive her man just a little bit crazy.

Back downstairs, she was peeling the potatoes for his favorite hotdish—creamy scalloped potatoes with ham and onions and peas—when she heard a car pull into one of the driveways. It didn't sound like the Explorer, and whoever it was hadn't pulled up far enough to be seen from the kitchen windows, so Laney put down her paring knife and went outside.

Rounding the corner of her house, she saw a silver Cadillac and a woman in a long black coat standing next to it, hands cupped near her face as she lit a cigarette. The sun had already set, but even in the twilight Laney had no trouble recognizing Jeb's manager.

"He's not home," she called with careful politeness as she walked toward the woman who'd been so rude to her on Sunday afternoon. "Can I help you with anything?"

"Where is he?" The demand was delivered in an impatient tone that made Laney blink.

"I'm not sure." The evening air was chilly, so Laney folded her arms for warmth. Realizing that she was still holding a half-peeled potato, she tucked it behind the crook of one elbow and hoped Shari Daltry hadn't noticed. What was it about this woman that made her feel like a gauche teenager? "I haven't talked to him since yesterday."

Shari turned her head to one side but kept her unfriendly gaze pinned to Laney as she drew on her cigarette and then released a lungful of smoke that curled artistically upward. "From what I've seen of this town," she said finally, "it's not big enough to disappear in."

Determined to live up to her etiquette training as well as her mother's godly example of answering insults with kindness, Laney was so focused on making a civil reply that her arms came uncrossed and the potato fell. It thudded against the concrete driveway and bounced a few times before rolling to an awkward stop next to one of Shari's glamorous high-heeled boots.

Shari tipped her head forward and peered down at it. "You dropped your potato," she observed with evident distaste.

"Sorry." Laney stooped to retrieve the traitorous tuber. "I was in the middle of making supper when you—"

"I need to speak to Jackson," Shari interrupted. "Urgently."

"He's not home," Laney reiterated with what she believed was remarkable patience. "Have you tried his cell phone?"

"Yes, I've tried his cell," the woman snapped. "He's not answering."

He was probably screening his calls, and Laney couldn't blame him. If he was with his new friends, he needed that fellowship a whole lot more than he needed his pushy manager harassing him about unfinished band business.

"I don't know where he is," Laney said, "but I'm sure he'll be home very soon." She hesitated for only an instant before adding, "If you'd like to wait in my house, I'll put on a pot of coffee and give you something to snack on while I finish getting supper in the oven."

"Well, wouldn't that be nice?" Shari drawled in an offensive monotone as she raised the cigarette to her lips. She inhaled deeply, her gaze riveted to Laney. "But, no." She flicked the cigarette away; its glowing orange tip described a long arc before dropping onto the grass. "I'm on my way to the Minneapolis airport to catch a flight back to L.A."

For crying out loud, this woman was even harder to get along with than Mrs. Lindstrom. Laney ached to invite her to get lost—and to take that still-burning cigarette with her. But somehow she managed to keep both her expression and her tone neutral.

"Maybe I could give him a message for you," she suggested.

"A message." A look of pure malevolence stole across Shari's face. "Yes, all right. You can give him a message."

Laney felt a tingle of foreboding. "I'll be glad to," she said uncertainly. "Is something wrong?"

"Oh, yah. You betcha," Shari confirmed in a distinctly insulting imitation of a Minnesota accent. "Something is definitely wrong."

* * *

"Mr. Rice?" Jonathan's gray-haired assistant stood just inside his office, one hand still on the doorknob as six people filed past her on their way out. "I'm afraid I wasn't able to get Mr. Bell a later flight, so he should leave within the next half hour." Her kind, intelligent gaze shifted to Jeb. "Unless you'd rather take a morning flight? I'd be happy to arrange that and get you a hotel room."

"Thank you." His gaze slid toward Jonathan. "But I need to get home tonight."

He had to see Laney. Had to hold her in his arms and tell her about all of this before he could begin to believe it was actually happening.

Skeptical Heart's rocket ride to fame had never thrilled him like this. Oh, he'd accepted the perks that had come his way: the limos and the alcohol and the drugs and the sex and the deluxe hotel accommodations. He'd partied like a rock star, that was for sure. But not for a minute had he ever imagined that anyone in that world genuinely cared about him.

Today, everything was different. Jonathan Rice and the six executives who'd just left his office were clearly interested in who Jeb was and in what he believed. And they had offered him a staggeringly awesome opportunity to partner with them and record Christian music.

"We'll get you home tonight, Jackson, don't worry. We just have one or two more matters to discuss." To his assistant, Jonathan said, "Have a car ready for him in twenty minutes." Then he clapped a hand on Jeb's shoulder and steered him back to the seating area by the windows, where just a short time earlier, Jeb had auditioned for the top management of Bright Hope Records.

The two men seated themselves in heavy leather armchairs on either side of the glass coffee table now littered with abandoned cups.

"Excuse me a minute." Jonathan scooted forward in his chair and reached for the notebook computer he'd left on the table. He pulled it closer to his knees and began stabbing at the keyboard with thick fingers.

While he waited, Jeb returned his guitar to its case and buckled it in. Then he sat back in his comfortable chair and stared out the 27th-floor windows at a sky filled with cotton-ball clouds.

What an amazing afternoon. Jonathan and his people had repeatedly expressed their eagerness to get him under contract. Jeb wouldn't sign any papers until his own attorney had looked them over, but in his mind the deal had already been sealed by handshakes all around.

This was the right thing to do. Jeb had felt God's approval settle over him like hot summer sunlight that passed through his clothes and his skin and sank deep into his chest, igniting an explosion of joy.

"How many songs did you say you have right now?" Jonathan inquired without looking up from his computer.

"Nine," Jeb replied. "The four you just heard plus five others. But the others are rough."

Jonathan's head jerked up. "Are you telling me you've written a whole album's worth of songs in just three weeks?

Jeb shifted uncomfortably in his chair. He didn't want to suggest he was somehow getting the songs from God, even if it sometimes felt that way. Because if God wanted someone to speak for him, would he pick a confused new Christian, one with a desperately wicked past, to do it?

"I've had a lot on my mind lately," Jeb said. "Reading the Bible. Going to church. There's been a lot of . . . emotion." That last word had refused to emerge without a struggle, so Jeb stretched his lips into a rueful smile. "I guess the songs are coming from that."

"Amazing." Jonathan's fascinated stare pressed Jeb like a physical weight. "Judging by the four songs you performed earlier, I'd say God definitely has his hand on you."

Jeb had no idea how to respond to that, and he could no longer withstand the other man's steady gaze, so he turned his eyes back to the window and the undemanding white clouds beyond it.

"I have an artist who's going through a prima donna phase," Jonathan said.

Startled by the abrupt change of subject, Jeb yanked his gaze back to the man, who was squinting at his computer screen and rubbing the cleft of his chin with an index finger.

"She needs a cooling-off period, so if we finalize your

contract in time, you can have her studio session."

Studio session? Jeb didn't even have a band yet.

"Here in Nashville. Seven weeks from now." Jonathan closed his computer's cover with a decisive snap.

"That's insane." It had never been Jeb's way to mince words, and at the moment he was too shocked to even try. "Finishing the songs won't be a problem, but it's impossible to build a band and have them rehearsed enough to start recording in just seven weeks."

"True." Wearing a sly expression eerily like the one Jeb had seen so often on Caroline's face, Jonathan sat back in his chair and propped his elbows on its broad armrests. "But you will do this impossible thing, Jackson, because I'm giving you Justin Kramer."

"*Justin Kramer?*" The man was a legend. Justin Kramer had produced some of the biggest rock stars in the business until five or six years ago, when he'd suddenly dropped off the radar screen. Was this where he'd ended up, in Christian music?

"I take it you've heard the name?" Jonathan's lips quivered; the man was struggling to suppress his amusement.

"Once or twice," Jeb said, fighting a grin of his own. For a chance to work with Justin Kramer, he'd put together a band and have them rehearsed and ready to record in seven *days*.

"He'll work you hard," Jonathan warned. "He'll be your harshest critic, but he'll also be your best friend. Nobody puts together a better record."

Jeb nodded dumbly. Justin Kramer could probably squeeze a good record out of a high school garage band.

"He's been working in Christian music ever since he got saved a few years back," Jonathan said. "In fact, his story's remarkably similar to yours. But I'll let him tell it to you."

Too amazed for speech, Jeb nodded again.

"Expect a call from him tomorrow," Jonathan went on. "I imagine he'll want you back here in Nashville by the weekend. We'll put you up in a hotel, and Justin will find you a rehearsal space. He knows everyone in Christian music, so just tell him what you're looking for, and he'll start sending you musicians to try out."

Jonathan said something else, but Jeb had stopped listening. His brain had snagged on that bit about returning to Nashville in just a couple of days.

He understood that he'd have to relocate. He could hardly build a band and record an album in Owatonna. But how could he leave Laney when she was just beginning to fall in love with him? For the next three months or so, he'd be working nonstop; there would be no time for even a weekend trip home.

On the other hand, what better way to give her all that time and space the Graces said she needed? If her new feelings for him could fade during a three-month separation, then Jeb wasn't the right man for her, after all.

He'd have to do some praying about all of that. But for now, he needed to pull his mind back to business.

"I'm not objecting," he said carefully, "but what's the rush?"

"Isn't it obvious? We want to drop this new album while people are still wondering why Jackson Bell left Skeptical Heart at the top of his game."

"But my name won't be an asset," Jeb pointed out. "In

the Christian market, it'll be a liability."

"That's where you're wrong, my friend." Jonathan's elbows remained on his chair's armrests as he brought his hands together and linked his fingers. "Christian music fans listen to secular music, too. Even the people who say they listen only to Christian music are still exposed to secular stuff in restaurants, in retail stores, and so on. Also, it's impossible to avoid entertainment industry news on TV and the Internet, so it's not just Skeptical Heart fans who'll recognize your name."

Jeb was beginning to understand. "So my notorious name will guarantee exposure for the new music," he said slowly. "Because people will wonder what a hard case like Jackson Bell is doing with a Christian band."

"Exactly." Jonathan nodded his satisfaction, but then his bushy eyebrows squeezed together. "Just understand that this album will need to be a cut above the ordinary. You know this business, Jackson. We'll do a big PR blitz and get you some attention. But if you can't hold onto it, there will be no second chance."

"Understood," Jeb replied.

"I think we're done for today." Jonathan braced his hands on the sides of his chair and heaved himself up. "I need to get to my kid's soccer game, and you have a plane to catch."

Jeb rose and followed him to the door, guitar case in hand.

"They'll have a car waiting for you downstairs," Jonathan said over his shoulder. He opened the door, and then turned to face Jeb. "One last thing. Those four songs you shared earlier are exactly what we want. Keep writing about what you're feeling and what you're learning as a new Christian. This album won't be a neatly packaged lesson in theology. It'll be raw and honest. Accessible. You have a tremendous talent, Jackson, so just sing what's in your heart and trust God to use it as he will." Smiling, he offered his right hand to Jeb.

"Jonathan." Overwhelmed by gratitude, Jeb gripped the man's beefy hand and struggled to form a coherent sentence. "This opportunity. I can't thank you enough."

"Yes, you can. Put together a good band and make a record I can take home to my sixteen-year-old daughter." Still clasping Jeb's hand, Jonathan suddenly tugged on it, pulling Jeb into a firm embrace.

Stunned by his very first man-hug, Jeb held himself rigid, his left hand clenching around the handle of his guitar case as he wondered how to respond.

And then something inside him broke. An odd tightening was followed by a sudden, snapping release, as if an old tether had been stretched to its limit and then given way, freeing something it had restrained for a very long time.

Jonathan thumped his back and let him go. "I'll look forward to our next meeting," he said. "You take care, Jackson."

Jeb's mouth worked, but a rush of emotion had swelled his throat, pinching off his voice. Helpless and embarrassed, he shook his head.

Jonathan eyed him with kindly concern. "What is it, Jackson?"

Jeb cleared his throat, but when he opened his mouth again, there was no need to force the words out. They came easily, escaping in a glad rush, and it felt so good, so right.

"My friends call me Jeb," he said.

Chapter Twenty-Three

SOMETHING WAS WRONG. Jeb knew it the instant he removed his key from the Explorer's ignition switch and saw Laney waiting just outside her kitchen door.

She stood on the top step watching him, her arms folded across her chest. It was a chilly night, but instead of shivering and stamping her feet to warm herself, she remained utterly still. In the cone of light from the fixture mounted above the door, her eyes were black holes in her face, unreadable.

She called no cheery greeting as he climbed out of the SUV.

Fear shoved his heart into his throat. *Please*, he prayed silently as he hurried toward her. *Not one of the Graces.*

"What's wrong?" he demanded as he jogged up the steps and reached for her.

She sidestepped, pointedly avoiding his touch. Her slender arms remained tightly crossed in front of her body.

"Laney?" He was now close enough to see her eyes; they were puffy and red-rimmed. "What is it?"

"Your manager was here," she informed him in a small, dead voice.

Relief flooded Jeb's heart. This was something he could fix.

It was no hard trick to imagine what had happened: She'd had another stressful day at the tearoom, and just when she'd come home to put her feet up and read the newspaper and decompress, Shari had shown up looking for him.

Finding him away from home, Shari would have been both annoyed and annoying. Laney would have made every effort to respond with kindness, but that wouldn't have saved her from been filleted by Shari's razor-sharp tongue.

"I'm sorry you had to deal with her, princess. She had no business bothering you about—"

"She needs to talk to you." Laney dropped the words like stones, each one heavy and hard and cold.

Jeb's temper flared. How many times did Shari need to be told that he was finished with Skeptical Heart? "Laney, whatever she said, don't let it upset—"

"You'd better call her." Laney backed away, stepping across the doorsill and into her kitchen. "It's urgent."

"*Laney.*" Jeb caught the door as she tried to close it in his face. "What exactly did she say?"

"It isn't my place to tell you. Go home and call her." She tried again to close the door, but Jeb managed to slip inside.

"Laney, please." Tamping down his exasperation, Jeb assured himself that he'd have this mess cleaned up in another minute, and then he'd share the exciting news about his day in Nashville. "Just tell me what happened."

She glared at him for a moment, and then she suddenly deflated. Her gaze faltered, her shoulders hunched, and her chin sank toward her chest.

"Oh, Jeb." Her voice wobbled on his name, and then it dropped to a horrified whisper. "Shari's pregnant."

He blinked. "What does that have to do with—" He stopped, suddenly getting it. "Princess, no. You've misunderstood something. What you're thinking— Well, it just isn't possible."

She raised her head and looked straight into his eyes.

"Obviously, it *is* possible," she said coldly. "And you know that very well, Jackson, because this isn't the first child you've fathered, is it?"

Jackson.

If she'd slapped him or spit in his face, he couldn't have been more shocked or more devastated. In all the years they'd known each other, she had never called him Jackson.

"You said you didn't have that kind of relationship," she accused, brushing away an angry tear. "You said it was all business, and I believed you. But it was a lie, wasn't it?"

"No, it wasn't!" he insisted.

Sure, Shari had hit on him a few times. And yes, he'd been tempted. But she'd been a valuable asset to the band, so he'd never have risked jeopardizing their professional relationship.

Unless he'd been too wasted to realize what he was doing.

As his inherent honesty forced him to acknowledge that possibility, his gaze fell away from Laney's.

She took that as an admission of guilt.

"I knew you did bad things." Twin tears slid down her cheeks, which anguish had stained a dusky pink. "But I never asked you about them because I knew that no matter what, you'd tell me the truth. So when you kept things from me, I never pushed, because I was afraid of what I might hear. But just this one time, I pressed you for an answer. I was jealous of her, I admit it, and so I asked you if—" Laney stopped and caught a ragged breath. "And you said *no.* I never thought you could lie to me, but you did!"

Jeb shook his head in desperate denial. He needed to pull her close and just hold on tight until they both stopped shaking and the world started making sense again, but when he opened his arms and swayed toward her, she swatted his hands away.

"Don't touch me! You lied!"

But he hadn't meant to do it. If he'd told her something untrue, he hadn't meant to do it. Why didn't she know that?

"Shari's going to have your baby and I—" Shaking her head, Laney emitted a harsh laugh. "But you don't want this baby any more than you wanted the other one, do you? Are you going to do what you did last time? Are you going to just walk away and tell yourself it's nothing to do with you?" She closed her eyes, squeezing out two more tears as she whispered, "You're just like my father!"

Appalled by that accusation, Jeb slumped against the doorframe.

"Go home," Laney commanded in a low, trembling voice. "Just go and leave me alone."

So this was the end. After sixteen years, Laney had finally lost her faith in him. She had stopped believing that underneath it all, he was a good person.

And if Laney couldn't believe it, then he didn't have a hope of ever making it true.

* * *

Alone in her kitchen, Laney pressed both hands against her face to cover her wicked mouth—too late.

What had she done? How could she have said those awful things to Jeb?

When she'd accused him of being just like her father, he had looked utterly defeated. He had offered not a single word in his defense, but with downcast eyes had turned and gone out and closed the door so gently that she'd barely heard it latch.

Laney swallowed convulsively, fighting a wave of nausea rolling in on a swelling tide of remorse.

She hated knowing he'd made a baby with Shari. And she hated that he'd lied about his relationship with the woman. But at least a lie could be forgiven and, in time, forgotten.

A baby was different. A baby changed everything.

In her mindless panic, Laney had said some unbelievably cruel things. But in her heart, she knew Jeb wouldn't make the same decisions he'd made last time. So the question now burning in Laney's mind was: How large a portion of his life would Shari, as the mother of his child, lay claim to?

Yes, Laney was jealous of the connection this baby would forge between Jeb and Shari. In the years to come, discussions would be held and compromises sought on things like education and where and with whom the child lived. And even if Jeb and Laney eventually married, Laney would have little or no say in any of those decisions.

She didn't doubt for a second that she would come to love Shari's baby. But this wasn't the sweet, uncomplicated future she had dreamed about.

She brushed tears from her cheeks and reminded herself that she wasn't the only one hurting tonight. Recalling the desolation she'd seen in Jeb's gray eyes when she'd ordered him to leave, she wanted to run after him and tell him how wrong she'd been and how sorry she was. But when she was still so upset, would that be wise?

She'd better give herself some time to calm down. And surely Jeb would need some time alone to process this shocking news—and to discuss it with Shari.

First thing in the morning, then. Tonight, she would pray for forgiveness—and for release from this awful, heart-twisting bitterness.

* * *

Still emotionally numb and hoping he stayed that way for a good long time, Jeb sat shivering on his screened porch in the morning twilight. Not counting the trips he'd made to the kitchen at regular intervals to refill his coffee mug, he'd been sitting there all night doing nothing at all.

Well, not nothing. He'd tried and tried to call Shari.

Then he'd booked a flight to L.A.

But otherwise, he'd just huddled in the wicker chair next to the back door, his old fishing coat buttoned all the way up, his bare hands wrapped around a warm coffee mug. He'd watched hundreds of stars crawl across the perfect black sky, and judging by the orange-pink glow now visible in the east, he'd soon see the determined sun heave itself over the horizon.

He had tried several times to pray, but he'd been unable to focus. So he'd given up and just sat on the porch drinking coffee and shivering.

He loved Laney with all of his heart, but he was beginning to be angry with her for giving up on him. He was fully aware that he'd never deserved her friendship. But considering that she'd forced it on him and then trained him to count on it, she had a lot of nerve revoking it now.

The wicker chair creaked as he uncrossed his legs. He was about to get up to refill his coffee mug when he remembered the pot was empty, and that he couldn't make a fresh one because he'd run out of ground coffee. He set the mug on the marble-topped table beside him, and then rubbed the whiskers on his chin and considered hopping in the Explorer to make a coffee run.

He could get some cigarettes, too.

No, better, not. He didn't want to risk running into Laney as she came out her kitchen door on her way to work.

He remembered his old man's stash.

Don't do it, his conscience begged, but he was already on his feet and making for the music room.

He sat down at the desk and opened the bottom drawer. For several moments, he just stared at the three bottles of whiskey his father had left behind. Then muttering one of the expletives he hadn't used in weeks, he scooped up the bottles and headed back to the kitchen, where he poured every bit of the stuff down the sink.

It smelled good. No sense in not admitting that.

It would have tasted even better. But as hard as he'd fought to clean up his life, he wasn't about to surrender now just because he'd gotten his pathetic heart stomped on.

He picked up the phone he'd left on the kitchen table and tried again to call Shari. It was two hours earlier in L.A., but he wasn't concerned about waking her up. After what she'd done to Laney, she deserved to lose some sleep.

She still wasn't answering.

He wondered if Taylor knew anything about this. An anomaly among rock drummers, who tended toward the psychotic, Taylor was a dropped-out sociology major who saw himself as Skeptical Heart's resident therapist. Whatever was going on with Shari, it was entirely possible that Taylor not only knew about it, but had already analyzed it.

Jeb placed the call.

"Jackson?" a sleepy voice inquired. "What time is it?"

"Early," Jeb admitted.

Taylor yawned. "Somethin' wrong?"

"Maybe. This is awkward, Taylor, but—" He had to force the words out. "Is Shari pregnant?"

There was a brief silence, and then in a wide-awake voice, Taylor said, "She told you?"

Jeb slumped onto a chair. "So it's true."

"Of course it's true." Taylor sounded almost offended. "Why would she lie about it?"

Jeb lowered his head and squeezed the back of his neck with his free hand.

Why had God allowed this to happen? Why *now*? Things had been going so well with Laney, and he'd begun to hope that—

"Jackson? You still there?"

"I'm here."

"Are you comin' back to L.A.?"

Jeb sighed.

Come to me, Jesus said, *and I will give you rest.* But since the night he'd fallen to his knees in that hotel room and offered his heart to God, Jeb's life had only gotten more complicated.

"Jackson?"

"Yeah," Jeb said wearily. "I'll be there today."

"For real?" Taylor sounded like a kid who'd just been promised a trip to Disney World. "So you're thinkin' about comin' back to the band?"

Thinking? That was a laugh. At the moment, Jeb's brain was so fried he didn't even know his own name.

Oh, wait. Yes.

His name was *Jackson.*

Pain slammed through him as he remembered how ugly those two syllables had sounded coming out of Laney's mouth. That utterance had flattened his spirit more effectively than any of the curses his drunken father used to hurl at him.

"Taylor, I'll talk to you later," he said, and ended the call.

He hadn't really doubted that Shari was pregnant. She was a hard woman, but she wasn't a liar. Still, he would insist on some tests before he made her any promises. He honestly couldn't remember being intimate with her, so he was going to need some irrefutable proof before he accepted this child as his own.

If it *was* his child . . . Well, he wasn't sure what would happen next, but he knew he couldn't let it be like before. He'd protect this baby at any cost. So if it took a promise of marriage to make Shari agree to carry it and allow it to be born, Jeb would make that promise.

Laney was lost to him in any case.

He knew he ought to pray, but bitterness had seeped into his ravaged heart, so he returned to his music room and sat down at the piano hoping to find oblivion. He considered for a few moments, and then he lifted his hands and—

Slammed them down, producing a loud, discordant sound to accompany his own anguished cry.

Chapter Twenty-Four

AT 7:30 ON THURSDAY MORNING, Laney phoned the Graces. She explained that she'd had a terrible argument with Jeb the night before, and said she couldn't face the day without first confessing her fault and asking his forgiveness.

If Caroline was shocked, she didn't let on. "You go mend your fences," she said. "Aggie and Millie and I will hustle over to the tearoom and find your baking list and get started on it."

"It's on my desk," Laney said. "Thank you." She hung up and resumed pacing in her kitchen, biting her thumbnail as she mentally rehearsed her apology to Jeb.

Ordinarily, she wouldn't have disturbed him at what was to him the middle of the night. But she suspected he was having as much trouble sleeping as she'd had, so she wasn't going to wait any longer to end this awful estrangement. She had just spent a heart-healing thirty minutes in prayer, and now she meant to march over to his house and pound on his door until he woke up and let her in and heard her apology so he could have peace, too.

She stopped pacing to stare out her corner windows at the breaking dawn. As soothing pinks and calm oranges flooded the eastern sky with hope, she prayed again, her eyes and her heart wide open.

"Lord, please let me be a comfort to him. Help me to say exactly what he needs to hear this morning."

A minute later, she stepped inside his screened porch. Like hers, Jeb's kitchen door was half glass, and through that window she could see him slumped at his table, both fists propping up his jaw. He was reading his Bible.

She tapped on the glass. He startled and looked up. She let herself in.

Haggard and even more unshaven than usual, he regarded her with wary eyes.

"I'm so sorry," she blurted. "I didn't mean it, Jeb."

He closed the Bible and stared intently at its cover.

She knew his silence wasn't meant to punish her, but it hurt all the same. When had Jeb ever needed to guard his heart from *her*?

"I don't remember everything I said," she confessed, twisting her fingers together, "but I'm sure it was all mean and untrue, and I'm sorry. I shouldn't have brought up that other baby. God has forgiven you for your past, and I had no business throwing it in your face."

"You couldn't help being reminded of your father." Still not looking at her, Jeb traced the embossed letters on his Bible's cover with an index finger. "I understand that."

"But you're *not* like my father, Jeb. I shouldn't have said that. It's just that I felt—" She squeezed her fingers, frustrated by her inability to recall the speech she had so carefully composed. "I mean, I was just so—"

"Disillusioned," he supplied.

"No, that's not—"

"Because all these years," he continued inexorably, "you've been clinging to the idea that I'm a wonderful person at heart."

"You *are*, Jeb." Determined to regain control of the conversation, she rushed on: "And what I said to you was unfair and mean, so I came to ask you to forgive me. If you need to be mad at me for a while, that's okay. I'll leave if you want. But not before I tell you how sorry I am."

"I didn't lie to you," he said quietly. "I could never do that."

"I know." Feeling a tear tremble on her cheekbone, she impatiently dashed it away. "It was stupid of me to—"

"But I've hidden some truths." He finally raised his eyes to her face. "And maybe that amounts to the same thing."

"It doesn't matter now. Honestly, Jeb." She pulled a chair away from the table and moved it as close as she could to his, and then she sat down and put an arm around his hunched back. "I love you," she said. "Right this minute, I love you more than ever before."

He tried to shrug away from her touch, but she wrapped her other arm around him, too, and held on tight.

"I *love* you, Jeb."

She didn't need a response. All she needed was for him to believe her. She squeezed him hard, wishing she could somehow push the words inside him and make him accept their truth.

"I wanted so much to be a good Christian," he said, "but I'm the same man I was before. I'm still angry and confused and—"

"But Christians aren't perfect, Jeb." Loosening her hold on him, she eased back to see his face. "We don't always think and act the way we should." She gave a self-conscious little laugh. "Haven't I proved that?"

When he tried to look away, she caught his face between her hands and made him watch as she shook her head slowly and emphatically. "You are *not* the same man. You've come a long way, Jeb."

He grasped her wrists and gently pulled her hands away

from his face.

"It's . . . possible that Shari's baby is mine," he said with obvious difficulty. "I was drinking and doing drugs. There are whole days and nights that I can't remember."

Sensing that he had more to say, Laney remained still and waited.

"Last night—" His voice had roughened; he cleared his throat. "Last night I told you I'd never touched Shari, but now . . ." He released her wrists and shook his head at the Bible in front of him. "I don't know if that's the truth." He raised tortured eyes to her. "Laney, I don't know anything."

"You should know this," she said firmly. "Even if you did father that baby, God has already forgiven you."

"Has he?" Jeb's deep voice was barely audible, but his longing couldn't have been clearer.

She leaned her head against his shoulder. "I know you've done some bad things, Jeb, but didn't you ask God to forgive you for those sins? And since the night you did that, haven't you been trying your hardest to live a life that pleases him?"

Jeb made a choking sound and wrapped his arms around her. When he bowed his head and pressed his face against her shoulder, she reached a hand up through the circle of his arms and stroked the soft hair at his nape.

"Regret's understandable, Jeb, but hating yourself for the things you did before you became a Christian is like calling God a liar."

"I'm not calling God a—"

"Aren't you?" She turned her head to study his face. "His Word says that if you confess your sins, he'll forgive you. So what business do you have trying to hold on to guilt God has already taken away?"

He raised his head and palmed the back of hers to tuck it under his chin. Snuggling against him, she felt a sigh ruffle her hair. They were both still for a few minutes, and as she felt his body relax in small increments, she silently thanked God for helping him find peace.

"Laney."

"Hmm?"

"When you said that you loved me." His rumbly voice was adorably hesitant; she hid her smile against his flannel shirt. "How did you mean that, exactly?"

"I think you know how I meant it," she answered carefully. "But you might be a father now, and I think you need to focus on that and save any discussion about the two of us for later."

"You're right."

He withdrew his arms and leaned back in his chair. Laney sat up, too, unease rippling through her.

"And anyway," he said, "I have to leave for the airport in twenty minutes."

The airport. "You're going to see Shari?"

His eyes remained locked on hers as his head moved almost imperceptibly: *Yes.*

Laney swallowed hard. "You were planning to leave without saying goodbye?"

He continued to regard her steadily.

A tiny sound of protest escaped her throat, but then she got control and said in an almost normal tone, "But you'll come back."

More silence. His eyes begged her to understand.

She didn't understand, but was it any wonder that she loved him? Jeb would never make a promise he wasn't sure he could keep.

His cell phone rang, startling them both. He picked it up off the table and checked the display.

"Not her," he said tersely, laying the still-ringing phone back on the table.

Laney drew a slow breath before asking, "So you haven't talked to her yet?"

He shook his head and then looked out the window, his expression bleak. "But I'll insist on some tests before I make her any promises."

Promises? Laney stared. Could he be talking about *marriage?*

What about the fact that Shari wasn't a Christian? What about the fact that Jeb didn't even like her very much?

What about me?

Laney pressed a hand over mouth to keep those selfish words from escaping.

She was no disinterested party to be advising him on this difficult matter. He was smart enough to call Pastor Jerry or Pastor Ted for counseling. She would just have to give her fears to God and trust him to work things out for the best.

"Laney." Jeb turned to look at her. "I am so sorry."

She blinked and felt a hot tear slide down her cheek. His tortured eyes followed its slow progress to the edge of her jaw.

His Adam's apple moved.

"The hockey game," he said, clearly desperate to change the subject. "I'll be sorry to miss it."

Laney opened her mouth to ask what game he was talking about, but then she remembered the tickets the

Graces had given him. Weren't they for this Saturday night?

"Maybe one of the guys from church . . ." Jeb let that sentence dangle meaningfully.

"No," Laney said. "I don't think I'll be in the mood to go."

"I hope you change your mind," he said. "But if you don't, you might offer the tickets to Ollie."

"Yes," she said without enthusiasm. "Crystal—his wife—loves hockey as much as he does."

"That's good, then." Jeb cleared his throat. "Princess, it would be better if you left now."

Better, how? she asked him with widened eyes.

He sighed. "I think we've said everything. I'm glad you're not mad at me anymore. I would hate to leave here knowing that you—" He shrugged and looked away from her.

"We're okay, Jeb," she assured him. "Just like always."

Deciding that he was right about not prolonging this painful goodbye, she rose from her chair and leaned over to press a lingering kiss on the crown of his head. He sat motionless as she wound her arms around his neck and hugged him, but she understood. This was all very hard for him, in part because he knew how hard it was for *her*. So he was fighting his feelings, just as he'd been doing all his life.

"I'll be praying for you," Laney promised in a shaky voice, and then she forced herself to let go of him and move toward the door. Aware that she was being followed by a pair of haunted gray eyes, she spared him further agony by not looking back.

He didn't say a word as she slipped out the door.

Chapter Twenty-Five

AS HIS PLANE TAXIED to its gate at LAX, Jeb turned his phone back on and tried first Shari's cell number and then her landline. She still wasn't answering, so he called Taylor.

"Hey, man." Taylor answered in a husky morning voice.

Jeb glanced at his watch. Subtracting two hours for Pacific Time, he noted that it was barely 11:30 in L.A.

Back home, Laney would be up to her elbows in flour and butter, keeping the tearoom's customers supplied with fresh hot scones. In Nashville, Jonathan Rice's clever minions would be hammering out a plan to divorce Jeb from his current record label.

"Sorry for waking you up twice in one day," Jeb said. "I'm trying to get in touch with Shari, but I'm not even getting her voice mail. Any ideas?"

Taylor yawned into the phone. "I would've told you before, but you hung up before I could explain. She started havin' trouble with her cell phone when she was in Iowa for her brother's wedding, and she didn't get back from there until late last night, so she hasn't had a chance to get it fixed yet."

"But she's not answering her landline, either," Jeb said.

"Yeah, 'cause she's stayin' at my place."

Jeb blinked. Why would she be staying with Taylor?

"I'd let you talk to her," Taylor went on, "but she's asleep right now. That trip was hard on her. Bad scene with her parents. And with her morning sickness and all the stress over wedding plans, she can't hardly—"

"*Wedding* plans?" If Jeb hadn't been hampered by a

seatbelt, he'd have risen to his feet in outrage. The woman was assuming an awful lot!

"Yeah, I think she wants to tie the knot three weeks from Saturday," Taylor said. "I told her not to wear herself out, but you know Shari."

Yes, Jeb knew Shari. But she didn't know *him* very well if she thought she could railroad him into marriage. He didn't know what God expected of a man in these circumstances, but until he did, he was going to be extra careful not to make any wrong moves.

"She didn't tell me she'd set a date," he said dryly.

"Yeah, well, she says if she's gonna do it, she might as well do it quick and get it over with," Taylor said. "Not very flattering, I guess, but any man would be lucky to get a woman like Shari."

Shaking his head, Jeb wondered about Taylor's definition of *luck.*

"So, you plannin' to be there?" Taylor inquired.

"I don't know," Jeb said, although his thoughts were flowing more along the lines of never, no way, not in a million years. "She and I will have to work some things out before I decide."

"What things?"

Jeb frowned at the uncharacteristic note of belligerence in Taylor's voice. "Personal things," he said shortly. Like a paternity test, for starters. "Listen, Taylor, I'm at LAX right now, just getting off a plane. I'd like to come over to your place and talk to Shari."

"Okay, man. Want me to pick you up? On the way home we could stop and get her favorite coffee and muffins for a surprise."

"A ride would be good," Jeb said. Taylor's place was less than twenty minutes from the airport, so he wouldn't have long to wait. "Thanks."

"No sweat. Just let me find my pants and write a note in case Shari wakes up. Be there in a few."

Jeb didn't have any bags to claim, so he got a cup of coffee and went out to the passenger pick-up area to wait for Taylor. He had just tossed his empty cup into a trash receptacle when Taylor's silver Jaguar convertible rumbled to a stop just a few feet away.

Jeb opened the passenger door, tossed his backpack behind the seat, and climbed in.

"So what's up?" Taylor asked.

Jeb pulled the seatbelt across his chest. "Like I said, I need to talk to Shari."

Taylor nodded as he eased out into the traffic. "She'll probably be awake by the time we get there."

"Yeah. About that. What's she doing sleeping at your place?"

"Exactly what you think she's doing." Taylor gave him a look of smug amusement. "Don't tell me you've gone and joined the morality police, Jackson. Not after all the times we—"

"It's a fair question," Jeb pointed out. "Why's she sleeping with you when she's making plans to marry *me*?"

"Marry *you*?" Taylor sliced him with a look of pure outrage. "What are you talkin' about?"

Jeb just shook his head. "All right, I give up. What game is she playing?"

Taylor hit the brakes and yanked the Jag back to the curb, where they came to a violent stop. "She's marryin' *me*!"

he shouted.

Jeb opened his mouth and immediately closed it again. "Awkward" didn't even begin to describe this situation. After a moment he asked, very carefully and not without a great deal of hope, "Do you think the baby might be yours?"

"*Might* be?" Taylor wrenched his door open and leaped out of the car. Stunned, Jeb watched him place a hand on the Jag's hood and kick his body over it like a guy in an action film. An instant later, he nearly tore Jeb's door off its hinges. "Get out!" he growled.

He wanted to fight? Well, fine. It had been far too long since Jeb had had the pleasure of hitting somebody. He jerked his seatbelt off and swung his right leg out of the car.

He never made it to a standing position. Taylor's roundhouse punch caught the left side of his jaw and sent him sprawling.

Lying on his back, his left foot caught inside the idling Jaguar, Jeb looked up at Taylor's furious face and tried to make sense out of what was happening.

"Get up!" Taylor snarled.

Jeb pulled his foot out of the car and sat up. Then he slowly shook his head, partly to ascertain whether Taylor's stunning punch had knocked his brain loose, but mostly because he had just remembered he was a Christian now, and Christians didn't pound the snot out of people.

Not even people who were begging for it.

"*Get up!*" Taylor kicked Jeb's thigh with the pointed toe of a cowboy boot.

Jeb rolled up to his feet and backed away, hands up and palms facing the irate drummer. "Hold on, Taylor! What's this all about?"

"You can't have her!" Taylor threw another punch.

Jeb ducked just in time to save himself from losing a few teeth. "Are you crazy?" he yelled, backing up some more. "I don't *want* her!"

"You don't?" Taylor rubbed his skinned knuckles and shook his long blond hair back from his face. "Then why do you want to see her so bad?"

Keeping a wary eye on Taylor's dangerous right hand, Jeb said, "Because she's pregnant and the baby might be mine."

Quick as a Texas rattlesnake, Taylor's left fist slammed into Jeb's belly.

Jeb staggered backward, bent double and fighting to suck in some air. "Taylor," he wheezed, raising one hand in surrender. "Come on, man. I don't even know what this is about!"

"You know what it's about," Taylor said, but he sounded less certain now.

"No, Taylor, I *don't* know." Jeb cautiously unbent his body, pulling himself up to his full height in front of the drummer who had once seemed to cherish an almost childlike admiration for him. "Shari came to Minnesota and told my girlfriend she was pregnant. But I never—" He stopped, remembering the haze of drugs and alcohol that had shrouded his former life, and decided to rephrase that. "If I ever spent a night with her, Taylor, I don't remember it."

"How could you not remember?" Taylor demanded, his face flushing with renewed outrage.

Jeb just looked at him and waited for him to figure it out.

Finally, Taylor nodded. "The baby's mine, Jackson. I

don't know how you got the hare-brained idea that—"

"She tricked me, Taylor." Yes, it was childish and unprofessional; Shari had been downright weird lately. "She wanted me back in L.A., so she made trouble between me and my girlfriend. I don't know if she just hinted or if she flat-out lied, but the message my girlfriend gave me was that Shari was pregnant and the baby was mine."

"The baby's *mine*," Taylor said through clenched teeth.

"Yeah." Jeb rubbed his bruised jaw with one hand and his aching belly with the other. "Yeah, man, I got that."

"And she's marryin' *me*." Taylor jerked a thumb toward his own heaving chest.

"Yeah." Jeb looked up at the blue California sky and choked back a hysterical laugh. "Congratulations."

* * *

Late Thursday evening, Laney sat at her dining room table and divided the "Paris at Night" puzzle into six large sections, which she carefully laid in the box she'd saved. If she ever changed her mind about hanging the puzzle in the hallway with those her mother had completed, it would be a quick job to put it back together. She'd make the tiny H-shaped hole in the midnight sky less noticeable with the black guitar pick Jeb had given her to glue behind it.

Rubbing the smooth plastic pick between her finger and thumb, she turned to look at one of the framed photographs on her mother's antique sideboard: Jeb at his piano, head thrown back and eyes closed, lost in his music.

She ached to know he was all right. He hadn't promised to call from Los Angeles, but she could call him, couldn't she? Just to see if he was okay?

No, she couldn't call. She was crippled by the fear that

he'd insist she was better off without him. And she just didn't think she could bear hearing him suggest, very gently, that she not call him again.

Her heart fluttered painfully as she laid his guitar pick on top of the puzzle and closed the box.

She was headed upstairs to bed when her phone rang. Assuming it was Ollie or Crystal returning her call about the hockey tickets, she grabbed the phone off her bedside table and didn't bother to check the display.

"Hi, princess."

Surprise and relief robbed Laney of breath. For several seconds, speech was impossible.

"Laney? Are you there?" Jeb sounded anxious and exhausted.

"I'm here," she said. "Are you okay?"

"Laney, it's not my baby."

Her legs gave out and she sank onto her bed. Silent tears slipped down her cheeks as gratitude broke over her in powerful waves.

Thank you, Lord. Thank you.

"Laney? Did you hear me?"

"I heard," she said faintly. "I'm glad, Jeb."

"She knew all along who the father was. She and I never—" He cleared his throat. "But she was mad at me. Frustrated. And she said something about hormones and mood swings and a huge fight with her parents. Whatever the reason, she deliberately misled you in order to make trouble for me."

What a dirty trick. Laney was amazed by the woman's callous deception, but she was too relieved to dwell on it.

"I'm just glad it's over," she said.

"Yeah. And I'm sorry about—"

"Don't, Jeb. We dealt with all of that before you left, remember? We're okay."

"Yeah." He sighed the word, still sounding dead on his feet. Had he even gone to bed last night?

His cell phone was picking up a lot of background noise. Laney could hear a male voice droning through a PA system that Flight Something-Something to Nashville was ready to board its First Class passengers.

Clearly, Jeb was sitting in an airport departure lounge. But he hadn't said he was coming home.

"Are you still in Los Angeles?" Laney inquired uneasily.

"Yeah." Jeb's reply carried a distinct note of reluctance. "The airport."

The fingers of Laney's right hand pressed down on her quilt and then slowly curled until she was gripping a handful of fabric. "Are you coming home?"

When Jeb didn't immediately answer, she knew. He was getting on a plane, but not one heading for Minneapolis-St. Paul.

She really ought to have seen this coming. She'd gotten an earful of this stuff from Sarah Jane and her other women friends: Men often pulled back the moment a relationship took a serious turn. Tell a man how you felt about him before he had accepted his own feelings, and you risked making him feel trapped.

And just that morning, Laney had uttered those three man-terrifying words: *I love you.*

"Princess." His deep voice was full of apologies. "I'm not coming home right now."

Squeezing her quilt even more tightly, Laney shot an

exasperated look at the ceiling. Sometimes she really hated being right.

Well, she would just have to prove to him that her love wasn't a cage. She'd back off; she'd give him all the time he needed to think things through.

He'd come home eventually. All she had to do was be patient.

"I know you have a lot to straighten out." She was proud of her calm, reasonable tone. "Your career, and all."

"Yeah," he said with palpable relief. "I flew to Nashville yesterday morning. I was going to tell you all about it when I got home last night, but then that other stuff happened. Anyway, I'm going back to Nashville to—"

"It's all right, Jeb. I know you're busy, and I—"

"Could you speak up?" he interrupted. "It's noisy here."

"I know you're busy," she repeated. "It can't be a simple thing to break up a successful band."

"No," he agreed. "It's going to be a mess."

Skeptical Heart was based in L.A., but since Jeb was going to Nashville, that must be where the record company was located. There was undoubtedly a great deal of money at stake in this breakup; it might take him weeks to sort things out. And for all Laney knew, he was already trying to hook up with a new band.

Her brain stumbled over that thought, but what had she expected? That he'd retire at the age of twenty-seven and settle down in Owatonna to raise tomatoes and hang out at the curling club? Jeb lived and breathed music. Of course there would be a new band.

Laney was suddenly a lot less sanguine about his coming home. With his heavy touring schedules, Jeb lived on the road for weeks or even months at a time. And it would be just like him to refuse to draw her into a relationship that would always be strained by the demands of his career.

She shook that disturbing thought out of her head and hastily changed the subject.

"I got an offer on my building today," she blurted.

"Did you? Was it a good one this time?"

"Yes, very. Just four thousand dollars less than the asking price. So I'll be—"

"Thank you, Mr. Bell." A woman's voice. "Enjoy your flight."

"I hate your phone," Laney grumbled. "It picks up every sound within a mile of you."

"Yeah, sorry. What were you saying about the offer?"

"Just that I'm going to accept it."

"I know that'll be hard," he said. "I'm glad about the money, though."

"I'll be okay, Jeb. I know it's time to move on."

"That's good." He seemed to hesitate, and then he continued in a deeper tone. "Laney, I won't be seeing you for a while. I'm trying to get a new project going, and if everything works out, I won't even have a free weekend for the next three months."

Laney's hand went to her throat. So this was it. He was making the break.

Telling her not to wait for him.

"Mr. Bell?" a woman drawled in a rich southern accent. "Could I trouble you to move up a row? This is seat 4B, and you're supposed to be in 3B."

Jeb mumbled an apology, and the woman said something that Laney didn't catch, and then Jeb was back on the phone. "Laney? I'd rather tell you about all of this later, when things are more settled."

She pressed her hand over her mouth, smothering an involuntary cry of distress. A tiny squeak broke through, but Jeb didn't notice because he was being distracted again.

"Jackson?" Another woman. This one sounded very young. "Aren't you Jackson Bell?"

"I'm on the phone," he said dangerously, and then he sighed. "Sorry, princess. I meant to call you earlier, but my whole day's been crazy."

"It's all right," she said.

"Are you okay? You sound—"

"I'm fine," she said firmly, because she *would* be, somehow. "But I have to go." A tear was rolling down her cheek, and she'd start sniffling at any moment now. "You get some rest, and call me sometime when you're not busy fighting off autograph hounds, okay?"

"Yeah, okay. But Laney? When you sell the tearoom, be sure to take some time to look around and think about what you really want in life."

She didn't have to think about it. She wanted *him*.

But he was being stupid again.

"All right, Jeb." She swallowed hard, but couldn't push the hurt down. "And you take care of yourself. 'Bye."

She pressed the End Call button and allowed her tears to flow unchecked.

Chapter Twenty-Six

SEATED AT HER DESK IN THE TEAROOM'S KITCHEN, Laney scanned the contents of a letter she'd just received from the Internal Revenue Service.

"Why am I surprised?" she said under her breath. Sighing, she set the letter aside and opened the rest of the day's mail—the tearoom's electric bill and the monthly invoice from the service that laundered her napkins and tablecloths. Both bills included notices about rate hikes.

"Blood from a stone," she murmured darkly, refolding those papers and tossing them onto a growing stack of unpaid bills. In the two weeks since Jeb had been gone, her money troubles had multiplied at an alarming pace.

"What did you say, dear?" Millie looked over from the prep counter, where she was slicing cucumber sandwiches into little triangles for the Graces' afternoon tea.

Laney sighed. "I just got a Notice of Audit letter from the IRS. Also, the electric company and the laundry service are raising their rates."

"Don't worry," Millie said. "We'll think of some more ways to economize until you get this place sold."

"I don't know what else we can do," Laney said bitterly. "I guess we could give up the tablecloths and start using paper napkins, but we kind of need our electricity." Pushing a mess of curls away from her right eye, she shared her biggest worry: "Millie, this buyer's financing is still looking iffy. What am I going to do if the sale falls through? It could be a long while before—"

"Hush, dear. It'll all work out. You'll see."

Laney startled as the phone on her desk rang, but she didn't pick it up. Caroline was out front; she would answer the call.

"Laney," Aggie said from the doorway. "The dining room's empty now. Do you want me to lock up?"

Laney glanced at her watch. "Yes, go ahead. Thanks."

Aggie grabbed the ring of keys off the counter and jangled them as she walked away.

"Laney," Caroline called from the dining room, "Your real estate agent is on Line One."

"There now," Millie said comfortingly. "That'll be good news."

Laney picked up the phone on her desk and forced a cheery tone."Hi, Ron. Do we have a closing date?"

No, they didn't have a closing date. The buyer's financing had fallen through. Holding the phone against her shoulder, Laney massaged her aching temples.

"Okay, Ron," she said wearily. "Thanks for letting me know." She hung up the phone, and then she folded her arms on her desk and laid her head on top of them.

Lord, why is everything so hard? I'm so tired of trying my best and being smacked down at every turn. It would be so much easier to bear if I had Jeb to share this stuff with.

"Is she crying or praying?" Aggie asked in a loud whisper.

"Both," Laney admitted as she raised her head and saw all three of the Graces watching her with obvious concern. She gave them a wan smile. "The building's not sold, after all. The guy didn't get his financing."

"Ah," Caroline murmured. "It wasn't God's timing, then."

That mild comment lit Laney's fuse. "Apparently not," she snapped. "Apparently, his plan is for me to go bankrupt!"

Instead of registering shock at that outburst, Caroline's eyes narrowed in keen speculation. "This is about Jeb, isn't it?"

"No," Laney said quickly, but then she realized that it probably was.

She'd told the Graces only that she and Jeb had argued bitterly about a personal matter, and that they'd made up just before he'd returned to L.A. on urgent business. She figured they had guessed the rest—that she'd fallen in love with him, and that she was afraid he didn't feel the same way.

"Stop trying to forget him," Caroline advised. "You've been best friends for most of your life, and you don't just forget something that special."

Aggie nodded sagely. "And the harder you try, the more miserable you're going to be."

Laney stared at her great-aunts. "Who said I'm trying to forget—"

"You don't talk about him," Millie interrupted gently. "And when we mention him, you always change the subject."

"I'm dealing with this the best way I know how," Laney said evenly. "He didn't promise to come back, and I can't just put my life on hold until he decides how he feels about—" She sighed and shook her head. "Anyway, I have other problems right now, so I'm not going to spend any more emotional energy wondering and worrying about Jeb."

Maybe if she kept telling herself that, her stubborn heart would get the message. It was worth a try, wasn't it?

"He'll be back," Millie said.

That earned her a sharp glance from her elder sister.

"We don't know that," Caroline said. "But letting that go for a minute." Her gaze shifted back to Laney. "We know you're upset about having to sell this place. But you need to stop thinking you've failed your mother's memory. Hannah couldn't have worked any harder than you've been doing, and she wasn't any smarter than you are, either. If she had lived longer, I'm sure she would have sold this place by now."

Aggie nodded her agreement. "Sometimes these things just happen."

"This business was your mother's delight," Millie chimed in. "But you're not having any fun with it, Laney. So why aren't you asking God to let you move on to something else?"

"Maybe I'm afraid," Laney admitted. Her folded arms slid off the desk and plopped into her lap as she leaned back in her chair. "Because when things change, you never know if they're going to get better or worse. And what if they get worse?"

"What if they get better?" Aggie countered with a touch of impatience. "What if things could be a *lot* better, but they're not because you don't have the guts to take a chance?"

"Don't be too hard on the girl, Agatha." Caroline removed her glasses and bent forward to polish them on the hem of her dress. "She's had one trouble after another since Hannah passed."

"And even before," Millie said. "Nursing her sweet mother and then losing her that way."

Laney shook her head, rejecting their sympathy. "When I remember how well Mom dealt with her troubles," she said quietly, "I feel so ashamed of my whining."

"I know what you mean." Caroline slid her glasses back onto her face. "Hannah had courage, that's for sure."

Aggie put an arm around Millie, whose eyes had filled with tears.

"She was barely twenty-two when your father left," Caroline remembered.

"She was heartbroken and scared to death," Millie said, slipping away from Aggie to pluck a tissue from the box on Laney's desk. "Her parents were killed in a car crash while she was still in college, so she had no family to help her."

"Except us," Aggie said. "But she didn't know that at first."

"But she managed to pull herself together," Caroline said, straightening her own back. "She had a baby coming, so she couldn't afford to sit around feeling sorry for herself. She worked hard and she prayed. And in time, her broken heart healed."

Millie blew her nose into her tissue and then said, "A Christian doesn't have the right to squander her life on bitterness, Laney."

"I hear you." Conviction thickened Laney's voice.

"When Hannah was fighting the cancer," Caroline said, "she worried about leaving you. But she wasn't bitter, even at the end. She knew you'd be okay."

Suffused with shame, Laney shook her head. She hadn't been okay since her mother's death. She'd been foundering.

She pushed her chair away from the desk and stood. "I need to be by myself for a while."

"Go ahead," Caroline urged. "We'll take care of every-thing here."

Millie smiled sweetly. "You go and have a good, long

think about all of this. When we sit down to our tea in a few minutes, we'll pray for you."

"Thank you. For everything." Her vision blurring, Laney hugged each of her great-aunts. Then she snatched a couple of tissues from the box, gathered her jacket and purse, and went out the kitchen door.

At home, she changed her clothes and then decided to go for a walk. She started to grab her jacket off its peg by the kitchen door, but reached instead for a hooded Minnesota Twins sweatshirt Jeb had left behind. It was ridiculously huge on her, falling almost to her knees, and she surprised herself by chuckling as she rolled up the sleeves—and rolled, and rolled.

She flipped the hood over her head and went out the door.

Her aimless stroll took her to Lake Kohlmier, where she sat on a bench facing the water. Raising her eyes to the sky filled with scudding gray clouds, she whispered a prayer.

"Lord, I don't want to fight you anymore. You know the desires of my heart, but it looks like you have other plans for my life. I want to be okay with that, but I'm going to need a lot of help. Please show me how to let go of Jeb and how to stop feeling so bitter about everything."

She sat quietly for a few more minutes and thought about her mother. Everyone agreed that Hannah Ryland had died bravely. But what was even more admirable, Laney now realized, was that her mother had *lived* bravely. She had learned to depend on God, and through obedience to him, she had discovered contentment and even joy.

"Lord," Laney whispered as she rubbed tears from her cold cheeks, "teach me how to trust you the way she did."

When the fresh autumn breeze pushed Jeb's hood from her head and tugged at her curls, she barely noticed. She sat very still, marveling at the warmth spreading inside her.

"Thank you," she whispered as peace seeped into her heart.

Chapter Twenty-Seven

AS THANKSGIVING CAME AND WENT, Caroline was proud of the way Laney held her chin up even though her heart was broken. The girl was maturing fast, and she was beginning to demonstrate a remarkable faith in God.

Her financial difficulties were only increasing. She was now thinking about selling her house and most of her furniture and moving into a modest apartment. And bless her heart, she wasn't even crying about that. Not as far as the Graces could tell.

Christmas arrived, and although Jeb hadn't called Laney in two whole months, he'd sent her a beautiful hand-sewn quilt that must have cost the earth. Caroline managed to peek at the card accompanying it, which read:

Merry Christmas, Laney.

I thought you might like this for your hope chest.

I want to call you, but I'm afraid I'd blurt out what I'm working on, and I want it to be a surprise. In the meantime, I think about you and pray for you every single day.

Love, Jeb

Caroline didn't know whether to be pleased or annoyed by the cryptic note. Whatever his surprise was supposed to be, the boy was making a big mistake by not calling. And what was that business about Laney's hope chest? Was he asking her to wait for him, or was he telling her to find another man?

Laney didn't appear to know, but she was holding up admirably. She was Hannah's daughter, that was for sure.

A week after Christmas, Laney's building sold for a decent price. The buyer paid cash and wanted possession right away, so at the end of the second week of January, Laney closed the Three Graces Tearoom for good. She sold the kitchen equipment and the furniture at auction, along with every bit of the pretty English bone china she had helped Hannah collect just a few pieces at a time.

Prior to selling the china, Laney had urged the Graces to choose a tea set for themselves, as a memento. They'd been glad to do that. But then Caroline had noticed the poor girl wasn't keeping anything for herself.

Some things hurt too much to remember, Laney had said. And Caroline, who hadn't been a crybaby even when she *was* a baby, had had to turn away and wipe something out of her eye.

But the girl would heal, and she'd get that tea set back just as soon as her great-aunts slipped away to Glory.

For now, though, she was still young, and it was high time she started chasing some dreams.

Especially that long-legged dream who'd stolen her heart and then forgotten how to use a telephone.

Caroline didn't think God had closed the door on that romance. No, those silly kids had just messed things up somehow. So wasn't it a good thing they had the Three Graces to help them find their way back to each other?

After spending weeks praying about the matter and considering it from every angle, Caroline had finally conceived a good plan. So one evening in late January as she and her sisters sat in their living room with their television blaring the evening news, she cleared her throat meaningfully.

Millie's knitting needles stilled.

Aggie lowered her newspaper.

Caroline settled Frankie Five more comfortably on her lap. "We're going to find Jeb," she announced. "And then we're going to bring him home."

A slow, satisfied smile curled Aggie's mouth. She folded her newspaper and laid it on the coffee table. Then she picked up the TV remote and turned off the news program.

"But how can we find him?" Worry deepened the wrinkles in Millie's forehead. "If we ask Laney for his phone number, she'll want to know why we want it. And when we tell her why we want it, she won't give it to us."

"True," Caroline said. "That's why we'll be hiring a private investigator to find him."

"That's your great plan?" Aggie rolled her eyes. "Caro, Laney's sure to have his number stored on her cell phone. All we need to do is get into her purse when she's not looking, and—"

"We are not getting into her purse," Caroline said sternly. "That would be sneaking."

"Sneaking?" Aggie snorted. "What would you call hiring a private investigator to find her boyfriend?"

"I'd call it fun!" Millie clapped her hands. "Let's do it!"

Aggie lowered her head and peered over her glasses at Caroline. "You already looked at her phone, didn't you?"

Caroline petted Frankie Five and stared at the blank television screen.

"So what was the problem?" Aggie persisted. "Doesn't she have his number stored?"

"She's got one of those fancy new phones," Caroline muttered.

"Ah," Aggie said knowingly. "You couldn't figure out how to access the directory."

Even at the grown-up age of seventy-nine, little sisters could be annoying. Caroline sniffed and tossed her head.

"Sneaky." Millie looked at Caroline with undisguised admiration.

"So we're agreed then." Caroline raised an eyebrow at Aggie to discourage further objections. "We're hiring a private eye."

"They're not called that anymore, Caro." Millie gave her head a regretful little shake as she went back to her knitting. "They don't wear suits and hats, either, which is a crying shame. I always liked seeing a man in a hat."

"Bogart as Sam Spade." Aggie nodded approvingly. "Now *there* was a man."

"Never mind that," Caroline said. "*Think.* Who do we know that knows a private investigator?"

Tapping a finger against her chin, Aggie suddenly brightened. "We could try Hillary Graham's new husband's brother," she said, referring to the best man at a wedding the Graces had brought about just last year. "Remember? The Minneapolis police detective on permanent disability after being shot in the back? I think Hillary said he was some kind of computer wizard, and that could be real handy."

"I'd forgotten about him," Millie said. "He seemed like a nice boy. If he's still not married, we should—"

"We'll find somebody for him," Caroline assured her. "But right now, our priority is Jeb. Let's give Hillary a call and ask her to put us in touch with the cop. If he can't help us, he's sure to know somebody who can."

"But what will we do after we find out where Jeb is?"

Millie asked.

Aggie's arms jiggled as she pumped two fists in the air. "Road trip!"

Millie looked worried again. "Aren't we getting a little old to be gallivanting around the country? He's probably in Los Angeles, you know, and that's a long way. We'd have to go over mountains to get there."

"Oh, don't be such a wet blanket." Aggie pushed her glasses higher on the bridge of her nose. "At our age, we could do with a little excitement."

"Just calling him on the phone might not get us the results we want," Caroline explained to her youngest sister. "We're going to have to show up in person."

"With pie," Aggie said.

Caroline inclined her head in agreement.

Millie still looked troubled. "So we just show up—with pie—and tell him Laney's pining for him and he needs to come home?"

"That's the plan," Caroline said.

Aggie nodded supportively.

Millie shook her head. "But what if he just eats the pie and doesn't come?"

"He'll come," Caroline said. "Don't you remember how that boy humbled himself to ask for our advice? Millie, only True Love could have driven him to that."

"All righty, then." Millie rolled up her knitting and stuffed it into the bag at her feet. "Let's get busy and hire ourselves a private eye!"

* * *

Jeb didn't need the burst of applause from the five people in the recording studio's control room to tell him he'd just laid down a great vocal track.

"Amazing. What a voice!" Seated at the mixing console, beefy and bald Justin Kramer shook his head at Jeb through the glass wall separating them. "I loved the raw edge on that last line."

"My voice cracked," Jeb told his producer as he reached for the coffee mug he'd set on a ledge in the tiny vocal booth. He swallowed some lukewarm coffee and then said, "Let's do it one more time."

"No, this one was really good." Justin traded glances with the audio engineer next to him. "Let's hear the playback."

"No, that's okay." Maybe Justin was right. Besides, the song was hard on Jeb's voice, and he'd already sung it five times. He couldn't afford a blowout when he had to track lead vocals on four more songs before he and the guys started on the background vocals.

"Let's move on," he said. They had already been in the recording studio three weeks longer than they'd planned, and they were over budget to a degree that gave Jeb the cold sweats whenever he allowed himself to think about it. "I'm sorry it took me so many tries to get this one right."

"It takes as long as it takes," Justin said with a shrug. "Jonathan believes in you, and my orders are to make a good record." Justin's gold tooth flashed as he grinned. "We'll just have to make sure the big guy listens to the finished product before we present him with the bill."

It felt good to be recording again, and it was even more satisfying to be doing it with a bunch of Christians. The three guys in Jeb's new band could practically read his mind, and their playing was so tight that everyone who heard them said it sounded like the band had been together for years. Along with Justin, the best producer in the business and Jeb's new prayer partner, the guys challenged Jeb to reach higher, dig deeper, and go far beyond anything he had ever accomplished musically.

He couldn't wait to share all of that with Laney. He thought about her constantly and prayed for her just as often, but he hadn't called her since that difficult day in Los Angeles.

He'd sent her a Christmas gift with a note, and that was the only contact he'd dared. He didn't have time to go home right now, and he wanted to be holding *her* and not a telephone when he told her about the amazing things God had been doing in his life.

Because after she laughed and cried and kissed him, he meant to ask for her hand in marriage.

Soon, he promised himself. Not yet, but very soon.

* * *

For more than two weeks after closing the tearoom, Laney had worried about the Graces adjusting to the loss of the job they had so much enjoyed. She'd called them at least once a day, just to say hello and to ask if they needed anything. In the middle of the third week, they had delivered the firm but loving message that she should stop worrying about them and get on with her own life. They had gently explained that while they had enjoyed the work, they'd taken the job only to get dear Hannah started, and then they'd stayed on to support Laney. It had been fun, but now they wanted to turn their energies in other directions.

After Laney digested that surprising news, she realized that she, too, was eager to move on.

Since closing the tearoom, she'd written a résumé and combed the newspaper employment ads for a job. She'd had three interviews, two of which netted job offers that she'd ultimately decided against accepting. The last thing she needed right now was to fling herself into a dead-end job or to take up an unfulfilling career. Now that her bills were paid, she could afford to spend another month or two exploring possibilities and deciding what she truly wanted to do.

She'd signed up for two online classes in journalism. She was reviewing her mother's recipe files and thinking about putting together an afternoon tea cookbook. She'd started an exercise program. She'd joined the women's prayer group at church and was considering a couple of local ministry opportunities. She was spending time with her friends.

She wasn't truly content, but she was determined to get there eventually.

Four days before Valentine's Day, she made some mouthwatering black-walnut fudge as a surprise for the Graces. They were away from home when she tried to deliver it, so she used her key to let herself in. She put the nutty confection in their refrigerator along with a hastily scribbled note: *Happy Valentine's Day (early) from The Fudge Fairy*. Then she went home to work on a writing assignment for one of her journalism classes.

At ten o'clock that evening, she was having a cup of jasmine tea and going through her mother's recipe collection when she realized the Graces had never phoned to say they'd found their treat. Since she hadn't talked to them in a couple of days, she grinned and picked up her phone, thinking to tease them about their shocking lack of gratitude to the

Fudge Fairy.

They didn't answer their phone, so Laney began to worry. It was rather late for them to be out, and she could see from her kitchen windows that snow had begun falling in huge clumps that would pile up quickly and make a mess of the roads.

Wanting to make sure they were aware of the weather conditions and that they weren't far from home, Laney called the cell phone they took turns carrying.

"Where are you?" she demanded the instant Caroline answered.

A pointed silence made her regret her shrill tone.

"I'm sorry, Caroline. It's just that it's snowing so hard, and I can't help worrying about—"

"It's not snowing at all in Indianapolis, Indiana," Caroline said pleasantly. "And that's where we are."

Laney felt her eyes bulge. "You're *where*?"

"We left this morning for a road trip," Caroline announced grandly. "We made good time today, and right now we're at a motel on the far side of Indianapolis. It's a real nice place, and not too pricey, either. They have apricot-mint soaps in the bathroom, and—"

"What are you *doing*?" Laney screeched. "You can't just take off like this!"

"Laney Ryland," Caroline said crisply. "We may be as old as dirt, but except for an achy joint here and there, we get around just fine. And we're certainly not feebleminded. We have a cell phone, and credit cards, and plenty of cash. And after Aggie got a speeding ticket in Iowa, we made a pact not to drive too fast. So you can just stop being horrified and trust us a little bit!"

It wasn't possible to talk to any of the Graces for more than thirty seconds without the phone abruptly changing hands, so Laney wasn't surprised when she heard a little grunt and a murmured entreaty followed by an exasperated sigh.

"Hi, Laney! We're having the time of our lives!"

"Millie," Laney said with relief. Her youngest great-aunt was usually the most reliable when it came to delivering a straight answer. "Please tell me what—" She gave up when she heard another scuffle for phone domination.

"We were planning to call you as soon as we got settled here in the room so you wouldn't worry," Caroline said.

"Just tell me where you're going," Laney pleaded.

"We're having an adventure," Caroline said. "You know how much we like driving. And Ollie Lincoln checked out the Buick before we left. So we're as safe as can be, and we don't plan to be gone more than four days. Now please let me go before Aggie and Millie claim the best bed."

"But Caroline, it's the middle of winter!"

"Laney, we're going to be just fine. And so are you. Go make yourself a nice cup of tea."

"But Caroline—"

"Oh, and we don't need you to feed Frankie Five. He's with us. 'Bye now!"

"'Bye!" Aggie and Millie chorused.

Caroline hung up.

Still holding the phone against her ear, Laney stared out her windows at the falling snow and wondered just how she was supposed to stop herself from worrying about her elderly great-aunts taking an impromptu road trip to heaven-knew-where in the middle of winter.

Chapter Twenty-Eight

SITTING ON A HIGH STOOL in the recording studio's vocal booth, Jeb clipped his lyrics sheet to the music stand in front of him and adjusted his microphone. Looking through the glass wall separating him from the control room, he met the sound engineer's questioning gaze and nodded.

Through his headphones, he heard the first notes of the intro to the album's title track. "Yours If You Want Me" was a love song he'd written for Laney, but it was also a message of surrender to God. Jeb believed it was the best thing he had ever written.

The guys had finished tracking their background vocals yesterday, and had already gone home to their families, but Jeb had one last bit of recording to do. On this special song, he was singing his own backup.

After he laid down a good track, they'd be finished recording the album. The next items on the agenda were the mixing and mastering: They'd drop in an embellishment here and there, and then they'd tweak the sound levels to add a final layer of polish to the record. But they'd have a two-week break before tackling those jobs because Justin Kramer had a commitment elsewhere.

So tomorrow, Jeb was going home. And as he'd told Justin, he intended to be an engaged man when he returned to Nashville to finish the record.

The intro to "Yours If You Want Me" built layer by layer. After several bars, the solo piano was joined by the bass guitar, then the drums, and then Jeb's lead guitar. Finally, he heard his own recorded voice singing melody on the first verse.

It sounded amazing. Laney was going to be so proud.

He'd decided against calling her to say he was coming home. Since he had already gone so long without talking to her—and it had *not* been easy—he thought it would be a sweeter thrill if he just showed up and surprised her.

Justin said he was making a mistake. But Laney was used to not hearing from Jeb for a couple of months at a stretch, so this wouldn't seem strange to her. Besides, hadn't the Graces advised him to give her plenty of time and space?

He would explain everything when he got home, and Laney would understand, just like always. Although from now on, he'd stay in daily contact with her, and he'd consult her before agreeing to any concert tour or recording session that would take him away from her side.

He had just pulled in a deep breath to begin singing harmony on the last two lines of the verse when the music abruptly stopped.

"Sorry, Jeb." The engineer jerked his head sideways, indicating that the interruption had been ordered by Justin, who was talking on a phone and frowning.

Jeb tugged off his headphones. "What's wrong?"

Justin pulled the phone away from his ear. "Jeb, Reception has three women causing a disturbance and demanding to see you."

Jeb couldn't imagine how any of his old fans could have found him here, but the bigger question was why a security guard wasn't already showing them the door.

"Little old ladies," Justin continued, looking both puzzled and amused. "They say they've come to take you home."

The Graces? Panic pushed Jeb off of the stool and onto his feet, but in the next instant, he relaxed. If anything had happened to Laney, the Graces would have called him, not driven all the way to Nashville.

So they'd come to escort him home, had they? Jeb thrust his hands into his pockets and just stood there grinning.

He didn't bother to wonder how they'd found him. Knowing the Graces, they'd probably been tipped off to his whereabouts by the brother of somebody's cousin's next-door neighbor.

Justin had the phone back against his ear, and was looking at Jeb and shaking his head in wonder. "They brought three pies," he reported. "They started out with four, but they gave one to the nice man who changed their flat tire in Clarksville."

Pies? Jeb's stomach squirmed in happy anticipation. "I hope they brought a strawberry-rhubarb," he said to nobody in particular.

As he listened again to whoever was on the phone, Justin's eyes widened in alarm. "Jeb, Reception says they have a cardboard box with something *alive* in it."

Jeb snorted. Of course they'd brought the cat. He threw back his head and laughed.

"Jeb, who *are* these people?"

Jeb wiped a tear from his eye. "Brace yourselves," he said to the men in the control booth. "You're about to meet the Three Graces and Frankie Five."

"The Three Graces and Frankie Five?" Justin scratched his bald head and then shook it. "Never heard of 'em. Are they a gospel band?"

Jeb laughed again. "No, the Graces are a force of nature. They make amazing pies, though, so if they'll swear they're not carrying a pink rabbit suit, invite them to join us. And have somebody start a fresh pot of coffee. We'll want it with the pie."

* * *

Was that someone at the kitchen door? In her basement, where she'd just transferred a load of wet clothes from her washing machine to the dryer, Laney paused to listen.

Five sharp knocks.

The Graces were back! Laney thundered up the stairs and tore into the kitchen just as Aggie, snugly zipped into a down coat and wearing a fuchsia knitted hat with matching mittens, opened the door and stepped inside.

"Where have you been?" Laney demanded, ignoring the open door and the cold air tumbling into her house. "I've been so worried!"

"Oh, Laney, we had the very best time!" Aggie's wrinkly, cold-pinked face wore a brilliant smile. "Come out to the car and see what we brought you."

Laney couldn't have been less interested in souvenirs. She was too busy processing her relief that the Graces were finally home. She moved past Aggie to look out the door for her other two renegade relatives.

The overcast day was slipping toward twilight, and while there was no wind to speak of, the temperature would soon sink into the single digits. Just an hour earlier, Laney had finished clearing six inches of fresh snow off her driveway and sidewalks. When she saw Millie barreling toward her, she was glad she had also taken the time to sprinkle deicer on the walk to prevent dangerous slips.

"Laney, come see!" Millie called. "We caught you a man!"

"Well, you can just throw him back," Laney said sharply. "I don't want a man." Not unless she could have Jeb.

"But this one's a keeper!" Millie insisted. "Get your coat on and come see him!"

Had they actually bullied some poor guy into coming here to meet her? They knew how she felt about their match-making. And wherever had they gotten the idea that she'd given up on Jeb?

She was worried about him, sure. Annoyed with him, absolutely. But she hadn't given up on him. Not yet.

Aggie grabbed Laney's parka off its peg by the door and held it out to her. "Come on!" she urged.

"Okay, okay." Laney shoved her arms into the coat's sleeves and yanked the zipper up. Then she stomped down the steps and started toward the driveway.

There had better be a good explanation for this. The Graces had been gone for four whole days and had worried her half to death. For crying out loud, they were *old*, and they'd left on their crazy road trip in the middle of February! What if they'd driven into a snowstorm and slid into a ditch and ended up freezing to death?

Caroline peeked around the corner of the house. "Come and see our surprise!" Her voice was muffled by a vivid blue scarf wound around her neck and covering the lower half of her face.

Laney sighed and shook her head and braced herself for a very awkward introduction. And then she rounded the corner and stopped abruptly, her breath catching in her throat.

"Hey, princess." Lounging against the driver's door of the Buick, his long legs crossed at the ankles and Frankie Five cradled in his arms, Jeb regarded her with transparent hope and a hint of wariness. "Happy Valentine's Day."

Laney was too stunned to speak.

"Sorry I had to be away for so long." His raspy voice deepened. "Believe me, I missed you every single day."

Oh, really? Then why hadn't he called?

She raised an eyebrow at him. "I'm not sure I *do* believe you."

He studied her face for a moment, and then his uncertainty vanished and he grinned, awakening the dimple in his left cheek. Settling Frankie in the crook of his left arm, he extended his right hand to Laney, beckoning. "Then come here, and let's see if I can persuade you."

No, he was going to have to do some explaining first. Laney slid her hands into her coat pockets and stayed right where she was, a good ten feet away from him.

His smile faded. "I have a new band, Laney. A Christian band. We just recorded our first album. Then the Graces showed up in Nashville and I hitched a ride home."

So that was the reason for the Graces' road trip. Somehow they'd discovered where Jeb was, and then they'd gone after him.

That rankled.

"I'm not so desperate for a man that I need my great-aunts to drag one home and throw him at my feet," she said loudly enough for the Graces, who were no doubt hovering just around the corner, to hear.

Jeb coughed into his gloved fist, covering up a laugh.

The wretch.

Laney tried to give him a severe look, but failed because his hair had gotten long again and the wind was blowing it over his left eye and she ached to smooth it back and press her lips against his dear face.

"I was ready to come home," he said, serious again. "The Graces just happened to show up in Nashville the afternoon before I was planning to leave." Frankie squirmed in his arms, and without looking down, Jeb stroked the cat's head with two long fingers encased in a leather driving glove. "I already had a plane ticket. For yesterday. I would have been here last night, but I didn't want the Graces driving home by themselves."

"We would have been perfectly safe driving ourselves!" Caroline huffed from somewhere nearby.

Laney rolled her eyes, and then she mouthed an emphatic *Thank you* to Jeb. When he grinned in perfect understanding, she felt an answering smile tug at her own lips. But then she remembered she still had a bone to pick with him.

"You didn't call me." Inside her coat pockets, she squeezed her hands into fists. "All these weeks, Jeb, and you didn't even . . ." As her voice faded to nothing, she shook her head.

"Yes, but when I called you that day from the airport, you said we were okay. And then I said I'd be busy for a while. Remember?"

"Jeb, that was three and a half months ago!" He'd sent her a lovely Christmas gift, but he hadn't called, not once in all that time.

"I know what you're thinking." His gaze remained locked on her even as Millie approached and relieved him of his feline burden. "You're thinking that if I loved you, I wouldn't have stayed away so long. But there were some things I needed to do, Laney. Some things I needed to figure out. And I think you needed time, too. And I was afraid that if I broke down and called you, I'd end up on the next flight home because I *do* love you, more than you'll ever—"

"You love me?" she interrupted, breathless with hope.

"Well, of course I love you," he said almost irritably. "I've loved you forever."

"Would you kids mind hurrying this up?" Caroline inquired pleasantly. "It's fifteen degrees out here, and we want our supper."

Jeb flung her an exasperated look, then turned and opened the Buick's front door with a flourish. "Don't let us keep you. I'm sure Frankie Five's hungry, too."

He walked over to Laney and pulled her into his arms.

Maybe she should have resisted, made him suffer until he realized how much he'd hurt her. But there had been too much suffering in Jeb's life already, so her hands came out of her coat pockets and she melted against him like butter on a warm scone.

"That's more like it," he said gruffly.

"Oh, Jeb," she sighed against his coat. She loved him too much to stay mad at him, but she had to make him understand what he'd done. "You've been stupid again."

"That's what I've been hearing all the way home." He squeezed her harder. "I wanted to call you, but I wouldn't let myself. In the last couple of years that got to be a habit—seeing how long I could go without calling you—and I guess I just kind of fell back into it. But you needed to hear from me, didn't you?"

"Yes." She nodded against him. "I really did. And I know I could have called you to ask what was going on, but I was afraid."

"I understand now. And I'm sorry." He sighed against her hair. "Laney, I think some parts of my brain are still screwed up. So please just tell me whenever I do something stupid and I'll try really hard to make it right."

"Deal," she said, snuggling closer.

"Jeb?" Aggie spoke from immediately behind Laney. "Now would be a good time to pop the question."

Laney groaned against his coat. "Make them go away."

"Ladies," he said over Laney's head, "I'm grateful for all of your help. But I've got this now, so just beat it, okay?" He found Laney's bare hands and pressed them against his chest, covering them with his gloved ones.

"Our work here is done," Caroline informed her sisters with smug satisfaction. "And it's my turn to drive."

"Shotgun!" Aggie yelled, pumping a mittened fist into the air.

Millie chuckled. "Happy Valentine's Day, you two lovebirds!"

Laney looked up at Jeb. "I can't believe you let them drive you all the way home from Nashville."

"Give me credit for having a brain," he said. "*I* drove. And this morning when they argued over whose turn it was to ride shotgun, I ordered them all into the back seat and let their cat-in-a-box sit up front with me. Frankie Five's not so bad."

By the time the Buick rumbled past them and backed out of the driveway, Laney was being thoroughly kissed. She wondered briefly if Mrs. Lindstrom was enjoying the show from one of Mrs. Schultz's windows, but then Jeb changed the angle of his head to deepen their kiss and Laney forgot all about Mrs. Lindstrom and absolutely everything else.

"I love you," Jeb said when they came up for air. "Marry me, Laney. Come live in my house and make it a home. We'll have fourteen children and grow old together."

She shivered. "Fourteen children?"

"Well, maybe not all at once." He dragged her hands away from his chest so he could unzip his jacket and open it to share his warmth.

She immediately pushed her arms beneath the jacket and around his lean waist. Flattening her palms against his back, she gloried in the warmth radiating from beneath his flannel shirt.

"Marry me," he urged in a low voice as he nuzzled the curls just behind her ear. "Please."

"Kiss me some more and I'll think about it."

He chuckled. "Sweetheart, if you can think when I kiss you, then I'm not doing it right."

She huffed out a breath. "I meant I would think about it after the kiss."

"Think about it . . . right . . . now," he suggested between nibbles on the tip of her frozen ear. "It's Valentine's Day, princess. Be mine."

Gently catching her jaw in his gloved hand, he turned her face up to his and waited.

"Oh, all right," she said, grinning.

"Thank you." He kissed the tip of her nose. "Now let's go inside where it's warm."

They walked arm-in-arm to her kitchen door.

"A Christian band?" Laney asked as they climbed the

steps.

"Yeah." He opened the door for her and followed her inside. "I have to go back in two weeks to mix the tracks and master the album, but that won't take long. You could come. You could see some new sights and meet everyone I've been working with. They're all Christians, Laney. We even pray together."

"I'll come," she said happily. She shut the door and they removed their coats. "I'm jobless at the moment. Did the Graces tell you?"

"They told me everything." Jeb tossed his gloves on the counter and hung his coat beside Laney's. Then he pulled her into his arms. "I'm sorry things have been so hard for you." He smoothed back her hair with one broad palm. "And I'm sorry for adding to your troubles. I was just so excited and so focused on what you'd think when I came home that I never dreamed you might not be sure about me." He leaned his forehead against hers. "But how could you not know? How could you not feel my love? Laney, you *know* me."

"I was afraid to believe it," she admitted. "I've fooled myself before, remember?"

"Stop beating yourself up over those other guys." His forehead lightly rubbed hers as he shook his head. "This is *me*, Laney. You know it's different with us. It always has been."

"Yes," she whispered.

"In one way or another," he went on, "I've been yours since the day I saw you in that blue dress and the tiara."

She raised her head, offering her mouth for another kiss.

"Wait." He touched a finger to her lips. "I have a present for you." His hand went to his pocket, and then he grinned and said, "Not an engagement ring. We'll go shopping for that tomorrow. But I think you'll like this." He withdrew his hand and brought it between them before slowly uncurling his fingers.

For several heartbeats, Laney could only stare in amazement at the tiny H-shaped piece of cardboard that lay in his palm. Then she picked it up and turned it over. And yes, the other side was shiny and pure black.

"Remember the dark gray suit I wore to your mom's funeral?" Jeb asked. "I had it cleaned after I got back to L.A., but I never wore again. I took it to Nashville in case I needed it for a fancy dinner with the record executives, and I didn't notice until I unpacked that there was an envelope taped to the hanger. The puzzle piece was inside."

"The cleaners found it in your pocket," Laney guessed. "You must have been toying with it the day of the funeral and absently dropped it in there."

"Or it fell in while I was sitting at the table."

Laney rubbed the piece between her finger and thumb. "I put the puzzle away."

"I know. The Graces told me. But even though you don't need it anymore, I thought you'd still be glad to have it."

"I am." The tears starting in Laney's eyes had nothing to do with the gift and everything to do with the sweet man who'd brought it to her. "Thank you."

He smiled tenderly. "You're an amazing woman, Laney Ryland."

"Hmm." Leaning away from him to put the puzzle piece in a safe place on the counter, she took the opportunity to dash away a trembling tear caught in the corner of one eye. "Don't you think 'Laney Bell' has a nicer ring to it?"

"Absolutely." He grinned and pulled her closer. "Hey, listen. I think I've figured out how to solve our geography problem."

"Are you talking about where we'll live?" Laney shook her head. "That's not a problem. I don't have to stay in Owatonna. Not fulltime. The Graces might be pushing eighty, but I'm beginning to think they don't need me to look after them."

"Some day they might," Jeb pointed out. "Besides, I need them to keep me humble, so we'd better stay here. You love my house, anyway. And we wouldn't want to leave our church, would we?" His dimple flashed as he added, "And let's not forget that all of my favorite fishing spots are less than an hour's drive from Owatonna."

"Oh, yes," Laney deadpanned. "The fishing spots would be the most important consideration."

"Hey." Jeb's dimple winked again. "Fishing *is* important. Haven't you ever noticed how often it's mentioned in the Bible?"

Laney smirked at him, then sobered to ask, "But what about your band?"

"We'll turn your house into a rehearsal space," he said. "Maybe even put in a recording studio at some point."

Was he be serious about installing a band in her house? The neighbors might have something to say about that.

"I take it you'll be sending Mrs. Lindstrom on a world cruise," Laney said archly. "She's still living with Mrs. Schultz, you know."

"Hmm. Tempting. But your basement's plenty big enough to rehearse in, and we can soundproof it. Your three bedrooms and two baths will make a nice living space for the band. Two of the three guys are married, no kids yet, so the wives will be able to come and go whenever they want. There will be times when we're rehearsing for weeks or even months at a stretch."

Laney was beginning to see some exciting possibilities. "So when you're not touring or recording, you'll be right here?"

"Yep." He grinned. "You can call me home to supper every night, and I'll come running."

"But could I travel with you some?" she asked hopefully.

"Like I've always told you, there's nothing glamorous about life on the road," he said. "But I'd love having you with me."

"That might be difficult after the babies start coming." As soon as the words were out, Laney felt heat rushing to her cheeks.

"Let's play that by ear," Jeb suggested.

"Okay." Laney snuggled deeper into his embrace. "How soon can we get married?"

The laugh that rumbled through his chest sent pleasant vibrations through Laney. "I'd suggest we hop in Francine right this minute and go catch the next flight to Las Vegas," he said, "but we can't deprive the Graces of a traditional wedding. Not after they insisted all the way home from Nashville that you and I are the best match they ever made."

"I can't believe they're taking the credit for this!" Laney huffed. "Remember that day at the tearoom? Whatever happened to that poor woman they were so eager to fix you up with? I never caught her name, but—"

Jeb was laughing again. "Haven't you figured it out yet? Princess, that 'poor woman' was *you*. They've been planning this for years!"

Chapter Twenty-Nine

ON A FINE SATURDAY EVENING at the end of April, Laney married Jeb in the church wedding of her dreams.

A former wedding-planner's assistant, she'd had a blast arranging things just the way she wanted. Unsurprisingly, Jeb had shown little enthusiasm for helping to make decisions regarding flowers and catering and so on. But when Laney wondered aloud which of her friends to have as bridesmaids, he'd made an extremely good suggestion.

After the ceremony, several guests told Laney how charmed they'd been when the music had begun and they'd looked expectantly toward the church door and seen Caroline on the threshold, a bouquet of white roses in her hands. Aggie and Millie, holding bouquets of their own, had immediately stepped in to flank their sister. And then with plump chins held high, the Three Graces—who were first-time bridesmaids, all—had linked arms and swished proudly down the aisle in matching gowns of sky-blue satin.

The wedding was perfect.

So was the honeymoon in Paris, where Laney spent the better part of two weeks indulging her enthusiasm for classic French cuisine while Jeb looked on in fond amusement.

"We can stay another week if you want," he offered one balmy evening during supper at a sidewalk café.

"We don't dare," Laney said. "Not when I'm gaining weight and you're losing it."

A subtle breeze ruffled Jeb's dark hair as he shrugged. "The bread's good here."

That was what he'd been subsisting on while Laney

had been enjoying mouthwatering dishes garnished with shaved truffles and swimming in exotic sauces.

"I'll make you some Minnesota man-food the very second we get home," she promised.

"Hotdish?" Jeb patted his flat stomach. "Now you're talking."

"You never said what made you decide on Paris for our honeymoon," Laney commented later as they left the café.

"I heard this was the place to go for French food," Jeb said. "And I knew you'd love seeing the gardens and art museums."

Was there ever a more exasperating man? Hugging the tissue-wrapped bouquet of purple lilacs he'd bought earlier at a charming flower stall, Laney gave him a piece of her mind. "Jeb, this is your honeymoon, too. What do *you* want?"

"I already have everything I want." He stopped walking and pulled her into his arms, crushing the lilacs and releasing their heady fragrance. "I spent years telling myself this could never happen, but just look where I am now."

"Yes, look," Laney said with tender sarcasm. "You're in Paris, eating food you hate and wandering through gardens and museums that don't interest you at all."

"I don't care about the food, Laney. It's who I'm sitting across the table from that matters. And if I don't seem very impressed by the gardens and museums, it's because I can hardly tear my eyes away from you."

"Oh, Jeb." She nestled her cheek against his chest and found the comfortable spot that belonged to her alone. "I can't imagine why you thought you needed the Graces' advice for courting me. You're the most romantic man I've ever met."

It was their last evening in the City of Light, and even though Laney's feet hurt from so much walking, it was too beautiful an evening not to enjoy one last stroll along the Seine. Holding Jeb's big warm hand as the nighttime sounds of Paris swirled around them, she was almost painfully happy.

When they stopped to admire a picturesque stone bridge spanning the river, Jeb shook his head in confusion.

"Are we walking in circles? Because this bridge looks familiar, and—" He broke off and squeezed her hand. "Laney," he said urgently. "It's the puzzle!"

She opened her mouth to ask what he meant, but then it hit her: The pretty bridge arching across the dark waters of the Seine was the very one pictured in her mother's "Paris at Night" puzzle.

"Over there," Jeb said, pointing to the opposite side of the street. "That's where the picture was taken from." He tugged on Laney's hand and together they raced across the street, laughing like children, breathless with delight.

Jeb suddenly stopped. "Right here."

"Yes," Laney breathed, hugging her lilacs and struggling not to cry as Jeb wrapped his long arms around her. "I can't believe we're actually standing here. I can't believe we found this place by accident. If we'd come here in the daytime, we wouldn't even have recognized—"

"We didn't find this by accident," Jeb interrupted, his deep voice rumbling above her. "Don't you see?"

"See what?"

"Laney, we were *led* here," he said with quiet conviction. "This is a wedding gift from God."

"Yes," she whispered, understanding at last. "And you know, I don't think it's Mom's puzzle anymore. She started it, but we finished it, so it's ours now. So the very first thing we're going to do when we get home is frame it and hang it in our bedroom."

"Wrong." Bending down, he pressed a brief kiss against her lips and chuckled suggestively. "That'll be the *second* thing we do."

Epilogue

One year later.

BACKSTAGE AT THE GOSPEL MUSIC ASSOCIATION'S annual Dove Award ceremony in Atlanta, Jeb cradled three gold-plated statuettes in his arms and tried not to flinch as he was mobbed by the media.

He was still trying to absorb the fact that he'd just won Dove Awards for Song of the Year, Male Vocalist of the Year, and Rock Album of the Year.

Spotting Justin Kramer over a TV cameraman's shoulder, his bald head reflecting the harsh overhead lights, Jeb caught the producer's gaze and then widened his own eyes in a silent message: *Can you believe this?*

The man who had become Jeb's close friend and spiritual mentor grinned broadly, his gold tooth flashing as he pointed one finger toward the ceiling: *This is all God's doing.*

Jeb shook his head at the interviewer in front of him. "Sorry. Could you repeat the question?"

"Just tell us how you're feeling right now."

"Overwhelmed," Jeb said. "Grateful."

He knew his one-word answers wouldn't satisfy the interviewers, but his attention had strayed back to Justin, who was speaking animatedly into his cell phone. When their eyes met again, the producer confirmed Jeb's hope by mouthing, "Laney."

"Excuse me," Jeb said to the people pressing around him. He quickly threaded his way through the clamoring crowd, his eyes on the prize in Justin's hand. Shifting his Dove Awards to one arm, he grabbed the phone.

"Laney?"

"I'm so excited!" she squealed. "Jeb, I can't stand it!"

He closed his eyes. "I know, sweetheart. I wish you were here."

"I wish that, too, Jeb. But you know we can't take her on a plane at this age."

Her. Their precious gift. The ten-day-old miracle they'd named Hannah Grace Bell.

Every time he thought of his daughter—His *daughter*!—Jeb's insides quivered with joy.

Someone touched his elbow. When he turned, a smiling entertainment reporter poked a microphone at his face.

"Congratulations, Jackson!"

"Thanks."

"When can we expect your second album to drop?"

"Release date is June first," Jeb said. "Please excuse me." Turning his back on the woman and the TV camera trained on him, he lowered his head and focused all of his attention on the sweet voice in his ear.

"I can hardly believe it!" Laney said. "First a Grammy and now three Dove Awards! I wish I could be there with you."

Her voice wobbled over those last few words, and Jeb pictured tears sparkling in her China-blue eyes.

"Laney, you *are* here. You're right here, in my heart. I take you wherever I go."

He heard a little sob, and then she said, "Jeb don't you *dare* make me cry when you're not here to hold me! Don't say any more romantic things until you get home, do you hear me?"

"I hear you," he said, loving her so hard it made his chest hurt.

"Good. So now I'm going to be all calm and wifely and tell you to be patient with the interviewers and give more than one-syllable responses to their questions, all right?"

"Yes, princess."

"And then go have some fun with your band."

His band. How could he ever express his gratitude to them? Not just for their professionalism and hard work, but for their companionship and encouragement. They had studied the Scriptures with him, and they had prayed with him for God's blessing on the music they made together.

Tonight he would tell them once again how much all of that had meant to him, and then he'd take his leave. They had families of their own; they would understand his eagerness to get back to Minnesota.

"I won't be on that flight tomorrow afternoon," he said suddenly. "I'm coming home tonight."

"Tonight? But don't you need to—"

"I need to be with *you*, Laney. I'll give a couple of interviews and then I'll do a quick round of back-slapping with the guys, but after that I'm heading to the airport. I'll call the hotel later and ask them to ship my suitcase."

"Not the awards," she said quickly. "Jeb, I don't want them lost!"

"I'll bring them with me," he assured her.

"Okay. But do you even know if there's a flight heading to Minneapolis that late?"

"There will be." He'd charter a private jet if that was what it took to get home in time for breakfast with Laney and

Hannah Grace.

"The Graces knew you'd win," Laney said. "So earlier this evening, they brought over a celebratory pie. Your very favorite."

"We'll have it for breakfast," Jeb said, grinning. "But you should go to bed now. You need to catch whatever sleep the little princess will allow you."

"You're right," Laney said. "I'll leave the kitchen light on for you."

Jeb told her that he loved her, and then he handed the phone back to Justin and turned to face the cameras.

Three microphones were immediately pushed toward him, and three people spoke at once. He managed to sort out the tangle of questions and give detailed answers to each one. Laney would have been proud.

When he'd had all he could take, he held up one finger and said, "Last question."

An attractive blonde woman elbowed her way forward. "Jackson Bell, you recently took home a Grammy Award for your chart-topping single, "Yours If You Want Me", and tonight you're walking away with three Dove Awards. Can you tell us where you're planning to go from here?"

Jeb knew she was asking about his music, and of course he had all kinds of plans for that. But looking straight into the TV camera and making no effort to hide his sappy grin, he said, "I'm going home to Minnesota to be with my family and eat some strawberry-rhubarb pie."

At the Atlanta airport, he made for the far corner of a deserted departure lounge where he wouldn't be disturbed. Loosening the tie Laney had made him promise to wear to the awards ceremony, he sat down and scrolled through the dozens of congratulatory text messages on his phone. The first one was from Shari Daltry, of all people:

You deserve this, Jackson. Your new music is amazing.

He hadn't heard from her in a year and a half, not since that awful day in Los Angeles, but he was still praying for her and for the guys from his old band. After all, if God could crack a skeptical heart like Jackson Bell's and slip inside it, anything was possible.

Two hours later, in the darkened First Class cabin of an airliner bound for Minneapolis-St. Paul, Jeb stretched out his legs and settled more comfortably in his seat. Staring at the bulkhead in front of him, he gave silent thanks to God for the remarkable success of his new music. Then he expressed his gratitude for the publishing contract Laney had signed last month for her afternoon tea cookbook. Saving the greatest blessings for last, he praised the Lord's unfathomable generosity in gifting him with Laney and with their precious Hannah Grace.

He turned his head toward the window and allowed his eyes to drift shut. Lulled to sleep by the steady roar of jet engines, he dreamed of a little girl in a long blue dress, a sparkling tiara perched atop her flaxen curls. The dress was too big, but she wasn't worried because her mother could fix it.

Tugging at a puffy sleeve that had slipped off one boney little shoulder, she tilted her head back and grinned up at him. *Do you like my tiara?* she asked as that accessory's fake jewels caught the sunlight and threw dazzling sparks at him.

I like it very much, Jeb said. *It's as beautiful on you as it was on your mom.* Then he looked over her head and into Laney's shining eyes.

Jarred awake by two loud thumps and the high-pitched whine of the aircraft's descending landing gear, Jeb rubbed his eyes and felt his heartbeat quicken.

He was almost home.

A Note from the Author

AFTER PUBLISHING FOUR MASS-MARKET PAPERBACKS with Harlequin's wildly popular *Love Inspired* imprint, I sent my editor a proposal for a story featuring a rock star hero. She didn't believe a character with that occupation would appeal to the established *Love Inspired* audience, but I had already fallen in love with the story and couldn't walk away from it. So I finished it on my own and published it as an e-book.

Six months later, *Her Minnesota Man* has become such a reader favorite that I am releasing this print edition.

Thank you for reading *Her Minnesota Man*. If you have enjoyed it, I hope you'll do me a huge favor and tell your friends about it.

I am currently working on another "Three Graces" story set in Owatonna, Minnesota.

Brenda Coulter
November 2012

WANT TO KEEP IN TOUCH?

E-mail
HMM@BrendaCoulter.com
I'll answer you personally, usually within a day or two.

Website
http://BrendaCoulter.com
You can read long excerpts from all of my books there.

Facebook
http://Facebook.com/Author.Brenda.Coulter
Do you like flowers? I frequently post pictures of my cottage-style garden.

Twitter
http://Twitter.com/BrendaCoulter
"Follow" me for fun links and stuff.

My four *Love Inspired* novels are currently out of print in paperback, but all are still available as e-books. Look for them at your favorite online bookstore:

Finding Hope

A Family Forever

A Season of Forgiveness

At His Command

May
the
LORD
richly
bless
you!

Printed in Poland
by Amazon Fulfillment
Poland Sp. z o.o., Wrocław